THE WANTED

By Lauren Nicolle Taylor

Clean Teen Publishing, Inc.

The Wanted
Copyright © 2014 by: Lauren Nicolle Taylor

Clean Teen Publishing
PO Box 561326
The Colony, TX 75056

www.cleanteenpublishing.com

YA content disclosure

For more information about our content disclosure, please utilize
the QR code above with your
smart phone or visit us at
www.cleanteenpublishing.com.

This is for you.

Prologue

2023
NADIR

I was eleven years old when they decided to save the world.

I stood pressed close to my mother, my sticky-with-sweets hand in her dry, calm one. Before the bombings, this wasn't how things were done, but now the safest place for the prime minister's son was under the watchful eye of the prime minister herself.

Four leaders crowded around a mahogany table, sweaty hands making vapory prints on the rich brown surface, fading in and out. Bottles of valuable, pure water glistened, slick with tears of condensation. I licked my lips as I stood close enough to touch one. The other first families lined the wall, probably all thinking the same thing—what would our fate be, and should we place our faith in the strange man dancing around the table? Unfamiliar faces wore recognizable expressions. Masks of restrained fear.

They listened to a man making big arcs with his arms speak in a grating twang. He gripped each and every one of them with his penetrating gaze and, I have to admit, I became entranced by his intensity. His deep blue eyes shone like sapphires. I broke from my mother's grasp and crept toward the table, the music of his speech drawing me closer like the pied piper.

"You see. It's perfect! It's the perfect opportunity. We have the chance to restructure society, all of it. Start fresh and stop all of this—" the man swung around quickly, "from happening again. Aren't you tired of worrying someone will kill you in your sleep?" People nodded. "Aren't you tired of worrying who you can trust?" They started to mutter.

I took a step closer to the blueprints they were taking turns examining. It looked like a maze. No, there was no way out. It was a prison.

"But why circles?" the black man asked, his deep voice rumbling like a marble in a barrel.

"Circles, squares, it doesn't really matter. It's the gates and the understructure that are important. Imagine if you knew there was a disturbance in one ring or section? You could shut it down, like that." The man clicked his fingers. "The perpetrators would be dealt with easily. No muss, no fuss. We will keep life above simple and keep all the messy, complicated stuff below." He wiggled his finger as he pointed to the levels underneath the ground. "Each ring can run independently, so even if there are issues in one, a lockdown will not affect the others' ability to run smoothly."

The complicated structure reminded me of plates spinning on narrow pieces of bamboo but on a much grander scale, rings balancing on long, metal supports, straddling the wide underground river that ran in loopy swirls underneath every town. "And see here, constant fresh water and easy waste disposal," he finished with a wink.

"I can't imagine the need for such a complicated facility. It will cost too much to build." The black man stepped forward, pointing at the various levels below the towns.

The American almost galloped over to the African president. "Oh, you'll want it. The population will grow, and waste disposal as well as the ability to isolate and control any disturbances will be an important aspect of this system. Besides, Sekimbo, money means nothing. Money is no object. This is about recreating civilization as we know it. Money is irrelevant." He leaned in, and the black man backed away. "I can't believe you even mentioned it."

Sekimbo grunted, stepping back from the table, and grabbed a precious bottle, taking a large sip.

"Can you taste it?" the American asked. "That is the sweet taste of change."

My mother cleared her throat, holding up one of the bottles and shaking it. Usually a flutter of silt would rise to the surface, but not this time. "So you're going to pollute what looks like one of very few pristine water sources left in this world?" She pursed her lips, a sign that she was unsure.

He pressed his hands to his forehead like he was frustrated. "No, no, no. We will ensure that everything is biodegradable or recyclable. We will process the human waste here." He pointed to a series of tanks hidden under the ground level. "These are details, details I've gone over, perfected and finalized. You don't need to worry about them; you only need to worry about your own survival."

My mother removed her glasses and cleaned them with her sleeve, giving herself a second to ponder what he'd just said.

The American paused for a few moments and then sprung into another speech, his eyes sparkling as if he were in love. "The rings, the circles, the Woodlands, it's beautiful, it's simple. It's a symbol of growth and change. The towns of the Woodlands will be set out like the rings of a tree trunk. And like a great redwood, we will become strong and unyielding." He made a fist with his pale hand.

I wanted to point out to him that there was no 'American Redwoodtown'. There were very few of his kind left.

"And this manifesto, this All Kind philosophy, do you think it will work?" my mother asked.

"Of course it's not the whole solution, but I think we can all agree it's a start. It's a new way of thinking that takes race out of the equation." He swiped his palms across each other, as if he were slapping dirt from them.

It sounded earnest, but it was too simple to even an eleven-year-old. Could we really leave all the prejudice behind?

"See, if we embed people with ID, we can always keep track of them. We can control where they go and when. No one would get through a gate to the next ring without us knowing, without us specifically *okaying* it. And if we shuffle the races between each town, we can start healing the human genome. Slowly start to rid this world of the racial markers that only cause fighting."

I started to wonder if he was a scientist. He certainly tried to talk like one, albeit a lazy one who used buzzwords to get people interested but didn't know much about the specifics.

"I already have the go ahead from Este and Poltinov; I just need your signatures..." He looked to my mother and the black man. "And then we can get out of this hell hole."

I remember thinking I didn't like the way he spoke to my mother, like they were friends, when really, they had been fighting each other for years. Killing each other's citizens. But I also knew everyone was tired of the death.

The American was energized, his hope and enthusiasm intoxicating.

The black man spoke again. "So, who has control?"

"That's the beauty of it, we all do. We remove the notion of countries and races… and we rule it together."

The word 'rule' stuck in my mind long after the American had stopped talking. I knew that word. That word did away with democracy.

The ground trembled, and people steadied themselves on furniture or each other. They didn't pause their meeting. Even though a ceasefire had been negotiated specifically for this gathering, some renegade groups had ignored it and were carrying on. The window was a view to sunlight trying to penetrate clouds of dust. The pictures of a green, fresh world were tantalizing, almost impossible to resist.

"How will you get people to come?" my mother asked distractedly as she held up a glossy photo of a stream running over rocks covered in moss, and giant trees shooting to the sky. I wanted to step into the picture and never look back.

The American nodded solemnly but it was overly dramatic. You could tell his excitement outweighed any seriousness.

"Well, you've all read the reports. Our planet can no longer support the current population. I'm sorry. I wish we hadn't made such a mess of things, but now we have to think about the survival of the species. It's too late to save everyone. We must look to the future." He didn't seem sorry, but he was right—the damage was done.

My mother flicked through the report, running her finger along the black text until she found the part she was looking for and stopped.

"But this number, President Grant, eighty thousand, can't be right. Is that really all we can take? And how can we possibly select those people?"

To think the world's population had been in the billions. Now we were down to a few million, and he was asking us to reduce it further.

"We don't make the decision; they will be randomly selected. And as for your first question, if you were given a choice between life and death, what would you choose?" His mocking laugh made me angry, and

I squeezed my toy until one of the side mirrors broke off.

With that statement, everyone started arguing. The noise in the room was deafening as desperate voices collided with one another. I crouched down on the floor and played with my toy Transformer, running Optimus Prime into my mother's advisor's foot repeatedly. He didn't seem to notice. I was used to the arguing. For months, they had been debating what to do. Then the American showed up in Brazil a couple of months back after escaping the Chinese bombing of the US. Now, they were just arguing about something different.

They went on and on and round and round in circles, trying to push their own agenda, trying to say their people had more of a right to exist, to go on, than the others did. Finally, the American stood on a chair and told them to be quiet. And for some reason, they obeyed. He seemed to have magnetism that made everyone listen to him.

"People. People. I don't mean to push you, but the decision's already been made. We are going. Construction has begun. You can stay here, but I guarantee you won't last a year. The world as we know it is over. The Woodlands embodies hope, a way forward. Join me, join us."

He spun a stack of papers towards my mother and President Sekimbo. And I watched as, with a deep sigh, my mother signed the death sentences of hundreds of thousands of people. All to save me. To save her family.

We didn't realize at the time that it was too late for us, and for most of our population. Radiation killed. Insipid, it ate at you from the inside out. My mother and father went first, my sister died shortly after, and now I was all that was left. The sickly and the dying were not permitted to migrate to the Woodlands. As I had been at a remote boarding school for most of the war, I escaped their fate.

President Grant flapped the papers in front of my face, urging me to hand over control to him. Although he wasn't really president anymore, his country was gone and he wanted to adopt mine. He promised me he would take care of my people, but I didn't believe him. There was no 'my people' or 'his people', that was the point of the Woodlands. But I was only seventeen. I would do as I was told because, although it broke my heart to do it, I couldn't lead. I couldn't do anything.

The Wanted

How did I get here?
It wasn't a miraculous stroke of luck. Some pointed finger that knocked
us into our places and forced us to walk forward.
Every minute I gained, I fought for.
I slogged out this life through a lash of ice and drag of pine. I swam to
the other side of the river of blood and kept myself.
Everything that's happened to me, good or bad, I earned.
I am not wanting.
I am wanted.
Which scares me most of all.

1

Little Pills

ROSA

The lost ones are holed up inside me. They might want to be free of my pocked and scarred chest. But right now... I need them more than their right for peace. They give me the strength to carry out my very simple plan.

...to live.

The too-bright light rustled me, my consciousness struggling to keep up with my surroundings. The unfamiliar feel of cold metal pressing into my back, a coffin full of my own breath, and the drag of blood on the glass shoved me to alertness.

One word floated around inside my new brain—pills. My thoughts flew aimlessly like someone had opened a case of live butterflies into my skull... *if... you don't do... something... in the next... fifteen minutes... you're going to... die... again.*

I pulled the words together and my hand tightened around the powder-crusted pills that burrowed into my palm like they knew, just as well as I did, what my fate would be if I didn't find a way to swallow them in the next few minutes. I clenched both my fists tightly, trying not to look suspicious. *But how do you do that when a Superior is peering at you with sharpened eyes? When you appeared from death?*

My eyes flitted from his face to his wheelchair and back again quickly, but he saw me taking in the surprising detail. Superior Grant was in a wheelchair. The small muscles around his mouth and jaw tightened slightly. He looked *off* sitting there lower than I was. Uncomfortable. I squirmed under his gaze like a rock was on my chest, pinning me under his stare and his authority.

I struggled because my energy was still wrapped around the being *dead* part. It wasn't quite awake or responding. I moved my hand to the glass surrounding me as if it were tied to my side with elastic, tracing the bloodied handprint above me and avoiding Grant's black expression. I needed to ignore the enormity of my predicament for one more second. Drawing my finger over each part of the large, reddish brown-painted hand, I wondered if it were my blood or someone else's. *Was it yours, Joseph?*

My eyes darted towards the wheels of his chair as they squeaked with movement, and Grant bent his head down to catch my gaze. "They're dead," he said flatly as he pressed back into his chair and awaited my reaction. Something squelched inside me, a splitting, but not all the way. I watched his countenance, the way he stared at me, his lips twisting like they weren't sure what face to make. The splitting stopped like a half-undone zipper. My heart didn't explode inside me because I could see the twitch in there, the irritation. His fist tight as an un-budded pinecone. I bit down on my lip to stop myself from smiling. He was a liar. They got away.

I let out all the air I didn't realize I'd been holding onto, so overjoyed that I almost forgot I was minutes from dying. My body jerked, my toes pointing straight down and my head hit the table. I closed my eyes slowly and tried to hang on. *Be far away from here*, I prayed and added, *just be.*

Grant wheeled back a little, almost as if he were afraid of me, then shook his head and grasped his jaw in his hand. Our eyes slid to the vacant, open window letting the wind blow the fluorescent light around like a solitary swing in a playground. I pictured Deshi and Joseph climbing out that window, Joseph's expression as he looked back at me lying there, dead, and I gulped air that stung like a mouthful of thumbtacks.

Grant ran a hand through his neatly cropped, greying hair.

"Let's get you out of there," he said in that awful twang like rubber bands over violin strings. The sound was muted through the glass, but it still smarted. I nodded in reply.

The pills stabbed into my skin. Grant seemed unaware of the urgency of my situation. He moved in a considered, slow manner. Unless he was just playing with me and waiting for me to die.

I chewed on the inside of my cheek, thinking in seconds, because that was all I had left. If Grant didn't know about the pills, there may have been a reason. And if that was the case, I couldn't let him see me take them.

I rolled to my back and stared at the ceiling; shiny, tinfoil pipes wound their way out of the room like worms. Escape was next on my list, but living was first priority. Grant wheeled backwards to the control panel, eyeing me like a bug pinned to a corkboard, my wings spread painfully wide, never to flap again. Not a butterfly—more like a dull, tatty moth with uneven coloring.

His finger rose and punched a button with a sharp tap. The glass coffin lifted, and the seal between the world and me broke with a clean suck. The cool air wisped at my bare arms and something feathered over my body, raising goose bumps on already shivering skin. I drew my knees up and covered my chest when I realized it was my clothing that had just slipped from my body. My hands brushed over a thick, plaited scar crossing my stomach. I shuddered as I remembered the knife going in and my life bleeding out so fast, the feel of being sliced open.

My clothes were torn from someone making way for all the needles. They were also somewhat singed, and when I drew my arms up, the fabric slid off me like pieces of burned cardboard. I was shedding my skin like a cricket. The image made me cringe.

When the glass lifted, I glanced around. A blood-soaked curtain splayed dramatically on the floor like a fan dipped in paint. I made a move towards it, but the tubes and needles twisted and splintered in my skin, halting me. With my spare hand, I started pulling the needles out with little ceremony, small, red dots forming all over my skin. I pulled a long one from my scalp and Grant winced slightly, but he made no move towards me. If anything, he was avoiding looking at my thin, naked body, my dark, legs swinging over the edge of the metal table like an underfed bird ready to take flight. When the needles were out, lying in a circle around me, I reached out to grab the curtain as I teetered on the bench. A spasm flowed through my arms again. *You're going to die.*

Grant cleared his throat and I snapped my hand back to my body, unsure of what to do.

"By all means, please, cover yourself up. No one wants to see that," he said, waving his hand at me as if I were a dead animal you stepped over and tried not to look at. He held up one knobbly finger, and I expected him to pinch his nose.

"I warn you not to run, child. The guards are outside the door. And I may seem incapacitated, but I am not. Dear."

The 'dear' part was spat out, flung at me with as much condescension as he could manage.

"Oh... kay," I mumbled, my fingers gripping the edge of the table as my body rolled and rippled.

I moved mechanically, grasping at what little control I had. My arms and legs were spastic with energy, shivering and wobbling like a newborn fawn. My eyes darted to the open window. A chill waved in with a misty rain. My feet hit the cool floor and I wanted to flee—kick his chair over and catapult through that window—but my body couldn't do it. Not now. I was too weak. And definitely too naked. I wouldn't survive the cold. I shuddered and bent down to scoop up the curtain. Before I could grasp my fingers around the corner, Grant was in front of me, handing the heavy fabric over with his eyes averted. I cautiously took it, so heavy in my hands.

This was my chance to take the pills. I turned away and brought the curtain, all crusted and wet in places, around my shoulders. The cold blood kissed my bare skin and my stomach rolled. With my back turned, I tried to lift my hand to my mouth to swallow the pills, but he clamped his hand over my arm and swung me around to face him. I snapped the curtain closed around me, and my body convulsed. I tried to contain it, but my limbs flung out, my hands opened, and the pills fell. His eyes were on my face, eyebrows arched. The pills landed in a fold of the curtain, out of sight. My mouth went dry as I started to panic. I had a minute or two at best.

Grant gripped the arms of his chair in alarm at the way my body was behaving, almost like he wanted to get up and help me. "Are you all... right?" he asked carefully.

Think. I bowed my head, feeling the poison churning through my veins, turning me blue from the inside out and eating at the lining of my body. I hunched down, pulling the curtain closer, the pills rolling under the cloth and to my feet. "I... I just need to use the bathroom," I stammered, my voice crackled and burnt.

He sighed with confusing relief, and his wheels creaked away from me. "Guards!" he barked.

As Grant turned his head and yelled, I picked up the pills, slammed them in my mouth and swallowed, my eyes watering as I forced them down my throat.

The door crashed open like they had been waiting for him to shout out. Grant groaned in irritation. They moved swiftly towards me, grabbed me under the arms, and pulled me to my feet. I coughed from the sudden movement, the bitter taste of the pills grating the inside of my mouth.

Grant growled at the guards, who both stood to attention as he spoke. "Be careful with her. She is not yours to harm." My stomach flipped, and my heart joined it.

"Wait!" I said around the bile pushing its way through my teeth. The men paused as I hung between their arms like a coat on a hangar. Grant stared at me incredulously but if I was going to die, I needed to know one thing, "The babies… are they okay?" Grant smiled, sharp like it was drawn on, turned away from me, and said nothing. My body jolted from sadness and nausea. "Bathroom," I pleaded desperately to the guards as I tried to suppress the heaving inside. The blue liquid was trying to leave my body the only way it could and if they saw me vomit blue, they would know something was wrong.

The guards dragged me down the hall, my feet galloping to keep up with their haste. It was darker than a secret in this part of Este's compound. The lights lit up as we walked and turned off after we passed under them. Strips of deep red and gold shone from the carpet as my body crimped and straightened like a cooked and then uncooked noodle. *Hold it in,* I warned my stomach. It shook its head in reply and folded in half inside me. I let out an anguished moan as the cramping worsened.

At this, the guard jerked me up close to his face and I thought he was going to hurt me, but he whispered in my ear, his breath hot and smelling of stale coffee. "He saved them all."

Then he suddenly let me drop, my knees burning as they dragged me across the carpet.

The last light clicked on over a gray metal door. One of the guards slammed into it with his shoulder so he didn't have to let me go, and then they hurled me into a bathroom stall, the curtain flying off as I tumbled towards the porcelain toilet bowl. I put my hands out on the seat before I hit my head, grasped at the curtain, and pulled it under the door. I kicked the door closed with my bare foot as I pulled the velvet around my shaking body and vomited blue.

Grabbing some toilet paper, I wiped the blue stains from the corners of my mouth. I searched out every blue splatter and quickly mopped that up too, flushing the toilet as the guard opened the door, his cheeks red with embarrassment at my pathetic state.

I stole a deep breath and tried not panic. My chest tightened. My heart was elastic, stretching thinner and thinner with every step Joseph took away from me. I knew I'd done the right thing, the only thing, but it didn't stop the aching, the fear of being left alone in this place, with these people.

2.

What Should Be

JOSEPH

I hadn't moved since I told them what had happened to Rosa. My back was against a tree, my body tense and rough. I pictured her blinking her beautiful eyes open to the white light, cold and stark over her bare skin. A lonely light. It would drive in the realization that I abandoned her. It would tell her—in certainty—that I wasn't coming back. I could feel her devastation. I could hear the empty sound of the glass moving away from her body. Exposing her, leaving her to fight without my help. *I should be there.*

My sighs lacked breath.

After a few pats on the shoulders and small bursts of tears, everyone had started to busy themselves. Move around me. But I was waiting for something, though I didn't know what. When they did look up from the ground, from their packs, which they were mindlessly rearranging, it was too much. Their eyes were red. Wet. Angry. I banged the back of my head against the trunk harder than I should and watched the sky, clouds tearing open to reveal the stars. My tears had stopped but the raw, empty feeling was only beginning. I wanted to wish for something, anything. A different outcome, a way through, but there was nothing. Just the bruises on my back and the blood on my hands.

Rash was missing, my fault as well. After Pelo pulled him off me, Rash shoved him too and ran deeper into the forest. They were sending someone to get him. I would have volunteered, but he didn't want to see me.

I wish I had the option of escaping myself like he had.

A shirt landed in my lap. "Put this on, you must be freezing, man,"

Desh said, attempting to sound light and failing.

"I'm not cold." *I'm as cold as stone, but I can't feel it because I'm not here. I wonder if I'm dying inside?*

"Please, Joe, you'll get sick," he said quietly. If I were myself, I would have told him people didn't get sick from being mildly cold. Cold was a state, not a sickness. But I was a man I couldn't recognize, so I sighed and pulled the shirt over my head.

Desh held a cup in front of my face. "Here. Drink."

I shook my head but took it. I knew he wouldn't leave me alone until I drank, so I took a sip. It tasted like blood and bitterness, stinging all the way down to my empty stomach.

"It's just water. Why the face?" Desh's head leaned to one side as he blinked at me, confused.

A man I hadn't learned the name of yet threw a metal flask at me. It landed in the dirt, the word 'courage' etched into the silver metal.

"Maybe he needs something a little stronger."

I picked it up and smelled the contents. It was pungent, like sterilizing fluid mixed with honey. I replaced the cap without sampling it, holding it in my fist. Desh yanked it from my hand and threw it back to the man.

"That's the last thing he needs right now!" The thick eyebrows skimming the mustard-colored beanie the man wore rose slightly, then he shrugged and put it in his pocket, patting it like an old friend.

I stared at my friend, kneeling in the dirt with concern plastered all over his face. It was hard to handle. I didn't want him taking care of me. I didn't deserve it. I planted my hands in the grass and eased myself up, looking left and right, but there was no direction I wanted to go other than the one I wasn't allowed to go in, so I collapsed back down.

How would I get a grip on this? I was a father too. I had to be better, for Orry. I owed her that at least.

"The handhelds," I whispered. Desh didn't know what I was talking about. I rolled my eyes and searched for Matt, finding him stacking packs against a tree. As I approached, he stopped, still bent over.

"Where are they? Where's..." Patiently, he waited for me to finish. Her name felt like a gravelly lump in my throat. "Where's Rosa's handheld?"

Matt's face fell as he stood up straight. "We hid them, past where the wolf carcasses were hanging, where we'd arranged with you. You didn't retrieve them?"

I stood very close to him now. "Does it look like I did?" I growled, my palms open and empty.

Matt put his hands on his hips and took a breath. "Right." I thought he was going to tell me I couldn't go back, but his kind eyes relaxed. "We better run then."

Desh stumbled across the campsite towards us. "I'll come with you," he said breathlessly.

I shook my head. "You'll slow me down."

He looked deserted. Scared. She would feel deserted. Scared. I closed my eyes and tried to shut out the windmill of emotions that kept turning in front of my face, never giving me a chance to catch up.

There was no guarantee, but I said it anyway. "I'll be back soon." We emptied our packs and put a single water bottle in each.

"We won't wait for you if you're late," Gus warned. He tapped his watch.

We nodded.

We wound through the black trunks of the trees, sprinting as though we were being chased. My muscles burned, but it was a welcome distraction.

Matt kept up easily, running next to me. He didn't try to talk. I got the sense no one knew what to say to me anyway. It was just the sound of our feet hitting wet ground and our own breathing.

I tried to pretend we were rushing back to the compound to rescue her. But I knew that was why Matt was next to me, his concerned eyes glancing sideways in my direction. He wouldn't let me do it. After what I'd done, they'd kill me before I reached her, but part of me just couldn't care. We ran in the direction of the hanging wolves, giving the compound a wide berth. They might be looking for us, although given the chaos I left them with, maybe not.

We got closer and our shoulders collided as we slowed to a jog, our attention elsewhere. To our right, the glow of a compound that would normally be sleeping slowed our pace. Sirens howled. A yellow haze of artificial light hung in the sky.

Matt stopped and put his hand on my shoulder, panting. "I'm not sure this is safe. They must be on high alert searching for you."

Between breaths, I said, "No. The place is in chaos. I think we probably have a good shot of going unnoticed tonight."

Matt was just a shadow in front of the glow and the trees. "Chaos? What do you mean?"

The words didn't want to come out my mouth. If I spoke them, it made them true. It released some of what was inside, and I wasn't sure I was ready.

"We need to keep moving," I said, taking a step forward and trying to ignore him.

He caught my shirt and pulled me back. "Joseph. What happened in there?"

Just say it. *I killed Superior Este. I killed all of them.*

"Superior Este is dead," I said.

Coward.

Matt's hands fell to his sides. Even as a shadow, his body language was clear. Shock. "How?" he asked, his voice high with disbelief.

I shrugged, unwilling to admit it to anyone.

Matt ran a hand through his hair. "Was it Rosa? Is that why they have her?"

I didn't answer. Which was as bad as saying yes. What was wrong with me? I was letting the girl who saved my life take the blame for my actions.

"Oh no," he said. "I think we should leave."

We were so close now. I could hear the red dot on that screen screaming for me. I needed it. Orry *needed* me.

"You can leave if you want. I have to find her handheld," I whispered tersely. I picked up the pace, pulling away from the glow, from my crimes that felt like they were written in the sky. I needed to know where Orry was. He was my home now.

Matt lagged for a few seconds but caught up with me. We jogged silently, one ear out to the compound, ready to sprint away if we heard soldiers coming.

Cold air cleaned my lungs. I concentrated on the pain in my side and the burn of needing oxygen to feed my working muscles. If I could focus on the mechanics, maybe I could forget the unnatural tearing my heart was doing. Matt puffed beside me. Then he stopped breathing and moving. His hand shot out and pulled me down to the ground with a sudden jerk.

"Look," he said mutedly, pointing his shadow of an arm. Twenty meters in front of us, torchlight crossed like swords in battle.

Loud voices whined through the dark. "This doesn't seem important. Este's dead for God's sake!" a woman complained, throwing her hands in the air in exasperation.

"Mmhmm. Superior Grant wants everything back the way it was."

Two women were tying the wolf coats back on to a newly raised line.

"Ugh! Who cares about this, though?"

"Maybe *they* will."

"Who?"

The woman paused and teetered on her ladder. "The murderers."

My throat closed, memories of loud shots and falling bodies clamping around me.

Murderer.

I gulped and tried to push it down, hide from it, until I could get out of there.

Matt signaled to me, pointing to a pile of rocks at the foot of the tree the wire line was tied to. My head rolled to the sky. Of course it would be there.

The women were still yapping as I crept closer, keeping my body low to the ground. One stood with the torch in her mouth, her hand clamped over the dried-up paw of one of the creatures. She put an iron peg in it and climbed down her stepladder. As she dragged it along the ground, I stole as close to the tree as I could. When they started talking again, I reached into the pile of rocks to find the handheld. My hand searched for something smooth and plastic and found nothing.

I turned back to Matt several meters behind me. He put his hands up as if to say, *I don't know.* Desperately, my mind started to hope that maybe she had managed to get here first. I withdrew my hand carefully. It was shaking from fear and hope meshed together. The rocks tumbled, the noise seeming louder than a landslide, and the women stopped talking. *Shit!*

I picked up a stone and threw it across the gap in the trees where they stood, just as the handheld nudged my other hand, which was still braced against the pile. The stone hit a turbine, sending a gong-like sound up the tube, and the women turned in its direction. I grabbed the handheld and retreated slowly. Equally crushed and relieved at the same time… more crushed.

We crept backwards for at least another twenty meters, painfully slow, our knees squishing in the mud and leaves. Once we were sure they weren't coming for us, we turned and ran back to the camp.

Running away from the compound a second time hurt just as much. It was final now. I would not be going back there, ever. If she were alive, she would have to find her way back to me. On her own. The words stabbed me—I was useless.

As we approached the camp a few hours later, I grabbed Matt by the shoulders to stop him from entering before I told him, "Don't say anything about Este and Rosa, please." My arm tensed at the lies I was telling, and I squeezed his shoulder too hard.

He shook me off. "I'll tell them about Este but I won't say how it happened, okay?"

"Thank you," I said, with no relief.

We walked into the camp, and I went straight to Desh. I whispered close to his ear, standing over him like the menace I was. "Have you told anyone what I did?"

He pulled back and made eye contact, shaking his head in disappointment. "Of course not, Joe. It's not my information to share. But I really think we should talk about it."

I laughed bitterly, "There's nothing to talk about, Desh. It's over. Done." I sliced the air with my hand.

"But…" he started to say, but I stopped him.

"Please man. Not now," I begged.

He let it go, but I could tell this wasn't the end of it. I pulled him down to sit next to me and turned the screen on. It remained black. I shook it, panic dropping a curtain on my restraint. I was about to throw it against a tree when a man came to me, someone I recognized from the Monkey City.

"It's on standby," he said, his breath sour and hot on my face. He snatched it from my tense grip and flipped it over, opening up the back and flicking a switch under the battery. "See." He held the screen in front of our faces until it lit up.

Icons gleamed in front of me. But when I went to the map, nothing came up. My frustration was boiling up inside me. I wanted to smash the thing against a rock until it was nothing but splinters of black glass. The man rolled his eyes and said, "Turn on the GPS signal."

Desh took it from me and manipulated the screen until he had what I wanted. A blinking, red light far away from here.

I pointed to it and nudged Desh's shoulder. "That's where the boys are."

We stared at it for a few seconds before it was snatched from Desh's hands.

"Now turn it off before they all get a lock on where we are!" Gus snapped. He switched it off.

Both of us sighed. Desh smiled. He'd been waiting a long time for this and now, Hessa was closer for him. Whereas I felt like a doll being pulled by the arms in two different directions. Soon the stitches would pop, and I'd be torn in two.

3

Eyes Opened

ROSA

I remember this feeling, my insides electrified, my head buzzing with healing. But I was safer.

With the blue comes the memories. People I hold onto, people I need. Safer than me, I pray.

I tried to dredge up a memory, a picture of when Joseph left me. The visions were muddy and blurred. Being dead must do that to you. Reviving your brain confused it.

In my dripping-with-mud memory, Joseph said, "What did you do?" with fear and disappointment. His face dissolved in front of me, his hair swirling into a golden haze, and then he was gone. I couldn't fill in those missing moments because I didn't exist in them. And if I was *somewhere* while I was dead, the door to those recollections had been slammed and locked.

I flushed the toilet again for good measure. The stall door banging into my forearm woke me up a little.

These guards were rougher. Much more annoyed at the inconvenience of me than the ones I'd dealt with so far.

One of them leaned his knee against the door and pummeled me with it repeatedly. "Hurry up!" he snapped. "Grant wants you escorted to his compound immediately." He shoved the door anxiously, until another guard pointed out that I couldn't get out until he stopped.

"Well, what's she doing in there anyway? Powdering her pointy nose?" he retorted, to cover his embarrassment.

The other guard just sighed. I touched my finger to my nose, the movement fresh and fast. My senses were heightened, the smell of bleach stronger than before.

Boots retreated and I un-wedged myself from between the toilet bowl and the wall, pulling the velvet curtain, heavy with dried blood, around my shoulders. Reality hit me hard, my naked body shaking like charged bones in a bag. I was alone.

Snake-like, yellow-green eyes searched me up and down as I stood in front of them.

"Let's go," the guard said, bringing his arm behind my back and nudging me as if I were a cow heading for the slaughter.

"Can I have some clothes first?" I asked uncertainly, pulling the velvet a little tighter around my slim body. I was drowning in scungy fabric, all its grandeur replaced with leftovers of violence and pain, flaking blood and tears.

They exchanged glances, and then one shook his head almost apologetically.

"We don't have time." His bluish eyes were cast down like he really was sorry. I took it as kindness and let myself relax a tiny bit, only to have the other one grab me by the back of my neck and shove me forward.

I pitched into the hall.

"Walk," he ordered. I wanted to salute him, but I couldn't give up my grip on my curtain dress.

The hall was now lit up end to end, a corridor of warm light swarming with people scrubbing, vacuuming, and carrying clumps of bloodied fabric. Stretchers were burdened with the bodies of men, their boots sticking out past the loose sheets covering them. I shook my head from side to side like the sad elephant in the zoo. Everyone was alive when I'd died. There was a big part of the puzzle missing. I dragged the twelve-foot-long curtain behind me like a nightmarish train, stepping aside to make way for the dead. My eyes trained on the shoes. No sneakers, no leather shoes, just soldiers boots. It reinforced my feeling that Joseph and Deshi were alive, and they were far away from here.

Someone stepped on the cloth behind me and I snagged, the curtain dropping down my back. I clung to it, trying to gather the fabric up and sweep it around me. I turned to see who was standing on it. Two men were carrying a stretcher behind me and appeared very anxious at being held up. Two pointy, patent red heels stuck up right in my face like sharpened poppies. I expected them to twitch, the body to squeal. My face drained of color. Este was dead.

I stood frozen, the atmosphere of absolute stress curling around me and poking me with sharp fingernails. I knew I should move and was surprised when instead of smacking me with their gun or shoving me again, one of the guards sighed loudly and began removing his jacket. He threw it at my gaping mouth.

"Here!" he said impatiently.

Thick, canvas cotton scratched my face. I grabbed the jacket and put it on as quickly as possible. It went down to my knees.

The guard bundled up the curtain with a look of disgust and plonked it on one of the passing stretchers without even checking to see if he'd put it on a body.

I blinked up at him. "Thank you," I muttered.

He rolled his eyes. "Just walk."

I cast my gaze down to the rich and colorful rug, mashed and scuffed from boot prints, and moved forward. My bare legs and feet jutted out like matchsticks.

As we left the chaos of the hall behind, I wondered, *What happened while I was dead?* Everything was unraveling like a ball of string tied to a bird-in-flight's leg. A Superior had been murdered! It was unsurprising these people seemed exasperated rather than mournful.

For no reason I could understand, the guards would sporadically shove my shoulder, sending me sprawling forward. It was like violence was just part of their job description, and they had to pepper it in every now and then to earn their titles. I shivered in my loaned jacket and scowled at them. It only seemed to amuse them further. The guard in shirtsleeves seemed to be regretting his choice and, in between shoving me, he kept his arms hugged tightly around his chest.

"Are w-we w-walking the whole way?" I asked through chattering teeth. My voice was so loud, it sounded like I had a megaphone pressed to my lips, another side effect of the healer. Cool air battered my legs, swirling under the loose jacket, and my feet pricked with the sharpness of the gravel.

The snake-like guard's eyes lowered to me as I jerked and shuddered in the cold. "We're on lockdown, thanks to you and your friends, so yes, we have to walk," he sneered.

We marched down Este's driveway towards two immense, ornate gates. The guards stopped and jumped in unison. Then, one of them laughed.

"She's not watching us anymore," he said, knocking the other one's shoulder lightly. "We don't have to do all that crap now." They laughed heartily at the demise of their loopy Superior and undid the padlock to the gate, pushing it open. I expected it to creak, but it opened gracefully.

"Zoo?" the jacket-less guard asked the other.

"Nah. Let's go around. I can't handle the stink tonight," the snake-like guard hissed, his eyes perching over me like I was a bad enough smell.

My eyes followed the disturbed path, the footprints, smudged lightly into the stones. One of those could have been Joseph's, Deshi's... I bent down to touch it without thinking and got a boot in the back.

The one in shirtsleeves, his voice calmer, humor hiding somewhere in there, pulled the other guard back. I turned to look in his eyes, the garden lights leaving them steel colored, almost grey.

"Leave her alone," he said quietly but forcefully. I started to hope maybe they weren't all bad, that they hadn't had all the humanity sucked out of them through their Guardian training. But then he laughed and said, "She's going to suffer plenty once Grant has her!" My heart tumbled into the sharpened ground and was punctured by the small rocks' tiny teeth.

Snake eyes chuckled. "That's for sure!"

At least they stopped kicking and shoving me as we made our way towards Grant's compound.

We arrived at the outer fence of the zoo, ten feet high and grazed with barbed and electrified wire. We followed the fence's perfect curve, the guards' boots crunching down on pure white stones the color and feel of giant rock salt, edged in by neatly cut, one-foot-high stone walls. My bare, aching feet made little sound.

The Indian elephant's sad, lamenting trumpet sailed over the walls. I clasped my hands together and tried to face forward. The hours between

Joseph and me lay in front of me like giant planks of wood. A barrier. *What had I got myself into?*

As we left Este's quarter, things changed dramatically. A neat line and gate defined the transition from one segment of the pie to the next. A single-bulb lamp hung overhead. The white gravel changed to a brick path, with round halos of light built into the bricks. The gardens changed to spiky grasses and architectural plants, pointless trees with no purpose other than to look imposing. They leaned over the path, their branchy fingers almost touching, forming a low, lit tunnel.

I knew without being told that this was Grant's section of the compound. It was far more orderly than Este's was. Each field fenced neatly, each section of garden aesthetically perfect, but there was no feel of life. While Este's seemed like it was a home for madness and nonsense, Grant's was stiflingly regimented.

As we rounded the curve, Superior Grant's house came into view, all angles and sloping roofs, sitting atop a grassy, man-made hill and lording over the ground below. It was nothing like Este's and nothing like home. The whole front was glass. My eyes scanned the floor-to-ceiling windows, and I jumped when I saw that Grant's shadow graced one of them. He sat in his wheelchair, staring down at me, his apathetic expression coming into focus as we neared the house. Warm, golden rectangles of light shone down on us from inside, and I found myself stepping over the shadows like they were solid. There was no gate to pass through, no extensive security measures. We walked down a short driveway and straight into an underground garage. The doors were already rolled up, waiting for us to enter.

Snake eyes pressed a button on an intercom on the inside wall and hissed, "Where do you want the, err, her?"

Grant's voice sailed through the speaker and itched at my ears with its twangy sound. "First floor, second guest bedroom."

Guest? I trembled at the thought.

"Lucky girl," the guard snarled.

I turned around slowly and spoke, my voice still wire-brushed and new to me. "Why am I not going to a prison? What does he want from me?"

They both laughed and didn't answer. I hoped it was because they didn't know.

One guard pressed the up button on the lift. The doors opened, and I caught a flash of hot, red, and shining chrome through the double doors of the lift before they closed. I leaned towards them in curiosity. The guard grabbed my shoulder and pulled me away from the view.

"Stand back," he said warily, his eyes searching out the corners of the lift. They both behaved as if they were being watched all the time. They probably were.

The lift glided upwards, strange moaning music playing, the singer caught in a trap he couldn't get out of by the sound of it. One guard clicked his fingers in time. The doors chimed and opened. A female guard stood to attention in front of the lift, jumping to life when she saw me, her red roots poking through her light brown dye job shone hopelessly under the round lights punched into the ceiling. She leaned in, grabbed my arm, and squeezed, yanking me out of the lift and away from the men.

"Thank you for delivering Miss Rosa." She eyed my clothing or lack thereof. "I'll have your jacket cleaned and returned to you." They nodded, and I caught one of them anxiously pressing the down button. He wanted to get out of there.

"Keep it," he shouted nervously as the doors closed on his narrow face.

I found myself missing them as soon the door closed. This woman's tight hold, the sleek décor, the fact that she called me Miss Rosa, were all more unnerving than the outward hostility and punches in the back. That, I understood.

She marched me down a hallway, lights glowing along the floor, and carpet the color of bruised lips and blood sinking between my toes. I looked up to see a large painting of a can of tomato soup and laughed. The squeeze got tighter, and her expression pulled her face in like purse strings. We came to a polished, wooden door with copper wall lights on either side. The woman, Red, as I had already nicknamed her in my head, punched in numbers on the keypad and scanned her wrist. The door unlatched, and I was dragged towards the bed.

My bony butt sank warily into the most comfortable mattress I had ever touched. A satin bedspread swirled around my dirty legs, which were striped with dried blood, the patterns almost wanting to eject me so I didn't sully their beauty. I gazed down at my hands, clasped over the heavy canvas jacket. The tarnished buttons and frayed pockets were almost a comfort. I put my hand into one of the pockets and fished out a folded piece of paper. Hope flowed through me too quickly, warm and golden. I had to clamp down on these feelings before they destroyed me because as I opened the paper, while Red was busy locking the door behind her, the short list of items caused my heart to shrivel inside me along with my faith. I remembered the last time I'd read a list like this. Black words scrawled on lined paper encompassed death, love, hope. This was just a grocery list: Tinned tomatoes x 2, rice, beef, tampons. I quirked my eyebrow at the last item. The soldier had a wife and maybe a daughter. It was something I needed to remind myself of—everyone had a family. Something, *someone* to lose.

Red huffed, standing over me with her hands on her hips. She held out her hand for the note, and I gave it to her. She scrunched it in one hand without reading it and shoved it in her pocket, her skirt so tight on her hips that I could see the little ball of paper bulging under the fabric.

Eyes wide and critical, she drew a breath and lunged at me.

I leaned back on the bed, frightened of this enormous woman pressing her breasts into my face. She dragged her fingers through my hair, and I struggled not to suffocate.

"Sit up!" she barked impatiently. "I'm not going to hurt you, child."

Still naked under the jacket, I felt vulnerable to say the least, but I sat there like a good girl, like someone else, and let her run her hands through my hair, inspect my eyes, and pinch at my skin like I was an animal on show. Because I promised. Even though every part of my dark, scrawny body wanted to smack her so hard I'd leave a bony handprint on her cheek, I knew I wouldn't get far.

"What are you doing?" I asked, my voice muffled through a curtain of my own hair.

She looked over the top of my head as she replied, "Getting your colors right."

"My colors?"

"Yes. What you need to change, what you can keep." *What I could keep?*

I gripped the quilt on either side of me like it was cement that could hold me in my place. Maybe I could hit her a little?

She seemed indifferent to my reaction and continued inspecting me, but when she made a move for my jacket, I put my arm up to block her, pushing back at her assault. I wasn't doing this again.

Her large head gave a tiny shake. I didn't have time to react before she whipped her hand into her breast pocket and tapped a black device to my arm. My body jolted, feeling and sounding like it had cracked in half like a dry branch.

My eyes rolled, my speech thick in my mouth. "Wha… why…?"

Her fuzzy image became larger in my eyes until she filled the whole room. Her thunderclap voice slammed against the walls.

"You didn't do as you were told." The words 'do as you were told' echoed and ran down the walls like dripping paint.

My arm stung with the familiar prick of a needle. My body slumped and gave in to a familiar feeling. I was right back where I started.

4

Captor

GRANT

I watched her treading or rather storming towards my garage. The look on her face was not what I had expected, and it irritated me. She should be afraid, trembling. Uncertain. Instead, her large, uneven, young eyes took in my home, my world, seeming more curious than afraid. That would soon change.

I cursed my inability to escort her myself. I imagined my hand clamped around her thin arm, my legs strong and quick. I would have dragged her here and heard her whimper. My ghost foot stamped and of course, there was no impact, no sound. But soon, I would walk again. I could almost feel my height growing. I would look down on everyone. Never again would people stoop to meet my eyes. It had not been so long that I couldn't remember what it felt like to stride through my own garden, to stand above most. Now, I looked up and despised my view.

She dragged her bare feet through my perfectly raked stones, her head up, proud. Stupid. She didn't know. She would soon understand. I was not Este, crazed, obsessive, and I certainly wasn't Sekimbo, a drunk, or Poltinov, stupidly agreeable, old, and clueless. My turn was coming. My way was the only way.

The chair moved awkwardly over the carpet as I wheeled right up to the window. They had recommended I change my home, lower it to the ground. But I knew this was temporary. They even suggested an electric chair, but I needed to feed my own movement. My toes bumped the glass; I couldn't feel it, just the resistance. From here, I could look down on them, but it was a pathetic victory. The girl's jacket swung below her knees, and I was reminded that she was a child. A foolish, insignificant child.

I clenched my fists on my chair arm when her eyes met mine. She didn't shy away from my gaze. She glared directly into them, those odd eyes, that spirit. It fueled me because it was begging to be broken. I wheeled back from the window, unused to anyone giving me such extended eye contact and smiled to myself. There was so much I wanted to show her.

5

Always

JOSEPH

I thought about her always. She was just there, in my mind, by my side, smirking, frowning at me. Because she was a ghost. I tried not to think of her broken, bleeding body surrounded by dead soldiers, toppled like Orry's blocks, but it was a flashcard wedged permanently inside my brain. I tried to bend it, push it aside, and think about Orry and what she had done for me. But the strongest feeling was wishing with every part of my hopeless body that she hadn't done it.

We sat around a campfire, except for Rash, who was standing as far away from me as he could. I was the plague to him, and I kind of agreed with his assessment. He glared down at me from behind the circle of crouching people. His face was pure hatred glowing behind the fire. It didn't sit right on his usually jovial face. He should be smiling, joking, and I took that from him.

For twenty-four hours, we'd done nothing but walk in silence. After they found Rash and convinced him to stay with the group, there was nothing to do but continue with the mission. I came because they wouldn't let me go back to the Superiors' compound, and they wouldn't let me return to Orry on my own. They didn't trust me.

Now, we were resting briefly before more walking.

Matt came and sat next to me, his whole form heavy with grief and responsibility. "How are you?" he asked warily.

"Do I need to answer that?" I replied as I drew circles in the dirt with a stick.

"No... you don't," he whispered, his voice small and broken into pieces. "So... we're heading to Birchton first."

My shoulders were set. I didn't want to talk. So I didn't. Matt sighed and rubbed the back of his neck. He wanted to get through. I didn't know how to tell him there was no point; there was nothing on the other side of this wall I'd put up.

Desh nudged my leg with his knee as he sat down on the other side. "Give him a break," he pleaded. I wasn't sure if he was talking to Matt or me, but silence followed, which was fine.

After about five minutes of awkwardness, Desh finally started talking again.

"I'm nearly finished adapting the projectors," he said to Matt over my dipped head. I continued drawing. An image of Rosa's dark face pushed out of the dirt, her forehead creased with pain and then suddenly peaceful. Even in sleep, she never looked peaceful. Only when she was dead.

I let out a huge sigh, trying to breath out the hurt.

"Great," Matt said. He turned and grabbed the bag of image discs behind him. The plastic rattled around like shell casings. "Here are the images. Will you be able to get this done by tomorrow?"

I saw Desh nod his head in the corner of my vision. He grasped the bag and put it by his feet.

"Easy," he replied confidently. Something other than the mush of crappy emotions I'd been feeling surfaced, just for a second. Pride. Desh was the smartest guy I knew.

Matt leaned across me. "Easy?" I tilted my chin up to see his eager eyes full of wonderment. "Can you talk me through it?"

Matt was almost as bad as Alexei when it came to new technology, new information. He ate it up like a hearty meal. I pictured Alexei holding Orry's hand and leading him 'up'. That was all she'd said, *Take him somewhere 'up'*. I shook my head. Somehow, everyone knew exactly what she'd meant. When her words failed, her eyes, the emotion in her voice, did the rest. Grief was as heavy as a backpack full of lead bricks. I slumped down further, my fingers swirling in the dirty pattern in front of me.

I don't want to forget her. I don't want to remember her.

Desh laughed, and I was pulled back to their conversation.

"Sure..." He put his hand on my back, and I flinched. "Do you need anything before I go?"

My back muscles tensed, and I stood up suddenly. I pulled my hands through my hair, scanning the group of people. They were all watching me, waiting for me to do... something. Rash mirrored my movements and moved around the circle away from me as I tried to exit it.

"Joe?" Desh questioned.

I grunted and made my way to a gap in the trees, leaving the smell of sweet tea and smoke behind.

Sharp, grey rocks tried to trip me as I climbed away from the group. Leaves rustled in the background and I swung around to Pelo's face, lit up by my torchlight. "Where are you going?" he asked, concerned.

Stop being nice to me, I wanted to scream, holler, punch into the ground, and wear across my chest. My fists vibrated at my sides. I wanted to do more than shout. I wanted to push him back towards the campsite, hard. Violence lived in me like a virus. I breathed in sharply though my nostrils. The shock of pine and crushed grass swirled around me like a memory I wanted to keep and forget.

"I'm not running away," I said through gritted teeth. "I just want some... space."

His eyes were so hard to look at. His sad, grieving face even worse.

I need space from everything and everyone except you, Rosa. Space between us is like a wall of knives.

I stormed away from him. I heard the branches snap back and his footsteps fade away.

Do you want me to be there for your father, comfort him? I shouldn't ask because I can't do it. I'm hollow. There's nothing left inside me to give.

My breath felt like a hard ball in my chest. Cold and concrete. Panic kept rising and subsiding with thoughts of her. Was she angry with me for deserting her? Was she suffering?

Putting a hand out, I grabbed at a jutting piece of rock to steady myself. I gulped back tears. If I started thinking about what they were doing to her, it would kill me. It *was* killing me. This guilt, this fear, was living and growing inside, trying to take over. I didn't know how to stop it. If it could just ease for a second, maybe I could breathe. Keep moving. Live. Like she wanted me to. I gripped the rock so hard I felt I could almost rip it from the ground.

Voices carried to me from below, a small, orange glow visible through the trees. Someone laughed. I couldn't stand the way everything just went on. Without her.

I kept climbing, desperate to escape their noise, until all I could hear were the leaves bristling against each other and the echo of wind deepening the curves of the stone.

My palms were roughed up by shards of rock. I was sweating even in this cold. The breeze picked up as I got higher, and I shivered. Her arm wrapped around my back, stretching to shield me. She could never quite reach, but her hand always found my heart. She patted it once. I put my hand through her ghost.

I climbed a few meters more, and was at the peak of one of the many rocky hills surrounding Birchton and Radiata. In front of me, swept with moonlight, were the craggy mountains we would have to climb over to get to Birchton and further below, the sleeping town lay nestled into the side of a cliff. Each ring shone softly.

Rosa's hand slipped from my heart to my palm. Her thin fingers threaded through mine. *Not that way*, she used to say. She hated holding hands like this; she always said my fingers were too large and forced hers apart painfully. *Like this,* she would say, placing her palm against mine. I sat down and shook it off. The feeling that she was here with me, that she was actually a ghost, was not true. It couldn't be.

"I won't give up," I whispered to the air.

The tower lights of the compounds glimmered like weak candles. We weren't far. I narrowed my eyes, imagining the walls exploding, people running through the gap. I would focus on that. Destruction. It matched my insides well.

I sat there for an hour. Breathing. Thinking. Remembering. Trying to suppress her and revive her at the same time. I looked to the sky, knowing she was probably boxed in. White, swirling flakes streamed towards my eyes.

Snow.

6

Unreality

ROSA

In sleep, I can have him. In the back of my mind, in the pretty little corners he opened up, he's waiting. I want to retreat to those corners forever.

If I could live there, I would.

"Bang! Bang! Bang!"

Gunshots clipped the air and shredded the curtains, tearing them into strips that dripped with blood. My blood. Wet and flapping against an open window. The streaks horrific, murderous.

"Bang!" One frustrated noise.

I pulled my knees to my chest, curling into a ball like a centipede tapped on its back, covering my head with my ineffectual fingers.

Bullets tear through everything, and when it's close enough, so does a knife.

I pulled in tighter; harboring my scar like it was precious. The movement caused satin to glide underneath and over my skin, and I shot up like a catapult. My dream receded. Reality cupped my chin and squeezed my jaw violently. It drew my face this way and that, stretching my eyes wide. *Look. Look where you are.* My dazed brain swept the room. Luxurious reds crept up the walls interspersed with strips of gold. The large bed was covered in a quilt spotted with pinwheel shapes, swirling and sucking me into its center. I leaned my head in and out as my eyes stared at the middle of the gold wheel until I felt dizzy. Shuffling back, I leaned against the wall. It was as soft as a satin ribbon. Rich honey timber glossed the corners in the forms of beautiful furniture. If I wasn't so scared, I could appreciate it. If I wasn't so disgusted with the opulence these people surrounded themselves with, maybe I could relax. My eyes followed the gold stripes up to the ceiling and found the black camera screwed to the wall. I felt like waving, but I was trying to suppress my normal wonts and behavior.

What was I wearing?

I bounded from the bed and looked down in horror at my clothing. My black, soldier's jacket had been replaced by a grey, knee-length skirt. My skin prickled beneath a high-necked, synthetic pink shirt and pink cardigan with tiny, pearlescent beads around the collar. Cracking my neck, I shuddered at the continuing weirdness. I would have been upset that someone dressed me, but I know I would have got myself in more trouble if Red had presented me with this outfit and forced me to put it on. I could just imagine the tug-of-war and grinned at my imagined victory. Pulling at the hem of the skirt, I wiggled in the cut-your-circulation-off stockings. No. They were coming off. I leaned down and unrolled them so my legs could receive their blood supply.

A bang on the door startled me.

"Miss Rosa?" A young, questioning voice.

Quickly shimmying out of the stockings, I put on the black shoes shining like pools of motor oil that were placed neatly by the bed. I was completely confused.

Gold-stemmed lamps rose from two identical bedside tables, the green glass shades painful to look at. I touched one tentatively, my finger bouncing off its surface. It was warm but didn't burn me. The colors were torture. Deep, forest green, gold. I felt like smashing it and holding it to my heart at the same time. I imagined Joseph's eyes blinking at me, him shaking his head with amusement at my strangeness, and it was all I could do not to sink to the floor, to allow myself to drown in the blood-colored carpet. To think maybe I would have been better off dead than here.

I undid a few buttons on my shirt so I could breathe and waited for the guard to barge in. I waited, but he kept knocking until I said, "Yes. Come in."

The door clicked open and I remained still on the edge of the bed, trying not to slide right off. I stared at the lamp for longer than I should have. *Joseph's face, his smile...* It was all running away from me, running out like the last, fresh spring in summer.

My shaky hands ran through my hair to tuck it behind my ear, but I came up short. *She cut my hair?* I pulled the strands through my fingers in front of my eyes, light honey-brown strands of hair! I cursed just as the guard stepped into the room. The look of surprise was quite evident on his face. I was sure I looked ridiculous.

I swore again, he stiffened, and I clapped my mouth shut. I needed to remember my promise—that I would live. So I sat neatly on the edge of the bed, looking up him expectantly, like a child ready to learn. I was never that child. I was the child wiggling impatiently on the rug until I'd nearly worn a hole in it. I was the child that asked too many of the wrong questions and never had any of the right answers. I chewed on my lip when the guard approached, wondering what they were going to do next. They'd changed my appearance. The next thing to change would not be so easy...

His hair was my color, my new color, and it swept across his face like someone had smacked his forehead with a large paintbrush. He swept it over his brow and blinked at me with strange, blue eyes. We stared at each other for a while, his hands moving unconsciously from front to back like he wasn't sure what to do with them. I got impatient and sighed. "What do you want?" I asked.

He snapped out of it and moved towards me, which caused me to brace myself in defense. One arm crossed over my chest, the other slipping on the bedspread as my body leaned backwards. He noticed my fear and stopped, again playing with his hands. It was strange for a guard to register anyone else's emotions. I waited for his hand to reach out and smack me. He stood with one hand below his ribs and the other behind his back like he might take a bow. I quirked an eyebrow.

"Superior Grant has ordered me to escort you to the dining room," he announced as he offered me his elbow.

I snorted. "Escort?"

He nodded, his hair falling in his eyes. Smoothing it over, he parted his legs slightly and waited. Voices echoed in my head and reminded me why I had to do as he asked. Because my arms felt heavy with the weight of a child who was no longer there. The ache of missing my child was the claw of a hammer, bluntly, blatantly tugging at my heart. I warned myself, *Just do as you're told. For him, for both of them.*

I rose and walked past the guard, ignoring the elbow I suppose I was expected to lace my arm through. In my mind, *escort* didn't need to mean touching. As I passed the young guard, who still had a pimple or two along his jaw, reminding me he was probably my age or younger, I anticipated his hand clamping over my arm and leaned away. He let me through, and I think he smiled. I grimaced as I tramped forward. He followed close behind me.

"Turn right," he said quietly when we were in the hall, confusingly allowing me a respectful distance.

I did as he said and followed the curve of the huge windows. I wanted to run my hands along the frames, wanted to ask about who built this place, but questions were for people whose opinions mattered and that was not me.

We stepped quickly. My shoes slid too easily over the carpet as if I were wearing two sticks of butter. My eyes ran over the paintings as we passed them. Everything was bright and primary, bold, strong shapes and thick, black lines. Orry could have painted them. I sniffed. The ache deepened.

The windows showed a bleak view. Close-to-black, night air pressed against the panes with a few garden lights dotting the ground below. I craved to feel it around me, chilling my shoulders and creating puffs of mist from my mouth. I shivered. I was trapped like the zoo animals, just in a fancier cage.

I stopped and turned my head to the guard. "How long have I been asleep?"

His eyes darted back and forth at the different cameras tuned to our movements and decided it was safe to answer. "About a day, Miss."

The 'Miss' made me cringe. This fakeness was surely going to end. Soon, I'd be thrown against bars, my bones would crack on cold stone floors, and I'd be forced to give up information. I shook my head slightly. They'd have to kill me. The plans lay in my stomach like iron brambles. They might try to drag them from me and it would sting and cut, but I'd rather set myself on fire than tell them anything.

Joseph was a day away from me. It made me smile and frown at the same time. He would still be a long way in time and distance from Orry. I tripped as I thought of us, like the points of an enormous triangle. So. Far. Away. If neither of us made it back, Orry would never know us. He would forget me. The pain of that realization was crippling, and for a moment, I struggled to move.

I pulled my hand across my stomach, the scar bending inwards. *You can do this. Keep walking.*

I stomped forward.

"Enter the door on your right, Miss Rosa," the guard said as he halted and waited for me to follow his directions.

I took a quick breath and placed my hand on the cool, brushed steel handle, trying not to be distracted by the silken beauty of the wooden paneling in front of my scared eyes.

Family. In Pau, the word meant very little. It was a threat wrapped in a warning: Don't get too close.

I had it in my slippery fingers for what seemed like less than a grain of time.

But I'm still tied to it. These ropes get stronger with every added piece of twine, each life I've added to my own.

The door swung open with just the minute sound of the glossy timber stroking the strands of carpet. I stared down at my bare feet in my court shoes and scratched my arm nervously as I shuffled into the room, pushing against a solid wall of my own fear.

Someone clapped once, hard, like a textbook hitting a table. My eyes snapped up.

His stare pierced my skin like a needle, drawing out what little bravery I had managed to strap to my heart.

"Ah! Rosa Bianca! Finally you wake." That voice like abused guitar strings rang out in a nearly empty room that smelled like talcum powder and fresh bread. My eyes swept across the large glass table. Its shining chrome legs polished like mirrors made my reflection even more narrow and bendy than normal. And at the head of it, Grant sat in a dining chair that looked as if it had been carved from a single piece of wood, seamless. His wheelchair lay folded in the corner and I arched an eyebrow, wondering how he got in the chair.

He cleared his throat, bringing my attention back to his needling eyes. I bowed my head.

"Superior Grant." I wondered if I should curtsy or maybe... throw a chair at his smiling face, smash a window, and run. Grant's smile was a twisted thing that cautioned me of the cruelty beneath, and it matched the painting behind him. A huge, gilded frame wrapped around a picture of Grant standing up proudly in military uniform without aid, his eyes searching the distance as if he were looking for more people to crush, just over the hill. My eyes moved up and down, comparing the painting to the real Grant, and he observed me silently. There was little difference, except for the legs. My mouth turned up inappropriately, and the table rattled as he gripped the edge.

My eyes passed over the glistening white plates, ringed with silver, the cutlery rattling slightly like they were scared of him too. The table was set for five people.

"Come. Sit by me. We have a lot to discuss," Grant said, beckoning with his hand as a shiny, metal watch jangled from his thick wrist. I stared at the dark hairs caught in the band, my head to the side, feeling like my feet were glued to the ground.

I didn't move.

He might as well have been beckoning me to walk over broken glass. The guard shut the door behind me, leaving us alone. I took a step backwards, my fingers searching for the door handle.

He frowned at my hesitance.

"Do I need to remind you what happens when you don't do as you are told?" he said, leaning forward with both hands spread on the table. I watched the condensation form around his disproportionately muscular hands. I pitied the wheels of his chair.

I took a timid step forward, feeling hot and uncomfortable as I passed under the blasting air conditioning. "No, you don't need to remind me, Sir," I said through gritted teeth. I didn't want to play this game. I wanted to smash the table with my fists and pull him from his chair.

One sturdy hand folded into a hard fist, and he hissed through barely open lips, "Then sit." He pointed to the chair beside him, straight down.

I moved slowly as his eyes tracked me across the room like a motion detector, his mouth pursing at my bare feet squeaking against the leather of my shoes. My eyes went to the high, narrow window above the buffet. Nothing but black sky. Empty. Grant's eyes were equally empty.

Below the window were photos of distinctively All Kind children of various ages. Some looked to be the same child, frames knocking against each other following the child's growth. Others were of a baby with no follow-up pictures. I was curious, but I couldn't spend time wondering. Grant's eyes were ready to slice me to pieces.

He patted the chair to his left, and I sat down. Hands folded in my lap, eyes downcast, trying to play the part I thought he wanted.

"Rosa," he croaked bitterly, my name a curse on his tongue. He tapped his fingers on the glass absently. "You've hurt your people," he said in fake seriousness, "and you've hurt me." He put his palm to where I suppose his heart would be if he had one. I tried to retreat into myself like a turtle to its shell before I reached out and slapped his face, holding onto my right hand with my left like it was not my own.

"Perhaps if you can tell me what you and your misguided friends are planning, there may be a chance of redemption for you." His voice held very little feeling. I was a pebble in his shoe, annoying but easily dealt with.

I allowed myself to peek into his soul-stealing eyes. "No." My lips formed the word and my heart stammered in my chest, telling me to take it back, to stop scrawling my death sentence all over the walls like it was nothing.

He leaned back and clasped his hands together, his moustache twitching slightly with irritation. I tried not to take pleasure in it and failed, my own lips rising into a smile.

"No?" he asked, his voice dark and dripping in the ink that would sign my execution.

"Never," I said plainly. I may have promised to stay alive, but I wasn't going to kill my friends to do it.

My eyes went to the floor, the safest place, and I noticed his chair legs were higher than mine by an inch or two. Red appeared in his cheeks and his forehead, instantly creasing like a dried riverbed. I winced, awaiting the force of his shouting. But then he took a deep breath and everything dissipated like blowing the steam off the top of a cup of coffee.

"We'll see, child," he said shrewdly.

I eyed the butter knife in front of me. It was blunt, but did he deserve sharp and quick? Its silver light promised revenge. I raised my hand to take it—

The door opened, and three people filed in. I paused. I couldn't fight three people. I wasn't even sure I could take a man in a wheelchair. Not this one anyway.

A girl about my age, maybe younger, entered, arm in arm with an older woman. A young man held the door ajar until the females had passed, his head dipped, white wires hanging from both his ears. All Kind colored, spiked hair sprayed over his forehead and grazed his ears. He glanced up slowly like his head was weighted, our eyes meeting briefly, then just as slowly he turned away from me.

"Rosa. I'd like you to meet my family," Grant announced in a voice so warm it burnt me. The polite host switch had flicked inside him. I stood as each member of this monster's family reached over the table to shake my hand.

"This is my wife, Camille."

The tall, blondish woman with perfect tanned skin leaned over the table, her ample cleavage bouncing in my face.

"Hello dear," she confidently greeted me. Dumbfounded, I took her hand. It was sweaty and slick with moisturizer that smelled like jasmine. She took her place at the other end of the table.

"This is Denis, my son," Grant muttered, watching Denis slowly and warily hold out his hand to me. His tall, lean body bent over the table resistantly, like a sapling being pulled over by a starving deer. I pictured him snapping back into place and covered my mouth before I laughed. He didn't say 'hello', he just let his eyes run up and down my torso until he met my eyes properly, the whole blue eye, brown eye thing causing him to pause. His hand finally made it to mine, too soft, warm. He shook my hand once and then dropped it, nearly landing it in the centerpiece, his caramel brown arm returning to his side. His eyes stared into mine, deep, dark blue like flint reflecting the sky. There was a smile teasing the corners of his mouth as we gazed at each other, but it was a shadow of a smile, his expression still guarded. I tried to stop the blush from creeping up my neck but was unsuccessful. He sat across from me. Dropping down in his seat perfectly, like he'd fallen from the sky exactly over his chair. He plucked the two earphones from his ears, and they dangled on either side of his neck like drops of water.

Grant groaned loudly.

From his seat, Denis tipped his head down and ran his eyes over his cutlery in a curious way. Like he was figuring out exactly how he was going to hold them, use them, before he even touched them.

"Take those off, Denis," Grant drawled with barely clothed disdain as he pointed to the earphones still pulsing soft music.

Denis nodded, muttering, "Yes, Dad," in a deep, hindered tone, and pulled the earphones from his green, V-neck sweater, winding them carefully around his fingers, knotting the cord together and placing it in his breast pocket.

Arms came from behind and startled me, wrapping around my shoulders and neck. Arms clad in a blue cardigan that matched my own. "Ooh it fits!" a nervous, almost-desperate voice spoke from behind me. I turned to stone in her arms. The girl released me, swung around, and collapsed in the chair next to me.

Grant's voice was dripping with sickly sweetness. "This is my daughter, Judith."

"Nice to meet ya," she said in an accent that perfectly matched Grant's, her skirt sliding up her leg as she swung it over the arm of the chair, draping her body over it like a discarded towel. She was small, willowy like Apella, but when she spoke, her voice was not like bells. The twang was like snapping wire, and I cringed noticeably. When she saw my reaction, she straightened up and pulled her hands inside her cardigan, just the tips of her rather orange skin poking through the ends of the sleeves.

Grant's head snapped to her but then he composed his voice.

"Judith. We have company. Place your hands in your lap like a young lady." I swallowed my laugh uncomfortably like a ball of air. She sat up straight and put her fingers to her mouth, about to chew on her fingernails. "Hands down," Grant instructed patiently, his hand slapping the glass table gently, causing the silverware to rattle. Everyone straightened. The atmosphere was light and wafting one minute and cold and frightening the next. They were aware of Grant's stretching temper, and no one wanted to be the one who made him snap.

Despite this, they seemed like a genuine family. I was in a dream, a painting, a life that shouldn't exist.

I watched quietly as they talked about their days and began to despise all of them. The chatter was inane, and I found myself wishing I were alone with Grant again. At least then, it was real. I had questions for him too.

Then Denis, who up till now had been slowly carving his food into small pieces and then carefully putting a piece of each type of food on his fork until he had a bite-sized cross-section, spoke.

"What is she doing here, Dad? Is she a replacement?" He looked suspiciously to his father with unblinking dark blue eyes, waiting for his answer.

Judith inhaled sharply.

The cutlery on the table vibrated softly as Grant put his glass of wine down firmly. "No, she's not a replacement, Denis. She's our guest." This word 'guest' did not mean what it should. There was a strangling threat behind it.

Denis nodded like nothing else needed to be said.

Everyone turned towards me like I should say something. I poked the creamy mushroom sauce that slathered a pork loin chop with my fork. Everything was ridiculous. They were ridiculous. *What do you say when your enemy has you over for dinner?*

"These mushrooms taste like dirt," I murmured at my plate, wishing instantly that I could pull the words back into my mouth. Silence capped over us like someone had placed a glass jar over the whole table. Flustered, I tried to cover my comment. "I mean, sorry. Like a nice kind of dirt. I mean," I tapped the plate with my fork, "I'm used to dried meat and stale bread…"

Everyone looked to Grant for a response. I got the sense they didn't breathe without his say so. His face was hard but he laughed, spitting it out like stale milk. When he finished laughing, his family stared at him, waiting for a more appropriate reaction. Camille looked down at her plate and then at her children.

"Poor child. She doesn't know what real food tastes like." She spread her arms over the table, and I wanted to plant her face in her mashed potatoes.

Denis watched me, his eyes distant but on my lips as I spoke. I felt like I was being measured.

"Yes. Sorry. You're right," I muttered as Denis shook his head minutely, almost like he was disappointed in me. *Measured and found wanting.* I was trapped in this painting with the rest of them, scratching against the scene and trying to force my way out without them noticing. I wanted nothing more than to yell at them, throw the plate up, and watch the sauce splatter their shocked faces as a slimy pork chop tumbled onto the perfect, white tablecloth. I could imagine Camille's gasp, Grant's roaring temper. I wanted to point at their well-fed, tinted faces and scream, *I don't know because you made me this way. You've deprived us, tortured us, and controlled us for so long. How can you live like this, you selfish, self-serving pieces of garbage?* But I said nothing. I ate my food, sipped my cider, and it felt like acid in my stomach. Not speaking was burning a hole through my insides, my personality leaching out of me and leaving me waned.

But I promised.

I promised.

An Ache

JOSEPH

The morning was frost cold, the fire almost out. The trees dripped water onto our faces from above. Poor Olga stretched and strained, dusting sheets of cracked ice off her jacket and pulling tiny icicles from her thin hair. She wasn't built for this kind of thing, but I was impressed at how hard she tried. She was always eager to learn, wanting to try new techniques and be involved. We could all learn something from her of how not to give up. I struggled with that myself, but I couldn't go to her for advice. I couldn't talk to anyone. I just wanted to talk to *her*.

You would laugh if you saw it. You'd nudge me and point at her, snickering, and then you would go over, crouch down on your skinny legs, and help her. I knew her, and I knew how she would do things. She stayed with me, even if it hurt more than healed me. Rosa was stubborn like that. I allowed myself to feel her for a second, and it slipped off my body like water before the second was over.

Today was the first day we would really risk our lives. It left us all feeling anxious to get started and apprehensive of the outcome. Desh spent most of the night adjusting the projectors. He made it look easy, although I was sure it wasn't. But the way that guy's mind worked, everything just came naturally to him.

I was the first to wake after Olga. Desh lay at my feet, curled into a frozen ball. I nudged him with my foot, and he snorted. A laugh rippled across my face and quickly disappeared, like a leftover heartbeat on an EKG. My smile felt alien, like it wasn't mine. Like I didn't deserve to have it.

We packed everything up. Donned our white clothes and crowded around Gus and Matt for final instructions. They made an odd team. Gruff and stoic paired with warm and heartfelt. They stood clear in front of us, Gus always doing something else while talking, sharpening a knife, cleaning his gun, or picking at a slice of jerky. He didn't like sitting still for too long. I understood that, being still left your mind to thinking.

Shifting back and forth on the balls of his feet, Gus addressed the group. "Bataar and Willer." He pointed at the men and they stepped forward. "Since this is our first attempt, we have the element of surprise. I want you to aim for the center circle for the video. I'll leave it to your judgment where to plant the bomb. It's timed to go off two hours after you press the green button. If you think it best to blow it quickly to ensure your escape, the minute button is red. For instant detonation press the red button twice."

He wiped his nose with the back of his hand and continued, "This particular mission is complicated. This was Gwen's stop, and as we know, she was unsuccessful and didn't return. Our Spider is still in there, and we need to retrieve them. They don't know you're coming though, so tread carefully."

"With the bomb, just make sure it's no more than a few inches under the ground and as close to the wall as you can get it," Desh added excitedly.

Matt connected with the men's eyes. "If there is any risk, any doubt in your minds during the mission, pull out," he urged. "Your safety is more important."

Bataar spat on the ground and chuckled. "I think we can all agree safety is not the first thing any of us are worried about! We just want this to work. The girl sacrificed herself for this..."

Heads swiveled in my direction, and I shrunk down. Olga's soft hand patted my back, and I wished I could run out of there or the ground would swallow me.

Gus cleared his throat, bringing their attention back to him.

"We don't know what will happen. *How* they will react, *if* they will react. But by the end of today, we will." There was sureness in his voice. And knowing Gus, he wouldn't have agreed to this if he didn't think it had a chance of working.

Everyone nodded solemnly, except for Bataar, who spat and joked with a knobbly grin on his face.

We held onto our hope and made the descent towards Birchton.

Soft ground gave way to sharp rocks as we stepped off the edge and down. Eyes always ahead, scanning the top of the walls of the rocky town for movement. It was hard to see though as the sun bounced off the rocks and snow blindingly.

The slope was gentle but slippery with ice. Dark caves stared at us as we carefully made our descent. It was easy to lose yourself and your friends in all this white. It would be easy to disappear…

We moved slowly, picking our way between loose sheets of rock, hiding, checking, and slipping on the growing ice. My nose was numb, and snowflakes clung to my eyelashes. I focused on what was just ahead of me and nothing more.

Desh clapped his hand on my shoulder and breathlessly said, "Well, it's certainly different to Bagassa."

I nodded, saving my breath for the climb. I felt bad that I wasn't talking to him very much, but the words stuck inside my mouth were not good ones. Until I could let go of my anger at him for pushing me to leave her, it was better to say nothing.

Rash came up by my side and slammed into me with his shoulder. "Move," he muttered.

I stepped aside for him, watching his dark head bob further down the rocky surface. "Rash," I said. He turned and glared at me, I leaned back from the razorblades emitting from his eyes. Not because it scared me, but because there was something of Rosa in him, and it cut me. "Put a hat on. Your hair stands out too much against the snow."

I caught him mumbling as he shoved a white cap over his head. "Yours doesn't, you blond jerk." I was no longer *beautiful blond man*. I shouldn't have been relieved, beautiful was much better than jerk, but jerk was what I deserved right now.

"Why do you let him talk to you like that?" Desh asked as he skidded on some ice and flew past me. I caught his arm and pulled him up.

"It's nothing less than what I deserve," I said, dusting snowflakes off his jacket.

Desh shook his head sadly. "That's not true, Joe."

I shrugged. He wasn't going to change my mind. Even if I had managed to save her, the ghosts of the men I killed and... Este... I gulped, feeling nauseous; they had a hold on me. I couldn't forgive myself for that.

I stopped moving. Frozen like their blood-spattered faces.

"Joe?" Desh shook my arm.

The image melted away as the glint of metal blinked at us from the top of the compound ahead. The walls of Birchton were before us, built out of huge bricks rather than one large concrete piece, as the rings lay over several levels, perched on the side of a mountain.

Matt halted us with an outstretched arm. "This is where we stop," he said, jerking his head towards a cave opening. He motioned to the two guys going into Birchton. "You two go on." They tipped their heads silently. "You know what you need to do."

Desh handed them their projectors and the small explosive device for the wall. They patted their packs and waved. We wished them luck and filed into the cave to await their return.

It was late afternoon when they left. It would only be a few hours and we would know if it had worked.

We took turns sleeping.

The cold never bothered me. But the others were shivering and huddling together. Rash especially.

The cave was quite deep, but we stayed near the entrance, ready to watch the show. The snow piled up in front of us and every now and then, the watch would kick over the pile so we weren't trapped inside. I liked the noise snow falling on snow made, like pouring sand.

I took off my jacket and leaned forward, wiggling it in front of Rash's glaring eyes. "Here, take this. You're shivering."

"Piss off," he snapped. I let the jacket hang there for a few more seconds and finally, he sighed and snatched it from my hands.

I smiled, which only made him angrier. He pulled the jacket up to his chin and turned away from me, swearing under his breath.

I tucked my back into the cold rock behind me, crossed my arms over my chest, and let my eyes fall. Faster than I expected, my mind crept towards sleep.

I'm buried, and I can't breathe. Weight is pressing down on me, warm, wet weight. I struggle to find a gap, pushing my hands up against obstacles. I suck in a shocked breath when my fingers get tangled in human hair.

The need to break free is overwhelming, though, and I keep pushing, digging my way out. It's dark, and I'm glad it is. Something warns me that I don't want to see what I'm buried under. When my arm pushes out and then my head, I immediately shut my eyes. I stumble over soft, uneven ground. My arm shielding my eyes from the view. My clothes sweat soaked.

"Wake up," she says over and over again in that soft, husky voice of hers. "Joseph. Wake up."

I woke, struggling for breath. *Would this ever end?* Was I always going to hear her voice, see her face, even in sleep? Could I live with what I'd done? The questions were unanswerable, hanging in the air like half-deflated balloons. I hated that I had no answers. I needed to solve this one and I couldn't. Breathing slower, I focused on my in breath and out breath. I just wanted it to stop for a while. Even it was only for a few minutes. As I breathed, my ribs felt soft, as if the weight of my guilt might actually destroy me.

I let out a sigh of resignation. I would not sleep again tonight. I sat up and felt around in the darkness for my sleeping bag zipper. Light snores drizzled down the walls, the dark shadow of the watch the only movement. Their peaceful noises made me crave empty, fresh air. The watch's shadow straightened at the entrance as he glanced at his handheld and checked the time. He stood up suddenly and motioned to me. "Wake the others. It's starting."

8

White As Snow

JOSEPH

*S*he always said we were guests. Intruders. I believed her, but I didn't really consider it. This world was not ours. It hadn't been for a very long time.

Sleeping bags rustled. People yawned. We were all frozen to our positions from cold but when the watch said, "It's starting," everyone jumped up and crammed their way into the cave entrance.

A weak, shooting sound echoed across the rocky valley. A single firework shot into the sky, exploded, and fronds of silvery light cascaded down, fizzling before they hit the ground. The first Signing Day firework for the year was as pathetic as I remembered. One every week in each town, for the next eight weeks, culminating in one last blood-red firework on the ninth Sunday in every town. It was unimpressive, but it was our signal.

Desh pushed his way to the front of the group, gripping his handheld tightly. He swiped the screen, typed in a code, and an enormous rectangular screen of light appeared in the sky over the town.

We all stared down at the movie hovering over the town, holding our breaths and wondering if the citizens of Birchton were looking up. Would this be a night marking the beginning of change or would they shy away from the images and return to their homes? Matt put his hand on my shoulder, and I stepped forward until he could no longer reach me.

The video started at the Classes. A student stepped out of line; a Guardian with a face as blank as an empty notebook strode forward and touched a stunner to her neck. She jolted once and collapsed in a heap at the Guardian's feet. He stepped over her, indifferent, and then the camera panned to the frightened faces of the other students. No one moved to help her. I remembered being that kid, wanting to intervene but completely unable to. I remembered the look on Rosa's face when it happened, the way she moved out of her chair but just managed to stop herself. I thought of all the time I'd lost when I walked away from her. I was an idiot.

The video moved on to the breeding facility. Quick clips of girls screaming, fighting against restraints. A baby was born and taken from the young mother. She barely noticed as it screamed, her eyes glazed over, her limbs floppy and weak.

Finally, the video pulled back to show at least a hundred pregnant girls walking in line. I stepped forward out of the cave, my feet sinking in the snow, halfway up my calves. Cold air hit my face, but I couldn't really feel anything. A pungent smell wafted towards me from the trees beside the cave, but I ignored it. I was chasing a ghost. She was there, up in the sky, her head dipped, staring at her feet as she shuffled through the queues of pregnant girls, her stomach, small, round, and perfect. I took another step, begging for her face—I *needed* to see her face. The somewhat transparent image wavered under the moon; the stars sat in her hair and across her bowed head like a crown. She was beautiful. As always.

I put my hand to the air, imagining touching her, feeling her soft skin beneath my fingertips, and I thought I might cry. *Where are you now?*

I had strayed several meters from the cave entrance. The others hadn't noticed my exit. Their faces were on the images too. Watching. Waiting. Listening for a roar, a cheer, something.

The only sound heard was of snow being compacted underfoot, which momentarily distracted me from the image. I glanced down for a second, but I didn't want to lose her yet. Beneath me, three figures frantically climbed upwards towards our cave. My eyes returned to the sky and her face was still downcast, her dark hair clumped together and knotted, her hands twisted together in an almost-prayer. Then a woman wearing a white coat blew a whistle and Rosa's head darted to the camera. I grabbed that picture and held on to it. Rosa's incredible eyes blinked back at me as big as houses. I gasped and took another step forward, my legs sinking deeper. Losing my balance, I fell forward onto my chest, cold ice spraying into my face.

The three people were closer now, clambering over the rocks towards me. It was Bataar, Willer, and the Spider.

From my position lying in the snow, I looked up and Rosa's face disappeared. My hands fisted and wrapped around the ice. *Was I always going to lose her? Over and over again.*

I couldn't hear the words from here, but I knew them. I helped write them. After the video playback, Pelo's voice would say, "The Superiors have been lying to you. They have poisoned your water to make you sterile. They are taking what little control you had away from you. You are not safe. Your sons and daughters are not safe. This breeding program is only the beginning. It's time to stop them. Fight. For your families. For the grandchildren you never got to meet. Tell them *NO*. We are the Survivors—we were not chosen, but we choose to live. There is a life for you on the other side of the wall. We wait for you to join us."

The light flickered and dissolved into the air. I stayed in the snow, my chin resting in the ice. I wanted to bury myself until my whole body was numb, but I had to get up, keep moving, and find my way back to Orry, no matter what kind of father I would be when I got there. I pushed up, about to jump out of the snow, when I noticed the three people were no longer running. They crept towards the cave just below me like they were afraid to approach it. I narrowed my eyes. *What was going on?* It was hard to focus, my brain still clinging to the image of Rosa floating in the sky.

They all stopped near the outcrop just below me. A girl's voice hissed in my direction, "Don't move!"

I froze, not understanding why but understanding the urgency in her voice.

Then everything happened at once.

Colliding. Smashing. Loud and confusing.

An explosion shook the ground. Debris spewed from the side of the outer wall of Birchton. I instinctively threw my head to the ground quickly and covered it with my arms. Everyone from the cave and in front of me shouted, "No!" Which confused me further.

Guttural, grunting sounds. Closer and closer. The snow crunched under something enormous. Legs as thick as tree trunks. I turned back to the cave from where I lay. Everyone stood outside, waving their arms and yelling. Rash's voice pierced through the other noises.

"Run! You idiot! Run!"

The screams of my friends faded into the background as my ears tuned to deep, loud breaths that seemed to echo inside a barrel. I scrambled, my legs grazing the rock underneath the snow and slipping back down. I couldn't get a hold. I pushed up with all my strength to standing and then fell to the ground on my back.

That was when I saw it from my upside-down position, hurling towards me, white as snow. Thick, wiry, white hair glistened under crisscrossed torchlight as it charged at me with gigantic paws that seemed to run over the snow and not sink into it. It was bigger than a bear, the shape of its head more dog like but with smaller ears. Its black lips pulled back to reveal massive white teeth—threatening, angry teeth. I couldn't move, for fear, for fascination, for lack of will.

"Get up!" Desh screamed.

It slowed as its head swung towards the people screaming at the cave entrance. But their shouts only enraged it further, and its eyes trained on me as it set into a calculated stalk. It was close, steam pulsing from its wet, black nose, its dark eyes wide. Fur bristled along its back, thick as straws. Its mouth opened in a threatening growl, showing gums pulled back in aggression and teeth ready to tear me apart.

Fear took over and whatever had stalled me released its grip. I tried to get up, to run, to escape this enormous animal. But I was out of time. It was over the top of me, and I could do nothing but stare as it reared back slightly, standing on its hind legs. Its body stretched to the sky, almost ten feet tall, its control almost human—its face nothing of the sort. I closed my eyes as its paws rammed my chest and its full weight came down on me. A rib cracked and my breath was thumped from my lungs. My arms flew up to cover my face. It snapped at me, but my feet planted in its chest, pushing against its heft. I barely held it back and its teeth dragged across my wrists and forearms without really digging in. I screamed in pain.

A shot would alert guards in Birchton of our location so the others approached from the cave, waving their arms in an attempt to scare it off. It took no notice, still straining against my arms to reach my neck. Its mouth knocked against my forearms with such force that it took every part of me to fight it.

Every part of me quickly lost the fight. I couldn't hold it back any longer. It was too strong. I was too weak. My arms fell down. My body exhaled and went numb. The urgency to flee left me.

The creature's saliva dripped into my eyes; its rancid, hot breath flooded my senses. Long, claws sharp as scalpels sunk deep into my chest, slowly piercing my skin and working their way deeper. I let out a sigh that hardly had any breath left in it. It was going to rip me open, and I wasn't sure I cared. Warm blood ran down my sides and into the snow, turning to pink ice.

I closed my eyes, saw the faces of the people I killed, the woman I left behind, and I made the wrong choice.

Just for a second, I gave in.

I let go.

And that was all the creature needed.

Words blinked overhead: *I have a son. His name is Orry. He needs me.* And then they floated away on the snowflakes with my life.

.9

Wrong Choices

ROSA

We were ordered to leave. Grant barked it like a dog. Camille jumped to his side, placed her jeweled fingers on his shoulders, and his hand reached up to pat her. The younger ones left. I understood his pride. He didn't want his children or me to see him being carried to the wheelchair.

I was relieved. Dinner was over. I couldn't have taken one more second of it before I jumped up on the table and kicked the plates into Grant's face. I pictured it now as I leaned against the smooth-as-butter door of my bedroom that the guard closed and locked as soon as I stepped inside. I still wanted it. Pressing my hands into the reassuring timber, I took a breath. I imagined his face dripping with gravy, a mushroom stuck to his brow. He would kill me. No, first, he would smile, and then he would kill me.

"Ugh!" I banged the door softly. Scared to attract attention.

I still didn't understand what the purpose of the dinner was. If it was meant to make me feel inferior, it did, but not in the way Grant would have wanted. I felt inferior to myself. Disgusted at my own behavior. If Joseph saw me now, he wouldn't know me. I ran my hands through my hair and let my imagination settle on his face. My mind always went back to home. What was once my home. Joseph in a chair with Orry, sleeping, safe, warm. I reached out to touch him, to feel a curl of his gold hair in my fingertips. I tucked the memory under my skin. He was always with me. They couldn't take that away.

I shook my head. At least they were both far away from here.

I moved towards my bed, kicking off my shoes as I walked. I paused, grunted in frustration, and picked them up, tucking them neatly under the chair by the door. I didn't want to annoy Red any more than I already had. Well actually, I did, but I knew I shouldn't.

Pajamas were laid out on the bed, pink and yellow, made of fabric as soft as a rabbit's ear. Pink daisies spotted the pattern, and it made me sick. What kind of nightmare was this? It felt like they were wrapping me in silk only to light it on fire. This comfort was a lie, and I was deathly scared of what my true treatment would be. I picked up the pajama top. Its pink, daisy-shaped buttons were nauseating.

I got into bed fully clothed, ignoring the toothbrush and other toiletries that had been put on the bedside table. I kicked the pajamas with my feet under the quilt until they fell in a heap on the floor.

My one pathetic attempt at defiance.

My chest began to rise and fall more rapidly, and panic crept up my arms like spider webs and wrapped around my throat. My eyes darted to the camera trained on my wreck of a body. I was trapped. Turning my head, I screamed into the pillow. *How was I going to get out of this?*

Sleep played with me. I'd close my eyes to nightmares. Something hurt deep inside, and I couldn't name it. I woke up in pain, and I slept in pain.

When the door opened, I was not surprised, as I'd woken up screaming so hard my voice was hoarse. When I saw who it was, though, I shrank back.

It was Judith. She walked in, barefoot, looking smaller, more fragile than she had at dinner. She rolled her head around, taking in the position of the camera, and then casually collapsed at the foot of my bed like she done it a million times. I immediately sat up and pulled my feet away from her.

"Ya don't need to be scared of me," she said, her words stretching out lazily, her hair falling in perfect waves over her shoulders.

I narrowed my eyes. "I'm not," I lied. She was maybe the scariest thing I'd ever come across.

"Dad sent me in to check on you. We could hear you screaming all the way down the hall." Hall sounded like haul, and it was grating my ears. I tried not to cover them at the sound of her voice.

"What do you care?" I snapped. I stared down at her legs, haphazardly folded over each other like she didn't know where they should go. She put her head down and stared at her hands. They shook, and she placed one over the other to still them.

"I care because I was told to care," she whispered at her lap. "I'm supposed to make friends with you." She tucked some of her golden brown hair behind her ears, and it fell forward again anyway.

She reached out to pat my leg awkwardly, and I sharply withdrew. I didn't want her to touch me.

"Please," she pleaded.

Her eyes were wide, blue discs of fear. A tear slid down her cheek like it didn't want to be there anymore. *Don't feel sorry for her*, I told myself. *Look at her. She has everything*. Even as I thought it, I knew it wasn't true, but I couldn't let this girl in. It was too dangerous.

Judith withdrew her hand, put her orange-tipped finger to her mouth, and started chewing at her cuticles.

"Dad says you won't break easily," she said with a mouthful of picked-off skin. I suppressed my gag reflex.

"He can't break me," I whispered, searching her eyes for something other than preened, parrot-like features. "I'm already broken."

She was so anxious, shaky... but there was something in there, maybe something I could use. Her face changed like someone was arranging her facial figures for her, from sad, to amused, and my hopes dashed against the wall and shattered.

She lulled me. I bought into her delicate, scared routine, then she said, "He will enjoy trying though," and I saw her father in her.

"Get out of my room," I said, glaring, willing her to move. She didn't. "Get out!" I said louder.

She went back to nervous, flustered by my temper. "I'm sorry," she said, her voice sawing my nerves as her eyes fluttered up at the camera purposefully.

I got to my knees, shuffled towards her, and shoved her shoulders. She flew backwards, her flannel-clad legs pointed to the ceiling, and she landed on her butt.

She sat there, propped on her elbows, breathing hard for a second. She shot me a disapproving stare, her face tight, her lips pouting. I growled like a feral animal, leaning over her from the top of the bed.

"You don't get it," she said, her voice snapped, full of haughtiness as she got to her feet. "You do as you're told. I do as I'm told. You don't have a choice!" She stormed away from me, her arms folded across her chest like she thought that was what you should look like when you were angry. She was as unreal as a mirage. As any vision I had of Joseph breaking this door down and taking me away from this place.

The problem was I knew she was right about doing as I was told. As she padded out of my room and closed the door with a clap, I whispered to the depressing air, to my prison, my words coming out like a thin stream of vapor, "I don't know how."

10

Punishment

ROSA

Maybe I'll wake up tomorrow morning with Joseph's arms around me. He'll nuzzle into my neck and kiss me. I'll swat him away half-heartedly because I want him just as much as I pretend not to... no... much more.

Orry will be asleep in his cot. His curls falling around his face like a lazy crown. He'll snore, stir, and smile in his dreams.

I'll be whole. Broken, but whole. Pieced together from heartbreak, from torture and love.

This mattress wanted to swallow me, its comfort of no comfort at all. I wouldn't know it was morning. When I swept back the curtains, I was staring at another manufactured view. The only way I knew was by the sound of Red, pushing her way through the doorway and screaming at me for—

"How could you treat Miss Judith that way?" she yelled, her eyes as red as her roots. She stomped her foot like a bull and charged at me. Taking one look at the pajamas on the floor, her nostrils flared. She grabbed my arm and wrenched me out of bed. I tried to pull away from her grip, but she was too strong. She pulled my cardigan from my body, ripping it, and threw it on the floor, dragging me to the bathroom.

"She was in tears when she came to me. She has a bruised... a bruised..." Red's lipstick clotted in the corners of her growling mouth.

"Butt?" I said through a wide grin before I could stop myself.

Red made a high-pitched noise, gasping in shock, and I knew I'd said the wrong thing.

She grabbed at me with chubby fingers trying to pull my shirt off, but I hugged it tight to my body. Each grab was like a punch. She was as strong as the ox she was acting like. Her curves were so tightly bandaged in her tight suit that she resembled a chunky, carved table leg. She kept hold of me with one hand while she turned the knob on the shower. There was no steam pluming off the tiles. I shivered and braced myself.

She kept pecking at my clothes like a nervous, lead-beaked bird, but I wasn't giving her my shirt. When she realized this, she threw me under the water, my back crashing into the tiles, my body making a hollow thud like a lonely drum. My muscles tensed at the shock of ice-cold water, and I spat as it ran down my face and over my lips.

"Clean yourself and change for breakfast!" she snapped. I heard the bathroom, then the bedroom door close and lock.

When I was sure she was gone, I turned the hot water tap on and removed my clothes, letting the hot water attempt to thaw my frozen body, inside and out. I tried really hard not to think of my last shower, with Joseph, in Este's house, but the memory was there, inside of me, and my body remembered before my brain caught up. My cheeks flushed red and I ran my finger over my lips, trying to bring back that last kiss. His arms wrapping me so tight because we knew it could be the last time. I turned off the taps. Drips of water ran down my nose and over my mouth as I let out a small cry. *It couldn't be the last time.*

He ruined my heart. But in a good way.

I was a patchwork of wounds and scars. He was the glue that held me together. And now, he was gone.

I pressed my palm to the tiles and waited to wake up from this nightmare.

When I got out of the bathroom, another hideous outfit lay on the bed. I put it on this time, grimacing at the purple blouse with diamanté buttons and the black skirt that flared at the knees. The sleeves were puffed and when I saw myself in the mirror, I couldn't help but laugh. A pair of blue contacts sat on the bedside table. I ignored them and sat down to wait for the guard. My hands were clasped neatly in my lap, mostly to stop me from throwing stuff.

The knock on the door still startled me. The politeness seemed so out of place.

"Come in," I yelled through the solid timber door.

The guard stepped in, giving me a nervous smile as he looked down at me through the light brown hair hanging over his eyes like vines over a cave entrance.

"Your presence is requested at breakfast," he said eagerly.

I rolled my eyes. "Faaantastic!"

The guard frowned. "You're lucky."

I shook my head. "No. I'm about the unluckiest person you'll ever meet. Don't get too close. I'm pretty sure it's contagious," I said, scratching my arms like I had a rash.

His eyebrows rose in confusion but he didn't say anything except, "Follow me," smiling with his arm extended.

I followed him down the long, curved hall. Large rectangles of light poured through the floor-to-ceiling windows, stretching across the carpet and creeping halfway up the walls. The timber glowed like amber honey under the sun. I paused to watch the tiny dust motes flying through the air in the clean-cut rays. They swirled and danced, landing on my arms. The air was thick and warm in here, artificial.

This was the first time I'd seen Grant's grounds in daylight. It was different to Este's in a lot of ways. Still vast, open, and stupidly luxurious, but everything outside was sharp, softened only by the light covering of snow, which a servant was busily dusting off with a hand-broom. Spiky, inhospitable sculptures made from concrete and rusty metal were scattered around the lawn. They were beautiful and raw, but frightening in their harshness. I imagined if you touched one that you would cut yourself, and then I shuddered at the thought that Grant would probably enjoy watching me bleed.

"Ahem," the guard coughed. I jumped. From here, I could see the outside world and my eyes, my heart, didn't want to leave it.

"It's alright, Harry," a cool voice spoke behind me. "I'll take her in."

Harry, the guard, grabbed my elbow and steered me towards Grant's son, Denis, letting him take me, or my reins I guess. Harry winked at me and said, "Enjoy your meal, miss." I smiled awkwardly. I couldn't tell if he was being sarcastic or not.

Harry walked briskly back the way we had come, disappearing around the curve.

Denis' hand slid around my waist, barely touching me, just kind of hovering there with a millimeter of air between his hand and my body.

"Shall we?" he asked, looking down at me from his very tall height, his eyebrows raised in question. I noticed a scar wrapped around the end of his eyebrow like a crescent moon.

The earphones dangled from his shoulders again. I stared at them too long, and he noticed.

"Do you enjoy music?" he asked. For him, this seemed to be a very serious matter.

I wondered whether I should lie, but then I thought, *What's the point?*

"It's new to me, but yeah, I do," I replied.

He tipped his chin. We hung around the door to the dining room. I didn't want to go in.

He put a hand on my arm so gently he could have been a mosquito resting there. "Don't worry. You have some time before…" His eyes moved to the tip of the painting next to us. A small camera buzzed on the frame like a housefly. Denis turned so his back faced the lens, his whole long body shadowing my own. "Don't show fear," he whispered.

His hand left my arm, raking over my skin like a breeze. His touch was so light but strong at the same time, like everything he did, he meant to do.

"Wait," I hushed, my lips barely moving. "Why should I listen to you?"

His mouth turned up in one corner, a crooked smile almost there. "Maybe you shouldn't."

I huffed and pursed my lips. My instincts pushed me to trust him. They were all I had left, and I needed to believe in something.

"Okay, tell me one thing," I said, looking up into his strong face.

It creased momentarily with irritation, his hand clenched around the handle. "Quickly," he hissed.

"What did you mean by replacement?" I said, leaning on my tiptoes to get closer.

His eyes closed briefly like he was remembering something unpleasant. When they opened, they were ringed with sadness.

"Let's just say, I'm not the first Denis Grant," he muttered impatiently. His words were quick and tinged with warning.

I blinked up at him. "That's not an answer. I'm going to need more than a cryptic sentence and a look," I whispered boldly.

He craned his head up to the ceiling and exhaled in exasperation. Licking his lips, an answer forced its way between his rigid, set mouth. "Dad has had several offspring 'made' as back ups. When one of us misbehaves or displeases him, we are 'replaced'. I have many brothers and sisters I will never meet. The photos on the wall are a warning," he said grimly, and sympathy sketched its way through my mind briefly.

Before I could respond, Denis turned the handle. When it coasted open, his demeanor stiffened. He bowed slightly and allowed me to pass through first.

Grant was in his wheelchair, rolling himself past a low bench laden with breakfast food. I tried not to drool at the smell of bacon and eggs.

When he heard the door close, he spun around slowly, a plate balanced across his knees. He didn't look at me, only at his son.

"Leave us," he ordered, holding up his hand.

No don't, I thought. But before I could blink, Denis was gone.

Grant wheeled himself to the table and placed his plate on the glass tabletop with a clang. "Would you like some breakfast, Rosa?" he asked.

I shrugged. "Sure." His face twitched at my response, but he nodded and wheeled himself back to the bench to serve me a plate.

"Sit down please," he said with his back to me.

I sat down like an obedient dog. He had this power over me, and I hated it. I clenched my teeth, fighting the words that wanted to spew from my mouth. I hated his control, his weird politeness.

I knew it had to end soon.

"I suppose you're wondering what you're doing here?" he asked, drawing out his words painfully as he took his place at the table and placed my plate in front of me.

I stared down at the steaming plate of scrambled eggs, the crispy bacon shining with fat, and sucked in my bottom lip. All of a sudden, I felt nauseous.

"I know you want information," I said, my voice as dry as cracked wheat, "but I can't tell you anything. I don't know what they're planning."

I lied unconvincingly.

He smiled at me, and I wondered if he knew how to smile for real or if his smile was only used to unnerve and threaten.

"Oh, we'll figure it out eventually. I'll figure you out eventually too," he said, winding his fork in the air at me. "The 'how' I figure you out is up to you." I placed a hand over my stomach protectively. He eyed me like a present he'd like to tear open. "How about I let you ask me a question and in return, you allow me to ask you a question that you must answer truthfully?"

I picked up my fork, pushing the eggs around the plate. This was a game. I could play a game. Jabbing the fork in his direction, I watched as his jaw clenched. "How could you be so selfish? Do you really think you're worth all those lives you took to get the healer?" I asked, my voice wavering with nervousness.

His fingers spread out and then clenched into a tight fist. "Yes. I'm worth ten times the number of lives I took," he stated. It was a stupid question. Of course he thought that. "My turn." He took a sip of his coffee and breathed in and out several times, making me wait.

"Do you really think your *cause* is worth all the lives I'm going to take in response to yours and your comrades' actions?" His tone was mocking, as if my *cause* were a childish faze.

My chest felt like ice. I tried to breathe, but there was something in the way. Guilt.

"No," I answered. "But the *life* you've allowed us in the Woodlands is not a real life. They'll see that."

He seemed extremely unsatisfied with my answer. His eyes rolled over me from head to toe, and found me lacking.

"You're a foolish girl. You think you're strong. You think I won't win, but I will always win." I was getting to him. The victory was small, but enough to fuel me, until he squashed it.

He composed himself quickly and said, "It is clear to me that you require a firmer approach." He rang the bell by his coffee cup with a sharp twist of his wrist and picked up a document next to his plate, running his eyes over it, and ignoring me. We were done.

Red appeared in the doorway. She grinned at me in a sick kind of way.

"Rosa here has chosen not to do as she is told," Grant said without looking up from his paper.

"Wait!" I said as Red gripped me under the arm and pulled me from my chair.

Grant raised his eyes to meet mine. My promise echoed in my head. I promised I would live.

"I'm sorry," I stammered. "I'll do as I'm told." I dipped my head down, in apology. My head felt like it would explode at the words. Every part of me wanted to scream.

Grant smiled, his teeth glinting under the slowly waving pendant light that hung over the table.

"Good girl." His voice was quietly satisfied. "Tell the others they can come in now," he said to Red. She looked put out by the change in events but left, returning with the rest of Grant's family.

I ate breakfast quietly, avoiding eye contact with Denis, who was staring at me like I'd killed his pet rabbit or something, and Judith, who was pouting.

What was I going to do?

The only answer was to play along, give them some of what they wanted but not everything. Ride it out and hope they didn't kill me.

It didn't seem like a very good plan.

11

Torture

ROSA

I *bang against the cell bars. Gripping the iron, I hold on so tight my* *knuckles turn white. I'm slipping away, a new, different person* *taking my place. Someone I don't recognize. Someone who's* *supposed to save me but is killing me at the same time.*

If I do this? If I stop being me? What's left if I manage to survive?

This was the second day of interrogations.

My fingers ached. They did small but painful things. I'd been warned that it could be a lot worse. If I didn't cooperate, the torture would be worse. I wasn't sure I cared. I'd lost myself. I'd retreated. There was a cage around me now.

I was bearing it. Just.

I scratched at the edge of my bandages as Harry stood next to me in the lift. He kept his eyes forward on the door. I looked up from my hunched position, the blood seeping around the edges of the white cloth like red ink blots. They were going to pull them off anyway so I removed one, inspecting the pink, raw skin around my nails. Harry flinched at the sight of them.

I held it up to the metallic light, the elevator humming in the background. "It hurts worse than it looks," I shot at him with a wink.

He grimaced, sighing in relief when the doors opened. I stepped out and he followed two steps behind me.

I distracted myself by taking in the details of the cars on either side of me as we walked through the under-house garage. Three red cars, one green, two black, and four silver. I breathed in the smell of motor oil and damp. Four convertibles, six hard tops. The chrome detailing glinted and winked at me. I gripped onto the wide headlights, shining like forced-open eyes. I wanted to be as vacant and empty of thought as the cars. I didn't want to go in there. I suppressed the panic as we reached the end of the line. Even if my brain was pumping its hands and calming me, telling me I could handle it, my body wasn't ready for this. I stalled. I couldn't take another step. But then I thought of Orry and I edged closer to the door, leaning into imaginary hands that were pushing me forward. The big, black door howled hollowly.

"Miss?" Harry asked questioningly, a hint of sympathy in his voice.

I put my hand to my chest, blood pulsing in my fingertips, the rest running away from my center. "Just give me a minute." He moved towards me, and I caught his eyes. "Please," I pleaded with a finger up as I bent over and tried not to vomit.

"One minute," he agreed.

I tried to slow my breath, compose myself. I had to take a few steps back into myself. It was small bites of pain, but it was constant. And I was afraid.

"Can he drive these?" I asked, attempting to sound light when my breath felt like coal bricks stacking on top of each other in my chest.

The guard stood straighter. "Yes, Miss. Some. But after the procedure in a few weeks, he'll be able to drive all of them."

I did a series of small nods, talking myself into moving. "Ok. Let's go."

Harry opened the door for me, and I stepped into my tiny nightmare.

My eyes adjusted to the darker room, the color of midnight. Navy with cold white stars.

Mr. Hun tottered over to me and took both my hands in warm greeting. "Sit, sit," he said, his round, dark face squishing into a smile.

He was a hessian sack with eyes, his dark skin rubbed and worn; his body low like his whole weight was sagging to the ground because his short legs couldn't hold him up. Small tufts of hair like those on old potatoes sprouted from the top of his mostly bald head. If you met him in the street, you'd think he was cute and completely unthreatening. But I knew better now. I hesitated but then the two guards leaning against the wall gave me a look and pointed to the camera that was always watching me.

Oh God.

Just breathe. Breathe…

I sank into the black, leather swivel chair and watched Mr. Hun sort through his various instruments lovingly. He picked up a small piece of metal the size of a toothpick and eyed it closely. A light attached to an arm was brought closer to my face. Mr. Hun dragged a stool in front of me and sat down, the air leaving the seat with a sad whistle. I allowed him to tie my arms to the chair and then he pulled my bandages from my fingers one by one, his face creased with concern when I winced at the cloth sliding over my newly scabbed skin.

He placed his warm hands over mine and patted me gently.

"Make sure you put some antiseptic cream on these afterwards." I nodded, a few tears pooling in the corners of my eyes. I squirmed in my chair.

"Ok, where were we…?"

A deep voice sounded behind me. "Her friend, the other escapee, sir."

Mr. Hun smiled kindly at me, his crinkled skin puckering around his mouth. "Oh yes, right. Now, Rosa darling, tell me about Careen."

I stared down at his fingers holding the metal toothpick. "Careen has red hair, she is about five foot eight, and she is my friend," I whispered, my voice rising in panic. *Retreat. Go somewhere they can't find you*, my mind whispered.

Mr. Hun held down one of my straining fingers and placed the toothpick under my nail. "What else?"

"I don't know where she is." Which was the truth. Mr. Hun pushed the toothpick under my nail.

"Ahh." It hurt so much the meager contents of my stomach were hurtling towards my mouth. I swallowed and dipped my head to my chin, struggling to focus. My hair fell around my face. He pushed it in harder. *Think of trees spotted with lichen, pale green and white.*

"More," he said, his voice losing its softness.

I tried to pull my fingers in, but he held them down hard. "She… she… is a hunter. Her baby died. She is in a romantic relationship with a Survivor."

"Who?" Mr. Hun urged. I gasped in pain as he took my next finger and drove a metal pin halfway under my nail. I screamed. "Tell me his name, dear."

The forest is warm, that springtime buzz of bees and pollen surround you. The trees are bending to tell you secrets. Arms wrap around your waist and you laugh.

I looked up at the ceiling. The black, padded walls that kept my screaming in seemed to expand like a pillow ready to smother me. *Don't let them see how much they're hurting you. Feel your bare feet pressing into the mud, the squelch of it seeping between your toes.*

"Pietre," I panted. Their list was growing. So far, I hadn't given them anything of consequence. But I didn't know how long I could hang on.

I closed my eyes and thought of Orry in their arms. I thought of stars, of green. Of fresh meat and fires.

Mr. Hun took my pinky finger, pulled it up at an angle, and held it that way, straining on the edge of breaking. My head flopped forward.

"Bring me the screen," he asked patiently. A guard walked forward and handed him a large reader the size of a book.

It was already paused on a video. He pressed the triangular play button.

Give me the pins. Give me pain, shredding hot pain. If the plan was to hurt me, then you've found your method.

The film was clearly taken from one of the many surveillance cameras placed around a Woodland town. I could see the images in the sky blocked slightly by people's shoulders, but they were looking. Gasps emitted from the crowd. Sighs of shock and rumbles of anger. A name was cried out, and then the camera focused on people's damning feet as they surged towards a group of guards.

Shots fired, and people screamed. The feet ran harder. The shadows of boots stomping furiously into the solid ground dispersed, and a circle of space opened up over a small child. His eyes were closed and his clothes dirtied—his body motionless. Trampled.

More shots.

Then an explosion.

It cut to another camera, one over a Ring gate. It followed a trail of smoke to a birch tree, alight. Its leaves curling and crackling. Chunks of concrete lay in the street. People screamed, pushed, but not to get out. They were running away from the wall. I didn't understand it. My eyes blinked several times, trying to take it in. They were afraid of *us*.

Mr. Hun handed the screen back to the guard, who put it on the desk and pulled it back to the image of the child in the street. Lying there, curled protectively over himself like he was hiding something, a secret he couldn't tell. The image shone bright in the dark of this tiny room.

Mr. Hun let go of my pinky finger, which was just about breaking, and I remembered pain. One by one, he pulled the pins from my fingers, cleaning them with alcohol wipes and placing back on his tray of instruments. He patted my cheek with his warm, dry hand and left me.

They all left me. To stare at the lifeless child whose death was partly my fault. They wanted me to take it. The responsibility. And I did. This hurt me more than all the small pains they had inflicted on me so far. I tried not to let it show. But as soon as the door closed, my mouth broke into a torn-up sob, my heart seized, and my head fell.

"No," I whispered. To myself. To them. To the child.

They were chipping away at me, wearing me down to a splinter they could flick to the floor. I couldn't let them win.

12.

Hang On

JOSEPH

I'm clinging to the end point of a snowflake, spinning round and round.
"Just let go," she tells me. "Just let go..."

"Hang on, Joe. Damn it. There's a lot of blood. Should there be this much blood?"

My legs were warm; my chest was cold, wet. Every bump felt like my skin was peeling away from my body. I opened my eyes to slits. Warm spots of light hovered over my head.

I wasn't dead.

I was flat on my back, my body sailing unevenly though the air. Up. Rocks slid and people stumbled. My leg fell off the stretcher, and I pulled it back up with a lot effort. I could use my legs. A good sign. They hurt like hell, but I could feel them. Someone's hand wrapped around my own. It was soft, delicate. I squeezed. I didn't open my eyes. It could be her. I'd keep them closed, and it would be her.

A smooth, feminine voice spoiled my delusion. "Hang on, Joseph. You're going to be ok." The voice was worried, but sure. So I believed it. I hung on. Until my mind slipped from consciousness again. But this time I knew I'd wake up.

Smooth fingers glided across my forehead. I flinched and opened my eyes. Staring back at me were two perfectly symmetrical, almond-shaped eyes, light green ringed with a darker green around the outside. She blinked and so did I, trying to change the picture. She smiled and ran a cloth over my chest. I shivered.

"Sorry," she murmured, shyly, as she ran the wet cloth over my wounds, her gaze on my chest rather than my face. "I need to clean your wounds." She pursed her pink lips and concentrated on her work.

I grabbed her wrist and stopped her hand before it touched me again.

"Who are you?" I asked, looking from left to right and searching for a familiar face. We were still in the woods. It was dusk or dawn; either way, the sun was leaving or returning and not giving much light. People moved around me, talking.

"Whoa there, Joe. She's trying to help you," Desh said, his face coming into focus behind this girl's halo of short, blonde hair. She smiled at me again, her small freckles dancing over the bridge of her nose. I narrowed my eyes.

"Who is she?" I said, coughing.

She held a bottle of water to my lips. "Drink," she whispered, her brow furrowed.

I snatched the bottle and regretted moving so suddenly.

Desh came to sit by my side. "Joe, this is Elise, the Birchton Spider. She saved your life." He grinned and patted my leg. I winced. I was covered in bruises. I took a small sip of water. It slid coolly down my throat.

"You make me sound much more important that I am," she said, shaking her head and muttering, "The Birchton Spider... sounds like the title of a bad book."

I pulled myself up to sitting, the sudden movement making me dizzy. "Book?"

Gravity caused blood to seep from the deep claw marks on my chest. The girl put both her hands on my torso and pushed me back down gently.

"You need to rest." She rolled up a jacket and placed it behind my head.

Desh's head bobbed up and down. "It was amazing Joe. After the blast, that thing, that huge, white bear came at you. Everyone was trying to get your attention, but you were totally zoned out. It jumped down on your chest and went for your neck. Elise ran out from behind a rock, slapped its big white, butt with a tree branch, and it just ran away." He was breathless from excitement but managed to calm down and look at me seriously for a second. Poor Desh, I'd put him through hell. "What were you doing out there, Joe? It was like you wanted it to kill you."

Did I? I wasn't sure, maybe for a millisecond.

Elise started spreading gauze over my chest and taping it down. I caught her eyes. "Thank you," I mumbled.

She shrugged. "Don't mention it. It's what I do," she said casually.

I groaned as she pressed down on my skin. Her touch wasn't reassuring; it just felt alien.

"You routinely slap bears on the ass?" I asked quizzically, raising my eyebrows.

"Ha!" Desh spluttered. "At least now we know he's not brain damaged!"

Rash shouted from across the campsite, "Based on current evidence, I'm gonna need further proof."

Desh shot him a warning look and I snorted. That was kind of funny.

Elise laughed lightly, ignoring Rash's comment as she tossed her head back to get her hair away from her face. "No. I'm Medical. Saving lives is what I do."

"Oh, right. Me too. Or at least I was. Medical."

"Shhh!" she said, putting her finger to her lips. "Get some rest."

Her face faded to a pale blur for a moment, and I shook my head. "Where are we? What happened after the blast?" I asked.

She didn't answer.

Matt's warm voice sailed in and his face followed. "How's the patient?"

"Superficial wounds to the chest and legs. Bruising to most of the lower body and also to the left eye," Elise replied, running her little finger down the side of my face. I jerked away from her touch.

"It doesn't feel very superficial, Matt," I said, managing a smile. "Now tell me what happened after the blast?" I insisted.

He nodded and faked a smile. "Nothing."

I clenched my fists and pulled my head up so I could see him better. Smoke from a campfire whirled around our faces and stung my eyes. "What do you mean—*nothing*?"

Desh patted my arm.

"Nothing yet, anyway. We always knew Birchton and Radiata were going to be a harder sell. We've left two of our own back there to wait and see. We do know people reacted to the film."

I glanced around the camp. Gus squatted down near the fire, poking the coals under a tin of beans. Rash leaned against a tree, quietly seething.

"Where are we now?" My voice was dry.

"Between Birchton and Radiata; we have two more nights before the next show," Desh replied, spreading his hands out and wiggling his fingers.

I chuckled despite myself. "Man I've missed you."

He grinned, his dark eyes flashing concern. "It's good to see you smile."

Elise stood up straight, and she was almost as tall as Desh. "I'll leave you boys to it."

Desh raised an eyebrow as she walked away. Matt's gaze followed her. I'd never seen him staring at a woman before and it made me laugh, which hurt my chest.

Desh elbowed him. "Like what you see, eh?"

I rolled my eyes.

Matt blushed and smacked his arm. "She's a little young for me."

I grimaced from pain and being uncomfortable. All this smiling, laughing, and joking was too much. I didn't like how easy they could pretend, or maybe they weren't pretending. All I knew was I didn't like it. I didn't want them to be sad all the time, but when they were joking like this, I saw her, or almost the absence of her. Like someone had cut a hole in the air in her exact shape, and I was just waiting for her to fill it.

I sighed loudly.

"You ok?" Matt asked, reaching for my wrist to check my pulse.

"I'm fine," I snapped, the pressure on my chest feeling heavier and heavier. "Seems like you are too."

Matt and Desh avoided my eyes. I knew I was being a jerk, but I couldn't stop myself. "How long do I have to lie like this?"

"Another day. At least until the bleeding slows."

I closed my eyes. I couldn't look at them. It was a reminder. The last thing I heard was Gus discussing the next move.

"If it goes the way I think it will, we won't be able to stay."

13

Advice

ROSA

There was no clock. But there was ticking in my brain anyway. I counted the little bursts of movement from the camera in the corner. It told me it was after midnight. It told me I wouldn't sleep tonight. My hands ached, and my heart ached. My eyes were like two purple, velvet pincushions.

At home, there was never a quiet place, no stillness where my body used to lay. Now silence smothered me like heavy-fogged poison. It pushed at me from every angle. That peace I thought I needed, that I craved, was all around me and I couldn't stand it. What I truly needed was gone. The slip of sheets moving across bodies, the clang and thud of metal, wood, stone. Gone. I wanted it now, more than anything else.

I pulled at the sheets in my clawing hands, wondering what I could throw at the cameras. A metal bowl grinned at me from the bedside table. I reached out to grab it, sliding my fingers along the cold surface, but once they made contact, they retreated. I had to be good. Obedient. To stay alive I had to not... be... me.

I drew my hand in under the covers and shivered with the need to break something.

The latch clicked and a slice of light cut the floor. A tall, long shadow wavered in the entrance like heat, and then moved towards me.

Immediately, I clicked the lamp on, lighting up a calm, young face. Denis.

I slithered up to sitting and watched him as he carefully approached me. Never not moving, but going so slowly that it was agony. I wanted to jump up and get behind him to shove him forward. But he continued in his sloping, loping way of walking. Like he was picking out each spot he was going to put his foot on before he stepped on it, the angle he would place his foot at, and how much noise his shoe would make. I ground my teeth together in annoyance.

He lifted his head slowly and connected with my eyes. "Look scared," he whispered, his deep blue eyes ringed with darker circles like someone had taken a pen to his irises. I was kind of scared but mostly impatient. If he was coming in to hurt me, I wished he would get on with it. I nodded, which he seemed to be irritated by. So I clutched the sheets in my fists and tried to look wide-eyed and scared.

He was wearing just pajama bottoms and no shirt, which could have been intimidating if not for the old man slippers. His body was toned but childish, as if he'd never seen a hard day's work in his life. Nothing about his demeanor suggested harm.

He stood two steps away from me. I found myself staring at his feet, trying to guess where he would step next. Left, left, right.

Finally, he reached me and I huffed. He kneeled down, neatly folding his legs over each other like a collapsible pram. Carefully, he put one hand on my shoulder and the other over my throat. I would have screamed but he wasn't really touching me. His eyes bounced to the camera and he shifted his head so he was blocking my face from its view. His held me down with one hand and the other was like a collar, taut and straining but hovering just millimeters from my skin.

"Wha... what?" I whispered. His eyes screwed shut, and he shook his head to the left.

"Look frightened," he whispered more urgently.

I was starting to be.

"Better," he said with a slight, lips-pressed together kind of smile. He stared down at my own lips, and I started to feel uncomfortable.

"I'll scream," I threatened half-heartedly.

"No, you won't," he assured me. And he was right. I wanted to know what this was all about.

His hand still fluttered above my throat, and then he pressed down a little. My breath caught as it tried to move past the blockage.

"Stop playing along," he whispered so quietly it was just air and small noise passing his lips. "If you keep doing as you're told, he will kill you." I raised my eyebrows. "The minute he thinks he's got you figured out, that he's broken you, you'll be executed," he said, his voice a whistle through his teeth.

I was about to nod, but he stopped me. "Don't nod, throw your head against the head board in three… two… one." I did as he said, and the hand on my throat moved with me but never pressed too hard.

Unfolding his knees, he stood with controlled movements. He turned his back to me and walked slowly out of the room, my eyes drilling into his back.

As soon as the door closed, I turned my head into my pillow and smiled. Grant's son had just told me to stop obeying, to stop being the opposite of *me*.

I picked up the metal bowl and flung it at the camera. It cracked deliciously and fell off its perch, hanging by a single wire like a hung prisoner. The bowl slammed into the dresser, teetering and scraping until it came to rest, hard and unforgiving against the polished wood.

14

Un-cooperation

ROSA

Apella rattled the bars of her cage, the tidy place I'd made for her and the others inside. She warned me not to go too far. Patting my chest, I shook my head. I never listened to her when she was alive, and I wasn't going to start now. *It will be okay*, I told my ghosts and myself.

Today would be the same. Breakfast. Escorted to torture. Lunch in my room. Dinner with the 'family'.

I took a deep breath in and flipped through the pile of clothes placed neatly on the chair by my bed. A lavender cardigan with blue flowers embroidered into the collar. I looked down at my pajamas and smiled. The devil had a hold of me today.

Twenty minutes later, there was a knock on the door.

"Come in," I sang loudly.

Denis' long leg slipped inside the door, followed by the rest of him. He eyed me and touched his finger to his forehead, rubbing it back and forth. "You ready for this?" he asked evenly. "It's not going to be easy."

I nodded, pulling my toes under my feet nervously.

He loped towards me and held out his elbow, casting his eyes up to the broken camera. "It will be fixed by the time you return, you know."

"I'll break it again," I muttered.

"Mhm."

I took his elbow to steady myself and followed him to breakfast.

The rest of the family was already seated when we arrived.

Judith looked up and huffed in my direction, "Why does she get to wear pajamas to breakfast?" she whined.

I steeled myself for the reaction, watching Grant carefully exhale through his nostrils like a horse that had just galloped a mile. There was heat in his eyes when he glared at me.

"She doesn't. Rosa, return to your room and change into appropriate attire."

I let go of Denis' elbow and collapsed in my chair. "I can't. My clothes are... er... damaged."

Grant ignored my comment and took a deep, impatient breath. "Why do you refuse to wear the contacts you were given? You are my guest and are expected to adhere to my rules and traditions."

Regression. All of my childhood was coming out to dance with me today. I covered my brown eye, letting the blue one gaze at the table. "Is this better?"

Grant frowned so hard his lips were close to leaving his face. His arms pushed back from the table. I smiled at him, big and toothy, still holding my hand over my brown eye, truly hoping that Denis was right. That the minute Grant thought he'd won, he would kill me. That this was the only way to survive.

I could almost hear Grant gnashing his teeth as I rubbed my hands together and said, "Food smells great!" I smacked my lips, grabbing forkfuls of bacon and piling it onto my plate. His anger was swirling around me in fronds. Any minute now, he was going to explode. The other members were glancing at each other nervously. Camille dabbed at her mouth with her napkin and cleared her throat.

"Coffee?" she asked, lifting the pot towards my cup.

I put my hand over my mug. "Ew! No thanks. That stuff tastes like crap!" I watched my hand vibrating, so shaky over the delicate porcelain cup ringed with silver, I wasn't sure I'd be able to lift the food to my mouth. *Keep it together. Don't let him see how scared you are.*

Denis let out a short laugh, covering it by taking a sip of his drink. And I started to wonder if this was a trick.

Grant picked up the bell next to his plate and rang it once.

Harry appeared in the doorway, his horrified expression showing what he thought of my behavior. "Sir?"

"Harry, please escort Rosa back to her room."

I grabbed a handful of bacon. "Some for the road." I smirked, winking at Judith, who looked like she might actually dissolve into a puddle of shock right in front of me, her mouth agape like she could swallow her whole plate in one gulp.

Harry ripped me from my chair, pieces of bacon flying through the air and landing in a greasy pile on the carpet.

"Ha! Whoops, sorry," I managed with my mouth full of fatty pork. I saluted the rest of them as I walked backwards out of the room with a fake grin plastered on my face.

As soon as the door closed, I started to shake.

Strength, find me. I know I'm not built for obedience, but this goes against what seems like the smart thing to do. I can't revel in this because I'm too scared.

Harry rattled me by my arm like he was trying to see what was loose inside. Everything. *Everything.*

"Not that I care, but what were you doing in there?" He was trying to sound angry but wasn't quite pulling it off. "Are you trying to get yourself killed?"

I sucked in my lip and scrunched my eyes, trying to decide if it was worth answering. But there was no one else. My words, my resolve, didn't mean much if no one heard me or believed me.

"No. I'm trying to live."

He let out an exasperated sigh and held me to his hip like a laundry basket while he punched in the code to my door. When it opened, he threw me to the floor and dusted his hands off like they were contaminated.

"If you keep this up, you won't," he warned as he slammed the door shut.

I swallowed, hoping he was wrong.

I shuffled backwards until I was leaning against the bed, but I didn't get up. I just sat there and swirled my finger through the plush carpet. Red like blood. I wrote my name and stared at it, then swept it away. Then I wrote down the names of all my family, ending with Orry. Twelve names. Twelve people who loved me and were counting on me to survive this hell.

There was no knock this time. The door swung open, and the edge of black rubber wheels appeared. I stayed where I was.

Grant wheeled into the room; his sinister expression, a lesson he was about to teach me.

"It didn't last long, did it, Rosa?" He waved his hands around the room. "I tried to be civil, tried to be charitable..." He paused, gazing down at me. "I like you there on the floor. It's where people like you belong."

I shrunk back, but something was pushing out of me. "Well, it must be rare for you to be able to look down on people from your reduced height," I quipped, my chin proud.

He slammed his fist down on the arm of his chair hard. "That's enough!" he yelled. Spit flew from his mouth, his eyes wild with rage. "You can't beat me, child."

Anger pressed out of me from every angle. He was trying to carve me away until I was small enough, weak enough, to crush. I had to resist.

"Why don't you walk over here and do something about it?" I challenged. "Oh that's right, you can't."

He combed his hair back with his hand, menacingly slow. "I will get what I need from you. And I will walk. You'll *see* me walk and once I have what I need, I will stand over you as you are executed."

I breathed in and felt the threat wrap around my chest and tighten, squeezing insolent words out of me like wood glue. "Can't wait!" I said with as much enthusiasm as I could muster.

He laughed in a small, mean way. "Oh, me neither."

When he was gone, calm left me. I breathed too fast and too hard until pain spread throughout my rib cage, and I thought my heart might stop.

I ran to the bathroom and retched, the panic flooding my body. Gripping the sink, I waited for it to pass. I needed to claw my way out of this if I was going to make it, but at the moment, it was hard to see a way through. I splashed some water on my face and promised just to get through the next day. Tomorrow could be a year away.

A knock at the door signaled the next part was starting.

"Miss Rosa, I have to take you downstairs."

15

Outcomes

JOSEPH

With every movement, my wounds grazed their loose dressings like I was wrapped in sandpaper. I touched my fingers to the edges of the tape, checking for heat in my skin. The last thing I needed was an infection. My skin was reassuringly cool. I pulled the blanket up, the cold eating at my fingers.

Elise appeared beside me when she noticed I was awake, running her hand over the old scar on my forearm. Her touch was light, a doctor's touch. Her eyebrows rose at the slightly caved in look of it. I never noticed it anymore, but every now and then, I'd catch Rosa looking at it, her eyes distant. I knew she was playing an image in her mind of me collapsing in front of her, dead, and was beyond my reach. I wondered whether history did repeat itself or we were just unlucky. I wanted to believe it was luck, and that it would change.

"How'd you do that?" she asked, blinking her green eyes. Her hooded, fur-lined jacket framed her face and made her look like a well-groomed cat.

"Spider bite," I grunted.

She pursed her lips. "Ooh, must have hurt a lot." *Like hell.* Her forehead creased as she investigated me like a body to be autopsied. She moved her hand and pointed a finger at the top of my heart surgery scar. "And this one?"

My scars were not something I cared to notice or talk about. They were signatures of the past. Things we'd moved away from. Under her hands, her gaze, I was captive and I didn't like it. I wanted to say, *stop touching me,* but she saved my life. So I guess I had to be polite.

"Open heart surgery," I muttered. "Performed by Matt." I pointed to Matt, who was walking on the other side of my stretcher.

Sensing my discomfort, he changed the subject. "So did you see our operative Gwen last year?" Matt asked as they talked over the top of my stretcher.

Elise shook her head. "No. They didn't even make it past the second gate before they were captured. I'm sorry; I wish I could have done something." She sounded genuinely sad.

Matt reached over me and patted her shoulder. "It's ok, Elise. It's not your fault."

I closed my eyes and tried to pretend they weren't there. I just listened to the frozen leaves grazing each other. Tried to boil my feelings down to simple things. The sun warming my body. The light stinging my eyelids. The blood pumping... *faces, dead, scraped faces.*

My eyes snapped open again. Elise placed a cool hand on my forehead.

"You all right?" she asked.

Her light hair fell down over her eyes as she leaned over me. From here, with the sun behind her head, I could barely make out her features. I squinted and replied in terse a tone, "I'm fine."

She took off her jacket and shaded my face. "Is that better?"

"That's not necessary," I grumbled. "You'll get cold."

"I don't mind," she chirped.

I do mind, a lot.

I groaned and rolled to the side, shifting my weight and causing the men carrying me to stumble. It hurt like I'd been burned all over.

"I'll just be happy when I can get off this stretcher," I said. I thought, *Happy? What a joke.*

"One more sleep and you can," she said, smiling, talking to me like a patient. It was a tone I had used many times myself.

After hours of walking, we left the dirt and the trees and descended, the rock rising higher on either side. We passed through a corridor carved from stone like someone had taken a log splitter to the earth and cracked it open. Tiny pines clung to little pockets of dirt in the cliff face. Sunlight streamed down from overhead as it was the middle of the day. I enjoyed the real warmth while it lasted because soon it would be freezing cold again.

Pelo stopped abruptly in front of us and leaned against the wall with his angular shoulder. Some of his movements were so like her because they were unpredictable, forceful. It was hard to watch. Pulling his reader from his pocket, he checked the time. He looked to Gus, who nodded. Everyone stopped moving and waited. Pelo switched on the GPS and immediately, it made a bell sound. A foreign sound. He held it away from his face, his eyes, *her eyes*, focused on the message. I propped myself up on my elbows and waited.

He cleared his throat.

"Get on with it man!" Rash snapped from his cross-legged position on the ground.

Olga waddled over to him eagerly. "Yes, Pelo, dear, tell us what it says," she asked, pressing close to him and straining her neck to see the screen. Her eyebrows rose and her mouth quivered. I braced for bad news.

"Right. It says around three hundred men, women, and children breached the wall of Birchton. Soldiers have lost control. Chaos. It's working … and…" Pelo paused, his eyes becoming wet. He blinked his dark eyelashes and swiped his face to clear the tears.

"And what?" someone asked.

His hand shook. Olga gently pried the handheld from his thin fingers.

"What does it say?" Rash asked impatiently.

Olga bowed her head as she registered the words. "It says: Praise Rosa."

Everyone bowed their heads. Except me. I looked to the sky. The clouds moved fast, creating dark shadows that blasted over the top of us and then revealed the sun again. I wasn't going to cry in front of them. I wasn't going to mourn her. Not yet.

Elise bowed her head with a puzzled expression.

Rash said what I wanted to say. "She's not dead. Stop bowing your heads like morons. Write back and then switch it off!"

Pelo oozed sadness. He was as dark as those clouds.

"What do I write?" he asked, sounding uncharacteristically unsure.

"Tell them to recruit able-bodied people to meet us at the designated place," Gus said gruffly. "And er, tell them good work."

"What place is that?" Olga asked, and Gus either didn't hear her or ignored her.

"What about the others?" I shouted, my voice bouncing off the rock walls.

Gus shook his head. The man needed a shave; his beard was starting to look pretty caveman-like.

"We've started the fire, now they need to feed it."

Pelo tapped out the message as I put my hand to my own face. I needed a shave too. He turned off the handheld quickly. We could only communicate once a day. Everyone got up and resumed walking forward.

Elise nudged me playfully with her elbow. "Cheer up, Joseph, it's only one more night," she said perkily. "Who's this Rosa anyway?"

I didn't answer. She was everything. She was mine. She was none of Elise's business.

Matt answered for me as he took over carrying the stretcher for a while. "She's one of us. This mission was her idea."

They launched into a discussion about the mission and about Rosa's brilliant idea. One more night stuck in conversations I didn't want to be in. I sighed and closed my eyes.

At least tomorrow, I would see her face again.

They marched all day as I lay staring at the sky, watching the weather and wishing I were somewhere else. I was a burden. They scaled a slim path that led out of the ravine and into the valley where Radiata sat. The snow had melted under the glare of the sun but was fast building up now that it had disappeared behind the rocks and the clouds had gathered like conspirators.

We retreated into a cave, high above the town. From my position, I could see the sweep of torchlight, scanning the flat terrain around the outside of the wall fervently as darkness gathered. It seemed they were expecting us.

"We better just blow the wall and forget about the video," Gus said, slapping the wall and wiping the pigeon blood from his hands on the rock in a grotesque finger painting. The bird crackled in the pan as the hollow sound of a gas cooker echoed through the tunnel.

"No," I said. Not really knowing how to explain myself because I had selfish reasons for wanting them to play it. Everyone turned to me.

Gus paused for a moment but then turned away and started talking to the Survivors who were supposed to enter Radiata tomorrow. I propped up on my elbows and said, "Gus, listen, it's not enough... you have to... she wouldn't want it this way."

Elise laid a hand on my arm, stroking back and forth with her thumb. I was exhausted, and I was too tired to fight her.

"What if you blew the wall and then planted the video amongst all the chaos? The explosion will draw people towards the outer wall. You could plant it near there so you don't actually have to go inside the town," she suggested.

Gus grunted. A good sign he was considering it. He yawned and conceded. "We'll vote on it in the morning."

Desh sidled up and slapped Elise on the back. "Nice one."

She laughed nervously. "Thanks." She nudged him with her elbow. He startled at the touch but smiled back at her. Desh was a bit like Rosa in that respect. He didn't give his affection away so easily, and he didn't like to be touched. The difference being, with Rosa, if you were one of those chosen few, if she allowed you into her space, she showered you with her touch, she slammed you with her smile, and she gave you everything she had. Inside her space was warmed by a bright sun. Now I was left out in the cold, in the shadows.

After we ate, we settled in to sleep. I couldn't. Sleep came with nightmares. I shuffled back and leaned against the cave wall, my legs slipping out of my sleeping bag.

Desh crawled over the sleeping bodies to get to me. He grabbed the sleeping bag and tried to pull it up over my legs. "You need to stay warm."

I scowled. "Yes, Mother."

He grinned in the dark. "Give it up; that attitude won't work with me." Sitting next to me, he chucked his jacket over my legs.

"Thanks, man."

"No, thank you. You didn't have to come back for me," he said, talking to the opposite wall, his face stiffly turned away from mine.

I replied to the wall. "Yes, I did. Hessa needed you too."

Desh sighed sadly, his shoulders slumping. "He won't remember me, Joe. It's been so long. I don't even know what he looks like now."

I fumbled around in my pack and pulled out Rosa's handheld. "Here, she took these just before we left because she knew you'd want to see him." I flipped through to a photo of Hessa standing in front of a fire. Rosa's hand was on his small shoulder, steadying him while she took the photo. I traced the curve of her dark thumb pressed into his knitted jumper. I remembered her touch with such an ache I thought I might be splitting apart.

Desh took the handheld from me. "Oh wow. He's so big and is he... walking?"

I nodded, a sad smile trying to move my lips, my feelings trying to claw their way out and seek comfort. Somewhere, my son was learning, taking steps and viewing the world without her or me in it.

"I miss him so much, and I miss her, God, I miss her, Desh," I let slip with some agony and pain I really didn't want to share.

"I miss her too," he said to the wall.

"I don't just miss her, Desh. I'm dying without her," I whispered.

He let out an exasperated sigh. "It might feel like that, Joe, but you're not. You'll go on. Eventually for yourself, but for now, keep living for Orry and for her, for what she did for you."

I knew he was right but it was hard to do when all I wished, all the time, was that she hadn't done it.

Putting a hand on my shoulder, he patted it once. He gave me back the handheld, rested his elbows on his knees, and stared at the cave wall with me.

16

Moments

ROSA

Sometimes a moment can steel you. It needs to be strong, something memorable. This moment I would catch and hold to sustain me. Keep it protected in my locked up palms.
The feel, the taste, the touch. It was like fresh air. Delicious.

Harry's hand on my shoulder guided me down the hallway like a blind person. It was a strong, yet gentle touch. I got the sense that Harry wasn't really a bad man... just a man forced to do bad things. He wouldn't hurt me unless I gave him reason to.

My eyes rolled to the bright, ceiling-high windows, the frost gathering in the corners of the glass like frozen breaths. Outside, the snow fought with the trees and plants, and was losing, with the sun as their back up. Thin sprinklings clung to the edges but slipped like melted icing. I tried to stop and look closer, but Harry steered me away. My hand crept up, trying to snatch a piece of the view and hold it. The air looked fresh, and I licked my lips at the imagined taste of it.

"Come on, Miss Rosa," Harry urged quietly. "We have to keep moving."

I sighed and shifted in my pajama pants and cardigan, my bare feet completely covered by the wide legs.

"Forgive me if I'm not in a rush to return to the torture room, Harry." I said his name warmly, like I'd laid it out on the table and smoothed its wrinkles lovingly. It was accidental.

His eyes were regretful as he turned me away from him and continued to march me forward. I walked as slowly as he would allow.

Wheels tearing up carpet didn't make much noise, but the huffing and puffing of the person pushing did.

"Move!" Grant barked as he stubbornly pushed his wheels while a soldier dressed in the black and gold uniform jogged next to him. Harry put out his arm and slammed me against the wall before Grant ran me over. I clamped my teeth together before I laughed. They looked like they were racing. I had the insane urge to declare a winner when they got to the end of the hall and had to stop to wait for the lift.

"Where?" Grant roared at the soldier, who jumped back a little. Grant's face was crimson, sweaty, and his hair flopped over his brow. I enjoyed seeing him rattled more than I could have imagined. A little smile started to tug and encourage my mouth.

"Birchton, Sir," the soldier replied, standing to attention.

"What?" His voice was a swinging trumpet that rose to a crescendo in disbelief. "Are you sure you're information is correct?" Grant's control slipped from him like rain over plastic. He was shining with beads of rage that sprayed from him as he screamed.

"Over three hundred escapees and at least twenty buildings destroyed, so far, sir." The poor soldier looked like he might wet himself.

My mouth danced happily. Who cared if he saw it? A smile spread across my face so wide that it was tipping off my head and flying into the air. Harry's arm still lay across my chest like a restraining bar and he turned his head towards me, warning me with his eyes.

"Stop smiling, Miss," he said through large, gritted teeth.

Harry's whispering caught Grant's attention. He turned his upper body to us and glared. It was too late to suppress. My smile wafted over to Grant and slapped him squarely in the face so hard I could almost see his head whip back.

He would have loved to have stormed over here and slapped me back, but he couldn't. My grin spread wider.

"So far?" His voice dropped low, but we could still hear him. "Close your stupid mouth, soldier. Do you want the whole compound to hear your lies?"

Too late.

The lift opened, and they entered. Grant turned to face us, his expression muddled. Smiling one second, menace the next. His world was changing without his authority, and it had unearthed him, roots bare and begging for water.

My face stayed the same, a grin slung ear to ear.

It was working. My idea, my plan, was working.

And even if I couldn't see it, I could feel its effect rolling over us like a wave, flooding the Superiors' compound and bringing their worst fears to the surface like lost treasures.

Radiata

JOSEPH

The problem is, I can't die. I can't let my feelings win. I have my son to get back to. I have to make sure Rosa's plans go ahead. I have to rise above the bodies. There are no choices that are my own now.

My dressings peeled back to reveal a scarred, scabby chest. But I was whole. I would heal. Physically anyway. There was no infection, just a lot of deep scratches. They would still hurt but getting up and moving was the best thing for my body. And my mind. Now I could get away.

"Looks good, Joe," Elise said, shaking her pixie hair. "You've healed surprisingly well."

"I always was a high achiever," I quipped. She laughed. She seemed nice enough, and I thought maybe I should give her a chance.

Rash sniggered near the cave opening. "Yeah, a high-achieving asshole."

I ignored him because I was in a better mood today. I stood up and rotated my torso, stretching.

"What's his problem?" Elise asked, narrowing her eyes in his direction.

I lied. "He's not a morning person."

Rash snorted and spat on the ground by his feet.

Gus gathered the group in the entrance and said, "We need to vote on Elise's suggestion. Who is in favor of detonating the bomb first, then playing the video near the outer wall of the compound?"

Almost every hand shot up except Gus's. He shook his head. "I think it's unwise but majority rules."

Matt and a Spider would head down to Radiata soon. It would be a slow, steep descent over loose gravel. They donned grey camouflage over their jackets.

I stood and tugged the grey plastic over Matt's pack to cover it properly. "Be careful," I said, not that it meant anything really. Everything we did was pretty far onto the opposite side of careful.

They left us mid-morning. We packed our gear, ready to run if we needed, and waited in the cave entrance for the explosion.

I couldn't see them, which was a good sign. The clouds were forming a gang over Radiata and the mountain. It had started to rain icy sleet that forced you to be alert.

After a lunch of more straggly birds Gus caught, we all went to our respective corners. I slammed a few things into a pack. I wanted to find a good spot to watch the show where I could be alone.

"I'm just heading up behind the cave, Gus." I waved as I stepped out of the entrance. Gus acknowledged me with a nod and a spit on the ground as he picked a feather from between his teeth. I laughed inside—that would have made Rosa giggle.

Desh's head poked up. "You want company?"

I smiled at him. "No thanks." The anger was easing now. I could see him for the friend and father he was. None of this was his fault. But I needed to be alone with her.

I stepped out, and the cold hit me with a blast. It felt good on my sore, itchy chest. Behind the cave were the remnants of a large landslide. Giant boulders leaned against each other, wedged in and hopefully stable. I pushed on them. Solid. So I started climbing.

My muscles were remembering what they were for. They flexed and burned as I heaved myself up, as I skidded on the loose stones and caught myself.

What are you doing now? Are you thinking of me?

I pulled myself to the crest of a large boulder that was split in half with one part lower than the other, making a perfect seat. The rain had eased but the clouds hung around, which was perfect. It would make her image clearer.

I sat back with my knees up and rested my arms across, hanging my head between my legs. I listened to my breathing. Fog poured from my mouth and joined the air.

Somewhere, Orry was probably being laid down to sleep. He would fight it. Like his mother. I reassured myself Alexei would be watchful over both the boys. Pietre and Careen would be doing their best. But it should have been us, Rosa and me.

I sighed and my back fell deeper against the rock. I wanted to blame her for our distance, but we made the decision together this time.

The sun was sinking below the level of the mountain now. Sunset lit up the clouds in a brilliant, bursting way. Violent strokes of red slashed through the purples, like internal bleeding under a bruise.

The sun fell and the lights flickered on.

I searched for movement, but I could see none. My eyes squinted and strained, staring at the side of the concrete wall. Smooth, dull, and perfectly curved.

A puff of dust pushed out from the wall like a hard cough. A few moments later, a small, popping sound followed.

Then sirens wailed thinly as if mildly displeased. The only indication of how serious the situation was seemed to be the way all the lights swung around to focus on the explosion site.

The screen opened in the sky minutes later like daylight had cut through the night accidentally. The clouds were the perfect backdrop for the show. I waited, barely breathing, as the video began.

I didn't notice Elise until she sat down with a thump next to me. "Great view," she said breathlessly, pulling her sleeves over her hands.

I wondered why she'd followed me up here, but I tried to hide my annoyance.

"Yes, it is," I replied absently. We were silent as the video played through.

She started talking just as Rosa appeared in the lines of pregnant girls. "How are you feeling? Should I check...?"

"Sh..." I said, putting my hand up to her face.

She crossed her arms over her chest and pouted like a child. "That was really rude," she muttered.

I groaned, pulling my hair back with my hands and froze, my hands fixed over my head. There she was. I stared into the clouds, trying to will them closer.

"Rosa," I whispered before I could stop myself. She blinked back at me, sad, disappointed. *How could you leave me?* she seemed to say.

"I'm sorry," I told the clouds and the image of her from two years ago. *That* Rosa loved a different Joseph. I tried not to think about the Rosa of now and what was happening to her at this exact moment, because my mind conjured horrible things.

Elise played with her fingers. "It's ok… you're obviously stressed about something."

"What? No." I wasn't talking to her.

God, she sounded like a doctor when she talked.

"Wow, look at that girl with heterochromia. Amazing eyes. She's beautiful." Elise said, pointing in the sky.

You don't even know.

I should have told her, *that's Rosa*, but I didn't. I was hoarding her memory. I didn't want to share it with anyone.

The image faded.

She was gone.

This was torture.

18

New Torture

ROSA

ry, crinkly hands like jerky. They were so much stronger than I would have thought. So much stronger than me.

A tub of water full of floating ice cubes shone in the bluish light. Blue like a gas flame but cold and harsh. The ice cubes rattled when a guard stood too close and nudged the tub with his leg. Tiny cute clinks, like glasses punched together in celebration. *I'm trying so hard to remember a good time, a better place than this.* The guard looked uncomfortable, scratching his stubble anxiously, which made me seriously afraid.

"Tell me about Joseph Sulle," Mr. Hun asked, his face close to mine, his breath smelling of rotten vegetables.

"No." *He was light, he was hope, and he was waiting for me.* Some things I had to keep for myself.

My hands were wrenched behind my back and tied at the wrists. I fought it, thrashing my head around until I could no longer see anything but my hideous hair slapping back and forth in front of my eyes. I breathed in. Panic stabbed me, in, out, in, out. My eyes went to the tub, just a plain plastic tub balancing on one, two, three bricks under each end. It was leaking, cold water seeping into the clay bricks. They were crying, or bleeding, weeping for me.

"Where is he?" A voice that warm shouldn't belong to someone who was so cold, flat, and without a soul.

"No." My teeth chattered and then clamped down. I wouldn't answer any questions today.

The two guards on either side of me tried to push me to my knees. I resisted. One of them stamped into the back of my legs and I collapsed forward, my hair dipping into the water.

"Take a deep breath, Miss," Harry whispered. I didn't know why he was in here with me. Usually, he just walked me to the door…

"Tell me about Mister Sulle," Hun asked calmly, softly, like he cared. A master of falseness.

I remained silent. Hun kneeled down next to me and grabbed my head, his palms cupping my ears. He tucked my hair behind them with his cruel fingers and shook his head at me.

Sadistic bastard.

"It doesn't have to be this hard. Stop fighting. Tell us what we need to know and it will end."

Yeah, you'll kill me.

It's coming, breathe. It's coming… breathe, breathe, breathe.

Soon, you won't be able to breathe.

I clamped my lips together and stared past Mr. Hun. The walls were covered in plump, dark blue quilted material.

Soundproof.

There was no count. Mr. Hun clawed the back of my neck, dug in, and plunged my head into the water so forcefully that my face hit the bottom.

Panic, panic, panic. I didn't breathe. I forgot to take a breath.

The shock was hard, like a baton to the face. One where you wanted to gasp, but you couldn't. I opened my eyes to bubbles in almost blackness.

I needed air. There was no air.

The cold crept up my nose, sucked into my ears. A dull thrumming, my heartbeat, surrounded by water, reminded me I was still alive. I bucked my head, but his grasp was like steel.

Bubbles. My voice. My head thrashing like a fish out of water.

Stop.

Please.

It was so cold. My head felt separate to my body. My lungs burning, scrabbling for air.

So cold.

My eyes closed. My mouth desperate to open, to draw in the liquid like it was air. I couldn't hold on any longer.

Mr. Hun's fingers pressed into my neck and drew me back. I surfaced and dragged in a breath, like a vacuum. Oxygen revived and hurt like hell.

I sat back on my heels and coughed out the water. The ice cubes danced on the surface. Battling, huddling on a sea.

He still held my neck and turned it so I was facing him. I watched his cracked lips move, his neck wobble as he talked.

"Tell me about Joseph Sulle."

A hot tear warmed a line down my cheek as I shook my head. *I won't let you take him from me.*

Mr. Hun sighed in disappointment.

One, two, three... Take a deep breath.

I am stronger than you think.

My hair clung to my face and neck in wet clumps. The top of my shirt was soaked. Mr. Hun cut my hands free and threw me a towel. Hands shaking, I dried myself as he studied me. His eyes narrowed to slits.

"Stay here," he said, pointing to the chair in the middle of the room.

I balled the towel around my hands and grinned at him. "Aw... d-don't go. Are the games over already?" My mouth quivered with cold. And fear.

Mr. Hun drew his shoulders up, and then released them in frustration. He shuffled out of the room, locking the door behind him.

As soon as he was gone, I collapsed in the chair, drew my legs up under me, and forced myself into a tiny ball. I curled into darkness.

How much more?

I leaned into comfort. Orry's arms wrapped around my leg, supporting me. I leaned back into the chair that had become Joseph's warm chest. His heart beat steady. *You can do this,* I told myself.

Feelings rose and fell, panic then strength, panic then strength. My heart either way.

The door opened.

Mr. Hun waddled in. I looked down at his feet and noticed his pants hung, crumpled, far over his shoes. He was a small, cruel man.

Insignificant.

Harry rolled in a table and set it in front of me, his eyes more sorry than I could take. I searched for instruments, but it was empty.

Mr. Hun placed his hand on my head and forced it against the back of chair, wrapping a band around my forehead and tying it behind the chair. He did the same around my chest and neck. The towel slipped from my lap and onto the floor.

"What are you doing?" I asked, my voice drained of any impertinence.

He tied my wrists to the arms of the chair and placed both his sickening hands over my own. He looked like a cooked turkey a week old, dried-up.

"Giving you some time to think," he said with a hacking smile.

Harry placed a screen on the table and loaded a video. He measured the distance between my chair and the table, and then chose to pull the table back a little further so it was just out of kicking reach.

He hit play, and then they quickly left the room.

My eyes darted from side to side, wondering what the next trick would be when I heard Este's voice, high and shrill, squawking from the screen, her thin frame teetering in those red heels. "I d-don't want b-b-blood on the carpets."

It seemed so slow at the time, as if I could catch every second and examine it before the next one came along. This was just ugly and violent and blade smashingly fast. The guard lunged at Joseph, and I stepped in front of him. Just like that.

I wanted to hold my stomach, but I couldn't. I wanted to look away. But all I could do was watch as the knife plunged into my stomach, the way it crippled me immediately. The disgusting gurgle and *aha* sound I made. My eyes wet as I stumbled forward, folded over, my hands fluttering over a wound that was just pouring blood like a faucet. I grabbed the knife and pulled it out with a sad grunt. Then I fell to the ground ungracefully like a pile of dirty laundry. My eyes still open. But dead. Dead.

I could feel it. The pain. The fear. The regret. Repeating. But worse than that, I could see Joseph's reaction when he realized what I'd done.

The worst thing I'd ever done.

The best thing I'd ever done.

He crumbled; he looked like someone had reached inside and

pulled his heart out.

"What have you done?" the Joseph in the video asked.

But I didn't answer. I was dead.

I died.

Emotions choked me as each one fought for release, and sobbing rattled in my throat.

The video went black, and I sighed in relief. But the anguish remained in me. I still felt the knife as it went in and the pain that started to ebb away so quickly as I pulled it out, because my life was leaving me. I remembered the blink and the absolute panic of knowing it was over. I was over.

I closed my eyes and wept.

Until I heard Este's voice, high and shrill, squawking from the screen, her thin frame teetering in those red heels. "I d-don't want b-b-blood on the carpets."

My eyes snapped open.

The video was on loop.

It had been three hours. Three hours of dying. My limbs shook and bounced against my restraints, my face hot but my blood lounging slowly in my veins like it was tired. I was so tired.

After the first hour, the panic started to strangle me. I tried closing my eyes but the noises were almost worse than the video. Instead, I started to focus on the details in the background, like Deshi's face drowning in horror, his arms drawn up over his body when the clatter and clanging began. He moved a few steps towards me before it happened, but when he saw the knife go in, he froze and then disappeared from the shot.

The guard that stabbed me looked as scared as everyone else. You could tell he didn't mean to do it. His round face, spotted with freckles, shook slowly from side to side in disbelief. When he released his hold on the knife, he stepped back from me and glanced down at his hands like they were separate from him. Small monsters.

In one moment, everything was ruined.

The video played and etched itself permanently into my brain. It stretched and pushed until there was nothing else in there but violence, pain, and blood.

It was damaging me, rummaging through my brain like a vandal, picking out the good memories, scrunching them into a ball and tossing them away.

When the guards and Mr. Hun finally re-entered the room, they could ask no questions. I was a useless heap. Sapped of anything. My mouth could form no words.

They untied my hands, and they fell limply in my lap. My eyes stung, my mouth dry, my arms and legs pieces of wood tied loosely together in a messy clatter.

Harry carried me back to my room. I clung to him. Pressed my cheek to his chest and refused to look up. He opened the door with his foot and knelt down, rolling me out of his arms and onto the carpet as if he were dumping an armful of firewood.

When the door wouldn't shut, he whispered, "I'm so sorry, Miss," as he pushed my body forward with his foot until it was out of the way so it would close.

19

Returning

JOSEPH

Maybe burying is the answer. Maybe if I pile enough earth, blood, and experience on top of them, I won't be able to hear them screaming or hear the 'ha' that forms around her last breath.

A weak ping rang out far below. Elise grabbed my arm and squeezed. "What was that, was it a...?"

"Gunshot," I replied, straightening and leaning forward.

Several shots fired close together. We couldn't see much from here, just a cluster of black, bobbing heads atop the wall, crossing under the spotlights. The lights moved frantically over the grey ground around the base of the walls. I caught what I thought were two people, running away. But I couldn't be sure, the light moved over them so quickly.

Another shot.

I strained to see, both of us leaning dangerously close to the edge.

"Do you think they're...?" She sounded alarmed, the pitch of her voice creeping up higher and higher.

"No," I grunted, "but let's go back to the others. They might need our help." I held out my hand, which she gripped tightly, and helped her climb back down to the cave. We slid down the rocks, tripping over each other as we went. I kept my eye to Radiata. The lights danced across the dirt. Then very suddenly, they turned inwards. I tightened my fist and pumped it once. They did it. Something was causing a disturbance inside the walls.

We swung into the cave, and everyone was getting ready to go.

"Did you hear the shots?" I said, out of breath.

Gus nodded, his voice as calm and blunt as ever. "We did. That's why we're leaving."

Desh's arms went slack by his sides, his face tangled in confusion. "What about Matt and Ermil?"

Gus shook his head. He did, for once, look truly sorry. "We can't risk it."

I moved right up to where Gus was standing, looming over him. "The lights turned inwards. I think the video is working. They might not have anyone following them." Gus looked up at me in annoyance, and I took a step back. Then he dropped his head and swore.

"You go then," he ordered, flinging his arm out towards Radiata. He picked up a backpack full of medical supplies and shoved it at my chest, avoiding my eyes.

"Take this, you'll need it. We'll wait for you five miles south of here."

I held the pack against my pounding heart with shaking hands. "Thank you," I whispered.

"We can't wait for very long, Joseph," Gus said, his voice full of regret.

I could feel Desh's eyes burning into my back. "I'm not coming with you, am I?" he said to the back of my head.

I shook my head. I wanted him to come but it would just be risking his life so I didn't have to be alone.

His hand clapped my shoulder. "Be careful."

Rash brushed past and stopped suddenly, turning to glance up at me. His eyebrows drew down, his anger hiding for the moment. "Yeah man, be careful." He then threw over his shoulder, "If you die, we've lost our punchline."

Gus grumbled and searched the back of the cave, singling one person out.

"Elise, you'll go with Joseph," Gus ordered.

"What? No!" I protested

"She goes or you don't go at all," he growled.

She grabbed her own pack and strode out of the entrance to the cave.

"Don't slow me down," she snapped as she quickly descended, her white blonde hair glowing as she skidded down the mountainside towards Radiata.

I jumped over several packs and followed her. "I'll see you soon,

Desh. Don't worry, ok?" I pleaded.

Elise was quick on her feet, moving from stone to stone, avoiding the slippery parts that were mostly gravel and watery mud. I struggled to keep up, but I wasn't going to ask her to slow down.

"If they're injured, it's probably gunshot wounds. Have you ever treated a gunshot before, Joseph?" She clasped a small tree trunk and paused, turning towards me.

"No. But I've studied them," I replied between breaths.

She snorted. "Not the same thing, honey," she puffed as she started running again.

I couldn't even be offended by her patronizing comments because she was probably right. Setting my lips together, I chose silence for the rest of the way down, running over procedures in my head and praying Matt was all right.

The sirens grew in volume and frequency as we descended.

The steep hill flattened suddenly, and we slowed our pace. Charred trees poked out of the ground with tiny, struggling branches pushing their way through the ruined bark. *Life always finds a way,* she would say. I ran my hand over one of the delicate new branches, feeling it bend between my fingers.

I heard a groan. In the half-light, trees looked like men stuck in the ground. Elise paused and we searched for movement, trying to pinpoint the source of the noise.

An arm moved.

"Hold on, Erm, just hold on," a voice whispered.

We ran towards the sound, our feet squelching in the puddles as we approached. I grabbed a flashlight from my pack and flicked it on. It swished over an agonized face, eyes tightened against pain.

Matt sighed in relief. "Joe, thank God it's you."

I kneeled down and swept the torch over where the two men were sitting. Ermil lay flat on his back. Matt had wrapped his shirt around a wound in Ermil's calf and was shivering uncontrollably in the cold while trying to apply pressure.

Matt's other hand was clenched in a fist. This hand had blood seeping out from between the fingers like he was squeezing a sponge.

"Oh Jesus, Matt, what happened?" I took off my jacket and placed it over Matt's shaking shoulders. He opened his hand; it was a mess of torn skin and blood.

"F-flesh wound," he stuttered, "s-superficial. They were following us but then got called back. R-riots."

Elise stood over me with her hands on her hips, triaging. "Right. Wrap a bandage around Matthew's hand to stop the bleeding. We need to look at this guy's leg," she stated matter-of-factly.

I carefully wrapped Matt's hand, pulling it tight.

"My fingertips are numb, Joe," he said in a broken voice.

I knew he was thinking nerve damage. I knew he was thinking he may not be able to operate again, but I just placed his bandaged hand in his lap and said, "You're just cold, that's all."

He nodded in thanks. There was no point in worrying about it now.

Matt held the torch while we laid out our instruments and moved Ermil's leg over a sterile sheet of plastic.

We cut his pant leg off until the wound was exposed. Ermil was lucky; the bullet had gone straight through the fleshy part of his calf. It hadn't hit the bone, which meant he would heal better. The problem was that it had left a giant hole that was pouring blood, making it very hard to see what was going on.

"Lift his leg above his heart level," Matt instructed. We rolled the backpack under the plastic and then under Ermil's leg.

"Pressure," I ordered, my voice tight as a coil, my brain doing what it loved, what it knew.

Elise nodded and grabbed a gauze pad, pushing down on both sides of the wound. Ermil moaned in pain as she applied pressure.

"You'll have to stitch the artery," Matt muttered in our direction, hoping Ermil was too out of it to hear him.

Ermil's head snapped up suddenly. No luck there. "Are you serious?" he said through gritted teeth.

All the doctors' eyes connected knowingly.

Elise held the torch over the wound as she removed the gauze. Blood bubbled up. "Hold it still so I can find the source of the bleeding," I said, my eyes connecting with hers.

Matt shuffled closer and dabbed as much blood away from the wound as he could. I sterilized my hands with hand sanitizer and alcohol wipes, pushing my fingers into Ermil's calf. He started to scream, and Matt put his hand to Ermil's mouth.

"I know it's hard but you have to be quiet, so they won't find us," he whispered.

Ermil's eyes were bugging out of his head but he managed to nod, and Matt released him. He gripped Matt's leg desperately, searching for comfort.

"It's going to be ok, Ermil. We won't leave you," I said quietly.

Warm blood ran over my fingers as I fished around for the torn artery. It was a strange, reassuring feeling: The flesh under my fingertips, the work that needed to be done. This was part of me.

I thought I could feel it and I moved upwards, tracing the artery, and then pushed down hard to stop the blood flow.

"Suction," I said automatically.

Elise laughed.

Matt understood what I meant and dabbed at the blood to see if it had slowed. We all relaxed a little when we realized it had.

"Quickly, sterilize your hands," I said to Elise.

"Already did, Doctor." She anticipated what I needed and moved her hand over to where mine was, sliding her finger into place behind mine and pushing down.

"How long before they take their fingers out of my leg?" Ermil gasped to Matt, his face sheened with sweat, his skin pale as the moon.

Matt flipped open the suture kit with his good hand. "You'll have to tie it, Joe. I can't," he said, holding up his injured hand.

Everything fell into place. My actions, my breathing, my timing. It was natural. I tied the artery easily, swiftly. I was at home with the needle in my hand.

I leaned back on my heels and stared down at the wound.

"Ready?" Elise asked all of our intensely focused faces, lit up by torchlight.

I nodded. "Do it."

Elise lifted her fingers, and we waited for blood.

Matt dabbed away at the wound again. It seeped a little, but it wasn't pouring anymore.

My shoulders sank a few inches, my body relaxed. Elise threw an arm around my neck and pulled our heads together so they knocked. "Well done. We make a good team."

Matt smiled. "You certainly do."

Ermil even managed a half-grimace, half-smile. "So I'm not going to die?"

I chuckled, something warm and unfamiliar growing in my chest, blotting out the sadder feelings. "Not today."

Cleaning his wound, we wrapped it tightly. We would have to carry him up the hill, but he would live. He would walk. We did that.

It was an amazing feeling.

Misery had been following me. I had been uninvolved and uninterested in everything around me.

No more.

As I packed up our gear, tumbling the bloodied gauze and dirty needles into the plastic sheeting, *she* came back to me. I tied a knot around the top and shoved the waste into a hole at the bottom of a tree, my hands scraping on the charcoal and coming back all black and slimy. I hadn't thought of *her* through that whole process. And I was ashamed to say that it felt good to forget.

"You coming?" Elise asked, turning around with Ermil's arm over her shoulder as she supported his weight.

I smiled a genuine smile at her. "I'm coming."

She seemed surprised but she returned my smile with a toothy one of her own, her freckles pushing high up under her eyes.

The sun rose over the peaks to our right. Shafts of light slipped through the crags of rock and poured through the brittle trees as I jogged to catch up to them. I slung Ermil's other arm over my shoulder, and Matt took my pack.

We did a good job last night. Apella would have been proud of me.

We saved someone's life. That had to count for something, push the peg forward one short inch.

I left any other feelings behind, jammed into that tree with the blood and contaminated instruments.

20

Got Me

ROSA

I wish I could hate you. I want to hate you for leaving me here.
I HATE you.
I love you.
I love you.

The door eased over the carpet. My face pressed against the floor, my knees folded over as if I were praying. I focused on the tiny little threads, bending, waving like red grass as the wood swept over the top. I would hold my heart hostage to lie in grass right now. I wanted the frozen spikes digging into my back. I wanted the melted snow to seep into my clothes.

I didn't want to feel dead, to relive dying.

A polished shoe wedged in the gap and Red's legs, body and face appeared. She glowered from her position above me. I hadn't moved in hours. It had taken me this long to remember how to breathe properly, to pull myself from a very real nightmare.

"I have to take you downstairs," she whispered regretfully, her countenance changing. Pity grimed the corners of her mouth. I had no energy to dislike her face. I was stretched past caring.

I turned my forehead to the carpet, rubbing it back and forth slowly. "Where's Harry?" I murmured, my lips picking up pieces of carpet fluff.

Red's voice was warmer than I expected, but disappointed as well. "Harry has been repurposed. He, er, wasn't suited to this position. You need to get up, Miss Rosa. I have to take you downstairs again."

Again.

I blinked, and tears met the carpet.

"You'll have to help me up," I whispered. I couldn't take another step. I couldn't willingly walk back in there.

She knelt down, a ladder in her stockings stretched wide over her knee as her weight pressed into the floor. She hooked her arms under mine and pulled me up. "Let's go."

I didn't answer. Most of me was still on the floor.

I love you.
Don't forget.
Please don't have already forgotten.

They strapped me down in the chair again. They asked the questions again. I refused to answer them again. They pressed play again.

My soul coiled inside my body, winding round and round in a tight dressing— protecting me, shielding me.

Este's voice, high and shrill, squawked from the screen, her thin frame teetering in those red heels. "I d-don't want b-b-blood on the carpets."

I closed my eyes and listened to the rest. I knew it by heart now. This was unnecessary. These images would never leave me.

"What have you done?" Joseph asked. I opened my eyes, waiting for the screen to go black and start at the beginning again.

But it didn't. This was the after part. The part I didn't remember because I was already gone.

A squeal, hard and piercing. Este stood on the tiles, her hands straight at her sides, her fingers anchored to her thighs. So taut, so distressed. Joseph leaned down to my body, his hands shaking. Before he could touch my neck to check for a pulse, a guard jumped on his back, his arms wrapped tightly around Joseph's throat.

My head shook from side to side as I watched in dismay. Maybe I was wrong. Maybe Joseph had been dead this whole time. The bottom fell out of everything. The floor rocked, the air swirled, and I knew I was going to be sick. But I couldn't stop watching.

Joseph's hands scrambled behind him, batting, grabbing, scratching at the guard. His eyes. They weren't *his* eyes. They were hollow, angry, absent. He got a grip on the guard and threw him to the ground. I watched as the guard skidded backwards over the tiles and his head hit the wall. I would have heard a crack, if there weren't so many other noises fighting for attention. Guards were coming at Joseph from every direction. Clawing, hitting, trying to pull him to the ground, but he was like a raging bull, his strength inhuman as he fought them off.

When his face flashed towards the camera, his eyes were still empty, and my body shuddered like a rickety shed in a storm.

A guard lifted the knife from the floor and held it out in front of him, my blood spitting from the end in splatters as his hand shook. He lunged at Joseph's side but accidentally slashed at the forearm of the guard holding Joseph by the waist. That guard dropped to the floor, screaming, gripping his arm over an open wound that was spurting blood like a sprinkler. My stomach crept up into my mouth at all the blood, the violence that seemed endless. The guard with the knife didn't seem to notice what he'd done and lunged at Joseph again. I gasped at the disconnection of these men grappling at each other, fighting for their lives, and Joseph, a body separate to his spirit, a hulk, a mass of rage.

There were two guards down. Este's piercing-as-a-bullet squealing was a constant musical backdrop to the scene.

A shot cracked the air, and Joseph ducked down. But it was nowhere near him. It came from somewhere else out of frame. The squealing ceased like someone had pressed the mute button, and Este lay across the couch like a dismantled puppet.

It dazed the men for a second and then I lost them all in the mesh of muscle, weapons, and blood. Joseph held onto a guard's hand tightly or around something... something black. I dug my nails into my palms, my body leaning forward and nearly pulling my chair over. I was a bird ready to take flight, straight into a wall.

Crack, crack, crack...

It didn't sound like it should. It sounded like a whip, like lightning. I could almost smell the singe, the burn, and see the scalded earth. But it was not something natural; it was something men made to undo men.

I searched the pile of bodies, slumped in a circle around him. Joseph was covered in blood. He was breathing like he couldn't get the air in quick enough, hunched over as if he were a seed that wouldn't grow.

The gun lagged in his hand, and then it dropped to the floor with an isolated, lonely clang.

What did I make you do?

I pulled at my restraints, thinking I might scream but knowing no one would come to my aid.

"What have you done?" Deshi asked in the screen, in a video I was struggling to believe was real, as he stood behind the bodies.

Joseph was lost. No color in his beautiful face save the color of others' blood. He moved to my body, silent and motionless through the whole thing, and collapsed. I watched and felt every punch, every splinter as he beat the tiles over and over again with his fist. I didn't know what to do. I wanted to cry out, I wanted to reach inside the screen and hold him, but I couldn't. I was lying there dead, and he was broken.

I broke him.

Everything shattered. A million tiny shards of ceramic the color of gold and dust rained over me.

I let out a moan. A shallow sound that was nothing. *Nothing.*

Mr. Hun pushed the door open. My eyes squinted at the light from the garage that didn't belong in here. I wanted to steep in darkness. Disappear.

His voice was soft and sure. "See, dear. You're protecting a murderer. Are you ready to talk now?"

My chin touched my chest, and I exhaled my soul in one breath. They would get nothing from me today.

I was done.

21

Reminder

ROSA

I fell in the hall on the way back to my room, my limbs so wobbly I could barely stand. They folded under me like poorly made chair legs and crumbled together. Red sighed and nudged me with her toe. I felt like any touch would disintegrate my form. I was a case. Inside me were dust, un-smelled air, and waves of sadness. I pulled my legs under my body sluggishly and whimpered at her impatient prodding. The pain I felt was scattered over my skin, like a lagging electric shock.

I could feel her body warmth closing in, looming, ready to grab me and jerk me up. She'd had her one sympathetic moment. That was probably all I was going to get. Besides, they were always watching and she couldn't show weakness.

A cough.

"Let me take her, Mrs. Kelly." A calm voice, slow like lava, but warm, bordering on hot.

Red's foot tapped once in front of my eyes, and then disappeared.

Lips close to my ear whispered, "You need to get up."

I can't.

"Get up." Strong fingers found my chin and forced it upwards. "Now. He's watching you."

Okay. Move your limbs. Pull one part in front of the other. Follow the thread of life left in you.

I heaped myself towards my door, moving like a kicked heap of wet towels.

Denis opened the door and walked straight into my bathroom. Pulling myself from the floor, I went inside, closing the bedroom door behind me. I heard a slight metallic clink, and then the taps running. Without even looking into the bathroom, I seized and shuffled into the corner with fear.

His concerned face appeared in the bathroom doorway, and I pressed closer to the wall. When he saw my expression, his eyebrows rose in alarm and he pumped his hands in front of him.

"No. I'm not going to hurt you, I…" He ran a hand over his close-cropped, spiky hair and sighed. "Have a shower, Rosa, take some time," he urged seriously.

I just stared blankly, not understanding anything. My mind was walled in on all sides by screens playing violent acts over and over. Then he checked himself, checked for cameras, and leaned in, kissing me briefly on the forehead.

"Let this be the last time you allow him to hurt you," he whispered, his breath a flush of peppermint on my aching skin.

Tears cascaded over my eyelashes and flooded my cheeks, a waterfall of disbelief.

He pulled back suddenly, as if he'd surprised himself, and backed away from me, opening the door behind him and slowly leaving the room. His eyes intense. His face finally showed some emotion—concern, but also… a challenge.

I waited until the door clicked and then rushed to the bathroom. Sitting on the basin was a candy-colored music player, the white earphones wound in a circle. The song was paused.

I traced the title with my shaking fingers, my head splitting with bullets and blood. 'The Work' by Catie Wings. It didn't sound like a real name.

I placed the earphones in my ears and pressed play, looking up at the girl in the mirror. She looked harrowed, hollow, wide eyes in a thin face, eyes as large as bowls and just as full. Full of more trauma than she could handle and struggling to get back to herself. To remember herself. I gripped the sides of the sink and listened.

If this was more torture, that would be it. I would wash down the drain.

The music was haunted. A floating voice sailed in the spaces between what I'd learned was piano. A dull thud. But then the vulnerability, the stress of the first words, hit me and I dissolved. My fingers slipped and I pressed them deeper into the porcelain. I watched the ghost in the mirror react and tried to recall that it was me.

"Clasp hands, you'll survive."

Her voice wavered as if she weren't sure of her words, the fear in there, the loss of something real.

"I'm on my own, looking in,
On the strife,
On the chaos."

I couldn't understand the next part, but her voice had me anyway. Something was over, she sung. It was about things that were out of her control. My tears fell into the basin, just water.

Insubstantial water.

Powerful water.

I can do this. I have to. My heart burgled all the strength it could. My head fell as I watched tears pour down the drain, my hair, waving, glowing light and wrong.

"Fate's taking the last of your strength,
But I know you've got a lot of fight left.
Fate's taking the last of your strength,
But I know you've got a lot of fight left."

Something was stuck in my throat, heaving panic. *Let this be the last time.*

"I can't cry for fear of what it means.
I can hope but it leaves me undone.
Regrets keep me standing alone.
Wondering what I could've done.
Wondering if I gave you enough."

There was more than just tears burning my throat; something else was stuck in there, my heart, my soul. I was trying so hard and then, I stopped. *This will be the last time. Make it count,* I thought. I eased myself down to the floor, the damp bath mat cool on my legs, the player pulling over the edge and landing on the floor. I wrapped my arms around my legs to contain the shaking.

"Please, my love, change this time, change this place."

She wailed, she pleaded. But it wasn't going away.

"Take this pain away." She threw the words at me, threw them into the atmosphere, and offered them to anyone that would have them. And I wanted to take the pain for her. I wanted to be stronger.

Grant. I hate you. I hate you. I hate you. I let myself feel it. I let the tears run over my lips and into my hands. I held them there.

"Leave me my memories.

Leave them here with me."

She asked. She told. She demanded.

I thought, *They're mine. You can't take him from me. You can't change my mind about him.* I won't.

I let the words roll over and over like racing clouds heavy with destruction. They floated in front of my face; they sloped over my forehead and smoothed down my hair.

"Fate's taking the last of your strength,

But I know you've got a lot fight left.

Fate's taking the last of your strength,

But I know you've got a lot fight left."

I knew.

This would be the last time I let him hurt me.

22.

Reasons

JOSEPH

We arrived at the camp after walking half the night, Ermil managing to support his weight but still needing a crutch. We were dirty, happy, and different.

The early morning clink of metal cups and the pour of hot water reassured me, brought me home. We were purposefully loud as we entered the broken-up camp; people perched between the trees of the thickly wooded area. Everyone reacted, jumping up, grabbing weapons. When Gus faced us, he broke into a wide smile.

"I knew you'd make it," he said, clapping his hands together. I couldn't help but grin, his happiness rubbing off on me.

Pelo ran up and offered an arm to Ermil so he could ease himself down. A drink was offered as soon as his butt hit the ground. Pelo looked up at me and his eyes again slapped me with their likeness to Rosa's. I shook it away, pressing her memory down and tucking it under other things.

"I'm so glad you're safe," he said, standing up and bringing me into his arms. "I couldn't lose you too."

My arms were at my sides. I held my breath while he hugged me.

"I'm fine, Pelo," I muttered, realizing I'd left him to deal with his grief alone because I'd been too busy with my own. I took a deep breath and forced myself to look at him. "I'm sorry I left without saying goodbye." I connected with his eyes briefly and then looked away.

Pelo waved his hand, steam coming from his mouth as he spoke. "No matter, no matter. You're safe, that's the important thing." He lifted a finger to the air. "That and the fact that our plans seem to be working marvelously." I caught myself starting to roll my eyes and stopped.

Matt came up behind us and broke the tension, his voice anchored in pride. "You should have seen him performing surgery on the side of a hill by torchlight! It was very impressive."

"I had help," I muttered, pointing in Elise's direction. I thought I caught a quick glare from Desh.

She smiled shyly and swept her short hair behind her ear. "It was mostly Joseph. I just held the torch."

I shrugged. She did more than that.

Clapping startled us, very slow clapping coming from the outer edges of the camp.

"Hooray for the hero," Rash exclaimed sarcastically.

I turned to face him. His eyebrows were pulled down; dark circles ran under his eyes like bruises.

"They never said..." I started.

"No, really you are," Rash said, shaking his head and stepping towards me, getting closer than he had since the night we'd left the Superior's compound. "You saved your own skin and left Rosa to rot. Now, look, you've played the hero, and you've got a new admirer. You can forget all about her now."

"Rash..." Pelo sighed.

He took another step, reached out, and poked me in the chest accusingly. "Isn't that right?" Each word was punctuated with a sharp tap to my heart.

I stared down at him. Tears pooled in his eyes. "No," I said sternly.

He desperately wanted to hit me. I could feel his fists burning to connect.

Matt spoke. "You don't know the whole story. Joseph did what he could, but she couldn't be saved."

Desh's head snapped towards Matt, his expression baffled. I took the opportunity to move away from Rash, but he followed me. I turned back to him and growled. "Not now!"

Rash put his hands up and smirked at me infuriatingly.

I grabbed Desh's arm and yanked him away from the camp, pulling him in between the thick trunks that barricaded us in like the black-clad legs of Woodlands' soldiers.

When we were a safe distance from the others, I spun Desh to face me. The look in his eyes was one of complete confusion and a little bit of fear. He was scared of me. I forced myself to relax a little and took a calming breath.

I sighed. "I'm sorry I dragged you out of there, but there's something you need to know."

Desh raised his eyebrows and waited for me to go on. I breathed in heavily. "I let Matt think Rosa killed Este." Desh's eye's widened and he opened his mouth to speak, but I cut him off. "But before you say anything just understand, I know it was wrong, but I couldn't have him look at me like I was a murderer. I know that's what I am, I know I have to face it, but it's hard. I wanted some time to deal with what I'd done before everyone knew."

Desh's face softened. "Joe." My name sounded like a sad sigh when he said it. He reached out to touch my arm, and I jerked away. "I think we need to talk about this. You know it's not your fault, right?"

I knew it was entirely my fault.

"Desh, please, I don't want to talk about it. It's too damn hard," I pleaded.

He seemed anxious when he tried again to talk. "But I don't think you understand…" I held my hand up to stop him. "I understand enough."

I stomped away, leaving him standing there, bewildered. He wasn't going to make me feel better about this, and I couldn't reopen the wounds. I was finally managing to move forward, and he wanted to drag me back.

We packed up and left for Palma. To keep them guessing, we were zigzagging across the compounds, not hitting them in order. We hadn't managed to sync with the fireworks at Radiata, but we would for Palma in five days.

Soldiers had poked around the bottom of the hill looking for us, but they hadn't come very far before they were called back. It seemed Radiata had exploded with anger and riots. No Survivor could stay this time. It was too dangerous. We had to leave them to it.

We walked in a zigzag as well. The Survivors were very good at hiding and avoiding Woodlands' soldiers.

I kicked a slice of shale rock down a grassy hillside, watching it skid across the other stones and disappear. Light snow covered any outcropping, but it wasn't building up as fast as we would have thought. It was actually a shame in a way because it would have hid our tracks. Gus predicted it would thicken over the next few days.

"How's the hand?" I asked Matt as we paused to get our bearings and rest. We were all on a high except for him. No one expected it to go this well. But then, no one really considered what would happen after. Matt was contemplative.

Matt bent his fingers slowly; two fingers didn't move. He watched them like they weren't his own.

"It'll come back, Matt, give it time," I said.

He smiled sadly. "How are your chest wounds?" he asked, peering at my shirt.

I tapped my chest lightly. "Itchy!" He laughed. I noticed several grey hairs running through the light brown.

"Itchy is good."

Elise strolled over and took my water bottle from me, taking a swig without asking. I cleared my throat. She ignored me.

"Yep, means it's healing." She daintily dabbed at her mouth with her sleeve.

Rash sat on a rock, listening intently, and then his face cracked into a smile. "So, itchy good, oozy bad?"

Everyone laughed. Even me. I tried not to look at him for too long though, scared I would ruin the moment. Our relationship had always been precarious, but without Rosa here, it was dangling off a cliff.

I stuffed thoughts of her back behind others, focusing on the next mission and Orry.

Gus clapped his hands together and looked at the sky, as if it were a clock he could read. "It's time to move."

Elise floated from group to group. She was easy to talk to and managed conversations with everyone. She was confident to the point of being a little annoying, but most of the time I didn't mind her company.

We were now one-day's walk from Palma. The time passed quickly. A lot of walking, talking, and shooting animals. I was training my eyes to search out game. Everyone did it and when Gus caught something, there was a lot of celebration and the bonus of fresh food.

I was at the back of the group today, when I heard a rustle to my right. The forest was dense in this area, although where we stood almost qualified as a stamped-out road. I thought I saw a flash of blue feathers. I grabbed Elise's arm and pulled her back while I kept an eye on the birds, three pheasants sitting between a couple of rotted, mossy logs.

"See the pheasants? Get Gus," I whispered.

Nodding, she lithely picked her way up the line until she reached Gus. She whispered in his ear and pointed to me. I beckoned him with my finger.

I silently pointed out the bird's positions, and Gus aimed his rifle. I watched him pull back the trigger and gulped, swallowing the nausea I felt at having a gun so close to me again.

A shot was fired and they flapped into the sky, a mess of feathers and noise as three birds rose unharmed into the air.

Gus never missed.

Ever.

Gus's finger was frozen, curled around the trigger. He hadn't taken a shot. "Scatter," he said through his teeth.

A man's voice slashed through the forest. "Did I hit it?"

"Now!" Gus said, his voice quiet but urgent.

I turned and searched for a hiding place. A hundred yards away was a thick-trunked tree with bushes sprouting around the base. I moved towards it, trying to put as much distance between the voices and me as I could. Everyone scattered, diving from the path as they were told. I saw Desh and Pelo dash towards a log and jump behind it. Olga floundered in the middle of the road, her head flicking from us to the direction of the noise until Matt appeared from behind a tree and dragged her from view. I exhaled in relief.

Luckily, the owners of the voices hadn't noticed us yet. They were too focused on the pheasants and still shooting at the sky like idiots.

I got about halfway to the tree when I realized Elise was just standing there, gaping. I groaned, looked to the sky, and returned to her, keeping low. Another shot fired and she had the sense to duck down. I grabbed her arm and pulled her away, moving from shrub to tree trunk to shrub as the voices came closer.

I leaped into the bushes, wet leaves brushing my face and hands, pulling Elise inside and onto my lap. I pulled her closer as I heard clumsy footsteps breaking sticks and crunching leaves, things I had almost learned to control.

"Don't move," I whispered in her ear. She flinched. Her body was as stiff as a board, but shaking. Her hair brushed under my nose. She smelled clean, but a chemical clean, like shampoo and hair products, things I hadn't seen or smelled in more than a year.

She shivered uncontrollably, her breath coming in and out in short, tight bursts.

"Calm down, you're going to hyperventilate," I warned. She nodded and tried to calm her breathing as the voices came closer.

Through the leaves, I could see black boots and black trousers with gold trim running down the sides. I held my breath and tried to silently shuffle backwards, bringing the shaking girl with me, until my back was pressed against the damp tree trunk. The boots seemed aimless, traipsing around and around in a circle until another shot was fired.

"Got it!" a man shouted gleefully. And then the boot moved away from us.

I let out a soft sigh. Elise was still shaking, her hands clamped together over a charm she wore around her neck.

We would have to stay there for a while, but the danger seemed to have passed for now.

"I think they're gone," I said, patting her arms with my hands awkwardly.

"I can't, not again," she stuttered.

"Huh?" I shook her arm and she jumped, the branches moving around us. "Elise, it's okay, you're safe."

She relaxed her grip on the charm and sighed, relaxing her body against my chest. "I'm sorry," she whispered, "bad memories, you know?"

Yeah, I knew.

"Yeah…" It seemed like an invitation, like she wanted me to ask her what was wrong. I was vaguely curious, but also really uncomfortable with how close she was. The soldiers' voices were softer; I could barely hear them anymore, just the occasional loud word. "What happened?"

She tilted her head to the side. "Oh you know, the usual, father murdered in front of you by soldiers because he's a Spider, mother disowns you because she's too scared to stay. Raised by strangers and constant, constant suspicion that you're going to follow in his footsteps."

I was impressed and saddened.

"Now that's a story," I whispered.

Her shoulder jiggled as she tried to suppress a nervous giggle. "I'm sure you have one too… Um… maybe you can tell it to me one day."

"You don't want to hear my story," I replied, closing my eyes.

"If it made you the man you are today, then I certainly do," she said, turning her head towards me.

She leaned closer, her big green eyes blinking shut as she closed the gap between our faces. I leaned away.

"Um… Elise, I…" I stammered, completely caught off guard.

She paused, a slight smile curling her lips.

"You're not ready," she stated, like she thought one day I would be. She turned away from me again, adjusting her position in my lap.

"I'll never be ready for what you want, Elise. I'm in love with someone else," I confessed. Someone who was lost to me, could be dead, could hate me for leaving.

Again, she giggled quietly. "Who said anything about love? I'm just looking for some fun, a distraction," she said, in an almost aggressive tone.

I shook my head, though she couldn't see me. "I can't offer that either. The best I can do is friendship, all right?"

The leaves rustled again, but this time it was just the wind. She didn't say anything for a long time.

"You'll change your mind, but I can be your friend until then." She was sure of herself. It reminded me of how I used to be, how convinced I was that Rosa loved me, even when she was constantly pushing me away. But I knew Elise was wrong about this one. I couldn't change my mind about this.

The tip of a rifle poked into the bushes and I gasped, trying to put my body between the gun and Elise.

Gus's gruff voice was a huge comfort. "You two coming out of there? Seems we're going to have to be more vigilant from this point on."

2.3

Siblings

ROSA

*W*hat will be left of me when I get out of here?
I should say IF…
IF. The word hangs there like a rusty sign.
Other words hang in line behind it, like NEVER and BLOOD.

Trusting Denis could be a mistake. He was Grant's son. And if he had anything of Grant in him, he might be desecrated on the inside, rotting charcoal lining his heart. But something whispered hoarsely against my ear, *Trust him.* Hope painted parts of him, even it was just the tips of his fingers, the edge of his nose. There was something there.

Denis cupped my elbow like a waiter holding a full bowl of soup, not wanting to spill what was left of me, as he accompanied me downstairs. Everything he said was a snatch, a snippet. Between cameras watching and listening, he fed me small lines, bite-sized morsels of information.

As he steered me towards the lift he spoke. "Focus on the background, not the action. I know you said you can't *not* watch, that the noises are worse by themselves…" He whispered this over the top of my head, his eyes front. "So watch but don't watch if you know what I mean. Pick a background image and count up the small details."

I didn't nod, but I listened. He had given me advice every morning for days, and it had worked some. Each time I returned to my room, I felt a little more broken and a little more sewn together. His other advice was to focus on the fact that he got away, that Joseph was somewhere out there, safe from Grant, from the Woodlands. I did that constantly, always, always, always.

The walk wasn't long enough. I never had time to prepare myself.

"We're here," Denis announced, running his finger along the hood of one of the cars; the smudging noise was like streaks on a window. The privilege these machines represented was sickening.

I paused with my palm on the door. *One, two, three. Just breathe.* I muttered to the door, "Why are you helping me?"

Denis collapsed on the hood behind me, the red car springing up and down with his weight. "I'm not sure yet," he said to his large, leather-clad feet.

The door opened and Mr. Hun grabbed my wrist without stepping into the light, gently pulling me inside. Fear murdered any thoughts about what Denis had just said. Now the exercise of not turning to vapor, to nothing, began. My energy had to be on keeping myself whole. At least on the outside.

Denis was waiting for me when I exited, sitting on the edge of a hood with his legs neatly crossed. His eyes were dark; he bowed his head, sorry at the sight of me. My legs had less wobble than three days ago but still, I struggled to stand and had to put my hand out to steady myself against the wall. Mr. Hun stepped out of the shadow of the door and looked up at Denis, who was suddenly standing by my side. "Tell your father we have made no progress, tell him…" Mr. Hun stroked his chin, white whiskers springing back under his fingers. I cringed. "Tell him I recommend termination or repurpose, though I don't know what for."

Denis' grip tightened around my waist, his fingers pressing the emptiness of me, I was skin stretched over air.

"I'll tell him, but you know my father. He doesn't like to lose," Denis said to the small, evil man.

Mr. Hun blinked up at Denis, who towered over him like a wavy weed. "Indeed," he muttered and then stepped back into the dark room, the door swinging shut. I wondered if he ever went outside or if he spent his whole life in the dark doing dark things?

Before I could wonder too much, Denis was marching me back towards the elevator.

The word 'termination' slammed over my head like a dropped

drawbridge. I stiffened, my legs locking. I turned up to him, begging with my eyes.

"Please. Take me outside," I whispered, my lips trembling with hope. If I was going to die, I needed to be outside, one more time.

He shook his head as he took in my camisole and shredded skirt. "You'll freeze to death."

"I don't care. Tell them it's part of my torture. Please, I need to breathe real air." I would beg if I had to.

He stood, statuesque, for the longest moment. His eyes on the ceiling as if he was counting nonexistent stars. *Stars.* Then he sighed deeply. "All right."

We moved around the cars and out, out into the open. He steered me around the base of Grant's house and into a garden, or more a frozen patch of grass surrounded by neatly trimmed hedges. The cold snapped at my skin, tiny shards of ice growing on the hairs of my arms. It felt so good. I breathed in and exhaled with the force of a hurricane. I savored every last particle. My bare feet dug into the grass. I cast my eyes up to the sky and took a mental picture, storing it with the others. The stars blinked down on me in sympathy. They were the same stars Orry slept under right now. The same stars Joseph was staring up at, wondering what had happened to me.

I wound my hand to the sky and tried to grab at them.

Denis coughed. "We have to go."

Just one more breath.

I turned to him, his thick, spiky hair making his shadow look like a cactus. "Tell me something about yourself."

He laughed, small, like a bird was caught in his throat. "I'm not good enough and I'm tired of trying."

I wanted to laugh in his face. Did he expect pity from me? But then he moved closer to me and took my hand. "I don't want to live like this anymore. I don't want *anyone* to live like this anymore." He squeezed my hand and kept it there. "There are people I love who are lost to me too, Rosa."

I gaped in response and continued to stare at the stars, not willing to give them up yet.

But too soon, he was pulling my hand and leading me back to the door. I wanted to ask him more questions but he was almost running, and he seemed uncomfortable already at what he had revealed.

We were silent in the elevator, silent as he walked me down the hall, deathly quiet until we passed my door and Denis put his hand on a handle that was not mine. He looked at me, pleading in his eyes, and said four words, "Give her a chance," and then he pushed open the door.

My eyes were assaulted by colors, by the rainbow that had seemingly thrown up on every surface of the room. Two single beds sat in the center and cross-legged on the tip of one sat Judith.

"Welcome, roomie," she sang, her voice like violins used as bats, as she bounced off her bed and came running towards me. I put my hands up to my face in defense, crossing them over each other as if she were, in fact, the devil.

Judith stopped short and whined to her older brother. "Denny, you said she would be nice to me."

I bit my lip to stop myself from laughing and peeked out from behind my arms. Denny?

Denis chuckled and pushed me deeper into the room. My feet bit into the carpet in resistance. *Was this my new form of torture?* I craned my head back to look at Denis, my eyes questioning.

"Dad wants you in here with Judy because you keep destroying the cameras," he said with a stupid smile on his face that I wanted to remove with sandpaper.

"I'm supposed to keep ma eye on you," Judith drawled, pointing to her eye and pulling down the bottom lid with her orange-tinted finger, her eyeball juicy and red. Miming it out like I was too stupid to understand the words.

I grimaced. "I'd rather they threw me in prison."

"Well, that's not vaaarry nice." Judith shook her head and pulled a pillow to her chest, hugging it like a teddy bear. I wanted to slap her pouting lips off her face.

Something vibrated in Denis' pocket, a patch of light appearing through the material. He patted it but didn't take it out. "I have to go," he said apologetically.

He didn't say goodbye, but then, he never did.

The door closed, sealing me in a bad dream like the lid closing over an airtight container. The air closed in around me, a cloud heavy with the smell of perfume and hair products. I wiped my nose with the back of my hand and took a step closer.

Judith's room wasn't real. She didn't seem real. Her perfect hair, her plastic-looking face. Perching on the edge of the bed, she watched me investigate my new living arrangements. She didn't say anything but she made a lot of noise, huffing, puffing, and sighing every time I touched something.

I made my way to her dresser, tapping my finger along the different bottles of perfume, makeup, and nail polish. Pausing on a white pill bottle, I picked it up to read the label.

"That's fer ma skin," Judith said.

I shook it like a maraca. "Is that why you're so orange?"

She pulled back, her hand to her heart like I'd wounded her.

I put the bottle down and pick up a lip gloss, rolling the sparkly pink tube between my fingers.

"You want to try it?" she asked, pinging me with the stretched rubber band that was her voice. I shook my head, a resounding no. "You know, this isn't my idea of fun either. You could make a little efferrrt."

I slammed the tube on the dresser, and she jumped. Her whole body pulling in like a startled slater bug. It seemed over the top. I watched her curiously, trying to decide what she was. Victim or foe. I wasn't sure.

I vibrated with the want to shout at her, pull her hair, make her understand what *my* life was. Fun didn't factor into it right now. The word was offensive to me. But I held it in. I needed to watch her, understand her more.

I simply said, "Please don't talk to me about fun. It doesn't exist for me."

She blinked up at me, uncomprehending. And then a smile spread across her face, her thin lips shining artificially with glittery particles. "Of course not, silly, I wasn't talking about you," she said, her voice and her thin arms shaking as she spoke.

Was this some kind of show-me-who's-boss kind of situation? Was she the dominant creature I was supposed to submit to? She didn't even sound like she meant those words. Denis said give her a chance, but I couldn't see why I should. Not yet anyway. I rounded the bed, eyeing the distance between us. What was Grant up to? I searched the corners for cameras.

"There are no cameras in here. Dad trusts me," Judith bragged.

I wanted to cover my ears. "But he doesn't trust *me*... What's to stop me from holding you hostage, threatening your life to save my own?"

Judith shrugged her shoulders, that sad slump returning to her posture. "Go ahead. It won't do ya any good. He'd let you kill me." She dabbed her nose with the corner of the cushion she was still hugging tightly. She looked smaller and fragile, bathed in the silky pinkness that radiated from the nauseatingly flowery light above.

"But you're his daughter," I stammered. But then I remembered Denis saying he wasn't the first Denis Grant.

"Yes I am, but there are more ware I came from." She laughed pathetically.

Pity for her was squeezing its way between my ribs. I tried to resist it but I said, "I'm sorry," before I could stop myself.

She hugged the pillow again. "It's fine."

"Denis said I should give you a chance, though I don't understand why," I managed through hard-set lips.

She laughed, her voice a bitter bark. "Yes, well, Denny is a bit of a dreamer in more ways than one. He has big plans." She opened her arms wide, her limbs perfectly bowed like a dancer.

I prickled, my skin ruffled with bumps like a plucked chicken. "What do you mean?"

She beckoned with her carroty finger. I turned and leaned towards her, the sweet stench of her perfume making my throat itch.

"He wants to take our father's place." She swung her arms around the room. "You know, so he can change all of this."

My fingers dug into the mattress. "But the only way he can do that is if Grant..."

"Dies? Yes. I didn't say his plans were reaaalistic," she muttered.

A thought pecked at the back of my neck like a bird. *I know how, I know how...*

I shuffled closer to her and tried to restrain the desperation in my voice. "If that's true, why wouldn't you tell your father of his plans?"

"I have plans too," she said, picking at her nails and not meeting my eyes.

I returned to my bed and let her simple words roll over me. Redness creeped up my neck and crowded my cheeks, my breath coming in short, painful bursts.

Could I do it? Could I help them plan a murder?

Could I trust them?

Did I have a choice?

I knew the answer. It dinged inside my chest like a dull bell. *No.* I didn't have a choice. If I had a chance to take Grant down, I had to take it.

I let her words sit in the air. I wasn't giving her anything just now. I didn't trust Denis wholly, and I definitely didn't trust her. Standing up, I twisted my hair in my hands.

"So what are we supposed to do now?" I asked.

She lifted her eyes to mine, her lashes crimped and unnaturally curly. She reminded me of one of those blinking dolls that you flipped the head back and forth to open and shut the eyes. Orry had one back at the Wall. Its lips were rubbed off and its hair was missing in most places except just over its ears like a balding man. I shuddered.

"We get ready for dinner," she said as she grabbed a hairbrush and approached me like it was a knife in her hand.

The next morning, Denis accompanied me downstairs like he had for the last few days. He coasted slowly next to me, his feet perfectly placed one after the other, his hand hovering near my waist but barely touching it. Then he broke from his normal behavior and dipped down to make eye contact with me. "How was your first night with Judy?" he asked.

"She snores, and she wears a mouth guard; it makes this horrible *squeaaak* when she grinds her teeth together," I replied.

He laughed quietly and his fingers tapped across the small of my back.

The sunlight was white, cold. Sinister. It lazered my face and eyes as we walked past the windows. My body started to seize up the closer we got to the elevator doors. Once I passed through, all joking and pretending was over. I wasn't relieved that at least this meant I wasn't being terminated. How could you be relieved that your torture would continue?

The elevator ride would suck the smiles off our faces.

We reached the elevator doors and I slapped at the button weakly, but I didn't actually press down. My lips trembled and my heart shivered in my chest. Every day it was harder. But I was getting harder too, my skin tougher, my eyes too used to violence, my body expecting pain and starting to understand it in a disturbing way. Denis went to push the elevator button, but I blocked his hand.

"I don't think I can keep this up. How much longer do you think it will go on?" I breathed.

Exhaling, he leaned down to my ear. "It only ends when he breaks you or..." He let the words run out of air, his breath hissing between his lips in a tiny sigh.

"Or he kills me," I finished for him. Breaking me meant me giving him the information he wanted. I would never do that. So death.

Then he did what I was hoping he would—he said the words that had rolled over and over in my mind all night as I listened to the squeak and grind of Judith's sleeping. The thing I had convinced myself I could do. That I had to do.

"We could do it first," he said so quietly I wasn't entirely sure I hadn't imagined it.

"Do what?" I mouthed, my hand still covering the button.

"Kill him. We could kill him first." He put his hand over mine and pressed my palm towards the button. It lit up, blinking like a warning light I would have to ignore.

I didn't say anything right away. I was silent in the elevator, my body straight, and my hands flat against my legs. He kept a distance. Two feet of solid air between us, piling up like concrete bricks. The doors slid back like a curtain to an operating theater and my fears were on the table, my life open and pinned back in gruesome positions for them to play with. I leaned back on my heels and then pressed forward, making my way towards the dreaded room.

One step—this was the man who stole me from my family.

Two steps—he drugged me, impregnated me against my will.

Three steps—he killed Addy, Apella, and hundreds of Survivors.

He was a bad man.

Four steps—he kidnapped Deshi, he took a father from his son...
but then that was what he did. He took a sledgehammer to peoples'
families, yet here he was, living with a perfect little family of his own.

Five steps—he was going to hunt down Joseph, Orry, and everyone
I cared about unless I stopped him.

Me.

Only me.

Denis' hand gripped the handle to the black door. His eyes searched
mine as his fingers threatened to push down. I put my hand next to his,
grasped the brushed metal, and stared up at him.

"I know how," I whispered, my eyes like two steel plates, my heart
fighting against me as I said the words. I opened the door before he
could answer and walked back into my torture chamber.

24

Palma

JOSEPH

"We'll have to split up," Gus announced, standing under a branch that kept waving in front of his irritated face. "It will be easier to remain hidden this way."

No one argued.

I laughed when I heard him mutter, "Can't believe we missed out on those pheasants!" as he waded through the group and separated them with his wiry arms. Chopping down on the space between us, like we were a pheasant to be quartered, and breaking us into four groups that would each take a different route to Palma.

I happened to be standing with Desh, Matt, and Ermil. Elise was right next to me, but Gus sliced us apart. I was relieved. Although flattering, her advance had made me uncomfortable. She didn't seem to be offended that I had refused to kiss her though, which was good. When she was separated from me, she sighed and rolled her eyes to the sky, but gave me a brief smile. I hoped it meant she was happy to be just friends.

Days of walking agreed with me. I liked the soreness of my feet and the ache of my wounds. It stopped me thinking about what I wanted. It kept Rosa's face at bay. I hadn't let her go, I wasn't sure that was possible, but she lived in the back of my mind at the moment. It was the only way I knew how to survive.

"How far now?" Desh whined, finding a tree and collapsing against the trunk dramatically. None of us were good hunters. We'd been eating rationed bread and dried meat for days, and it was affecting our strength.

I paused and pulled the handheld out of my pocket. "Can I?" I asked Matt. He nodded. I quickly turned the GPS on, Orry's light was still blinking in the same position it had been last time I checked. Still mountains and rivers between us. The handheld told me we were only half a day's walk from Palma. It felt like the trudging would never end, I felt like I could barely lift my legs. Raising my foot, I stared down at my heavy boot print and scuffed it up with my toe. I turned to the men, "We need to tread carefully."

We walked, quietly, lightly, turning circles through thick brush for hours. Brambles snagged our clothing and scratched our skin, but we were hiding our tracks better.

A thick wall of blackberry bushes crossed our path. It tumbled and rolled on itself like a prickly wave. Frozen berries glistened from the middle, the ones closest to the outside picked clean. A group of deer startled to our left, their muzzles stained purple from the berries and, before we could stop him, Ermil limped forward, pulled out his gun, and shot at them. The bullet ripped at the bark of a tree and they cantered off, unscathed.

"What the hell did you do that for?" I whispered tersely.

"What? I'm hungry," he said, shrugging his shoulders and spitting on the ground. "What's your problem?"

I shoved his shoulder gently, although I wanted to shove him harder. "Because according to the handheld, Palma is right on the other side of that blackberry bush."

We scattered, finding hiding places and awaiting the swarm of soldiers that was sure to come for us.

We waited for four hours.

Crouched down in a bush, my pants soaked in muddy water, I watched as Desh stood up and ran his hands over the bark of a stark-looking tree, its branches like the bronchi of an unhealthy lung, covered in dark brown lichen and scars.

"What are you doing?" I asked in time to see him hoist himself up into the fork of the tree. He looked out of place up there. That was *her* spot. Desh was more at home on the ground, surrounded by cables and computer screens.

"I'm tired of waiting; it's ridiculous," he muttered. "I want to get a better look."

Curious and with aching backs and legs, we emerged from our hiding places and crowded around the base of the tree.

"What do you see?" Matt called up.

Desh's legs were precariously spanning two thin branches as he strained to see over the giant blackberries. "There's a break in the blackberry bush about a mile down, um… I'm not sure I can explain the rest."

I groaned. "What?"

He wobbled and I threw my hands out like I would catch him, which was stupid. His hands skidded down the branch, and he steadied himself.

"It's just, well, it's very different from the others."

"What do you mean?" I asked impatiently, my neck getting sore from staring up at him.

"I think it will be easier if you come see it for yourself." Elise's smooth voice sailed over my shoulder. I jumped, turned around suddenly, and bumped right into her. She threw her arms around my neck, pulling me into an embrace.

"I'm glad you're safe," she whispered, smiling broadly. I patted her back awkwardly, shuffling out of her hold and into a circle of the rest of our original group. We must have arrived last.

"Stop playing around and get out of that tree. Let's get on with it," Gus grunted up at Desh.

Desh slipped down the trunk, and we followed them to the break in the bushes.

The gap was narrow, my shoulders covered in thorns as I bristled through sideways. Purple streaks ran across the arms of my jacket as I collected leftover berries every time I snagged. Elise walked in front of me. Being thinner, she wasn't catching every single branch like I was. She stopped suddenly and reached her hand into the thicket, retrieving a single berry. Turning around, she held in front of my eyes.

"Here, try this."

I held out my hand for her to drop it into my palm. She reached for my lips. My cheeks went red. I grabbed the berry from her hands and stuffed it in my mouth, embarrassed. Someone shoved me from behind.

"Keep moving, jackass." Rash's irritated voice pelted me with disapproval.

I stumbled forward, Elise giggling as she strolled forward too casually.

We walked a few more meters and broke free of the bushes. The group squatted down in the high grass, leaning against fencing wire, waiting for stragglers. Olga waddled through the opening last, looking annoyed, her face covered in tiny scratches. We were huddling at the fence of a large field. A field that looked organized. Wire dissected it into neat squares. A frozen crop jutted out of the ground, seemingly snap frozen mid-grow. My eyes struggled to take in all the unexplainable images, particularly what appeared to be a road. A road that led directly to a gate. A gate in the side of the wall of Palma.

I gasped despite myself, crouching closer to the ground.

"Yep. See what I mean." Desh elbowed me in the side. "Different."

"We knew it would be different, but not quite like this!" Pelo announced, his eyes shining the way they used to, before Rosa.

"I don't get it. Look at the guards." I pointed to the soldiers stationed on the outside, the *outside* of the concrete walls, in surprise. Their large guns were slung over their shoulders. Bigger guns than I'd seen before.

We observed silently, passing water between us and waiting. The sun shifted from overhead, to bobbing above the tops of trees.

Pelo shifted on his long legs and whispered, "What are we waiting for?"

Gus, who was eyeing the gate like it was a deer he was stalking, lifted his finger to silence Pelo and then pointed directly at the gate as it opened and about ten citizens, dressed in colorful clothing, were ushered outside.

"That!" he said sharply.

We all peered over the tips of the grass in fascination. The citizens had baskets in their hands or on their heads. One of the guards shoved a woman in the back with his gun, and she stumbled forward. We'd all seen this before. A soldier hurting a citizen. I closed my eyes, awaiting the sound of gunfire. I waited a few seconds and when I heard nothing, I dared to open them.

"You watching this?" Desh whispered, elbowing me in the ribs. Our clutter of people was too close, heat and the smells of unwashed hiker wafted up my nose with the sourness of the berries.

I nodded and kept my eyes on the soldiers.

A tall, dark man with a bright orange and brown patterned shirt turned to the guard and yelled at him, pumping his fist. He received a gun butt to the head for it but the man got up, spat at the guard, and helped the woman to her feet. The guard hovered over the pair, but he didn't shoot. I expected him to shoot.

Why didn't he shoot?

The other citizens had paused and were watching the altercation, hands on hips, standing tall. Not cowering or running for cover. I couldn't see their faces but I got the feeling their eyes were proud, unafraid, and it baffled me.

"Holy shit, that dude's got some balls!" Rash muttered, shaking his head from side to side.

Gus actually laughed, well sort of. He held his stomach and coughed with a short smile on his weary face.

We watched the group dig in the frozen ground with sharp, metal implements, retrieving roots and putting them in the basket. When they finished, they got up and were escorted back inside. Just as the last man passed through the gate, I watched as a tall, lean woman, her bones jutting from her skin, offered the basket to the soldier. He rifled through it, took out a handful of roots, and then he pulled cash from his pocket and offered it her. She shook her angular head, and the man fished out some extra coins, dropping them in her basket. She bowed her head and walked inside.

My mouth hung agape, the cold freezing my lips open. What we'd just witnessed, apart from being contradictory, was extraordinary. This place was different in a way I could never have imagined. These people had some independence.

Desh tapped my chin, and I closed my mouth.

"You all right?" he asked, his tone more joking than I'd heard in a while.

"Um, yeah, just surprised," I answered, my eyes scanning the top of the walls of the Palma compound, coils of razor wire crowning the wall. We didn't need that kind of barrier in Pau. No one ever tried to get over the wall. The concrete also looked damaged and patched in places. I ran my hand over my jaw; the stubble was now long enough to be more of a sketchy beard now. I stared down at my other hand, pressed into the mud, and thought, *Rosa would have loved to see this.* And then I pushed the thought behind other things.

We retreated from Palma, creeping backwards slowly until we were at the blackberries, and then we moved quickly into the forest to a safe place. The big question pulsing through the whole group was—did this change our plans?

Pelo grabbed my arm excitedly.

"Did you see that? It's change. Things are changing…"

I turned to face him, avoiding his eyes, my mouth not wanting to even utter her name. "From what I'd heard, Palma was always a bit different to the others."

Gus joined us. "What have you heard?"

Desh stared down, his memories pushing up from the dead-looking ground.

"Clara, this was Clara's home," he muttered.

I didn't want him to say it, Clara led to Rosa, and thoughts of her led me into darkness. A picture of her, slumped against a tree after Clara died, entered my mind, her thin arms wrapped around her tiny body, wearing nothing but her underwear as I washed her clothes of Clara's blood and wished I could wash her pain away with it. She didn't shake with cold, she didn't cry—her eyes were two wells of nothingness, empty of feeling, like Rosa had left her own body.

I wouldn't have thought it possible but my feelings for her deepened in that moment. The way she loved her friend Clara so fiercely and the fact that she took it that hard when she died, made me love her so much.

I took a step back from the conversation and watched, unable to contribute anything useful as Desh explained who Clara was and what we knew of Palma. The Spider filled in some of the blanks, but he also said the gate was new.

"You ok, friend?" Elise asked, her eyes sincere, her hands hovering over my shoulder but not touching me.

I swiped the air like I could clear the vision like smoke. "Bad memories." *And good memories and everything I've lost rolled into one.*

"Things have changed a lot since the retrieval mission," Matt said. It became apparent our intel was pretty outdated after only twelve months.

The Spider from Palma smiled wide. "I didn't know it would change this much. But I'm happy to see it!"

We listened. We voted. We decided it changed nothing. We would do the same as we had done in the other towns.

That night.

25

Change

JOSEPH

The clouds moved in. Thin ones that weren't about rain. They just kept the small amount of warmth from the day in.

The atmosphere at the camp was more relaxed than normal. Maybe we were getting used to it or maybe it was because we had more hope with this particular mission. Either way, we sat on rocks or in the dirt, surrounded by brittle trees with dresses of thorny bushes, making our plans. Some of the men pulled out their precious flasks and offered them around as we jumped from foot to foot, trying to stay warm. There could be no fire tonight as we were so close to the compound. Small battery lanterns or torches sat by people's feet.

Gus flashed a warning stare in our direction as the flask flew around. "Take it easy, men. We still have a mission to complete."

Olga stood up, flask in hand, and pushed it at Gus's face. "Just one drink, Gus. It won't kill you."

She was braver than I was, but then, that wasn't hard. We held our breaths. No one talked to Gus like that. He stared up at the patch of sky above us, the branches encroaching on the view, and swore. Snatching the flask from her chubby hand, he gazed into the opening. He sniffed it once, and his face relaxed. Raising the flask, he said, "moy syn," and took a large swig. I watched him roll it around in his mouth and swallow it like it was a spoonful of honey. Man, he was a tough guy.

I leaned towards Matt and asked, "What does moy syn mean?"

Matt glanced down and I noticed he was flexing his injured hand, testing his fingers. They seemed sluggish.

"It means my son, Joe," Matt whispered sadly.

"Oh."

When the flask came to me, my head was already dark with memories: Cal's crazed eyes when I'd burst into his hospital room, ready to tear him apart, a fan of perfect, dark-brown hair, blood. But I also thought of Gus. Most of the time, I forgot he was a father too, that he had lost both his children. He was just Gus, strong, gruff, and unemotional. I didn't pause for long before I placed the flask to my lips and drank. The harsh liquid burned down my throat like charcoal-flavored acid. I coughed and spluttered while the older members of the group laughed at me.

I wiped my mouth and let myself smile, my eyes stinging with tears from the burning fluid. The alcohol pooled in my stomach and created an unfamiliar, warm sensation. The darkness got darker, shrouding my memories in a wavy fog and putting me in the present. I liked the feeling.

I passed it to Matt, and he declined. "Not a path I can go down again," he muttered, still staring at his hand. I shrugged and took another small sip. It didn't taste as bad the second time. Elise watched me from across the circle of Survivors and Spiders, curiously, with a small smile playing on her lips.

Matt stood. "Now as you know, poor Ansel was supposed to be the accompanying Survivor for the Palma mission." Everyone bowed their heads. It seemed so long, though it was only weeks ago that Ansel was killed by those brutal men on our journey to the Superiors' compound. Matt cleared his throat. "I would volunteer but... my hand..."

I jumped up, the sudden movement causing me to sway a little. I forced my body to straighten, to look confident, competent.

"I'll go." I was desperate to keep that distraction going, focus on the action outside of my brain, not the destruction going on inside.

"But you're wounded, Joe," Desh said, shaking his head as he hugged his body against the cold. *That's never going to change*, I thought.

I made eye contact with Gus. "I'm fine, I feel perfectly fine," I told them and myself. Moving closer to Gus, I talked in a hushed, pleading tone directly to him. "Please, let me do something."

He groaned, and then his head fell into a begrudging nod. "All right, boy," he conceded.

I clenched my fist and pumped it at my side. This would be a good thing for me. I blinked up at the stars, peeking out between branches that looked like spidery veins tangling across the air. A door was opening, but I had to close one first.

The Palma Spider stood and held out his hand. "My name's Nafari," he said, his strong handshake out of proportion to his small size. He looked up at me with almost black eyes like buttons and grinned. "My friends call me Naf."

I shook his hand and returned his smile. "Ok Naf, where do we start?"

He threw his head back and laughed, his voice was deep and roaring, like an engine.

"I said my *friends* call me Naf." He poked my chest with his brown, scarred finger, which hurt. "We are not friends... yet."

I shrugged and forced a smile, which gradually became less fake as I stared into his strong, rebellious face. "By the end of this mission, I'll be calling you Naf."

He slapped his leg. "Oh, I hope so!"

"So Nafari," I said, annunciating every syllable carefully, "where on the wall do you think we should place the bomb and the video?"

His eyes were as round as the moon, but more intense, brighter. "We are not going to place the bomb on the outside. We are going to stroll right in and we're going to blow the gates open from the inside." He swung his elbows dramatically and raised his legs up high, doing his strolling impression while he laughed.

My face froze in disbelief, which made him laugh harder.

"Don't worry. Trust me," he said through giant, white teeth. One tooth was missing, a black square punched through his mouth. He grabbed the flask and licked his lips before drinking. "This is going to be fun!" he garbled with a mouthful of alcohol.

The others didn't argue. We had let the Spiders run each mission. They were the experts on their own towns after all.

The videodisc seemed heavy in my pack. Even though it only weighed about two hundred grams, its importance and my responsibility dragged me down until I felt like my feet were making deeper impressions with every step. Now that the alcohol had worn off, I felt less brave and more nervous. Nafari slapped my back, his springy steps making me even more tense, and began to push me through the gap in the blackberries.

"Let's go, big man!" He laughed as he threw me a colored shirt to pull over my camouflage one.

Pelo and Desh waved me good luck as I turned around one last time. Matt and Gus had already told me to be careful a dozen times and were now packing.

We were swallowed in thorns and rustling leaves.

"Now, you remember what we practiced?" he whispered as we moved through the briar.

I nodded my head more times than necessary. "Yes."

We burst through the other side and made our way to the dirt road that led right up to the gates. Our feet un-quiet, strolling casually or, in my case, trying to look casual and looking more stiff and edgy.

Nafari's head swung from side to side like he was looking for something as he sauntered towards Palma under the light of the cloud-shadowed moon. Suddenly, his upper body darted down and he snatched up a discarded basket. It was rotted and crusted with dirt, a large hole worn through its side. He pressed the hole against his body and poured the frozen berries we had collected into it. He did it swiftly, never breaking his gait, brushing the dust off as we moved.

The cloud cover made it hard to see the road, but above the gates, two lights streamed over the opening, giving us quick illumination as they flicked on and off when the guards walked in front of sensors. I slowed as we approached. Those giant guns slung over their shoulders would make a hole in me the size of Nafari's basket.

Nafari clipped the side of my head and yelled, "Hurry up! See, they've already closed the gates. Idiot!" He smacked me again, almost having to jump up to reach the top of my head. I flinched and ducked as his palm slapped my skull.

"Ouch," I growled.

"It has to look realistic," Nafari murmured under his breath as he grabbed my shirt and dragged me towards the gate.

I held my breath as they raised their guns and one of the guards shouted, "Stop!"

Nafari ignored him and kept walking. And I braced myself for a bullet.

"Stop!" the guard screamed, his voice peeled of aggression, sounding afraid.

A warning shot fired at our feet, dirt and gravel spitting at our knees. I leaped into the air like I could avoid it.

Nafari shot me a glare with his moon-like eyes and then turned to the guards, swearing at them, waving his fist around in anger while I tried not to gawk in horror. "Is this what I get for spending my outside time collecting berries for Ursra?" He cursed again, and the guards lowered their guns in confusion.

Nafari kept storming towards the gates, dragging me with him, blaming me for slowing him down.

By the time we were at the gate, the guns hung slack across the guard's stomachs and the looks of puzzlement and almost apology on their faces had me struggling not to laugh.

"Are you going to let me in or what?" Nafari asked, his tone so convincing and demanding.

The guard paused under the lights. We stood still for so long that they turned off. When he moved to get his keycard, the lights clicked back on.

I kept my head bowed, my eyes narrowed.

"Wait," the guard paused, flipping the card over in his fingers. He pulled a scanner from his holster and held it out. "Your wrist, please."

Nafari rolled his large eyes and stuck his wrist out. The barcode was there, but a thick, red line ran across it, making it unreadable. I took a deep breath. This was it. We were going to be gunned down. My muscles tensed, ready for the fight.

The guard stared down at the red mark, his scanner shaking in his hand. He made eye contact with Nafari, who smiled wide.

"What's taking so long, man? I'm cold and I've got a drink with my name on it waiting for me inside," the other guard snapped, jumping from leg to leg and rubbing his arms.

The guard holding the scanner pressed the trigger, looked at the screen, and said, "Nothing, let them in," without giving me a second glance.

The iron gates opened with a creak, and we were inside. Walking fast, but not too fast. Once we were out of sight, Nafari pulled me into a gap between two buildings and pressed me against a wall.

"What the hell...?" I started to ask. I had so many questions that I didn't know where to start.

"Sh!" Nafari grinned in the dark, his white teeth glistening like they were painted on. The black gap looked solid.

"But... how?"

"Let's just say, our resistance has a few officials in its pockets," he whispered, his voice whistling, his face slanted in shadow.

I swiped my forehead with my shaky hand. "I can't believe it. Nothing like that would ever happen in Pau. I was sure we were going to be shot!"

I took a wobbly breath. Palma was more than just a *little* different.

He nodded, I think. His teeth moved in the dark anyway.

"I think they're getting just as tired of fighting us as we are of fighting them. We threw cans, they took them away. We threw bottles, so they took them too. If all we'd had was the spit on our tongues, that's what we'd throw." I watched his dark lips pass over his teeth and listened to a true rebel. "Now we are forced to scavenge for food because they keep taking every potential weapon from our hands before we even use them. Our biggest problem has been access to decent weapons and large enough explosives. This," Nafari said, patting the bomb in his pack, "will change everything. Come on." He pulled me away from the alley and into the main street.

"Where are we going?" I gasped, my heart galloping with excitement.

"To place the videodisc."

26

Far Away

ALEXEI

The decking creaked underfoot as I reached out and pulled down a handful of evergreen. Crushing the needles in my hand, I lifted them to my nose.

Apella, darling, we wanted this life. And now I had to live it without her. It seemed... unfair, sometimes... empty.

Apparently, this place used to be a 'ski chalet'. An old chair lift hangs overhead, frozen in time. It boggled my mind to think of the lives people led before, both fascinating and frightening.

Faded pictures of families long gone hung on the timber walls. Dressed in shiny suits and holding black sticks in their hands. I missed my reader. *You'd understand. To me, it was like an appendage.* I remembered 'skiing' from the archives. People would shoot down snow-covered hills wearing long shoes. It looked terribly dangerous.

Two very different pairs of arms wrapped around my legs. I felt joy. Joy and then guilt. I didn't want to move on. But these boys, these beautiful children, they forced you whether you wanted to or not.

I bent down and opened my hand. "Smell this."

Hessa pushed his whole nose into the pine, green bits sticking to his chubby face. "Mmm."

But Orry, he had so much of his mother in him. He stood back, looked up at me with those incredible eyes, and squinted suspiciously. I moved closer. "It's ok, Orry. It's safe."

He poked it with his finger, swirled it around in my palm, and lifted his own finger to his nose. I couldn't tell if he liked the smell or not; he didn't smile or react. Hessa tried to pull on Orry's arm. Orry shrieked, but then he laughed. They tumbled about on the deck play fighting. *They can laugh.* I was so glad that after everything they'd been through, they could still laugh. But they needed their parents.

I need you, darling, but I'm coping. I knew my role, and I was doing my best to fulfill it.

Orry shouted, and I heard crunching in the snow. I knew it couldn't be them, but I always hoped.

"Reeeeen, reeeen!" Hessa waved frantically at Careen as she marched up the hill, three birds slung over her shoulder.

I tell them about you every day. I tell them about Rosa, Joseph, and Deshi every day too. Our adopted family. My biggest fear was that they would forget them. I wasn't so worried about Orry. But Hessa hadn't seen Deshi in more than six months. There was a time when I would have done anything to be called Father or Dada. Now, I dreaded it. I bowed my head in silent prayer.

I had to believe they would come for us.

Careen climbed the stairs and threw her prey on the deck. She pulled up a chair, selected a bird, and began plucking the feathers. I cringed a little at her ruthless efficiency when it came to butchering. But then, she'd kept us well fed this past month. I took the boys inside to spare them the gore.

Careen blinked up at me, her hood falling down to reveal her sad eyes. "Any change?"

I shook my head. "Sorry, no, he's not worse, but he's not getting any better. He's..."

She put her hand up to silence me. I stopped talking and ushered the boys inside.

I kneeled down to them and said, "Who wants to help me turn the lights out and light the candles?"

They jumped up and down and followed me, giggling and jostling each other, playing with the switches. We only had a small amount of solar power we could use every day.

I moved to the bedroom door and knocked. No answer. I turned. "Boys stay here." They nodded and ran to play on the stairs.

Pietre lay so very still. I dipped my head down just to check he was breathing. He was, barely.

*I'm praying to you, Rosa. I know you're the one I need to count on,
the one that's so stubborn, strong, and willful that you'll get here.
We need you.*

2.7

Plot

ROSA

I don't know this girl. This girl is younger, stupider… she's losing her grip on what she's learned like a kite not tied to its spool. The string unwittingly unraveling as the colorful cloth gets caught in the wind and soars into a cold, blank sky.

Torture was over for the day, but was I in for more?

Denis closed the door and leaned his back against it, locking it with a swift flick of his fingers behind him. I drew a sharp breath as I started to worry that this had been a trick. I was an idiot to fall for the line. He'd just wanted me to threaten Grant, catch me out. Then I'd be thrown into a real prison. Not this pretty cage. Not that it mattered—the containment, the lack of freedom was the same. I was a bird clipped of her wings wherever they put me. I imagined bars and grime, placing my hand to my throat. No, they would just kill me.

Denis' movements were unconsidered, brief, which was odd for him. His eyes had the intensity of a sun flare. He took a large step towards me. I glanced around, wondering where he had shoved me so suddenly. I shouldn't have just let him take me. I should have fought. The room was darker in color than mine. Heavy, black curtains hung from the windows, the bedspread black and white stripes. It was a very masculine room. A music player rested on the bedspread. I was in Denis' bedroom.

I shuffled backwards, my hands reaching out behind me and finding a desk. Two computer screens startled to life when I knocked something.

He stalked closer and closer, until he was hovering over my bent back body. He wet his lips and spoke. "How do we kill my father?"

I wasn't relieved. Tears pooled in the corner of my eyes. *Could I be a murderer?*

I think I'd wanted it to be a trick. I had wanted this decision to be definitively ripped from my hands.

I glared up at him. "Back up," I said flatly.

Suddenly realizing how close he was, how scary he was acting, he jumped back and unrolled himself like a poster, slotting back into his controlled persona once again. When he carefully sat on the edge of his glossy bed, I sighed, in a shivery, dreading way, and told him how to kill his own father.

"When I was, er, revived, there was one step Grant seemed to be unaware of, one that my friend Deshi made sure I had here." I tapped my hand. "I'm sure Deshi wanted me to hide it, and I did."

I swear Denis flinched at the mention of Deshi's name. "Did you... know him?" I asked slowly.

He shook his head and flicked on a lamp. "Not very well but we worked together for a short time towards the end of construction on the healer. Dad wanted me to take it over when... um..."

"When they terminated Deshi?" My anger pulled and played with me. The reasons stacked up as to why I should do this.

Denis nodded.

"So you know how the healer works, but you didn't know about the final step you must take before healing is complete?" I asked, suspicion putting a block between my words. *Trust.*

I hesitated. This was a big move. One I wouldn't be able to retreat from. "I don't know..." I mumbled, struggling with whether to tell him or not. It was my only leverage. Could I hand it over to him?

He shuffled forward on the bed until his knees nearly touched mine. I leaned away, my back anchored to a squeaky computer chair. "You can trust me on this. I want things to change. Neutralizing Grant is the first step."

Neutralizing. We weren't tying his hands behind his back—we were plotting to kill him.

I shook my head back and forth slowly. "And what will happen to me when it's done?" I was scared of the answer. I wanted it too much.

Denis' face was earnest, a murdering, earnest face. "I am his successor, and I will have the authority to release you."

"And my family?"

"Rosa, if we pull this off, I will make sure you are free. Your family and everyone you care about will be safe from harm. You will not have to live in the Woodlands. You can go where you please." He widened his arms and spun them around like the whole world would be mine. *If I did this one horrible thing, the whole world would be mine.*

How could I be certain he was telling the truth? I needed something from him, a guarantee. Him bouncing up and down like excitable child was not enough. I needed...

"Tell me a secret," I said, pointing at him. "Tell me your darkest secret and then maybe I'll know I can trust you."

He stopped twisting and suspended his excitement. His eyes dark, sad. He stood up and paced back and forth on the plush carpet. He turned to the wallpaper and ran a finger down the golden stripes. His voice sounded young, cracked with apprehension.

"I'm in love," he murmured as he pressed his forehead to the wall.

I scoffed. That wasn't a deep, dark secret. "So?" I snapped.

He turned, his head still resting against the metallic paper, the lamp lighting his face all kinds of sad and scared. "I'm in love with Deshi."

"Oh." That was a deep, dark secret. Grant would never allow it.

I checked his eyes, looking for the lie, but all I saw was regret and restraint. I recognized it in Deshi; it took him a long time to relax and be himself. He still struggled with it now.

I moved and sat on the bed, and Denis sat next to me, causing me to bounce up on the mattress. "Your father doesn't know that once the procedure is complete, you only have fifteen minutes to take the voiding pills."

"What will happen if he doesn't take them?"

I squeezed my hands together, wishing there was another way. "He'll die fifteen minutes after leaving the machine." I didn't know what would physically happen to him, only that it was horrific. When I'd asked the doctor after my first time in the healer, it was reflected in her avoiding eyes. It would not be a nice way to go.

Denis tapped his chin and turned to me. "This presents a rather large problem."

Before I could ask, a knock at the door interrupted us and we were told to get to dinner.

"Where are we going?" I asked Denis anxiously.

After another very tense dinner with Grant and his family, Denis had leaned down towards Grant and whispered something in his ear. I'd strained to hear it but couldn't pick up anything. All I knew was it couldn't have been good because of the way Grant turned his head and smiled at me. It made me shiver with ripples of terror.

Now we were hastily striding down the hall and entering the elevator. "Denis, what the hell is going on?" I shook his arm.

The guard next to me raised an eyebrow.

"Dad and I thought you should visit our holding cells. We think you need to be a little more grateful for your current living situation," Denis said, his voice dipped in sarcasm.

I wanted to ask him questions, like what was the large problem? Did he not think my idea would work?

The door slid open, and Denis held out a small, black piece of plastic the size of a coat button. He pushed on it and one of the cars blinked its lights and beeped at us. I stifled my mild hysteria enough to be excited about riding in a car. Denis opened my door for me and the guard shoved me inside, bumping into me as he pushed his way into the backseat.

"Kinesh, you can ride in the front with me," Denis said, eyeing us both through the rearview mirror. Kinesh grunted and got in the front seat, throwing a black sack at my face.

"Put this on," he growled.

I looked to Denis, who nodded slightly. Doing as I was told, I put the sack over my head. I sensed the car taking off and found the armrest. Music started blaring from the speakers and drowned out the gravel crunching under the tires.

I sank into my chair and waited.

Grant's eyes kept floating to the top of my thoughts. The way he smiled like he knew a delicious secret and was dying to tell me. I pictured the smile melting off his face as he died in front of me. The feeling was completely frightening. Because I enjoyed the vision. I was scared of it, but I wanted it just as much.

28

Sacrifices

JOSEPH

I followed Nafari through the outer ring of Palma where old people sat together on their porches, talking, drinking, and pointing at the stars. Someone began to sing and other voices joined in. A guard yelled for them to stop. They did for a moment, and then they laughed and started up again. Palma was where the Superior's iron grip was loosening. The people were not as afraid as they should be. It was only when a warning shot was fired into the air that the old men and women ceased their music.

There was defiance around every corner.

I glanced back to see pipe embers floating in the dark, lighting up the worn faces, mischievous eyes that shouldn't be so bold. My heart felt less heavy, my hope more realistic.

We got to the gate, and it was already hanging open. I didn't ask. We passed through every gate easily and were in Ring Four.

Drums like bells, is the only way I could think to describe what I heard.

It was about eight o'clock. At this time, in Pau, everyone was inside, doors locked, curtains closed. Guards always patrolled the streets, but there was never anyone to catch.

Not here.

Soldiers guarded the streets but they had to wind their way through the groups of people—the children playing in the street, the parents sitting on their lawns, clustered in groups, clapping along to sounds I'd never heard before.

I watched as a soldier tried to stop a man from dancing. They warned him, he bowed, and stopped only to start again as soon as their backs were turned. It was only when they grabbed him and dragged him off that people calmed. But then we'd turn the bend and more music and dancing continued. They were clinging to what little freedom they had and risking their lives in the process. I kept tightening my jaw to stop my mouth from falling open.

Nafari relaxed more and more as we passed through these groups. Some people he knew or seemed to. He joined the dancing for a moment, and then side stepped out and kept walking. I kept my distance but found myself relaxing just a little too.

We walked up the path of a plain, standard-looking house. Nafari turned and said, "Wait here," in a sinister voice.

He turned the knob and went inside. The room was dark, but I could hear voices.

Turning around, I ran my eyes over all the Palma I could see. I took it in and held the possibility of it in my heart. They were bright. Color hung off the people like dumped paint. But they wore it well. They were more ready for this than any other town. I patted the disc in my pack. The firework would go off soon.

Nafari came back quickly; he was still talking as he passed through the door, bobbing his head and talking in a strained tone. "Yes, yes, all right, woman."

A woman's voice muttered in the dark. I couldn't quite make out the words.

"Who were you talking to?" I asked as I watched Nafari kick off his shoes and swing himself up into the palm tree that grew in the front yard, leaning towards the roof.

Between grunts and heavy breathing, he said, "My wife." Then he chuckled as he paused and held out his hand, beckoning me to follow.

I took off my shoes and climbed after him, my soft feet getting cut up on the rough bark. The tree struggled under my weight but luckily, it just leaned closer to the roof. Nafari held out his hand, and I grabbed it. The palm tree sprung back into place as I met the roof. "How are we going to get down?" I asked, my skin prickling from sweat and the cool wind that ran over the tin roof.

"We jump." Nafari jumped high and landed firmly on his feet, while the roof vibrated from his impact. His wife shrieked and swore inside the house. The door swung open and a small, dark woman with her hair swept into a colorful rag stomped down the path with a bag on her back. Nafari watched her leave in silence.

I put my hands out to steady myself and followed him to the apex where we sat down to wait. Nafari placed his hands down on either side of his body and leaned his head back to gaze at the stars. He sighed, the sound like an empty water tank.

"Do you miss *your* wife Rosa?" he said, his round eyes still staring at the sky.

I miss her like someone performed open-heart surgery on me and forgot to sew me back up. They cracked my chest and left me that way, gaping and in danger of infection.

"I'm not married," I replied.

He punched my arm. "The way you stare at her face in the sky. How you feel about her in here," he punched his chest, "you are joined even if you're not married."

I know.

"Have you missed *your* wife?" I asked, desperate to change the subject. At this, he laughed hoarsely, a whistle coming from his gappy mouth.

"I don't miss her. We are not joined. We are married, but I don't love her. We were forced to marry. The one thing I do miss is our child." His head fell between his knees. "I don't even know where she is or if she's alive."

"What was her name?"

"Zawadi."

"Beautiful," I whispered.

"It means 'gift'." Nafari clasped his hands tightly, and quiet floated between us for a few minutes.

"Joseph, when we start the playback, I will run to the gate. You can stay here if you want."

I shook my head. "No, I'm coming with you."

He nodded.

We stared up at the sky and waited for the firework.

I placed the disc on the chimney of Nafari's home, my finger hovering over the play button. Once I pushed it, we had five minutes before it started.

In Pau, on Signing Day, everyone was forced from their homes. Kids stood in their pajamas in the street, shivering. We lined the sidewalk like mannequins arranged to look awed. The firework went off, we clapped, and then we were told to go back inside.

Here, the firework popped and shot into the sky. I watched the streets for the peoples' reaction. But they continued to talk and sing as if nothing had happened. Shuffling around their fires, their hands and faces reddened from warmth. No one even looked up.

I pressed the button on the video disc, and we skidded off the roof. Nafari took off running.

Just as we passed through the first gate, the playback started. I didn't look up tonight. I followed Nafari's dark form through the streets, the lights catching us in quick snapshots of action. My legs burned to keep up with him. He was a small ball of muscle, fast and determined.

"If you want to see your girl, look up," Nafari urged, barely panting. I couldn't answer; I was so out of breath. I just shook my head, which he couldn't see. I couldn't look at her now. Whatever this was, this risk, this action, was keeping her under my thoughts. It was making it easier to smile, easier to laugh. I wasn't ready to give up on that. So I had to keep moving. She would slow me down.

By the time we reached the next gate, the streetlights were flickering on and off. Noise was building. Voices, wails, broken glass.

Halfway to the last gate, the lights went out permanently.

People streamed past us. Angry people carrying boards and shards of glass. A woman pushed past me to get through the last gate and slashed my arm with a broken bottle. I put my hand to my bicep, glanced down at my blood-covered fingers, and stopped.

I lost Nafari in the crowd.

I knew where he was going, so I kept on towards the gate, the swarm of people thickening around me. The angry shouting was a mix of oppression and freedom forcing its way out the end of a bottle, squeezing and then bursting.

A shot fired.

Emergency lights flooded the Outer Ring with amber light.

I thought, *This is where it stops*. Fear would stop them. But people followed the shot, poured over the soldiers holding the guns until suddenly they were the ones putting their arms up in surrender. I watched one soldier, still holding on, blinking desperately, moving his gun frantically back and forth as he was forced against the wall. A woman stepped towards him, her palm up.

"Put your gun down. We don't want to hurt you," she shouted.

I started running towards her. I don't know why. Before I had even taken two steps towards them, there was a crack and she crumpled. The people surged towards the soldier, and he was swallowed by tearing arms and grieving screams.

My heart knocked on my chest wall, reminding me I had to find Nafari. My eyes scanned the area near the gate. There he was, pulling his pack from his back. He plunged his arm into the bag and a shot rang out. His arm jerked and fell limply to his side. I could do nothing, only twenty meters from him, but about a hundred people deep in the crowd. Doggedly, Nafari gripped the explosive with his other hand.

I searched for the gunman and found him, hiding behind a brown, velour lounge that had been dragged into someone's front yard. I swam through the crowd to get to him as he lined my friend up in his sights.

This bomb was about to go off. I could see it in Nafari's steely eyes. I could get to the gunman and stop him from firing at Nafari or I could try and clear the area of innocent civilians.

We hadn't expected this. This amount of people, this response.

I screamed, "Clear the gates! They're going to blow up the gates!" Over and over, as loud as I could.

People started to move away from the great iron gates. They pulsed and surged backwards, spilling over furniture and soldiers. The smells of sweat and copper-tasting blood filled the air, mixed with a waft of smoky, fragrant spices I'd never smelled before. The gunman aiming at Nafari was lost in the sea of people.

The crowd pushed me back until I was pressed against the front wall of a house.

My eyes picked out the tip of a gun still aimed in Nafari's direction. It shot again, hitting him in the leg. My heart dove into my feet. *I couldn't stop this.* I was going to watch him die.

"Nafari!" I screamed as I pushed against the crowd and tried to get to him.

His eyes found me. He put his hand up, *stop*, and yelled, "Call me Naf!" Then he grinned and turned away. He pushed the button twice for instant detonation, and the air around him flashed white.

2.9

Remember Me

ROSA

From my blind position, breathing my own fear-scented breath, I guessed we had driven for about thirty minutes. I couldn't hear anything over Denis' loud, thumping music. The only thing I could tell was that the journey had been mostly in a straight line until this sudden jerk to the left. Now we were still. The engine running, the music decreasing in volume.

The guard yanked the bag off my head so violently that my neck did that painful snap you felt when you turned too suddenly. Pain coursed through me like a hot rod was shooting up my spine and poking my brain.

"Ow!" I shrieked, rolling my neck from side to side to ease the lava-like pain. The guard sniggered. The Superiors truly chose their soldiers well. Most of them seemed to truly enjoy inflicting pain. I rubbed the back of my head gingerly.

"Rosa, are you all… ahem… Kinesh, that was unnecessary." Denis covered his concern for me poorly, and I shot him a warning glare.

I blinked my eyes and tried to adjust to the streaming, harsh light pouring over the black sedan. It was sleeting, the light picking up every drop of rain clashing with every snowflake as it rolled over the black metal of the car. I gazed up at the long, metal poles holding up the lights and followed them around a semi-circle of high fencing back to where we were parked. Automatic gates swished closed behind us, pulling lumps of mud with them. I inhaled the rich, mushroomy scent and let my brain fool itself that we were somewhere else for a moment. But then I had to open my eyes. Illusions were smashed to splinters as I stared in front at the muddy path, pockmarked with pools of freezing water leading to a glass door splattered with rain and dirt.

Denis pulled up the handbrake. "Time to get out."

The holding cells reminded me of the underground facility in the most vivid, lacerating way. From where I stood, gripping the car door like an anchor, all you could see were two windows and a door punched into the side of a slick, green hill. The difference being we were not surrounded by towering forests and birds didn't circle above. I couldn't hear the rustle of creatures scratching their claws through the undergrowth.

Squeezing the car door harder, I cocked my head to the side, my body rigid with cold and reluctance. I was inside one of Addy's babushka dolls. A prison within a prison within a prison. No escape.

Kinesh pried my fingers from the door and slammed it. I startled at the noise and blew air out my pursed lips trying to calm myself.

"Kinesh, you can stay with the car," Denis ordered, squinting through the frozen rain.

You didn't have to tell him twice. He was in and starting the engine before I could blink.

Denis beckoned with one arm. I shivered. My clothes ballooned around my skinny legs, and I instantly regretted my choice of outfit for dinner: A formal dress so long and a little too big that it dragged across the floor. Although a smile did tease my lips as I remembered Grant's horrified expression when he watched me tugging the sleeves up and his aggravation when they kept falling down to reveal my bra strap and bony shoulder. Denis watched me curiously as I hiked my dress up, tucked it into my underwear, and walked towards him, allowing myself to be cradled in the bow of his arm. *He's not going to leave you here*, I told myself in short, puffy breaths.

Muddy water had soaked into my dress and frozen my ankles. I shuddered. Denis pushed a code into the door handle and it opened. Fingers of warm air and light reached out and grasped us, pulling us inside. The shiny white tiles were mussed by my dragging, dirty dress.

"These are the holding cells. Follow me," Denis announced grandly, as if he was giving me a tour of a palace ballroom and not a clinical, bleach-scented room used to process criminals, people like me.

The small receiving room was lined with red-cushioned chairs. A small cubicle sat in the corner with a window perforated with small holes like gunshots. Denis went to the window and spoke through the holes.

A person's face appeared. "Yes?"

"We need two passes to go downstairs, level four," Denis demanded loudly, like she wouldn't be able to hear him from her fish tank.

The woman nodded and typed something into the computer, looking up and appraising me once, narrowing her eyes around my dirty, frozen blue ankles.

"New inmate? I'll need processing papers," she said, taking her thick headband off, plucking hairs from it and dropping them on the floor, then sliding it back over her dark blonde hair.

"No. Visitors' passes." Denis held up his wrist and pressed it against the glass. "Do you need anything else?" he asked, irritated.

She flustered like a cat being brushed backwards. "Oh no, no, that won't be necessary, Master Grant." She hastily printed out two barcoded tickets and passed them through a slot under the glass.

I smiled at her, trying to assure her she wasn't in trouble, but when Denis turned his back to her, the woman scowled at me.

So she should, I guess.

I wonder if sunlight is the fundamental thing that keeps you sane. When it's snatched away, you start to feel less human. You can't remember. You're a starved plant that can't grow.

We entered the lift and Denis scanned the passes. When the buttons lit up, he pushed four.

"What's on level four?" I asked, my hands seeping nervousness and dripping from my fingers.

Denis kept his eyes forward and said, "It's who. And I don't know." But his hand flicked and flattened like he was telling me not to ask any more questions. He knew something, but the cameras froze his tongue.

I rocked back and forth on my heels as my stomach bottomed out and my heart refused to calm. The lift so fast, I thought maybe my organs were sitting in a disgusting pile at ground level.

Within seconds, the lift stopped abruptly and the doors slid open with a chirpy ding.

I stepped out, expecting moldy, rock corridors and single bulbs swinging in cages. Instead, clean, white halls glowed before my eyes. Long, fluorescent lights shone overhead. To our right, in front of locked glass doors, a plush, green lounge the shape of plump lips faced a bunch of screens. The small, carved-out area was painted in soft colors like beige or cream. The only way to describe the color was 'blah', as if they had mixed every dull color together to create one super-dull one.

A guard sat on the couch, his legs spread wide. His attention was on a book rather than the screens. When he saw Denis, he shot up and saluted him.

"Master Grant," he said, flustered. He looked from me to Denis in confusion, and then he chose to ignore me. "Haven't seen you in a long time. Are you taller?"

Denis gave an easy laugh. "Probably, it's been two years, Solomon."

Solomon laughed with him, his dark, bald head catching the light as he dipped down, grabbed a remote, and blacked the screens.

"Yes. Not since Superior Grant brought you down here to scare you straight." Solomon winked as he spoke. The wink too long, too familiar.

Denis swallowed uncomfortably and fiddled with his earphones. "Ah, yes… anyway. Similarly, Miss Rosa is in need of a wake-up call."

I scowled at the guard; his jolly exterior was as unnerving as his thin face and nonexistent eyebrows. In their place were two bulges of skin like he'd stuck brown dough above his eyes.

"Doesn't look so bad," I lied, trying to appear blasé. "It's nicer than my actual home!" It was nothing compared to my home. The home I would never return to.

Solomon snorted and I wondered whether you could fit a Ping-Pong ball up his nose, his nostrils were so large.

"Tickets, please." Denis held them out, and Solomon scanned them with a reader. There was a shake to his hands. "Do you want the tour?" Solomon said, waggling his soggy brow.

Please no!

"No thanks, Solomon, just open the doors, please," Denis said, tipping his chin.

Solomon pulled a chain from around his neck and lifted a small, numbered pad that was dangling from it. He punched in a code, and the doors opened.

"Have fun!" he said, waving dorkily.

We stepped over the red line painted in front of the doors, and they closed quickly after us. As soon as they did, I felt squeezed, like someone's hand was around my throat. We were sealed inside a corridor smelling strongly of chemicals that barely masked other horrid odors like sweat, urine, and things I didn't want to think about. Denis put his sleeve to his nose and started placing his earphones in, then he glanced down at me, remembering I was there, and muttered, "Sorry."

I breathed in deeply and repressed the urge to gag. This might be my home soon, if they let me live. I guessed I'd better try to get used to it.

The thick, metal doors, spaced every few meters, were plastered with giant barcode stickers. You could see the tears and leftover paper from previous inmates underneath the current barcode. When you were a prisoner, they took your name as well as your freedom.

We walked hesitantly down the aisle, and my eyes caught glimpses of the inmates through the wire-infused glass. Huddled in dark corners. Lying with their backs to the door, their knees pulled to their chests. They were shadows, thin and barely human.

My skin shuddered over my frame loosely, like it was trying to escape my body. *This could be my life.*

"There are no mics in here," Denis said as he ran his hand along one of the doors and rubbed the microscopic dust between his fingertips. "I think they got sick of listening to all the screaming."

I imagined the desperate pleading of shadow people scratching at their last shreds of humanity.

My dry mouth spat out a curse, making him flinch.

How many people did they keep down here? It went on for at least twenty doors on both sides but not all were filled.

A sharp bang made me jump.

"Git, git, git, me out of here!" A muffled voice came from my left. I walked closer and saw a raring face pressed up against the glass, his eyes bulging with need.

"Please, please, please…" he whispered softly like a song, like a prayer no one would answer. When I put my hand to the window, he suddenly head-butted it. "Devil bitch!" he screamed. I pulled back my hand like he might bite me through the glass or infect me with his insanity and shook my head in shame. Denis placed his hand at my waist and pushed me past the door. We increased our pace, the sad thump of his head hitting the glass continuing as we moved away.

Before I could ask, Denis answered. "Level Four is for those who have lost the ability to mentally cope with imprisonment."

"You mean it's for the ones who've gone crazy," I snapped. I knew I would end up here after a few days of imprisonment.

He nodded. "Look, they're still watching us, even if they can't hear us. Dad instructed me to put you in cell seventeen." We stopped in front of the door. It had no barcode on it and must have been empty. "Just for one hour he said, to give you a scare. I have to do it, Rosa, or he'll suspect something is up." His eyes looked less sympathetic and more uncomfortable.

I shrugged. What choice did I have?

Denis leaned in to punch the code Solomon had handed him.

"Does our attitude offend you?

As do our glorious, defiant eyes?

Coz we laugh like we've got the world's riches

Piled under the place we lie.

You can test us with your swords,

You can hurt us with their cries.

But we'll surprise,

Surprise you when we stand up,

When we stand up,

Up together in our misery and our triumph

You'll hear it in our voices,

You'll see it in our eyes, eyes, eyes,

In our eyes…" sung the prisoner.

A voice from another time. A place I tried not to revisit because it hurt too much. My body shook with the fear that it might not be her. It shuddered at the thought that it could be her, because when my eyes slid to the small slide tag under the window, it read, *Test Subject*, in large, lazy marker.

I rattled the handle, my sweaty hands slipping. I pushed against the door with my shoulder like I believed I was strong enough to push it open by sheer will.

Denis snapped his hand back and stared down at me in shock.

"What are you doing? I didn't think you *wanted* to go in?"

"Open the door," I screeched, blowing my hair from my eyes, my limbs heated with anger and anticipation. "Open the damn door!"

He moved around me and quickly punched in the code. The door clicked, and I barged inside, breathing hard, breathing clouds of pins and metal triangles.

In the corner, sitting on a suspended bed with her legs out in front of her, a long plait hanging over one shoulder, was a thinner, sallower girl than I remembered, but her voice was as strong as ever. Out of key, but filled with a love for the music and the words.

My lips quivered, two tears spoiled my cheeks as I whispered, "Oh Gwen," in a voice, split open and chopped into pieces.

Two concave eyes nested in purple and suffering glanced up, and my hatred for Grant scored my bones a little deeper. I was serrated, sharp, boiling with anger and disgust. Because he wanted me to come to *this* room and witness *this* scene... and he *knew* what it would do to me.

30

The End of the War

JOSEPH

I know what the end of war sounds *like.*
It sounds like broken glass crashing against metal. Shrieking and cheering. It sounds like clapping and sighing at the same time.
I know what the end of war feels *like.*
It feels like relief trapped inside death. Wanting freedom. Knowing the cost of freedom. Celebration and agony wrapped together in bloody bandages.
I should know by now what it is to lose someone, but it's always fresh. Like a retractor, it opens old wounds again and again.

I let my hands fall from my face and my ears began to ring dully. The lights slammed on, showing the devastation and the success. Torn apart by the blast, one gate hung pathetically from a twisted hinge, the other lay flat on the ground. People stopped for about five seconds before they flooded the opening in elation, knocking my shoulders in their haste to get through.

The people of Palma were ready for this. They stepped between the bars on the ground like they were playing hopscotch. Most of the soldiers were already lined up against the concrete wall, disarmed with their hands on the back of their heads. The gunman who'd shot Nafari had been taken down too.

I rushed to where I'd last seen him.

The ground and wall were scorched black. There was no body. I started tipping up debris and calling out his name. "Nafari! Nafari!" I screamed, my voice disappearing, my ears thrumming.

A hand gripped my shoulder. "What are you doing, my man?"

I flinched and swung around, my fists up, ready to fight.

"Whoa, let us help you," the man said, his voice deep and tinny, his face scored with age. He had kind eyes, and I latched onto that.

I tried not to cry as he waited for me to speak. The whole situation was pounding down on me like an enormous fist from the sky. "The man who freed you, who blew the gates is here somewhere..." I managed breathlessly, sweeping my arms over the piles of concrete and segments of iron, pointing to the vague area where I'd seen his smiling face before a blanket of white.

"Nafari!" I yelled again.

The man nodded and started yelling Nafari's name. Somehow, word traveled, and soon there were twenty people upturning bits of gate and rubble and shouting his name. All the while, others were leaving the compound.

I looked up at the where the gate used to be and saw Desh standing there, beaming. The others were picking their way over the debris too.

"Here!" someone shouted.

I ran to them, my legs grating against sharp rubble. A twisted arm protruded out from under a collapsed shed. The guard's shed. I kneeled down and grabbed his wrist. A thin pulse blipped under my fingers.

"He's alive," I said, relief pouring out of every pore in my body. He was alive.

The others ran towards me, and we pulled the sheets of tin from his body. I gave him a quick physical assessment. He was bleeding badly, but he would live. Some men lifted him up and laid him on one of the sheets of tin. "We'll take him to our hospital, friend," one of them said.

I lifted his dangling, broken arm up and placed it over his chest. He opened his eyes and managed a smile. "You did it, Nafari," I whispered.

"I said call me Naf," he managed before his eyes fluttered closed.

It had turned around in a matter of hours. Now we were sitting inside one of the cottages in Ring Eight with some residents of Palma. Laughing, drinking, and celebrating freedom.

Pelo slapped me on the back. "This is what we wanted," he said, sweeping his arm around the scene we could see from the window. Soldiers were being marched to a holding building. People were cleaning up the debris. The thing that made my heart swell was watching the children running between the legs of their elders. I memorized that sight and stored it away for later. I captured it in my store, the one I kept for Rosa.

I sighed. I hadn't been thinking of her. It had been good to have a break from the torture, but as soon as I let my mind wander, it always went straight back to her.

"Does it hurt?" Elise asked as she dabbed my cut with antiseptic.

Yes.

"No."

Cups were offered and we cheered to Naf and to the huge success of the mission as we sat on borrowed dining chairs.

Desh shook his head in disbelief. "I never thought we'd be celebrating inside the walls." He clinked his cup with mine, and we drank. The cider flew down my throat and relaxed my mind. I locked the store for Rosa and filled my cup again.

A Palma local knocked my shoulder and laughed. "Now that you have helped us, are you going to return to your home?"

Home. To me, home was two people, one who might be lost to me forever. I was homeless. The bubbles swirled around my brain. They begged me to let it go. *Forget her. Forget it all.* I turned to the man and laughed too loud, too hard.

"I don't have a home, man, I'm homeless." I hit my leg and chuckled more. "I'm homeless!" Desh's shaking head caught my attention. "What? It's true. Isn't it? We're all homeless."

Some of the men laughed, others ignored me. But I didn't care. I had no grasp on what I actually did care about.

Clink, drink, clink, drink.

Someone patted my back gently, whispering, "I think you better slow down, Joe."

I shrugged them off.

Everything seemed funnier.

Everything seemed stupid.

I was weightless, in muddy water, sinking lower and not caring.

Laughing too loud and not caring. Allowing Elise to put her arm around my waist and lean her head on my shoulder and not caring.

I let the alcohol carry me off into a dreamless sleep.

31

Old Friend

ROSA

Gwen lifted her head slowly from where she stared at her knees. A nightdress lay over them but every bone, every angle, of her jutted out like the dress was her skin and underneath was just a skeleton. She didn't jump up to greet me, but I was already running towards her anyway. I rushed her and skidded into the bed, falling to the ground as I tripped over my dress.

Denis shut the door on us as I whispered hoarsely, "Gwen, Gwen, what... how can... are you?" Each question was cut short with the axe of redundancy. It didn't matter. She was here. *She shouldn't be here.*

She put her hands in my dyed hair and lifted it to the light.

"What have they done to you?" She smiled and those familiar dimples formed high in her cheeks. But there was falseness to her humor.

I blew my relief through my lips like a whistle. "Oh, thank God! You know who I am."

She laughed sadly. "I'm not crazy, despite my accommodation. Apparently, singing is for loonies," she said, winding her finger in circles at her ear.

Was she crazy? I cocked my head to the side and examined her like crazy was something I'd be able to see on her face. But then I remembered—I knew exactly what crazy looked like. I knew what crazy sounded like. Crazy squealed and stomped its red, leather-clad foot. Crazy made you jump and turn in circles before you passed through the door.

I doubled over, clutching my stomach, as Este's squealing echoed through my head and I felt the knife going in and out, looping, never-ending.

No, Gwen wasn't crazy. But I started to wonder whether I was.

Gwen touched my hand, and I snapped up.

"You ok, Rosa. Where'd you go?"

I laughed unconvincingly. "Sorry, I just can't believe you're here."

Why was she here?

I wrapped my arms around her neck and pulled her forward into a hug. She returned it, but she was weak and didn't move very well. I sat on the edge of the bed, my eyes roaming over her diminished frame. Her sunken eyes, her dirty face. She had a bag hanging of the edge of the bed, and I noticed a tube poking out from under her thin, cotton dress.

"Are you sick?" I asked shakily.

Her bare feet were a purplish blue. I pulled the blanket up over her legs and tucked them under her feet. Watching my hands closely, she shook her head. She couldn't meet my eyes. I put my hand over hers, which was resting on her leg.

"Gwen, what is it?" I asked, even though I didn't want to know the answer. I wanted to grab her hand and run—push Denis aside, kick the guard in the groin or the face or whatever I could reach, and run. I could feel the bad answer; it was already carving a deep pit in my stomach. They hurt her. They hurt her like they'd hurt me, and then they'd hurt her more.

Still staring at our hands touching, she said dully, "I can't feel your hand on my leg." A sob caught in her throat, and she coughed. "I can't feel anything from my waist down. The bastards paralyzed me."

The air sucked from the room, gravity inverted, and I thought I might explode with anger.

Grant, I hate you. My hate is a searing sun. It's going to swallow you and turn you to ashes.

I knew it. But once she said it, the last pieces slotted together. Any doubt I had was swept away. Grant was using my friend as the test subject. He broke her back and then he showed her to me like some sort of twisted trophy. He was evil.

Grant had to die.

"I'm so sorry," I wept.

"It's not your fault."

"It is." I put my hands to my head and rocked. My head was being crushed in a vice of guilt.

Gwen grabbed my hands and jerked them down, locking eyes with me. "Listen to me, Rosa, and stop crying. Evil is never your fault."

Okay. Okay. Just stop. Gather up the frayed, pilled edges of your sanity and pull it together. She needs you.

I drew in a large breath from this airless room and wiped my tears with the back of my hand.

"What do you know?" I asked, leaning in.

"That's better." She smiled with effort. "I know I'm Grant's guinea pig for the healer," she said, gripping the edges of her blanket. "I know he's a selfish prick!" she screamed towards the door. "I know neither of us will survive the process, but he won't listen to me."

She gasped from the screaming, her starved eyes wide, her lips dry and cracked. A glass of water was placed on a table just out of her reach. I retrieved it for her, and she grabbed it greedily.

"Oh, it'll work, Gwen. It worked on me," I said loudly, not trusting that they weren't listening to me.

Her eyes peeled back further, her sharp cheekbones pressing out of her skin like tent poles. I couldn't say anything else. I just looked at her, trying to convey with my eyes that somehow I would get her those pills.

She raised her eyebrows and opened her mouth.

"You may push us down
In the very dirt
That grows your fruitful lies
But you should fear us
When you hear us
When you hear our cries,
We'll rise, rise, rise."

Her hand was a fist, pumping with each 'rise'.

I rose from her bedside.

The door opened and Denis hovered in the doorway, his face a mixture of worry and something else I couldn't quite discern. "Something's happened," he said. "I have to take you back."

"I thought I had an hour?" Panic drove through me like a rusty spike, plunging deep into my ribs. I couldn't leave her. She was injured, alone, and she was my only anchor to my old life. The life I wanted back.

I shook my head and returned to her side. "No. Let me stay here. I'm a prisoner anyway, shouldn't I be in *prison?*" I pleaded, my fingers digging into Gwen's mattress. She stared at me with carved-out eyes, her frame wavering like vapor. She needed food.

"Rosa, please." Denis sighed in exasperation. "We don't have time for this."

I didn't turn around and just waved one hand behind me. "Then leave me."

Please don't take me away from my last beacon of sanity.

Gwen wrapped her hand around mine and gripped it. "Don't go, not yet," she whispered. She blinked, but there were no tears. She was too dehydrated. Then she lifted her chin defiantly and snapped, "Who's this clown?"

"I'm Master Grant," he said authoritatively, and then he glanced down at me. "Rosa, we have to leave now!" He was moving from leg to leg like he needed to pee.

"Why?" I snapped, so sick of being dragged from place to place, being a pawn in their sick games. This was my friend lying here, broken. I choked on all the tears I couldn't cry as Denis' shadow encroached on me.

"We've lost Palma," he stated. "We have to go home. Now!"

"Home?" I laughed. I had no home. And Palma. Lost. We. *We*, like I was part of *his* people. No, *we* had gained Palma. *They* had lost Palma.

Gwen grinned. Her skin was paler than clean sheets. She was suffering, but God, she was so strong. Much stronger than I was.

"I'm not leaving yet." I filled her glass again and handed it her. I searched the room, my breaths getting shorter and more hysterical. "Why doesn't she have any food?" I yelled, my voice uneven, shrill as a drill bouncing against metal.

Denis strode towards me and yanked me up by my collar, the silk fabric tearing at my neck. "Get up!" he growled.

Gwen's grip was tight, but she was too weak to hold me against Denis' pull. I scratched and hit but he held me out from his body as if I were a rat hanging from its tail.

"I'll see you again," I screamed as he dragged me from the room.

She shook her head. "You won't see me until Test day."

My eyes widened. She would die if we didn't get those pills. "You know I'll do what I can to help you?" I shouted as I held onto the doorframe. Denis pulled on my arms.

She sung loudly, bopping her head along with the tune. And if you didn't understand what it was about, I guess you would think she was crazy.

"Your love is a pill,
It's bitter and still.
I'll take it,
I'll swallow it.
I'm addicted to you,
Addicted to you."

She understood. She knew.

Her grin stretched to my face as the door closed, and Denis dragged me down the hall.

I would save her. If I could do nothing else, I had to find the rest of those pills.

"Let me go!" I snapped.

Denis still had a hold of my collar, my dress now barely covering my upper body. He suddenly dropped me, and I fell into the wall. He reached out to grab me, but I slapped his hand away.

"Don't touch me," I said, backing away from him and rubbing my sore, scratched neck.

His eyes were severe, dipped in rage. He stepped towards me quickly and slapped my face hard. The breath was knocked from my mouth. The sting instantly radiated over my whole head.

"Don't ever speak to me like that. And when I say it's time to leave, you do as you're told."

My chin fell in understanding. *Do as you're told.* I forgot who he was. He was Superior Grant's son. While I had to work with him and even though he'd told me his secret, he had been raised by a cruel man. And now I knew the cruelty lived inside him also.

I pulled myself up from the floor and crept past him to the glass door. It glided open to Solomon standing there, his expression indifferent to the violence just as I would have expected.

I shuffled towards the elevator door, my hands stubbornly at my sides, even though I wanted to cradle my pulsing face, and waited. I felt beaten in every way.

Denis spoke to Solomon in a detached tone. "My father expects a healthy, well-fed test subject. Your care for the prisoner is unacceptable. Rectify the situation or I'll report you."

We didn't speak on the ride home.

I ignored any attempts he made to help me, maneuver me, or touch me when we arrived back at Grant's compound. My trust in him was dented, and I hated that I needed him.

We made it to Judith's bedroom door, and I turned to look at him. He winced at the sight of what he had done. My face felt swollen, my lip bulging.

I spoke from one side of my mouth. "Find those pills," I whispered. I thought about Deshi. *Where he would have hidden them?* It was so hard to picture without being in his office.

"You'll have to help me," Denis said quietly.

I nodded. "Don't worry," I hissed. "I'll do as I'm told."

He looked at the floor. "Rosa, I'm sorry," he barely mumbled. I open the door, stepped backwards, and slammed it in his face.

Leaning against the buttery timber, I breathed in and out violence. I was starting to wonder whether it was something about me that made men want to hurt me. Some men, anyway. But I quashed the thought as quickly as it had appeared. It was not me... it was them. They were 'less than' and violence was their only power.

Wanting comfort, I reached out for Joseph's arms to crawl into. I strained to hear his warm, rumbling voice telling me it was all going to be ok. *Please let it be ok.* I banged my head gently against the door as I slid down to the carpet. I wanted to dig through to the ground. I wanted to feel the damp dirt between my fingers.

This was not where I belonged.

Judith sat up in her bed, rubbing her eyes groggily.

I let one tear slip before I padded my soul with steel bars and strengthened myself. Palma was free. Free. It was working. I smiled and my face hurt.

As Judith peered at me through the glow of her hideous fairy nightlight, I thought about my father. I wondered where he was when Palma was freed. I imagined him celebrating, marveling at the power of the people. But I also knew he would look to his side and want me there. I pictured his wiry arm over my shoulder.

I'm sorry, Dad.

32.

Splitting

JOSEPH

This was definitely the way to forget, but it came with a price.

My head lolled to the side and I startled awake, my eyes resistant to opening, my mouth dry and desperate for water. I licked my lips and unfolded my arms, stretching them behind my back. Dried blood crackled on my shirt. I needed to change.

The room was spinning and I blinked several times, trying to sharpen my dulled senses. Some people were still awake, hovering over the kitchen bench and whispering, but the house was almost empty. Most people probably returned to their homes once the celebrations had died down. I did a quick head count and noted that everyone was here, sleeping on the floor or crookedly in chairs. Elise's blonde head stuck out from under a blanket on the worn, yellow sofa.

I got up and wobbled over to the kitchen to get water, tripping over Desh's sleeping body. A murmur in the corner caught my eye. Olga sat with her back against the wall. She looked anxious, shaking her head from side to side, her small eyes darting around the room like she was also doing a head count.

"Olga, are you ok?" I whispered hoarsely, clearing my throat of its fuzziness.

She nodded and waved her hand dismissively. "Just tired," she replied.

That was good enough for my cloudy brain. I stumbled and tripped on the spot where the carpet met the kitchen tiles, water calling to me from the dented sink.

As I lurched over the tap and drank directly from it, Rash's voice hit my ears like he'd clapped tin lids together over my head.

"Feeling a bit under the weather are we?" he asked triumphantly.

I took a few more sips and raised my head, wiping the water from my mouth. The other men who were whispering wisely moved away from the counter. Rash sat on a stool, his arms clasped neatly in front of him, a big grin on his face, his speech a little slurred.

"What did you do to me?" I asked, my own words sounding garbled.

He raised his eyebrows. "Nothing, you dumbass. You did this to yourself. You're drunk."

I leaned my elbows on the counter and dipped my head down between my shoulders. It made me feel worse. The room started bobbing up and down like I was on water. I looked up and caught his amused expression.

"I'm glad my pain gives you comfort," I groaned.

He clapped his hands together and chuckled when I flinched at the noise. My head was splitting open.

"Oh it does, man, it does." He opened a can of beer and handed it to me. "Here, drink this; it will make you feel better." I eyed him suspiciously but took it. I couldn't feel any worse than I already did.

I took a few swigs and soon, I could feel it doing its job.

"Are you ever going to forgive me?" I asked, watching him pick at his brown hands.

He laughed sourly. "This is not about forgiveness. I'm grieving. I miss her. I need her. You're just the obvious target for all my misdirected anger." His head sunk down.

I shook my head from side to side. "You're... you're in love with her..." My hand curled into a jealous fist.

Rash's eyes narrowed. "You know, you really are an idiot. You need to realize you're not the only one suffering. I love her, yes. I'm not *in* love with her." His voice started to rise in volume. "You think...You think..."

I slammed my fist down on the table. "What?" Violence pulsed in my fingertips. I was tired of him blaming me for everything.

"You're so sorry. So sorry for yourself, you don't..." he started. It wasn't even true. I felt the burden of what I'd done to everyone. To him, to Pelo, and everyone who'd lost her. "You're not the only one who lost her. And just coz I wasn't sleeping with her, doesn't mean I didn't love her just as much as you did!"

That was it. I was so sick of his attitude. His damn, stupid, glaring face. I snatched his clothes with my hands, pulled him across the counter, and close to my face. My heart thumped loudly; my ears pumped a sea of blood.

I stared into his eyes and whispered, "You think this is about sex?" I shook my head, sorry for him. "Screw you, Rash," I said, throwing him away from me. He fell off his stool and onto the floor.

My hands were still begging to hit him. I paced back and forth, my fists tight against my sides.

Suddenly, Elise was in front of me. She put her hands on my shoulders, and I nearly punched her. She ducked back from my angry expression.

"Come with me," she said, taking my hand and pulling me away from the kitchen and down the hall of the small cottage.

I let her lead me because if I'd stayed there, I would have stomped on Rash's face. Rosa wouldn't want that. I ran my hands through my hair. She wouldn't want any of this.

Elise pulled me into the bathroom and closed the door. She daintily put down the toilet seat lid and sat on it.

She handed me a balled-up wad of cloth. "Here, I found you a clean shirt."

I turned away from her and quickly changed, my eyes roaming over the blue glass tiles bordering the shower that were clearly not standard issue.

"Sit down," she said, pointing to the bathtub with tumbled-down toiletries gathered around the plughole.

I sat down on the edge and sighed, trying to expel some of the violence inside me.

"I just don't want to feel like this anymore," I admitted.

She leaned in, her eyes so sad, welcoming and understanding. "Feel like what?"

I shrugged, my shoulders sinking. "So guilty."

Elise crossed her legs and rested her head in her palm. "Right. I think you should tell me what happened."

I started from when Orry got sick. She nodded. She asked the occasional question but mostly, she just let me talk. She was being exactly what I needed, a friend, and I was grateful for it.

When I finished, she gazed at me gently. "She sounds amazing, Joe."

I nodded. "She was. I mean… she is."

"You've been through a lot together, and I understand the bond you must have with her. But let me ask you this—do you really think she would want you to torture yourself like this? You love her, and that's not going to change, but it doesn't mean that your life just stands still when she's not here, does it?"

No. I knew this, but hearing someone else say it, sort of giving me permission to keep living, was good.

"It's not just about her. I've done some terrible things, Elise. To escape, I had to…" My words ran out and dripped to silence.

She pursed her lips, tipping her head to the side. "You can tell me, Joe. No judgment."

I tried to say it, but it just wouldn't come out. Confessing to her seemed a step too intimate. "I can't."

She tucked a strand of fair hair behind her ear. "You don't have to. But just listen to me. You *have* to find a way to move past it. If not for yourself, then do it for your kid. At least try and let go of the things that you can't control. Hopefully, she'll come back. You can hope for it, but you can't count on it. You have to keep living your life."

I laughed sadly. If only it were that easy.

"Try," Elise said more forcefully.

I dipped my head in agreement. "Okay, I'll try." I said. Lifting my eyes to meet hers, I whispered, "Thank you for stopping me."

She stood and patted my head. "Don't mention it."

I wondered if I could do it. Move on while still holding hope that I'd see her again. It seemed like a candle burning at both ends. It was going to burn no matter what end I picked up.

I found myself following her out of the bathroom and back into the kitchen. Rash had passed out on the floor where I'd shoved him, his arms wrapped around the stool like it was a woman. She took two metal cups, one pink and one green, from the cupboard and poured us both a drink from her own flask.

I took it. I wanted it. Didn't want it. Just didn't want to think about anything anymore.

She clinked her glass with mine, the only other sounds the murmurs of people sleeping satisfied and safe. "To living your life," she said, and then she sculled the brown liquid in one gulp with a smile.

I couldn't smile back, but I didn't feel like I was going to explode anymore, which was a step in *some* direction. I wasn't sure there was a *right* direction. Putting the cup to my lips, I drank.

33

Cowards and Heroes

ROSA

"Rosa, what's wrong with you? Are you all right?" Judith shook my shoulder as if my body were a door she couldn't open, her big blue eyes blinking away sleep and crusted mascara grit.

I was somewhere else. In the trees, my feet pressed hard against a branch, the scent of smoke and sweet pine rushing over my face and teasing through strands of my hair. My mind sought escape for one small moment. But the normal sound of her voice shattered my dream.

"Your voice..." I started.

One daisy-shaped pajama button pinched between her fraying fingers. "Dad prefers it."

I gazed down at my dress, muddy and torn. "I should change," I said, uncomfortable under her stare and her sudden admission. I didn't want her to confide in me. I had enough secrets poking holes in my flappy existence without adding hers to my list. It was liable to squeeze something important out.

"I'll get some ice for your face." She smiled softly. I couldn't tell if she enjoyed seeing me this way or she felt bad. Then she flipped her hair and muttered, "I can't wait to tell Dad what Denny did. He told us he was the only one permitted to hurt you."

She put her hand to my bruised cheek and cocked her head. I winced as her fingers brushed over my hot, raised skin. I retreated from her touch. Her hands were laced with poison. She was much worse than Denis was. An evil layered with crazy, beneath a sweet face.

I grabbed an armful of clothes without really paying any attention and ran to the bathroom to get away from her. I heard her say, "ice," and the bedroom door opened and closed. I turned on the shower and quickly washed, eager to fall into bed. I was so tired even Judith's teeth grinding wouldn't keep me awake tonight.

I wrapped a towel around my aching body and sighed at the clothes in my hands. I'd grabbed two pairs of pants and a bra. I tried to open the door and it hit something. When I pushed harder, the door clanged against metal.

I pressed my face to the small gap. "Judith, did you put something in front of the door?" My eyes took in the small slice of view afforded by the crack. I looked up and then I looked down, my heart jumping into my mouth. I leapt back from the door in fright.

A slither of Grant's dark face smiled at me. "You should come out, dear. I have something to tell you." His voice was dripping with sickly sweetness, drawn out like the stretch of molasses.

I lingered on the other side of the door, quivering in a towel. No way was I going out there.

"I'm good," I said, pulling the towel tighter.

"I heard what happened with my son. You can rest assured, he is being punished." He was a slick of oil, bright with rainbows playing across its surface, but dangerous, one wrong step, a slip, and you'd break your back.

I was sick of this game. Groaning, I pulled my hands through my wet hair. "What the hell do you want from me?" I knew it was pointless but I said it anyway, my voice hollowing out at the end. "How could you do that? How could you break someone's spine for your own benefit?"

Silence followed for so long that I thought he was gone. I moved to the handle slowly, and then he spoke. "Well, the test had to be accurate. The fact that you know our test subject... well, that's just a bonus."

I wanted to scream, but it was futile. I knew he did this to Gwen because of me and I hated him for it, the hate extending and wrapping around my own wrist too. It was my fault.

"Your time with us is nearly ovvver. My procedure has been moved up. The test will be in one week and then... I will walk again." He clapped his hands together once.

I laughed bitterly. "Forgive me if I don't celebrate with you."

He pushed the door hard, and I flew backwards towards the

bathroom wall. He leered at me sitting on the tiles in a towel, shaking despite telling my body to straighten up.

"Since you have refused to cooperate," he growled, "you've left me no choice other than to execute you and your friend." I knew this. "And since you've been so stubborn, your demise will not be an easy one. No…" He held up one finger, pointed like a knife. "You've helped me make an important decision."

"What are you talking about?" I asked, my voice losing its tiny edge.

His eyes were steel, nothing in them but cold, hardness. "Let's just say, your reunion will be a short one."

What did that mean?

"What do you mean?" I asked, scrambling to my knees, gripping the towel with one hand.

He rolled backwards, his eyes on his feet. The guard holding open the door let him pass while I crawled after him screaming, "What do you mean? Reunion with who?"

He ignored my screams. I tried to follow him, but the guard pushed me back. He shook his head, muttering, "Stop, Miss."

I watched him roll away from beneath the arm of the guard. Judith passed him, a bag of ice and a tea towel in one hand. She leaned down to kiss Grant on the cheek. "Night, night, Daddy," she drawled, using her twanging voice again. I cringed.

"You're such a good daughter," he crooned, smoothing her hair down.

She skipped towards me. "Let's take care of that face," she said once we were inside.

I breathed in, my lungs expanding too far.

What did he mean?

I breathed out, my lungs scrunching down flat.

What did he mean?

Electrified chills ran through my body like I'd stuck a fork in a toaster.

The next morning, after breakfast, I went back to our room. Judith skipped off to bake a cake or paint Grant's toenails. I didn't know—whatever a suck up did. I sat on the edge of the bed and waited for Denis to take me downstairs, seething. Half my face was purple and all of my insides were blaring red with rage. I tried to remind myself that I needed him. Gwen needed him. But all I wanted to do was shove whatever alliance we had made deep into the rubbish bin and jump up and down on top of it.

When the knock on the door came, I considered ignoring it. But then the dragging and pulling would start. *I had no choice.*

Denis' face was dark as shadows of shadows. He'd kept up a good act at breakfast, but now the mask had slipped off.

"I'm sorry," he dribbled, and I wanted to slap him.

I glared at him, making sure the whole bruise was right in his field of vision. One blue eye crinkled in pain at the sight of me.

"I know you're sorry. You already said that," I snapped, stepping past him and into the hall.

Strips of white light cut me in half. I was dressed in black and red, and I was half-dark, half-light and on fire, standing in the cool sunlight. Denis shifted uncomfortably, like a beanpole in the wind. I ignored his guilty face and stared out of the window. It was a dirty winter, made of mud puddles and brown ice. I wished I could jump through the window and feel it—smell the rich earth, taste the crisp air.

I turned, and Denis was still standing there awkwardly.

His eyes swung to the camera in the corner carefully. "I just remembered, I need to borrow Judy's music player before we go. There are some songs I need to download from it."

Shrugging, I followed him back into the room. Suddenly, he shoved me into the bathroom and closed the door. He twisted on the taps and stared at himself in the mirror, bracing his hands on the sink.

"No amount of staring is going to change your stupid face," I snarled as I caught my hideous expression in the mirror behind him, purple hate. Thin, angry, and not who I wanted to be.

"I'm really sorry, Rosa," he said again.

I was getting annoyed. "Stop saying that! What do you want? Forgiveness? Fine, I forgive you for being just like you father, a violent bastard."

He crumpled like my words were rocks thrown at his gut. "No. I'm sorry because I can't go through with it. He's watching me. He's suspicious. I won't be able to get the pills for your friend." He exhaled loudly, as if it was so hard to say.

I wished I had rocks to throw. I wished I were strong enough to punch him. I clenched my fists at my sides. "So you're going to let Gwen die because you're scared of your father?" I shook my head. *I should have known this would happen.* "You could never deserve a man like Deshi. You are... beneath him," I said cruelly.

He hung his head and muttered, "I know."

My mind stretched and strained. I couldn't let this happen. I turned to the wall, rich black and white tiles with swirls that looked like parsley leaves rolled in front of my eyes. Grant was suspicious. He was watching us both now. He was already distrustful of me. But his weakness was what he thought of me. He thought I was nothing, an insubstantial mess he could play with.

I strode out of the bathroom with a purpose tucked into my pocket. Denis stood there, looking pathetic. "Let's go downstairs."

I knew what I had to do.

34

Backwards

JOSEPH

S he's almost out of reach to me now. Slipping below the horizon like the setting sun. And I can't tell if it's good or bad. All I know is that it puts the pain on hold.

A helicopter passed over our heads as we walked away from Palma. I ducked instinctively, as if it were close enough to touch me. Desh laughed. There was an old memory there, but I didn't even need to shove it down. It was already buried. My head still swam in what Elise called *hangover territory*.

"Shut up!" I said as I elbowed Desh playfully. His look was suspicious, and I knew what it was about. My smiles were an endangered species. *My smiles were a betrayal.*

"Sorry, it's just good to see you smile," Desh said, slapping the tops of the ferns that whipped our legs with melting ice.

"We did good, didn't we?" I grinned, thinking of Palma. The people had control. They were so ready for it. We didn't even need to light the match, just give them the packet and let them start the fire all on their own.

Desh nodded. "That we did, man. Can't believe the way those helicopters flew away from there. It was like, one look and they thought, *No way are we even going to try and go in there!*" He was giddy. We all were. We were floating on a high after the success of Palma.

I glanced up at the sky as the helicopter disappeared from view, wondering what we would find when we got to Pau. I knew it wouldn't be like Palma.

A deep, dark wish had been working its way to the surface like a splinter as we got closer—I could find my parents. The other, even deeper wish was maybe I could find *her* mother. But that was a small wish. The problem was the more I thought about it, the more I started to chicken out. Seeing my parents meant facing what I'd done. I wasn't sure I could handle it or them.

I frowned, my headache pulsing in my temples like a heartbeat.

"Yeah, that's the face we've come to love," Desh joked.

Elise sidled up next to me and smirked at Desh. "You just don't know how to bring it out of him. The guy just needs to relax a little."

Rash snorted ahead of us. "Yeah, I bet you know exactly how to *relax* him!"

Desh strode closer to Rash and opened his mouth, ready to shout highly intelligent abuse at him.

I stopped him. "Leave him. I know he's full of it, so does everyone else. I'm not going to let him get to me anymore, so neither should you," I said.

"That's the way!" Elise said chirpily, slapping me on the back.

I pulled in at the contact. "Did a mosquito just tap me on the back?" I asked.

She slapped me harder and a memory crept up and held me, angry, desperate hands trying to pull me down. Cuts, blood, fingernails digging, digging. I reached for Elise's flask that she kept in her backpack pocket. I snatched it, and she turned around. When she saw the flask, she jumped to get it from my hands, which I held high in the air.

"Hey," she giggled, her hair flapping up and down like a birds wings as she jumped.

I took a drink, letting it warm my stomach and calm my head. She was still trying to get the flask from my hands. I chuckled as she tried to hit me again.

"What was that? Oh wait, nah, it was just the wind," I teased. Desh laughed along with Elise, but there was something off about it, strained.

"Here." Desh offered his bottle of water. "Slow down."

I took a large gulp of the spirit, ignoring the concerned stare coming at me from my other side and the water being tucked back into his bag.

"Give it here," Elise said, taking the flask back.

Two drinks were enough for now—enough to keep bad thoughts in the background.

We stopped for lunch in a sheltered spot under cracked birches, shading large boulders. Thankfully, we'd been given ample supplies from the citizens of Palma. They'd refilled our packs and our flasks. I pulled my jacket around me as the clouds came over.

Gus threw his pack on the ground with a thump and turned to face me. Some of the others moved away from us like they were anticipating something. "Joseph." he sighed my name.

I took a step backwards because I thought I knew what he was going to say. "What's wrong, Gus?" My hands were two fists of rock.

Matt approached me, with Pelo shadowing him. Everyone else fanned out and away.

"We had a chat about your, er, situation…" My situation? *What did that even mean?* "And we've decided that you shouldn't go in to Pau with Pelo. One of the others will go."

My fists crumbled at my sides. "Why?" *I knew why.*

Matt put his injured hand on my shoulder. "We're just not sure you're coping so well at the moment. We know how much you miss Rosa and Orry." *Don't say her name.* "We're worried you're not thinking straight. Grief is… well…"

I took a shaky breath and threatened Matt with my eyes to finish that sentence. It wasn't just about missing her. It was about facing her.

Pelo put his hand on my head and patted me like a dog. "I'll find your parents, I promise. We all feel that maybe you should sit this one out, son."

I wasn't sure what to say. "Did I do something wrong in Palma?" I asked, knowing full well there was no point in arguing.

Gus shook his head. "No, but this really is for your own good."

I pulled my hands through my hair and exhaled. "Jesus, Gus, don't talk to me like I'm a child." I wanted to say more but I left it. Nodding, I walked away.

Everyone was a bit annoyed, a bit uncomfortable, and it spurred our feet to move faster like we could escape it. The happiness from Palma seeped away as we neared Pau. The small chatter leaked to nothing as we headed towards the railway track.

By nightfall, we'd reached the rails and decided to camp in a tunnel. It didn't worry me like it once would have. I was numb to memories. I wasn't allowing anything past the solid barrier I'd built.

A small fire kept us warm and we hunched down over the tracks, the cold biting into our butts. A bearded man nudged me.

"I don't know what Gus is on about," he muttered. "You did a great job in Palma."

I shrugged. The decision had been made and in a way, I was grateful for it being out of my hands. I wasn't sure I wanted to go in, and now I didn't have to. I tried not to examine my reasons too closely. Packed it away with the other feelings that kept trying to drag me down. I shivered as a cold blast of air shot through the tunnel and put my hands out to the fire to warm them.

The bearded man handed me a bottle, its contents sloshing around the bottom. "This will warm you up."

I put my hand up to decline, but then changed my mind and took it. *What did it matter?*

I caught Rash's eyes across the fire, and briefly, I thought I saw something other than anger in his eyes. It looked like pity, which was so much worse.

35

Brave

ROSA

Today I'm going to be brave. I am my only chance. I am strong. Today, I will turn every slap, every break, every time they shake me and turn me upside down to see what will fall out, into bloody action. There is no choice.

I wound my strength tighter. Turned it over and over like a bandage in my hands, until they were wrapped like a boxer's. They didn't think I would do this and that was where they'd fail. I was bigger than stunts and stupid outfits. I could be bigger than all of them.

Denis led me downstairs. I talked as I normally would. I snapped at him. In the elevator I said, "Well, at least I don't have too much more torture left to deal with, huh?" Denis' shoulders pulled in, and he stared at the door. Yeah, guilt was an uncomfortable feeling, it dug in, constricted you like a too-tight, high-necked jacket, each regret pulled the buckles and straps tauter, each wrong action dragged the zip nearer to your throat. He had a lot to feel guilty about.

My thoughts were not on Grant. They were with Gwen. *Save. Gwen's. Life.*

You can do this.

The doors slid open and I walked through the garage with Denis close to me, his hand always hovering at my waist. My eyes glanced at the dark door, the one that opened into nightmares. My body twitched like someone flicked a switch inside me, sending a sharp slap of pain up my spine and out my nostrils. I looked away and turned in on the one thought I had to sustain. *Do it.*

We took two more steps and my desperate eyes found what I needed, lying there like a cut snake, silver, heavy, perfect.

I pretend to trip, knelt down, and snatched the piece of metal from beneath the front of the gleaming, green car. Denis leaned down to help me, and I swung around.

I hate the noise. I hate it.

The 'crack' as I hit Denis as hard as I could burrowed into my head and made a nest so it could stay there.

He appeared confused. His eyebrows drawn down like brackets around his rolling eyes. He put his hand to the side of his head like he wasn't sure if it was still there. Regret crept up my throat, but I swallowed it. I searched his pockets and found what I needed, his handheld. He resisted me but softly, flopping around like a fish on a jetty. I grabbed his wrist and pulled back his sleeve, quickly taking a photo of his wrist tattoo. He didn't make a sound. Staring at me with urgent, weeping eyes, he mouthed, "Run." Then he rolled to his side and coughed.

I slammed the handheld into my pocket and ran.

All I could hear was my own breath and the crunch of ice beneath my feet. All I could think about was Joseph and Deshi running just like this, hearts pounding and breaking together.

I arrived at the gate to Este's compound and fumbled around for the handheld. I knew they would be able to track me, that didn't matter. I knew they would catch me. I just needed to get there a few minutes before they did.

Pulling up the photo, I prayed it would work. I held it under the scanner, turning it back and forth, trying to get that beep. My body was ready to press itself through the wires if it didn't hurry up.

Beep!

I exhaled in absolute relief and pushed through the gate. It locked after me. I took a rock and smashed the scanner on the other side, hoping it would slow them down.

Please let something be on my side today.

Quickly, my toes pressed down in their shoes and I sprinted for Este's house. Crunching. Sweat dripped down my neck from fear, from exertion, I wasn't sure. I let the cold air in like it was medicine. It was. It filled me with lost freedom. With hope.

As I rounded the curve, Este's home came into view. The giant, two-story stone villa looked different in the light. Beautiful and too old for this world. I hugged the zoo wall and waited for the guards to pass the gate. There was just one. He strolled down the drive rather than marched, casually arriving at the iron bars and grabbing a set of keys from his pocket.

I felt like slamming my head through the concrete wall of the zoo. A lion roared and echoed my frustration. *The padlock.* I'd forgotten about the padlock.

The guard opened the gate. I prayed he would forget to lock it after him, but he didn't. The lock clipped back into place, and my hopes were squashed and splattered all over the gravel. I inched closer, my eyes squinting for another way in.

The guard stared at his feet, hands behind his back, bored from what I could tell. My foot slipped along the gravel, the grazing sound causing him to look up. I sighed. It was over. My short escape was pointless. Gwen would die and I would be executed for assaulting Master Grant.

The guard took a couple of steps in my direction and froze, his warm eyes meeting mine in recognition. Harry. He glanced away just as quickly, reached into his pants, and got some gum. The keys fell from his pocket and hit the ground, heavier than an asteroid. He didn't retrieve them, though he must have heard them fall. He put his hands behind his back and sauntered around the corner away from me.

I didn't think, I sprinted for the keys, scooped them up, and collided with gate, which shuddered from my impact.

As I flayed the keys and picked, one red ribbon rippled across my eyes and slid down my arm. Death markers. I remembered them from Pau. When someone died, there was no funeral, or occasion like the Survivors had, but people would tie red ribbons to the tree in front of the deceased's house as a show of respect. You'd think a Superior's house would be drowning in ribbons, but there was just this one. I picked it up off the ground where it lay like a streak of blood and wound it through the bars.

After three keys, the padlock opened.

The sound of footsteps shoved me in the back and urged me to keep moving. I slammed the gate shut and locked it, throwing the keys in the rambling garden. As the group of guards came around the curve, I managed a grin through the bars and then I took off.

Este's house was a tomb. As I approached the door, the soundlessness of it hit me. The place was as empty as a robbed grave.

I didn't even bother trying the door. I picked up a rock and smashed a window to the right of the giant, wooden entrance. Instantly, alarms squealed like an arrow shot through my ears as I turned to see guards shaking the gate and yelling at me to let them in.

I screamed, "Jump up and down four times and turn in a circle!" Which made them pause for a second, before rattling the great gate again. I slipped into the darkness of a home deserted, avoiding the broken glass, and ran to where I remembered Deshi's office to be. My hands clapped over my ears, which felt like they must be bleeding.

This was the site of my death, the undoing and breaking of so many things. I drew my breath in small, panicked bursts as I crept across the rug. I had minutes, at best, before they got another set of keys and came after me.

I left the room and entered the hall, my hands running along the tapestries, searching for pictures I remembered. I poked my head down one hall, and it didn't look familiar. Sweeping my finger along a dark, mahogany hallstand, I was surprised how much dust gripped my fingers.

I turned again. This house was a maze of halls and doors.

The alarm sound switched from squealing to a low whooping noise.

I moved faster, my head snapping back and forth, searching. And then I caught it—a flash of white snow, brown-grey fur against burdened pines. I ran to it like I could save its life.

The deer in the snow.

I was close.

I couldn't stop to stare. I cut a sharp corner, my shoulder bumping hard into the stone wall, and was faced with Deshi's office door. A dead space, echoing voices of the ones who left me behind.

The keypad blinked in front of me. I punched in the only code I knew that would mean something to Deshi—Hessa's birthday.

The green light gleamed happily, and I felt like laughing hysterically. Pushing inside, I locked the door behind me. I switched on the light and the scene flickered to life. It was an uncomfortable feeling, like the air was not mine to breath. I climbed onto the wheeled stool from his desk and stretched to pull the camera from the wall, though it didn't look switched on.

I took one very brief moment to be shaky, to miss them and want them and then, I ransacked the office.

I emptied the drawers and tipped them on floor. Papers covered in numbers and symbols I would never understand rained down and covered the entire floor. I pushed at the ceiling squares and pulled down the piping that wound its way between the metal support bars. Reaching my arms, I desperately flapped my hands over the top surface of the bars, hoping he'd taped them up there, but there was nothing. Nothing.

Damn it.

"Damn it!" I screamed and kicked the stool across the room.

It landed on its side, the wheels swinging uselessly back and forth, trying to grip the air. I pulled at my hair in frustration, tears burning. These would be my last tears. Gwen was going to die. I would never see Orry or Joseph again.

I walked over to the stool and picked it up, slamming it down on the floor in anger. Over and over. "Damn it! Damn it! Damn it!" I screamed until my voice felt tiny and wasted.

As I slammed it again weakly, my anger giving in to fear, the wheels cracked. I lifted it up to throw it and one wheel fell out of the leg and onto to floor, a small tuft of plastic protruding from the hollow leg. I teased it out. Little white pills danced before my eyes, and I cackled like a crazy person.

Bang!

"Miss Rosa, open the door immediately!"

Bang!

I took four pills from the plastic bag, shoved the rest back in the leg, and replaced the wheel. Placing the pills in my sock band, I rolled it over, shaking my pant leg down to cover it.

Bang!

I righted the stool, placed it under the desk, took one deep breath, and opened the door.

36

Human

SUPERIOR GRANT

I suppose I should be nervous. I'm not. There is nothing that can stop what's about to happen. I'm like the rising moon. Strong, powerful. The controller of the tides.

I rolled out of the bathroom, my hair wet, my robe tied tightly around my waist. Camille sat on the edge of the bed, waiting for me. When our eyes met, her plump lips rose in a sweet smile. There was certainly one thing I was looking forward to when I had my legs and my whole body back. She blushed as my eyes ran over her body. She was beautiful. Perfect for me. Supportive and loyal. I held out my hand, and she took it.

"I'll help you dress," she said, standing and making her way over to the closet to find me a shirt.

"Thank you, darling," I whispered.

"Of course," she replied dutifully, pulling a shirt out and holding it up for me to approve. I nodded at the second one.

I wheeled closer, grabbed her hand, and pulled her gently down to my level so I could look her in the eyes. "I want to thank you for standing by me," I said, suddenly not wanting to look in her eyes.

Her eyebrows rose briefly. She seemed surprised but as per usual, she hid it well. She composed herself and unwrapped my robe, placing her soft hands on my chest.

"Soon I'll be able to do this myself," I said.

She leaned me forward and put my shirt over my back, doing up the buttons, even though I certainly could do that on my own.

"I don't mind, dear," she said, gazing down at a button and rolling it between her delicate fingers.

I put my hand over hers and leaned in to kiss her cheek. "I know."

The door flung open, and Camille jumped back from me.

"What the devil!" I shouted, aiming my voice towards the soldier standing shakily in my doorway. "Even if this isn't the most important information you've ever had to deliver, you're still going to be repurposed, boy. How dare you barge into my bedroom!"

Camille stood angrily and stormed over to the soldier. "What is your name?" He told her, and she made a note of it. Yes, she was perfect, but then I had made sure she would be exactly what I wanted.

"What is it, soldier?"

"It's the girl. Miss Rosa," the soldier began. That name. I was looking forward to deleting that name from the register personally. My finger ached to press the key that would signal her existence terminated. But not yet.

"What about her?" I snapped impatiently.

"She escaped."

37

Shrug

JOSEPH

The nights were blending, bleeding into each other as the alcohol flowed. Distance grew between me and what I should be. But I didn't mind the sinking. The forgetting. It kept the nightmares away. It kept the feelings from drowning me. I just didn't care. About anything.

I could be a lonely star in the sky. I could be a leaf, trampled into the dirt. I am as light as air and as heavy as lead.

If I stood in front of an x-ray right now, I wasn't sure what you'd see. A heart not beating strong, lungs shriveled from lack of real air.

I was afraid of losing her, and I was afraid of finding her.

If I do find you, Rosa, I'm not sure if you'll be able to find me.

38

Helpers

ROSA

Ten minutes ago, I was listening to a conversation.

"*You* can tell him," the younger guard said, holding Denis' handheld up. Grant's number flashed, bold and intimidating on the screen, the photo, a generic silhouette of a man.

The guard shook his head, pointing a knobbly, scarred finger towards his partner. "No way. You."

My wrists ached, the plastic ties digging in and shredding my skin. "Is Denis, I mean, Master Grant, is he ok?"

They ignored me. "There is no way in hell I'm going in there. Let's just make the new guy do it."

They laughed together.

"Great idea."

I stood like a stump in the ground, solid and dying. My hands stretched tightly behind my back, lost in Grant's stifling office. A long window framed the view at the back of his grand, architectural home and called to me. Frosty, green grass carpeted the hill and slipped down to meet a rectangle of frozen water. Bright blue, shimmering tiles bordered the pool. Two long chairs, open like books and dusted with ice, stretched out under a wooden pergola. I leaned closer; a ladder perforated the ice. I squinted at the water, fascinated by what its purpose could be. The guard grabbed my bindings and pulled me from the window. I jerked away from his touch. Some of my boldness from my escape clung to me like sawdust after a clean cut. But it wouldn't last.

Towers of books climbed the walls. Books with titles like "Your Power", "Success is Simple", "The Psychology of Influence." I raised my eyebrows and small smile poked its way through my armor. Nestled in a small corner behind a step stool were a few fiction books. Two rested against each other and seemed like they were leaning away from the others. A bookmark poked out of the top of "Black Beauty" and "Oliver Twist" lay against it. I wished Joseph were here, he would know these books. He would laugh. He would...

I stopped still, and my breath left me. *I'm never going to see him again.*

I didn't turn at the now-familiar squeak of wheels.

"Untie her please." Grant's voice was scarily calm.

The guard severed the tie with a knife, and my arms snapped back into place. I rolled my shoulders.

"You may leave," he said to the guard, wheeling around me and parking behind the chair-less desk.

I stood motionless in the center of the room. My feet were caught in the quicksand of this opulent rug, the pills still rolled into my sock. I shifted to one leg.

"There were many other ways to try and get what you wanted," Grant said, his hands flat on his desk, his arms cutting a sharp right angle at the elbow.

I eyed the letter opener lying across the green, vinyl desktop. A computer screen shone to one side. I could just stab him. He was going to kill me anyway. My hands wouldn't move.

He noticed me eyeing it, placed his hand on the letter opener, and swept it into his desk drawer, shutting it with a bang.

"I saw your hysterics at the holding cells on here," he said, tapping the screen. "You wanted to be with your friend, Gwen is it? Ransacking a dead woman's home was not the way. It was..." He paused, stroking his beard, and I wanted to slap it from his face. "...unacceptable. Have you no respect? Now you will not be allowed to view her procedure. I had wanted you to see her heal, to see that I'm not the monster you think I am."

I pressed my lips together. This man was so arrogant, so sure of himself, that he wasn't even going to ask me why I broke in to Este's compound. He just assumed he knew the answer and presumed he was right. I stepped forward and he arched an eyebrow, a dark smile tugging at his bristled lips.

My voice grew in my throat until it was too loud for me to hold in. "What do you care what I think of you?"

His eyes narrowed. He slicked his hand through his thinning hair and shook his head, as if he wasn't really sure either.

"You represent an element of rebellion, an exercising of will that I need to understand to quash. It is a threat to the health of our society."

I snorted. I was just one girl. I didn't represent anything. He wanted to see me suffer. That was the only reason for any of this—punishment. He could push me as far as he liked, but he would never understand me.

"Is Denis all right?" I asked stupidly.

"My son is perfectly fine. He's my son; he's designed to be resilient."

I wanted to say, *No, he's designed to be afraid of you.*

"What are you going to do to me now?" I asked.

He stroked his jaw; he was enjoying teasing this out, stretching me over the rack. "Nothing yet. I have a few more things I need from you. Come here." He beckoned with his finger.

I approached him out of pure fear. My body moved like a puppet. He had a hold of the strings and he jerked them forward.

"Give me your hand," he said, holding his own palm upward.

I did as I was told.

He ran his forefinger over my bony wrist and turned it over. Taking a scanner from his desk, he scanned my code. It had been so long that it felt like a stab in the guts.

It beeped, and he released me.

"Now go to your room," he said, waving me away.

"Wh… what?" I stammered.

"Leave!"

I stumbled out of the room, dreading each step, wondering what horrible plan he had for me. Because there was no way I was getting away with this. None at all.

Judith met me at the door to our room. The guard tagged her and left. I was always accompanied, never alone.

I hoped she would tell me. "Where's Denis? Is he badly hurt?" I asked, gripping her arm. My hand slipped off her satin shirt.

She eyed me suspiciously for a moment. "He's in the hospital. Broken nose, bruised jaw, mild concussion. He'll be fine."

I sucked in my bottom lip, completely ashamed of myself. This was not me.

She ushered me inside and shut the door. Her eyes intense, her face stripped of its usual mask.

She pushed me against the wall, suddenly stronger than I would have thought possible. Her perfume stung my eyes, and her breath smelled like candy. Her face was so close when she whispered, "Did you get the pills?" I gasped, closing my eyes and trying to make sense of her asking me that question.

"Rosa, this is important. Did you find them?"

I nodded. *Had I been I wrong about her?*

"Give them to me," she demanded.

I shook my head slowly. I was swimming in a pool of disbelief, barely keeping my head above water.

"How do I know you won't give them to Grant?"

"Listen to me very carefully, Rosa. Denny told me what you're planning. He trusted me. So you can trust me. Besides, you won't be leaving this room until…" she paused, licking her glossy lips, "until Daddy's procedure. You have no other way of getting them to the test subject."

I straightened my back and dusted off the shock. "Her name is Gwen."

Judith jutted her palm towards my face, frustrated.

"Whatever. You know you don't have a choice. You know I'm tired of pretending. We all are. I can help you."

I leaned down and pulled the pills from my sock. They were heavy in my fingers. They were the solution and end to so many of my problems and yet, I didn't want to let them go. She shoved her hand at me impatiently, like a teacher waiting for you to surrender your contraband. I winced as I dropped them in her palm. Fingers with nails painted in rainbows folded over Gwen's only chance of survival.

"I don't trust you," I whispered, fighting back tears at my complete lack of control in this situation.

"You don't need to. You just need to trust that I will do this one thing. I know it's best for all of us," she said.

I'm not one of you. I'm not part of your 'us', I thought, *but I'm not sure I know who I am anymore.*

She stepped away from me, tucking the pills into her breast pocket of shiny pink satin. "I have to go," she said, pausing at the bathroom mirror to fix her hair and lipstick.

I caught her arm as she started to open the door. "Wait. When *is* the test day?"

She looked confused as she answered, "I thought you must have known they've changed the dates. It's today."

I let her go. Everything rushed past me, and the air sucked from the room.

I fell to my knees and prayed someone would tell me what happened to Gwen.

39

Judgement

JOSEPH

Two more days and I'd be home. Although home was not the right word. No, I'd be back where I'd started. Changed so much, I barely recognized myself.

I am years older and miles sadder.

Elise balanced on the railway line. Every now and then, she'd steady herself on my shoulder. She seemed happy. I tried to be a mirror. I wanted to be in the moment like her, not looking back and definitely not into the future. There was nothing to be gained except pain. I cringed when a small window opened onto images I was trying so hard to forget. My past was filled with the faces of lives I'd stolen.

My eyes dropped to the orange gravel beneath my shoes. We never walked this part of the line the first time. I knew *she* rode the Spinners to Pau on this part... I shook my head and stared out over the forest below. The snow was still having a hard time getting a grip on the branches, but every day it got colder and bleaker.

Pelo strode up to me and clapped me on the shoulder. "Tell me, young Joseph, can you remind me what your parents look like and their names? It's been a long time since I last saw them." The future. I didn't want to think about the future.

Desh answered for me. "Didn't you always say your dad looked just like you except he didn't have a broken nose?"

"Yes," I nodded, tipping my head to the sky. The pale blue reminded me of Orry's one blue eye. It had always been lighter than *hers*.

"Oh, yes, that's right! I remember now. Such a big man, just like you," Pelo recalled, his eyes gazing on some far away dot on the horizon.

Dad had felt so bad about breaking my nose. Memories were trying to break the bag I'd shoved them in. Her sweet, angry face when I'd told her how I'd broke it. Her small fingers curling into a fist like she was going to hunt the culprit down and make them pay.

Stop. Please stop it. I want you out of my head, please, just for a moment. There was no peace.

Pelo coughed, his hand still gripping my tense shoulder. "And their names were Jonathan and...?"

"Jonathan and Stephanie Sulle," I replied. "My mother looks like, well, she looks a lot like Apella, except taller. Thin, fair hair, blue eyes."

Elise winked and toppled off the tracks. "Like me!"

I smiled flatly. "I guess, but older, wrong eye color... so no, not really. You really love being the center of attention, don't you?" I jabbed her ribs playfully. She giggled.

I tried to force that giggle to be something I wanted.

I thought I saw Pelo narrow his eyes in her direction but then he smiled gently. "Yes. Yes. It's coming back to me now. I'll find them, Joseph," he said reassuringly.

I sighed.

Olga toddled forward, pushing between us and grabbing Gus by the sleeve. "Can I go with Pelo? I know I'm not a Survivor, but I'd dearly love to contribute."

Gus didn't break stride, and she struggled to keep up with him. "You're not in the best shape," he said, casting a critical eye over her round body.

She wheezed as her short legs struggled to take a railway sleeper at a time. "All right, well, give me something to do."

Gus grunted and tapped his chin. "Communications."

She seemed to jump in excitement. "Yes! Fabulous! Communications."

Olga was a strange woman, but lovable. I stopped and left the tracks to find a tree to piss on, and Desh followed me.

We were engulfed in foliage immediately.

"Hey man, wait up," he puffed, snapping the branches back.

"Desh, what do you want?"

He stopped, waist deep in frozen bracken. "I just wanted to check on you. I thought it may be hard walking the tracks, you know..."

It was. "It's not, I'm ok. You can stop worrying."

He shifted from side to side, unsure.

"You're sure?" he asked.

Make an effort, I told myself. I moved to him and punched his arm lightly.

"Stop fussing over me." I gave him a strained smile. "I'm doing okay."

He took the smile on my face at its word and seemed to relax. "Good. But if you're not, you can tell me. We still have a lot of things to talk about, Joe."

I waved him off. "And I still need to pee, man. Seriously, can't a guy have some privacy?" I laughed.

Desh jumped. "Oh sorry," he said, and he walked away.

I couldn't keep up with my lies. I didn't even know what the truth was anymore.

After, I caught up with them and slung an arm over Desh's shoulder. I joked and laughed, until soon, I'd almost fooled myself.

We camped just off the tracks at the beginnings of a black rock seam that would lead us all the way to Pau Brazil. It shone wet with rain and gleamed sharply like a threat under the moonlight.

This was our last night of being able to relax a little, and some people were taking full advantage. A large fire roared and warmed the already pink cheeks of most of the group. We hadn't seen any signs of Woodlands' soldiers, choppers, anything.

My head was swimming. Whenever I moved, the ground shifted beneath my feet. My thoughts were muddled but kind of clear—clear in their intention to keep this feeling going anyway. So when Elise handed me another drink and knocked it with her own, I gladly took it, drinking it quickly. Anything to hang on to the numb, almost happy, cloud I was on.

She put her hand on my knee. I looked down at it like it shouldn't be there, but my brain didn't care to stop her. I let her lean her head on my shoulder, and the flames warm my flushed face. Across the fire, Matt's eyes darkened with concern, but instead of acknowledging him, I turned away. I laughed a hollow laugh and threw my head to the stars, which swirled like a tornado above me.

Her hand moved up and down my thigh slowly, in a caring way.

She stood and offered her hand. I took it. I let her lead me away from the group, through the wooded area, and up to the entrance of a railway tunnel. Warning feelings spiked for a moment, but I poured my drink over them. The heady, underwater feeling resumed and I stumbled after her, her pale hand pulling me gently into the entrance.

She tittered. "It's so dark in here."

I wiped my mouth with the back of my hand and dropped my can. "Well it is a tunnel."

The noise of my drink hitting the floor startled her and she grabbed my arms. "What was that?"

I stood facing her. She was so tall that her eyes almost met mine.

"Nothing, it was just my beer," I slurred, my voice thick and stupid sounding. I shook my head, trying to clear it. It had the opposite effect, making me dizzy. I stumbled back, and she came with me. She still had a hold of my arms, and she was running her thumbs up and down my biceps.

"Well, at least I've got you to protect me," she said. I winced. I couldn't protect anyone.

I took a step away from her. "You can take care of yourself, Elise."

"True, but I'd rather you did it for me."

She moved closer, only a little air between our bodies. I took another step back and was up against the tunnel wall with nowhere to go.

"Just pretend for a second, that I need your help, your protection..." Her voice was light, playful.

"Mmhm," I managed, rocking a little, the alcohol moving from a nice feeling to a sick feeling.

Her breath was warm on my face. "I don't need much from you, Joe, just this..." She took the last step so there was nothing between us.

For a moment, it felt good. Her lips were soft and warm on my neck. There was no small callous, in the corner, where she chewed on it when she was thinking. She pressed me against the wall, her breasts squashed against my chest. The wet stones behind me seeped into my shirt as she ran her hands under my clothes, her smooth palms gliding over my back.

Her hands were like silk. She didn't have a chipped fingernail that always seemed to catch on my skin.

I moaned and grasped at her waist. She felt strong. Her hipbones didn't jut out. I grabbed her hips and pulled her closer. She didn't put her ear to my heart. She just pushed against me harder, until I was bending into the curve of the stones behind me. Her lips went to mine, and our mouths parted. The taste of her lips was wrong. I breathed in through my nose and the scent of her hair, like artificial lemon, was wrong. My chin dipped to meet her head, but I didn't need to lean down very far to reach her. *Wrong.* She didn't need to stand on her toes to kiss me. *It was all wrong.*

I battled with myself. The swirl of too many drinks and my self-pity was winning.

And I didn't care.

I switched places with her, so her back was against the wall, and pulled her shirt over her head. She was breathing hard. I didn't know what I was doing. I had ceased to be. Nothing mattered, because I just didn't want to feel this way anymore. I kissed her neck, and she gasped. Her short hair didn't get in the way. *Wrong.* She started unbuttoning my shirt. *Wrong.* I stilled her hasty hands and pulled it over my head in one swift movement. She touched me, and it felt warm and cold at the same time.

Her hands moved down as she toyed with my pants button. I paused. But I was fast tipping over into oblivion, which was what I wanted. *Right?*

Was I going to do this? My body answered and I allowed her to flick the button open, her hands dancing over my waistband.

A rustle near the entrance caused us both to freeze, but then nothing followed.

"I've wanted this from the day I met you," she whispered breathlessly, which sounded cheesy.

I tried to ignore the blaring in my head. The voice and the warning. It was louder now as the alcohol started to wear off. Because I didn't really want *her*, I hadn't been thinking of *her*, of *this* at all. She was a distraction and I wanted her to stop talking, to stop making me think about things.

Before she could say anything else, I closed my mouth over hers.

She moaned in approval as my hand moved to her bra, and my fingers fumbled with the clasp.

A crunch on the gravel and a loud sigh stopped me dead. "You've given up," he said, just a shadow in the entrance of the tunnel. "You think she's dead."

My arms dropped to my sides like lead weights. Because that wasn't even it. This had nothing to do with how I felt about Rosa and everything to do with how I felt about me. What was left of me.

Rash stepped into the tunnel, collected Elise's clothes, and threw them at her.

"Leave," he said flatly.

"Joe?" she questioned.

It was all wearing off now, my legs started to shake, and I crumpled to the ground. I reached out my hands and grasped the rails in front of me. "Please. I think you should go. I'm sorry."

She sighed haughtily. I felt bad that I'd dragged her into my mess. It wasn't fair.

"I think you were right all those weeks ago, Joe. We should have just been friends." She patted my back gently. "I hope it's not too late for that."

God. I didn't deserve her kindness. She pulled her shirt on and left.

"Wait!" I shouted after her, and I heard Rash groan. She turned around. "Can you find your way back?"

Her head bobbed. "You're a good guy, Joe. Don't worry about me. I plotted this route hours ago. How do you think I got you here so easily?" she said, unapologetically.

Right. I was just a clueless idiot. She tramped down the hill towards the camp.

What the hell had I done?

I heaved but nothing came out. I couldn't even get that relief.

Rash put his hand on my back. "I'd punch you, but at this point, it'd be like kicking a dog when it's already chewed its own legs off and it's begging me to end its suffering."

No one could end my suffering. I gripped the rails like I was trying to pull them from the ground. Rash stood over me in judgment. As he should.

"I haven't given up. I know she's alive," I said to his darkening shadow.

He took a step back from me, in disgust.

"You know, she chose *you*. And I guess I'd always assumed it was for a reason, that you deserved her."

"Maybe I did. But I don't anymore."

"And what? You thought you should just add an extra nail to your coffin? Why the hell would you do this, do... her?" He pointed down the hill.

A self-pitying sob escaped my lips. "I don't know. I was trying to forget."

Rash's exasperated voice pinned me to the ground. "Forget what? Rosa?"

No and Yes. I shook my head, empty of answers. "You don't know what I've done, Rash."

"Do you?" he asked sharply.

I sat back in the gravel. "What do you mean?"

"Do you actually remember what you did?" he challenged, pointing a finger at my heart.

"I remember enough." Their faces after. All the blood.

He ran his hands through his hair, clasped them behind his head, and a landslide of curses poured from his mouth. "Get up."

"What?" I sniffed.

"Get up, man," he snapped angrily. "If you really believe she's alive, then stop being such a dickhead. Ugh! What the hell do you think you're doing? Get it together. Like now. And I suggest you talk to Deshi, like really talk to him about what happened. You're an idiot. And right now, I should kick your ass for it."

I stood up. He was right. I nearly did the worst thing I could have ever done to her. We wouldn't have come back from it.

I was broken. But if I'd slept with Elise, there would have been no way of putting me, or us, back together. I'd like to think I would have stopped myself, but I just didn't know.

I owed Rash my life.

40

Sentence

ROSA

Colors cross my life unexpectedly. They come in streams and strokes. But at the moment, in this part, where I can no longer find myself, they are broad splashes of red against black with deep fingernails scratches dragging across the surface. Nothing else. Because I am losing my light.

I had to fight off darker thoughts. I had a shield in my hands. It was gold; it felt light and warm in my hands. I paced around Judith's room, picking up random items, inspecting them and throwing them back into place. If this didn't work, I didn't even know what would happen to Gwen. Dr. Yashin never told me. I could tell from the way she hugged herself, the way her eyes pooled with moisture, shining like glass, that it was bad. Really bad. Gwen didn't deserve to die like that. I shook my head and tried to stop myself from going back to the thought that continually plagued me. Did anyone *deserve* to die?

"No. Stop," I said to my reflection, slapping my hands down on the dresser, beads and necklaces jingling and swaying in front of the mirror me. I couldn't think like that.

I sat on my bed and clasped my hands tight, then released them, throwing my hands above my head. I didn't know what to do with myself. Falling back on the bed, I closed my eyes.

Joseph, where are you now? I know you're thinking of me. I feel it. It presses out of my chest like rays of light splitting my ribs. I want you to know that you're always on my mind, in my heart. Memories will keep me going, but they're like feeding a spoonful of rice to a starving person. It's not enough, never enough. I need the real thing.

But they were all I had.

I breathed in. Filling my lungs with something other than false air and perfume.

Do you remember our first kiss?

To me, it was an explosion. A realization that maybe I could be more and have more than scowls and disappointment. *Your lips...* I clutched my chest, a sharp pang stretching and snapping over my heart. This hurt almost as much as it helped. His lips had felt like a home I never thought I could have. One I definitely didn't deserve.

I let out a strained, "Oh."

I didn't feel that way now. Joseph was mine. It took me a long time to believe it, to accept it.

I reached out to the air and felt him settle beside me on the bed. If he were here, he would wiggle his arm under my torso. I'd complain that it was digging into my back. I'd roll towards his chest, and he'd fold over me. I'd say, *Your arm weighs a hundred kilos! It's suffocating me.* He would chuckle, and I would revel in the sound. I would want to make it solid and wear it. I'd sling my leg over his and try to cover him with my small, insubstantial body. His heart would beat steadily; mine would rattle and jump impatiently.

'I love you' were words I wouldn't need to say. They existed in our intertwined limbs, our mixing breath. Our beautiful child.

"Orry," I whispered. It had been weeks. Was that too long? Would he know me?

A tear slid across my cheek and into my ear.

She didn't knock. She slipped through the door and stepped lightly over the carpet until she was standing over the bed, her hands pressed into the sheets as she leaned over my still frame.

"You're sleeping?"

I opened one eye and grimaced. "No." I was dreaming. Awake but dreaming.

I sat up on my elbows and waited. Judith smiled. Which could have meant anything from 'my hair looks good today' to 'Gwen survived.'

Judith handed me a sandwich, which I unwrapped and took a large bite.

"Well?" I snapped, my mouth full of bread. I was getting tired of her stretched grin.

Her face composed as she flicked crumbs from the quilt. She looked at me through slit eyes, silver eye shadow stuck in the folds of her lids.

"Your friend survived. I managed to slip the pills to her before the procedure. And then, when it was time to take them, I made sure everyone was looking at me," she said grandly, pointing to her chest. "I also made sure she had privacy when it was time to void." Her mouth screwed up unpleasantly at the word.

"Where is she? Can I see her?" I asked desperately, clutching the quilt.

She laughed, or more like cackled. "Of course you can't *see* her. She's back in the holding cells. But I can tell you she walked there. With her own two legs!" Judith said proudly, as if she'd performed a miracle.

Relief stuck in my throat. Gwen was alive, she walked, but her safety was very temporary. Each part of this plan was like climbing a crumbling staircase. Each step you mounted left the one behind disintegrating just as your foot left it. I was hanging in midair, mid-step, wondering what to do next.

I swallowed the sweet-tasting bread and asked, "So what happens now?"

She went to her dresser, sat down, and started pulling pins out of her hair or her head, who knew?

"Daddy's procedure will take place tonight. He wants you there."
Tonight.

I let my head fall back against the headboard. It was so soon. Too soon. My face must have said it all because Judith commented, "You needn't look so panicked. You don't have to do anything. In fact, the only thing you must do is *nothing*."

Just do nothing.

Do nothing and watch Grant die.

41

You Were Wrong

JOSEPH

I did manage to vomit. All the alcohol hit at once and all my disgust in myself came charging out of me.

Rash jumped back. "Watch the shoes, man," he yelled.

I wiped my mouth with my shirt. "Sorry."

My head cleared enough for me to realize something. "Hey, you said I should talk to Desh about what really happened. What do you even know about it?" I asked, my words still slurred.

Rash swore and helped me up, yanking me away from the tunnel. "I can't think clearly with that damn smell. God dude, have you eaten anything except beer and spirits today?"

I shook my head.

We stood on the railway tracks facing each other, well, me looking down on him. The clouds cleared a little, and I could just make out his stern expression.

"What do you think happens every time you disappear for some of your 'alone' time?" he asked, making air quotes.

"You make it sound so dirty," I said, instantly regretting it.

Rash shoved me in the chest. "Don't make me hit you."

I kind of wanted him to. I slipped my hand through my hair. "I'm sorry. I'm an idiot."

"Something we can all agree on!" Rash swore again and stared up at the stars. "Deshi is worried about you, and so are the others. He needed to talk to someone, and I was there. He told me what really happened. And don't worry, he didn't tell anyone else. I don't even want to get started on the fact that you blamed Rosa for it when you told Matthew."

I took a step back, preparing for him to punch me. But he didn't. He sighed and reached out to me, awkwardly patting my arm. "Look, I understand guilt," he muttered. I shook my head, I doubted it, but let him continue. "I know the faces are always there, waiting in your dreams, ready to torture you. You've got to let it go. You have to understand that part of the night was not your fault. You were trying to live." He took a deep breath. "And I know I've given you hell, but it's not because I don't understand *why* you left her. It's because I miss her, and I wish it had gone a different way. Honestly, I wish it had been you left on that table."

I stepped towards him. "I wish that too, Rash. Every day."

Rash threw his hands up in the air. "Ok. That's enough heart to heart for me. I think I'm gonna be sick myself. Just talk to Deshi, get yourself sorted out. She's going to need you."

He stormed away from me, swearing and kicking rocks as he went. And it hurt me to watch him, because he was so like Rosa. But this time, I let it in. It was better to feel something than nothing at all.

He was right about everything. Look where hiding from my problems had got me. But facing them seemed impossible, like if I tried, I would lose whatever was left of me.

I had to talk to Desh.

I stayed under the bath of moonlight for a while, letting my fear subside before I moved. And I cried. I cried for what I'd lost, what I might lose, and what I might learn.

The camp was quiet. Most were sleeping. Olga was propped up in her sleeping bag, grasping a handheld. When she saw me, she blinked up, her mouth crinkled, her eyes startled.

"Sorry Olga, I didn't mean to frighten you," I whispered.

She clicked the off button atop the screen and dropped the handheld in her lap. "Joseph! Where have you been? I was just sending a quick message to Palma letting them know of our next move and where to meet if they want to join us for the liberation of the children and pregnant girls." She made it sound like a party she was inviting them to.

"Right... well, I just needed to talk to Desh." I picked over the snoring bodies until I found him, sleeping neatly on a rolled-up jacket, his hand clasped over his stomach, his face peaceful. I nudged him with my foot and he snorted.

"Desh. Wake up."

His eyes opened slowly. "What?" he groaned, still half asleep.

"I'm ready to talk," I murmured, aware of all the listening ears around us.

He properly awoke and sat up on his elbows. "Okay," he said warily.

"Not here," I insisted quietly.

We got up and walked away from the camp.

Out of the corner of my eye, I thought I saw a screen light up. But the moon was fully exposed now. It was probably just light reflecting off a saucepan or cup.

We walked for about half an hour. Desh huffing and puffing nervously. Streaks of pink showed through the trees. Their icy branches looked splattered in purple and pink paint as the sun started to rise. We stopped and Desh turned around, his face anguished, a couple of tears rolling slowly down his dark cheeks. He sniffed and wiped them away.

"What's wrong?" I asked, scared of what he might say.

"I need to tell you something," he began, and then he stared down at his feet and wiped his eyes again. "Este tortured me. She threatened me. She told me they knew where Hessa was and if I didn't finish the healer, they would go after him and the rest of you. I took my time, made mistakes I would never usually make, so you had longer to get away from the Wall. But every hour I wasted, she made me pay for, dearly. I hated her. She was a crazy, obsessed monster," he rattled off so fast I could barely keep up.

I put a hand on his shoulder. He was shaking. "It's all right, Desh, I know. But she can't hurt you anymore." *Because I shot her.*

He glanced up at me, his eyes red. The sun filtered through the bleak, black branches and hit me in the face. I closed my eyes.

He shook his head vehemently. "No Joe, you don't know. I watched you; I didn't help fight off all those men. Those men were going to kill you. They tried to… But you were so strong, like a bull being speared over and over, but you kept fighting. I saw you pull one off only to have another jump on you. Every single thing you did was in defense of your life. Every… single… thing." He annunciated each word slowly. "I could have helped you, but I didn't. I was too scared to die."

I flinched at his description. I couldn't remember much. I just remember the part after, where they were all dead in front of me.

"It's all right, Desh. I'm not angry with you for hanging back."

He avoided my eyes. "You don't understand. Este was watching you so intently that she didn't even notice me. She didn't see the gun in my hand. She had no clue. You were fighting for your life and instead of helping you, I calmly walked over and shot her."

My legs weakened. I leaned back and braced myself against a tree. "You killed Este?" My voice was as rough as the bark I was leaning against.

Desh looked at me then, his brown eyes completely still, calm. "Yes. I killed her, and I'm not even remotely sorry about it. She threatened my son, my family." He paused for breath. "You know that's one of the reasons I love you, Joe. You've been taking this so hard because you're too good inside. You're a good man."

I wished people would stop saying that.

I stumbled and gripped the tree with both hands behind me. "You're a good man too, Desh," I managed.

"I know. But not like you, which is fine. I just wish you'd let me tell you sooner. Maybe I should have tried harder to get you to listen, but part of me was happy to put it in the past. I'm sorry."

I waved my hand at him. "It doesn't matter. I still… um… those other men…"

"Would have killed you."

But I still left her behind. I still nearly slept with Elise. It would not be that simple. These deaths and actions were not written in chalk that could be washed away. They were carved all over my skin.

I could have kept it to myself. Maybe I should have, but I felt like I had to change the way I'd been dealing with things.

"Desh, I nearly slept with Elise," I confessed. The words tasted like vomit as I said them.

He raised his eyebrows and took a deep breath, sighing. "She'll forgive you."

I leaned my head on the tree trunk and stared up at the sky. The pink was fading, yellows the color of yolk taking over, shining like gold.

"I don't deserve it."

His voice was solid and sure. "Yes, you do."

I chuckled because I didn't know what else to do. It was like he'd plucked a pebble off the two-ton weight I was carrying. Maybe I used to be a good man. Maybe that was why this had been so hard for me to accept, to move on. But I liked who I used to be, and I missed being that man. "I'll try and believe you."

I worried that the Joseph she fell in love with was unreachable. But I had a choice. I could let what happened with Elise drag me further down. Or, I could use it as a push to grab a hold of the rope and pull myself out.

I turned my head to the clouds. The sunrises and sunsets I'd seen since I'd lost her had washed right over me. I couldn't see beauty. I was motionless. But for the first time, I could see hope in that gold streak in the sky. I wasn't going to mend instantly but talking about it had eased my pain and made me see the truth of that night. Each step was a small one, but at least I wasn't standing still anymore.

42.

Devour

ROSA

Judith held a dress up in front of my body, so just my scowling face stuck up from the frill-necked collar. "I think this will please him."

I wanted to ask her how she could be so calm when she was about to witness her father's death, but I held my tongue. There was something chilling in the way she moved around the room. The way she meticulously did her hair and makeup. I tried my best not to engage.

Snatching the dress from her fingertips, I went to the bathroom to change.

In the mirror, my reflection held too many secrets. I needed to compose myself and change my face. I stripped down and put on the hideous dress, the taffeta fabric ringing my throat intimidatingly. My roots were starting to show. Dark brown, almost black, hair ran in a stripe down my part. I smiled, a small part of me was returning. Then I took a cavernous breath that scraped the bottom of my diaphragm and tried to convince myself that it was going to be okay.

A knock signaled it was time to go.

I was surprised to see Denis' face when I opened the door. His nose set in plaster, his eyes ringed with deep purple bruises. He tipped his chin at me, and winced at the effort. He held the door open for his sister, each movement controlled and calm. We joined him in the hall and walked towards the lift.

There were no nervous glances exchanged—nothing. Just calm breaths mixed with my panicked ones. They were ready for this. I was not. I smoothed my dress and tried not to see rivers of blood running between the delicate folds of fabric.

When the lift opened in the garage, Grant and his wife were waiting by a car. The green one. We were told to turn around while the guard helped Grant into the driver's seat.

"Get in," he barked, while I stood there agape, agitated and itchy. I scratched my neck, and he rolled his eyes at me.

Judith got in, then Denis opened his arms and ushered me inside. The engine roared to life and I shuddered, wedged shoulder to shoulder with Grant's murderous children.

Grant grinned as he revved the engine. It looked strange on him. Like the Cheshire cat had loaned him his teeth. Camille, his wife, patted his leg. "Shouldn't we blindfold the girl, dear?"

Grant pressed a button on the dashboard, and the car rolled backwards. "No need." His eyes found me in the rearview mirror. I gulped at his gaze. His plans for me were in that gaze, cutting me into bite-sized pieces like a laser. He didn't need to say more. It was clear my time was nearly up.

Camille wrapped the fur around her shoulders a little tighter. The fox's glass eyes stared at me in the backseat, seeming to say, *You don't belong here.* We drove out of the garage, followed by another car filled with soldiers.

Judith picked at her nails and Denis sat upright, rigid. His earphones were missing. *He* was missing.

Grant drove at a snail's pace, cursing every splash of mud that sullied the paintwork and every squeak of the windscreen wipers. It was sleeting until it turned to flurry. I shivered as ice pelted the windows, barely paying attention to where we were going, only that it was away from Grant's home. We went through gates, which the soldiers had to open for us, futilely covering their heads with their arms as they tried to shield themselves from the weather. I exhaled sadly, missing the forest, fires, and wolves. Wondering if this was my last winter.

Suddenly we dipped, the suspension creaking. Grant drove down a well-lit concrete slope into an underground park. He slammed the brakes on when we reached the bottom, our heads surging forward, and ordered us to leave the car. He seemed a little nervous. A guard quickly came to Grant's door with the wheelchair. We turned before being asked this time.

Grant was arranged in his chair. He wheeled ahead of us eagerly. "Come!" he said excitedly. I could tell he was picturing himself walking, striding proudly out of this place. Guilt. Displaced, misplaced guilt crept up my skin like ants searching for a crumb.

We followed, with ten guards in our wake, their boots thudding on the concrete in unison.

This was the end, the beginning.

I crumpled my dress in my hands and held my breath as the lift shot upwards. Mirrors lined the four walls, so all I could see were many sets of Grant's excited eyes dancing under the harsh light. He turned his head slowly to me and his lips spread wide. His glare was cruelly triumphant. I let out a small, hysterical laugh, wondering if he wanted his legs back just so he could kick me with them.

The doors parted, and the smell of a hundred dishes twirled together into one delicious stream hit my nose. A banquet flush with flowers toppling over vases as centerpieces and tall candles wavering in the air conditioning slapped my eyes.

People were gathered in small groups but when Grant rolled into the room, they all turned and started clapping. Beaming, proud faces with an undercurrent of fear of the terrible man glistened in the warm light. I stared down, hiding behind the siblings. Diamond shapes and messy scratches printed on the garish carpet greeted my eyes.

The Grant family stepped forward and I followed like a baby elephant holding the tale of its mother, taking in the table, the plastic chairs with brown velvet cushions, and the glass window that enveloped one whole wall of the large room. Below the window, metal glinted and the glass coffin hung suspended in the air. We were in some sort of amphitheater.

He was going to have a party and then make us all watch as he died.

Two guards grabbed my arms relatively gently and took me to a chair. The eyes of the guests trailed me across the room.

One guard leaned down and spoke to me slowly, like I was slow myself. "Now you stay put, Miss."

I nodded briefly, distracted by the party and the guests. I recognized with shock that both Superior Sekimbo and Superior Poltinov were present. They looked older than their posters, but still. I shrank smaller into my chair as Sekimbo noticed and approached me, rolling over like a giant dark pudding. He held a plate of food in front of him like an offering.

"So you're *the* girl?" he bellowed, his voice like smooth stones being rubbed against each other.

"I am *a* girl. I don't know if I'm *the* girl," I said, leaning away from his alcoholic breath.

He grabbed my cheeks and squeezed them. "So small, so thin," he muttered, his large cheeks wobbling as he shook his head. "Here, take a cake." He shoved a small cupcake at my face. I shook my head. I felt too sick to eat.

He placed his hand on top of my head, his broad, flat fingers squeezing as he tried to hold me still. I could feel the violence in his voice as he said, "Wyatt said you were... uncooperative." He was going to shove that cake down my throat.

Grant's stringy voice sailed over the crowd and Sekimbo released me, the cake tumbling to the floor. He leered and swayed from drunkenness as he twisted to face Grant.

"I'd like to thank you for coming to this meeting and this celebration." People clapped. "We'll discuss business first. I know you are concerned about recent developments in the towns. It is true we are struggling to keep control of Radiata and Birchton. We have lost Palma. Helicopters have been unable to approach, and a significant portion of our army has defected. The citizens of Palma have weapons and are firing."

The crowd murmured, and Grant's face showed slight frustration.

"Please, please..." he started, pumping his hands. "We are still in control of the majority, and I have complete faith that we will regain it in the towns that are rebelling. All is not lost. We know the terrorists have recruited some of our residents. But," he put his finger to the air, "we have our own operative and have just received word of the terrorists' next target." I leaned forward.

His eyes found me and bored into my head like black drills. "Isn't it wonderful when everything just clicks into place?" he said, ignoring the confused faces of the other guests. "Like it was simply meant to be." He swept his arm in an arc and looked to the ceiling. "Written in the stars."

Sekimbo laughed heartily, holding his belly and slurring, "Get on with it, Wyatt. I have women waiting for me at home."

Grant's eyes snapped to him in irritation. "As we know, the terrorists have been projecting a video showing a very one-sided view of what we are trying to achieve here. It has upset the community unnecessarily, but I fear it is too late to use reason to calm the situation. No…" He shook his head like he was sorry. But I knew he wasn't. "We must send a clear message that uprisings will not be tolerated." He paused for effect.

"Tell them, Daddy," Judith encouraged.

"I suggest we make our own video," he said, weird mischief in his tone.

Everyone was still very quiet, hanging on his every word, and he loved it. He clicked his fingers and someone brought a large roll of thick, blue paper to the front, laying it down on an empty table to Grant's right.

The guests moved in like moths to a flame and Grant hungrily absorbed their attention, grabbing at their silken wings and shoving them in his pockets. "I had already selected Pau Brazil as the site for personal reasons." My hands dug into the underneath of my chair. It felt gummy and strange. "But now that our operative, Olga, has told us Pau Brazil is the rebels' next target, it seems like the perfect opportunity to strike. We can show the terrorists what we're capable of and issue the most severe of warnings to the other towns before the terrorists have a chance to reach them."

Olga? No, no, no. That can't be true.

"No," I whispered, feeling everything I knew being shaken and poured down the drain.

Poltinov spoke, his aged voice slipping over his words. "Er, how do you propose we, er, strike? *Cough, cough, ahem.* We don't have their kinds of weapons." Then he muttered, "There never, er, seemed a need, *cough*, to develop them."

"And Wyatt let the one man go who could have whipped us up a few bombs and high tech guns," Sekimbo shouted.

Grant's stare was the sharp end of a knife when he looked at Sekimbo, who in turn, was unflappable.

"Come," Grant said, beckoning with his finger, which then flew in semicircle and landed on the large drawing. "These are the original drawings President Grant commissioned before Signing Day. See here…" I couldn't see what he was pointing at. "We haven't had to use this before, but I think now is the time."

"Which Ring and how many people are we talking about, Superior Grant? We can't afford to lose too many workers," someone I didn't recognize asked.

Again, Grant's eyes slid to mine when he said, "Ring Two. Roughly three thousand citizens." My mother's Ring. I stood to try and see what he was pointing at, to understand the plan, but a guard pushed my shoulder down.

"If you think, er, it will work then that, er, seems like an acceptable loss."

Acceptable loss? I screamed on the inside until my lungs started to peel away from my ribs.

"How does it work?" Sekimbo asked, pushing himself to the front like a barge.

Grant smiled, though it was more like a snarl.

"It's very simple. But it must be done manually from beneath the town. I will do it myself. We already have cameras all over the Ring that can record the incident. We simply flick the switch and show the people what happens when you rebel against the Woodlands."

What switches? I couldn't see anything from where I was forced to sit; all I knew was thousands of people were about to be killed in a 'simple' way, and my mother and sister were part of that number of acceptable losses. It was my fault he chose Pau. Mine and Olga's. That unassuming, egg-shaped woman had deceived us all.

I writhed in my chair, impotent, and clamped my mouth over the indecision hooking into my lips.

The three remaining Superiors voted unanimously for Grant's plan.

After the vote, they strolled around the room, eating, drinking, and socializing like it was easy to kill. They didn't see us as people. We were numbers, workers, losses and gains. We were the foundations they stood on with their swollen, over-fed bodies. That was all.

Judith approached me, squatting down to reach my eyes, which were wide and panicked like a gun was to my head. She placed a plate of food on my lap.

"Rosa, eat, you'll need your strength," she crooned as she pulled out her lip gloss and applied it while she spoke. "You know I've enjoyed having you around. I might actually miss you."

I stared down at the colorful, oily food, and my stomach turned. I wanted dried meat and stale bread. Fresh game roasted on the fire. Not this. I poked it with my finger with distaste. "What do you mean, miss me?"

She stood and covered her mouth with her dainty, peeling hand, her eyes filled with devilish delight. The secret on her lips was so delicious.

"You'll see," she said, stepping away from me and swaying her hips as she walked. When no one was looking, I picked up a cream puff and threw it at the back of her head. She stumbled forward, and then snapped around to glare at me. She was about to turn me in when Grant cleared his throat and called for everyone's attention.

His hand shook, just a small tick, tick, tick, as he waved everyone over. The guard dumped me out of my chair and pushed me forward. The crowd of drunken gluttons laughed and then whispered as Grant hushed them.

"Dear friends and family, it has been years since my accident. Just one misstep, one literal slip in my life, has caused so much pain and suffering. I must admit I have struggled daily with my condition. It has not been easy." He paused for dramatic effect and wiped his mouth with his hand. "But now, through great personal sacrifice and commitment, I have found a cure." I couldn't help myself. I scoffed. The laugh quickly turned to hatred emanating from my eyes like fire. So many people had died to get him here. "Today... I walk!" he shouted proudly. I leaned in, ready to slap his face, but the guard had a hold on me.

"Please join in my triumph as I am placed into the healer a paraplegic and step out on my own two legs."

Everyone clapped and cheered. Denis and Judith the loudest of all. For a moment, I forgot what was about to happen and all I could think was how selfish he was. How could a person put his need to walk above other peoples' lives?

I was cracking open with anger like a breaking stone, my anger parting me with fissures of red-hot light.

43

The Biggest Fear

ROSA

He was ready. Nervous, but it was like he was already standing. Standing on the inside. I didn't feel ready. I turned to Denis, and he gave me the slightest of nods. He was prepared for this. He'd been planning it long before I got here. I just gave him the key. Judith beamed proudly at her father below. He looked small, almost frail from up here, in a hospital gown and black socks. Just a man.

The guard had been instructed to place me right in the front, so I had the best view. *I didn't want to see this.*

Doubts swirled around me like shards of glowing embers, stinging my skin and branding me with finality.

I clenched my fists and wrapped my legs around the legs of the chair. It wobbled as I struggled to contain my shaking and nervousness. I glanced up at Denis, who was standing by an intercom, staring down on the glass coffin.

"Good luck, Dad," he said happily, his voice nasal from the break. His head snapped to me, and his eyes narrowed in warning. I needed to control myself.

Grant's eyes flicked up to his son and daughter. Judith made an apathetic show of pressing her hand to the glass and letting it slide down, making a squeaking sound. She smiled, but it was a fake smile. A hardened smile appeared across Grants lips as he smoothed his hair from his forehead. Even from here, I could see the beads of sweat twinkling under the fluorescent lights. When his eyes lit on me, they solidified. This moment was doubly pleasing to him. After I watched him heal, he planned to execute me in some horrible way, I knew. The word 'execute' hung there like a nothing word, a word you said over and over until it lost its meaning. Grant walked, and I died. That I understood. That was always the plan. But something other than fear was creeping up on me.

Men in white coats stood around his wheelchair, holding a printout and checking through a list. Grant's hospital gown flapped under the air conditioner. The socks pulled halfway up his hairy calves making him look old.

I was there when Judith flushed the two remaining pills down the toilet. I watched as they'd circled the porcelain and disappeared. Any chance Grant had of surviving this had bobbed along in the water like tiny life preservers and dissolved with the disinfectant.

Grant's eyes were still on me. His eyebrows furrowed as he watched my reactions. My inner struggle was bubbling up onto my face. But to him, I probably looked exactly as he would expect. But *I* didn't expect my reaction. I looked scared to him because he knew *I* was about die. But I was scared because I knew *he* was about to die.

A whitecoat put his hand on Grant's shoulder and squeezed. Grant jerked and glared at the man. It was time to be lifted into the healer. One man held him under the arms and the other under his knees. Grant's butt sagged down. He looked pathetic, helpless.

Finally, Grant's eyes left mine as they laid him on the table and I thought I would relax. But everything inside was screaming.

I gripped the chair arms and tried to steady myself. Talk myself out of it. This was stupid. This could change everything. *Murderer*, whispered in my ear. This would change me and I was already so broken that pieces would go missing.

Denis took a step towards me.

Grant closed his crinkled eyes, his forehead, for once, un-furrowed. I remembered the pain of the healer and wondered what would happen when it all went wrong. Would it hurt more? I turned away from the glass. A guard placed his hand on my head and forcibly turned my face back towards the coffin.

"He wants you to watch, miss."

I hated him. He hated me. Despised me. I would hate myself if I became like him.

Nausea pressed out of me as the leftover smells of the banquet started to sour like they were sitting in a stomach. "He's going to die." It came out like a desperate, hoarse whisper.

The guard laughed. "No. That's you, Own Kind."

I shook my head, my blonde-tipped hair hitting my face. My freedom tied up with this murder was too high a price to pay. Denis took another step towards me shaking his head and smiling.

"She's trying to ruin Dad's big day," he said casually, bruises like war paint smudged under his eyes, then he leaned down and took my face in his hands, squeezing my cheeks together. His cool blue eyes danced over my face. "Don't worry. It will all be over for you soon," he said as he pushed my head back into the headrest violently, warning me to keep my mouth shut.

I bit down on my lip until blood pooled in my mouth.

I tried.

I watched them insert the needles into his back and legs carefully. Grant's face was calm. He didn't know. The men stepped back when they'd finished, and the glass case lowered. Grant's upper body flinched when the seal closed and then everyone left the room below us except the technician, who stood behind a thick piece of glass.

"Are you ready, Superior Grant?" the man asked through a microphone.

Grant laughed nervously. "I've been ready for years!"

The crowd tittered awkwardly.

Camille inhaled sharply as they started the countdown, her hands knotted together.

"Right. The machine will be activated in 3... 2..."

Something inside me burst, my heart, every bubble of air left. My voice broke and soared over the nodding heads of the onlookers to what would be a murder.

"Stop!" I screamed as I stood, slapping my palms against the glass wildly like a bird attacking its own reflection. Everyone gasped in shock and the technician paused, his eyes blinking up in surprise at the crazed girl screaming. But he wasn't going to stop unless I did something big, something that made it impossible for them to continue. Picking up the chair, I smashed it against the window. It bounced off the glass and scattered the crowd.

Sekimbo belly-laughed. "My, she is spirited!" he said, directing a guard to hold me down.

The guard wrapped his arms around me in a bear hug. My legs kicked and dragged across the glass. My dress tore as I struggled in his grip, the layers of taffeta ripping sounded like pain, like death. "It's going to kill you!" I screamed through the glass. Grant's head turned in my direction, but he couldn't hear me. He spoke to the technician, who pressed the intercom button.

"Bring her to the mic," he ordered.

I was roughly lifted to the mic, arms still hugging me so tight my ribs felt ready to crack. Breathless, I shouted into the speaker. "It will kill you! You don't have the pills. Without them, you'll die after the procedure."

People exchanged nervous glances. Denis' hands were shaking but he calmly moved the speaker to his mouth, about to utter words of reassurance to his father like, *Don't listen to her. She's crazy. She's unhinged.* Judith's steady hand had taken her mother's, and she was stroking the woman's wrist calmly. Before Denis could open his mouth, Grant's laughter shredded the room with its iciness—it's pure disrespect for me.

"Do you think I would listen to anything you have to say, child?" he said coldly, so amused at my attempts to stop him from getting what he wanted. "You're nothing." Words spat. "And I will be everything I once was when this is over. You fear that, as well you should. Your death will not be quick." There was a small bridge of silence. I watched it build and grow as people's panic quickly turned to disbelief in me—the nothing girl from Pau Brazil.

I surged towards the glass again, managing to break free of the guard's grip for a moment.

"Please!" I begged. "Listen to me." Tears streamed down my face. I was pleading for myself. I couldn't watch this. I couldn't be a part of it.

He turned away from me and I thought, just for one second, that maybe he was considering my plea. Then he said, "Gag her." His voice was sharp, like a dagger.

The guard grabbed a scarf from one of the women and stuffed it into my mouth and my scream of, "No!" was muffled. The clean silk cut into the corners of my lips as he tied it tightly, and I was silenced. Denis sighed in disappointment, and Judith regarded me with wane sympathy.

The technician started his countdown again. "Three... two..."
This would follow me forever.

44

The Past

JOSEPH

I felt lighter as we walked towards Pau. Not unburdened, more like I wasn't alone. I still carried a heavy weight, but with my friends next to me, it seemed slightly easier.

Matt stopped ahead of us and pointed down; I could barely see him through the sleety rain. But his torch cut a line through the forest. We would trek all night. The trees were sparser here, so we needed the cover of darkness to get closer.

Rosa and Careen had told us there were caves to hide in. I imagined her battling her way through the snowstorm they encountered, and I swelled with pride. She was tough.

Pulling my hood down over my brow, I skidded down the wet hill.

I had a purpose now. It was to get myself together. Try to accept what happened on the night I lost her and regain parts of myself I hadn't let live and breathe since then. I had time. I was going to complete this mission, get Orry, and find her. In that order.

"This weather is atrocious!" Olga exclaimed as she waddled past me. She seemed in a hurry. I'd never seen her rush for anything.

Elise slung her arm over Olga's shoulder and shielded her from the rain with the flap of her jacket.

"Yep, it's going to be a looong night."

They were the last words I heard from anyone for the rest of the night. It was too hard to talk through the rain when we needed every last ounce of energy to keep walking. Pau held more meaning for many of us—our former home, family, memories.

My mind was on Rosa.

When I'd thought of her these past few weeks I'd stopped at the pain part, shut myself down. This time I allowed the pain to rise, but then I dug through and found that underneath, there was still comfort, warmth.

I hugged my arms to my chest and watched Pelo almost galloping forward through the churning storm. He was like her in so many ways, but not in the quiet ways. I remember when we first met; those days of walking where I did all of the talking and… She. Just. Listened. And I could tell she was listening because of the flush that crept up her neck when I complimented her or the warmth in her eyes when I told her about my parents. My heart skipped to life at thought of that blush. That was the best color in the world to me. It told me I had affected her. All I ever wanted to do was affect her, impact her life, and make her feel something.

If you're thinking of me, please know I'm thinking of you. I want to wrap you up, shield you. But I know you're strong. You'll do what needs to be done. I'll make this promise. I am in pieces, but I will slot them back together. I will be as whole as I can when I see you again.

45

I Tried

ROSA

Grant lay on the cold metal bench, his fists clenched, his legs flopped apart casually. I bit into the silk and tasted the salt of my tears that just wouldn't stop. Denis had isolated himself from me as if I were a hysterical, catching disease. He stood as close to the window as possible. His body locked into place by will. He was able to fool everyone, and it was frightening.

I leaned back in my chair, straining my neck to focus on the corner where the large window met the bumpy, pilling carpeted wall. No one's attention was on me now. I was a fly buzzing haplessly in the corner. All eyes were on the man with wasted legs and muscled arms. *My* eyes were the only ones that wanted to turn away but couldn't.

"…one…"

Watching it from the outside was a very different experience. But a memory of pain still ran a routed course through my veins. I could *feel* the searing burn of blue liquid under my own skin as I watched Grant's body convulse when it entered his. He was silent, his mouth a punched, hard line, but the scream lay plain across his face. His eyes pooled with water, and his arms lifted slightly as he gripped the seams of his hospital gown in his hands. He thought the agony was going to be worth it. He thought this suffering was a means to healing… *not* a means to his end.

I pulled my legs up to my chest and rocked back and forth, trying to shut it out. But it was useless. Thoughts banged in my head, clanging like an empty drum. He had said my death would not be easy. *When was death easy?* I was trapped between my fear of dying and my fear of what I was about to see. There was no avenue to escape, no wall to climb. I would have to watch my actions play out in front of me, just as I had watched myself die over and over again.

"I tried," I told myself, my lips stretching over the green and pink silk flowers. "I tried." Words dried up.

I tried, I tried, I tried.

The guard slapped my shoulder and told me to shut up.

Five minutes of pain, and he thought it would be over.

The glass coffin lifted and people gasped before Grant had even moved or spoken. A whitecoat moved to him and attempted to mop Grant's forehead with a washcloth. Grant waved him off in irritation, pulled himself up to sitting, and laughed.

The crowd shuffled closer, pulled in by the maniacal laughter, and for a moment, I couldn't see him. I didn't want to see the joy on his face. But I could hear it.

Camille's voice passed through the crowd. "Oh Judy," she sighed happily. "Did you see that? He just wiggled his toes."

"I did, Mother. It's amazing!" Judith crooned. "This will change his whole life." Her voice had taken on a very considered tone.

He had fifteen minutes to enjoy his legs.

People took turns congratulating him through the intercom. Sekimbo shoved through the guests, shouldering a woman out of the way, and slobbering drunkenly over the intercom. "Well done, Wyatt, well done, friend. Now you can…"

"Daddy, wait!" interrupted whatever uncouth thing Sekimbo was about to say as the guests jostled like tenpins. Judith's breathless, willowy body pushed through and she landed on the intercom, her thin fingers hanging off the plastic rectangle like she needed it to hold her up.

The crowd pulled back from the window, and I could see clearly again. Grant sat up on the edge of the bed, delighted by his own, working legs, lifting them and rolling his ankles. His face lit up with a genuine smile that fell into a grimace at the sound of Judith's voice.

He signaled the tech to open the mic. His voice stretched as taut as a set catapult when he barked, "Wait for what?"

From a pocket in her dress, she produced two white pills sealed in a plastic bag. Denis stumbled backwards like they were going to blow up in her palm. I didn't know what to feel. Relief I wasn't involved in a murder? Dread I was going to be executed? Every emotion whirred together like a cyclone and sucked into the sky, leaving me an empty shell, watching this play out like a video, a play, a plot.

"Daddy, they tried to make me do it, but I knew it was wrong. They threatened me and Mother, and I didn't think I had a choice." She held up the pills and showed them to everyone. "Denny was plotting to murder Superior Grant by withholding these pills." Her eyes narrowed and her true self was revealed. It had been hiding beneath a layer of taffeta and torn words. She betrayed us.

Camille sat down and put her head between her legs, whispering, "My own child, my own child."

Confusion dominated the room. Grant's voice, thick with anger, rose above the crowd.

"Judith, come down here immediately. Guards, detain Denis."

Quickly, everything flipped like a coin. Denis was a prisoner, Judith was the hero, and I was still pinned in the corner. The clock above my head ticked. He had five more minutes. I held my breath and waited for the door to open downstairs.

Grant swung his legs on the edge of the bed like a child. Bright lights bounced off the metallic surroundings and made his sweaty skin shine. When the door finally opened, he jumped down and I sensed the power he felt as his legs supported him. He drew strength from the ground as if it were electric as he strode towards Judith's tiny figure. He eyed the pills and his daughter suspiciously. She talked fast, her head bobbing up and down, and her eyes welling and spilling over with false tears. She moved to hug him and, after a moment of rigidity, he wrapped his arms around her and patted her honey-colored head gently. He swallowed the pills without water while still in her embrace and then turned to the crowd, who were all almost leaning on the glass as they tried to read the situation.

Grant strode proudly over to the mic and flicked the switch. The intercom vibrated with his energy and fury. "Judith has relayed a plot to assassinate me in which she was an unwilling pawn." My heart rattled in denial. "She has come to my aid and has proved her worth in my eyes. Denis, on the other hand, has proved wanting at every turn since he came to me, and perhaps that is why he has now reached this depth of deception and depravity. Working with a rebel to murder his own father is despicable and unforgiveable." Grant shook his head and swiped his forehead. "I have no choice but to disown him and sentence him to death along with the rebel." He didn't even look at me. He had won. I could be swept down the garbage chute now.

Denis managed to yell, "She's lying!" as they dragged him away.

Judith took a step back from her father as he began to address the crowd above. His head tilted upwards, his expression glinting all kinds of sharp angles and cuts.

"Friends. See what is possible." His leg wobbled, and his foot dropped flat when he stepped towards the window. He straightened it. "See what our great society can achieve with the right motivation." He cringed inwards and coughed, a blue drip appearing at his nostril. "I am healed..." He stumbled. "I am..." One knee collapsed, and he reached down with his strong arms to pull it back up. But as he leaned down, his other knee buckled.

Camille whispered, "Wyatt," and reached her arm out towards him. He fell forward, bracing himself with his hands. His legs were once again useless. He rolled to sitting and grabbed at them, pinched them, shaking his head.

The guests breathed in one collective breath and held it.

"No," he wheezed. Another cough sprayed blue liquid down the front of his gown. I retreated deeper into my seat, the second hand pounding over my head.

In the corner, leaning against the door, Judith smirked. No one saw her but me. Then she rushed to him.

"Daddy!" she screamed. Her voice was over the top, her screams strangled and full of huffs and gasps as she sobbed hysterically.

The mic was still on and we heard every word.

"What's happening?" he rasped, his voice weak, desperate, as he sat staring at his hopeless legs.

Judith kneeled down. "I don't know, Daddy. They should work. Unless she gave me fake ones." She pointed up at me and I shrank back, the events leading up to this moment sifting through my mind and landing in a neat and ordered stack.

I gave Judith four pills. She took two to give to Gwen and I watched her flush the other two down the toilet. Initially, when she rushed to Grant's aid, I thought she had somehow kept the pills I'd given her. I was wrong. All she'd done was give Grant fake pills. The only possible reason—to get Denis out of the picture so that she would be named Grant's successor.

Grant was incapable of doubting her in his last minutes. She held his head and stroked his hair as his fingers swelled and turned blue. I watched in sickening horror as it eventually tracked up his veins and across his face.

The last thing he said was, "See it through."

His head fell to his chest, the whites of his eyes bright blue. I recoiled and shuddered, my fingers finding the bumps in the carpet and counting them one by one. Judith threw her head up and wailed. The whitecoats crowded around Grant, suddenly pushed to action by her siren-like voice. Camille shed silent tears as they grabbed his body and dumped it on the table, attempting to resuscitate him. But when blue liquid started pouring from his mouth, eyes, and ears as they pumped his chest, they jumped away, pulling a kicking and screaming Judith with them.

Camille let out a dry, withered moan and shriveled like a blade of grass scorched by the sun.

The whitecoats exited the room screaming, "Biohazard!" One of the techs hit a red button, and the alarm drowned out Judith's howling.

The guards left me and ushered the guests out of the viewing room. I stared down at Grant's lifeless body. He cried tears of blue. He had one moment of pure joy and then he was gone. *Maybe that's all you can hope for.*

Maybe I shouldn't care.

One arm hung limply off the table, his nails and finger bulbous like frogs' feet from the pressure of the blue trying to escape anyway it could. A guard grabbed my shoulders and pulled me away from the glass, lifting my trembling body and carrying me to the lift. Grant was abandoned, broken and bleeding like he had left so many of his citizens. A picture he would have flipped like the page of a book without a second thought.

Superior Grant was dead.

And in his place was an evil, unhinged teenager who had fooled us all.

46

Seeing it Through

ROSA

Maybe I can't learn. Maybe my brain is set in concrete now and there's no undoing it. But then, maybe I was never going to get out of this.

At least I tried.

The rain whipped up by spinning chopper blades gave me hope I shouldn't have. Gwen, escorted by two rough guards, the wind and sleet pelting their harried faces, gave me strength I shouldn't have. A swollen, beaten face that I barely recognized as Denis brought me crashing back down to earth.

A small man clutching a metal suitcase to his chest scuttled past me and hopped into the waiting chopper.

Before I could comprehend what was happening, we were forced into the chopper, our harnesses were secured, and we lifted off the ground.

I passed a look to Gwen, who shrugged, but had a slight squish to her expression. It was too loud to speak with the chopper blades, the wind and rain slapping the sides and streaming in the open door. Denis appeared completely baffled. Everything he'd carefully planned was left in the shrinking mud below.

A guard strapped to a thick, nylon line stumbled towards the door and closed it, shutting out some of the noise.

The little man rested his chin on his case and gazed out of the window at the lightening dark and the glow of floodlights getting smaller and smaller. "Well, this is exciting isn't it?"

No one answered.

It was close to dawn when we lifted off and now a sunrise lathered in blood reds and failing purples spread before us like a flapping, silk scarf over the land. I counted eight soldiers plus the pilot strapped to the sides of the craft. All inwardly focused, sunrise washing their cheeks in color as they avoided our eyes.

"So where are we headed?" Gwen asked, her legs pumping up and down on the hard, black floor.

Nothing.

The small man laid the case flat on his lap and opened it, a small chime sounding from within. A computer sat in one side and sixteen flat, plastic rectangles the size and shape of handhelds nested in the other.

"What's in the case?" Gwen asked, hoping she could get some response out of someone.

The man scratched his nose and pursed his lips, squinting at the screen. I didn't think he even heard her. I'd had enough. I stomped my foot and everyone looked up, their eyes fiery red from the sun's rays.

"Where are we going?"

Denis spoke, his mouth struggling to form words through his bruised lips. "I assume we are headed for Pau Brazil, right? My father has always been very creative with his punishments." He spat blood on the ground in front of him and wiped his mouth on his already crimson-spattered shirt.

All Grant's cryptic statements rolled out of a sack with a clunk, and I pieced them together. There were no hard parts to this puzzle; it fit together easily with sharp edges and straight lines.

"So your psychopath sister is having us dropped in Ring Two with my mother and sister," I said resignedly. My punishment was to watch them die and know I couldn't save them. Judith was honoring his sick wish.

Denis nodded.

"Do you know what the plan...?" A sharp punch to my stomach blew the words from my mouth.

"No talking!" an older soldier snapped.

I connected with Denis' eyes. The warning in them was huge,

lighting the clouds. I closed my mouth and gazed down at my cracked, purplish fingers.

Joseph would be there. The thought drove me into the sky and pulled me through the dirt. They knew he would be there because of Olga. I wanted to crack her open, peel her shell off, and show everyone what she'd done. He was in danger—the whole group was. But the only thing my heart would hold onto was the idea of seeing him again, despite the million obstacles between us.

It was all part of Grant's twisted sense of justice. He wanted me to have hope. He wanted me to fight. And I would. I would find my mother and sister, and I would try to save them. Even from death, I heard his cruel laugh and pictured his calculating eyes.

The rain eased and the sun rose chillingly over the vast forest beneath us. Gwen put her hand over mine, and I was pulled back to the last time I was in a chopper, Joseph's warm hand over mine, his reassurance. We were scared and didn't know what was ahead, but in that moment, the future was immense and could have been anything—there was promise in the sky. Things had changed. I shook my head and laughed, causing some of the soldiers to glance in my direction in surprise.

There wasn't much I could do, little I had control over, but I promised I wouldn't give up. *Never.* I would always fight. It was the only certain thing. A solid, glowing part of me that had endured every single atrocity they'd thrown at me.

I didn't know any other way.

I couldn't *be* any other way.

I curled my fingers around Gwen's hand and she squeezed them tightly. She was with me.

I was ready for my lungs to burn, to scream with the force of the turning blades above me. To survive.

I wish I could have slept. Most of the soldiers closed their eyes at different times, resting for their mission. Their hunt-down-my-friends-and-kill-them mission. It made me smile a dark smile to know this would not be easy for them. They were in for the fight of their lives.

My eyelids were peeled back with pure adrenaline as they took in the lush green beneath. The river. The places I'd stepped in and over. I could hear the water over the rocks, the patches of ice shifting and cracking on the surface. It brought me home, gave me strength.

I searched for the Survivors, hoping to catch a glimpse of them walking, but of course, they weren't there. They would hide well. They weren't likely to be caught in the open.

Gwen and I whispered to each other as we passed over the first town. "When we hit the ground, we will have to run, like really run. How are your legs?" I asked.

Gwen raised them in front of her and wiggled her bare feet. "Better than ever!"

The soldier snorted next to her and rolled his eyes.

I stared down at my dress, torn and muddy. I had court shoes on, better than nothing, but they would slow me down.

The small man spoke, his voice sounding like the air being let out of a balloon slowly. "Unless you have super speed on your side, I don't like your chances. Once you touch down, you'll have thirty minutes before the tip, the…" He stopped midsentence and pulled his top lip into his mouth.

A few soldiers jerked their heads in his direction but then the older soldier growled, his teeth sharp and gappy. "No talking. No questions. Those were the orders."

"Yes sir," several said in unison.

Denis slept, and I wondered what I was going to do with him. *Did I owe him anything? Should I include him in my plans?* The truth was I felt very little for him, but he had promised to save my life in exchange for my help with Grant. He had said he wanted to change things…

The chopper jolted over an air pocket. Below, the rings of Bagassa darkened the perfect forest. We were close now. Pau was next.

Just before Pau, the helicopter slowed and hovered, bouncing lower and lower, sending us flying up out of our seats. The soldiers started unbuckling their harnesses and hooking themselves to ropes. The chopper lowered until it was quite close to the ground, hovering like a dragonfly.

Denis startled awake when the body of the chopper tipped as

soldiers shifted their weight around the craft.

"What's going on?" he asked.

The door slid open and the soldiers jumped out one by one without answering. Only two were left behind, plus the pilot and the computer man, who glanced up from his screen. "An ambush works better with the element of surprise, don't you think?"

They were going to sneak up behind Joseph and the others.

I grabbed at my harness and started unbuckling it, ready to hurt someone, push them out of the door, scream a warning, anything, but the soldier next to Gwen braced me with his strong arm and pushed down on my chest until the last soldier dropped and the helicopter rose higher. When we were high above ground, he violently shoved me against the wall and re-buckled my harness, sneering.

"Wouldn't want you to fall out and kill yerself, now would we?" he growled.

I closed my eyes and banged my head back in frustration. *They won't find them.*

It took very little time to arrive at Pau.

The chopper brushed over the walls and headed for the center circle where it touched down. The soldiers undid our harnesses and shoved us out of the door. Denis fell flat on his chest, the saturated sandstone pavers absorbing more blood. I heaved him up and stared at the chopper, everything coming full circle. I was back. *Changed. The same.* My hair whipped around my face as it rose. I shivered and tugged my ragged sleeve up over my collarbone, an insubstantial gesture against the cold morning. The small man shut the case and waved happily at me.

"Good luck!" he shouted before a soldier slammed the door.

Thirty minutes.

47

So Close

JOSEPH

We walked through the night, collapsing at the edge of the forest, nestling in several small caves that punctured the rocks leading to Pau. I woke after a short sleep to hear Pelo's voice echoing off the walls.

He was electrified, bouncing up and down, peppering Desh with questions about the mechanisms behind the technology. He was nervous. I started to wish I were going with him, if only to keep him safe for her.

"So… let's get down to the nitty gritty," he said.

"The what?" Desh didn't understand what Pelo was talking about, so I stepped in.

I slung my arm over Pelo's bony shoulders. "Pelo, all you need to know is how to set off the bomb and where to place the video disc. Do you know those two things?" I held two fingers in front of his eyes.

He nodded jerkily.

"And where to find your parents!" he exclaimed, his finger pointing to the ceiling.

"Yes, if you have time. Please, Pelo, don't risk your life for them. I know them, and once that bomb goes off, they'll find their way out all on their own."

Pelo slowed to a sway, his head bowed over his clasped hands.

"I'll find Esther and the baby first, then your parents. I… I just want to do her proud."

I pushed through my uncomfortableness and said, "You will. You have already, Pelo."

He seemed to accept this and started rousing the others.

Gus was crouched at the entrance, quietly. His hand braced against the wall. I shuffled towards him and his shoulder tensed as I approached. Quickly, he grabbed his handheld and sent a message.

"What's going on?" I asked as I squatted down beside him.

"What do you suppose they're looking for?" Gus whispered, pointing through the trees. I froze, my face caught between the lighthearted grin of before and the panic rising up my throat. Fanned out, scanning the forest, were ten Woodlands' soldiers, their gun butts pressed to their chests, swinging back and forth.

I didn't need to answer, but I did. "They're looking for us."

Gus nodded slowly. "Tell everyone to arm themselves swiftly and quietly."

I cursed internally. "Wait, what are you going to do?"

"What I have to," he muttered from one corner of his dry, bristly lips.

I told the others and soon the cave entrance was crowded with gun tips.

Olga leaned over the men and whispered worriedly. "Can't we just let them pass? They may not notice us if we're quiet. Gus, you can't kill all those men!" Her voice was high with panic.

He ignored her and took aim. "Who said anything about killing them?" he grumbled.

She shook his shoulder just as he pulled the trigger, the shot hitting the dirt in front of one of the soldiers. They scattered and took cover.

Gus swung around, his gun still loaded, and leaned in on Olga. "Damn it, woman! Why did you do that? I was aiming for shoulders and legs. Disabling shots, not kill shots."

Olga's pale face turned anemic. Her lips trembled. "I'm sorry. I didn't want you to... I was worried you would..."

As I watched, everything rolled into place, and I understood why Olga tried to stop Gus. I could see it plainly on her shiny, white face.

Shots fired and chipped the rocks around us as we backed further into the cave. Olga slid along, her hands creeping backwards, but there was nowhere to go.

"How did they know we were here?" I demanded as shots pinged around the cave entrance.

She took way too long to answer. "I... I don't know."

Gus pressed the rifle to her chest right over her stuttering heart, and she gasped.

"We've disabled three of them," someone shouted from the front. "The others are too well hidden."

Gus swore. "Take this," he said, pushing the rifle into my arms as he returned to the entrance to help the others, pulling a handgun from his waistband.

My hand shook and slipped over the black plastic.

Olga blinked up at me. "Let me go and maybe I can negotiate with them to get Rosa back."

Don't trust her.

"I can't believe you betrayed us, Olga," I stammered, my finger grazing the trigger. I was so glad Rosa wasn't here to see this.

She narrowed her beady eyes and smiled, revealing nubs of teeth. "Are you even sure you're on the right side?" I paused. She was just messing with my head. "I can find her for you, Joseph. I can help you." Her voice sounded strange, hissing like a snake.

I considered her as another shot clipped the rock above me, and I ducked.

Rash crept up beside me and snatched the gun from my hands, turning it around and smashing Olga in the side of the head, knocking her unconscious.

"Don't listen to that bitch," he said, flashing me a worn-out grin.

He was right. She couldn't be trusted and I was never going to betray my friends, no matter what promises she made.

I crawled towards the entrance just in time to see the last shot fired.

Some of the Survivors had already jumped down to remove the soldier's weapons. Most were writhing around in the dirt with shots to the legs and arms. Matt pumped his hand a couple of times. "I'm going to administer some quick first aid," he said as he jumped down.

Elise skidded down the rocks from the other cave, and I joined them to help.

"Why are you helping us?" a soldier spluttered as I put a pressure bandage on his arm.

"I'm a Survivor," I answered proudly. He grimaced at my answer. He didn't understand.

We tied the men to trees and promised to return later. Their eyes betrayed how confused this situation made them.

We gathered, away from the soldiers, to discuss what we should do.

"The video is out of the question," Matt said. I'd expected it to be Gus. "It's too dangerous. I'm not even sure we can plant the bomb. Obviously, they know we're coming." Matt's sad eyes went to the cave, where his friend Olga lay unconscious. "I can't believe she..." He hung his head in sorrow.

Pelo sounded crushed when he said, "You mean I can't go in?"

Gus stared at the sky, counting the clouds. "I'm sorry."

We decided to get closer and assess. But just a small team—me, because I begged, Pelo, Rash, and Gus.

We followed the rocks until they petered out, the huge turbines suddenly shooting into the sky before us.

A noise we'd heard before pulsed through the sky.

We stopped and hugged the large pillars of the turbines as a single chopper flew overhead, its spinning blades mixing with the turbine shadows and looking like a giant star on the forest floor.

Gus eyed it like prey. The rest of us cowered. We moved closer, hiding behind the one clump of bushes.

The chopper flew to the center of Pau and slipped out of view. Minutes later, it rose and flew to the outer wall. It hovered close and landed carefully in a small clearing, its nose nearly touching the outer wall. We retreated into the scrub, our eyes trained on the small man who clambered awkwardly from the chopper, holding a silver case in one hand. He scurried to the front of the chopper and suddenly disappeared.

"Where'd the little guy go?" Rash exclaimed.

I knew from when Rosa and I had entered the Superiors' compound that the man had gone underground.

"He's entered the tunnels beneath the town," I muttered, still grasping the ends of a branch and pulling the leaves off stressfully.

We waited anxiously for him to reappear or for the chopper to leave for about twenty minutes when an agitated Rash sprung up and said, "To hell with this! I'm getting us a chopper!"

Before we could stop him, he was stealing closer to the back end of the craft confidently like he knew what he was doing. But I knew he didn't have a clue, so I followed him. Letting Rosa's best friend get killed was not going to help my situation.

48

Patterns

ROSA

The earth rocked beneath my feet, even though it hadn't started yet. My body was anticipating the scramble, the fight against whatever Grant had planned. *My mother. I had to find my mother.*

The chopper rose and peeled away from the center circle. I whipped my head towards the others. *A flash of Orry, a tight grip on an image of Joseph waiting for me on the other side of the wall.* They were photos scrunched in my hand as I uttered, "We have to run."

They both nodded and we took off together with me in the lead, leaving the bloodstained bricks behind. I hurdled the low wall and headed for the first gate, all the while whispering, "Please open, please open."

I skidded up to the gate and stuck my shaking wrist under the scanner. The infrared line wobbled over my wrist tattoo, and the lock clicked. I shook my head realizing that, of course it worked. Grant knew that was where I would head, to rescue my mother. He was counting on it. The gate creaked open, and Gwen and I stepped through. Denis faltered. I didn't have time for this.

"What are you doing?" I panted, my breath cloudy like smoke, my head clear as the sky.

"If I go in there, I'll probably die." He wrapped his hand around the bars, holding it open, though it strained against him.

I searched nearby, found a rock, and wedged it in the gap.

"You have a chance to save people today, to do something good," I said, challenging his dark blue eyes, squished almost shut on one side from the beating.

I didn't wait to see if he followed, I spun around, and Gwen and I ran. I shouted over my head, "Warn as many people as you can."

When I hit the main street of Ring Two, the smell of cut grass and bleeding sap made me pause. It was Sunday. People were maintaining their gardens. A woman walked passed me with an armful of groceries, staring so hard she tripped on a crack in the pavement. I caught her elbow, and she snatched it back like my skin stung her. "You need to get out of Ring Two, Ma'am. Something bad is about to happen." She huffed and walked away, paying me no attention at all.

No one was going to listen to me.

Denis jogged into the street and headed to the first home, knocking on the door impatiently. No answer.

Gwen shook her head, her dimples looking like little frowns under her dark eyes. "They're not going to listen. Look at us," she said, motioning to her bare feet, prison clothes, and my taffeta frock.

She was right.

I pressed back on my heels and pushed forward, heading for my mother's house, cursing the fact that her home was so far from the gate.

Pau Brazil trees capped with ice rustled in the freezing breeze. Wide eyes followed us, mouths hung open. One barefoot girl in pajamas and one in a shredded taffeta gown, decorated with mud speckles streaming down the street was probably the weirdest thing any of them had seen in their whole, controlled existence.

As I ran, I wondered what I could say, how I could get people to at least come out of their homes, to give them a fighting chance. I rounded the bend and my elbow clipped a letterbox. The man shouted abuse at me from his yard.

"Sorry," I shouted, my stupid shoes skidding on the icy bitumen.

Gwen yelled happily, "Superior Grant is dead! Superior Grant is dead!" The man dropped his shovel with an empty clang and followed us a few meters.

I joined in screaming, "Superior Grant is dead! Superior Grant is dead!"

Doors creaked and slammed as curious and alarmed people poked their heads out of their homes, following our noise.

In front, a plain house with cardboard-thin walls leaned towards me. Yellow and purple curtains waved at me like the finishing flag, but we were far from finished. They were tied back for once. My reflection blurred across the yard like a different person, a crazed, wild person, running towards the house, torn taffeta spilling behind me in ribbons.

We kept screaming.

We kept running.

We had about fifteen minutes.

I caught a flash of my face as I ran up my mother's driveway. This girl with bleached hair and wide, underfed eyes. I stalled at the door as I attempted to smooth my hair down, to look less insane.

"Rosa, darling, get away from the door. You've been told before about playing with the locks." My mother's voice sounded calm, sweet, and it open-palm slapped me, stinging my cheeks.

Gwen turned to me, her face muddled. "This is your house, right?" she said as she bent over purple feet to catch her breath.

My own breath was gone. My nerves frayed to a million points of nothingness. What was on the other side of that door? My birth. My death. My future.

I raised a hand to knock, holding my breath. The door swung open, and a child collided with my leg. A dark face framed in strips of taffeta glanced up at me from my knees.

"Rosa!" My mother's face was smacked of color, her eyes round with disbelief. She grabbed the collar of the small girl and pulled her back inside the door, stepping back herself.

The little girl looked up at her mother, *my* mother, and grasped at the woman's waist, digging her chubby fingers into her skirt's waistband, begging to be picked up.

Gwen and I followed her in and shut the door behind us. "I don't have any time to explain," I said, walking closer until my mother's back was pressed against the kitchen counter. She pulled the child into her arms, and tears formed for all three of us.

"Rosa. It's so good to see you. I thought you were dead." She shook her silvering head in shock, and my head rattled with it too. *Good to see me?* Last time I saw her, she'd pushed me away. She'd said no. She reached out to take my hand, and I let her grasp it briefly. It felt... odd.

"Mother, there's no time. The Superiors are planning to destroy Ring Two. We need to get out of here now!"

Her eyes widened, and she tightened her grip on the little girl sitting on her hip. My sister.

I thought I'd have to fight, convince her, but all she said was, "Thank you for coming back for us."

I couldn't respond; we'd wasted too much time already. I grabbed her arm, and she shivered.

"Rosa, your fingers are like ice!" Her voice was a bruise that couldn't heal. Her life was in my hands. She reached up and retrieved a coat from the rack by the door. *My* grey, wool coat. "Put this on," she ordered quietly. "And this young lady needs shoes," she said in a pitch strings higher than usual, her calm hanging off the precipice with the rest of us. I sighed, exasperated, somehow already falling into a pattern that was years old. I pulled the coat on, my hands brushing over the rust stains at the elbows while she fetched shoes for Gwen and threw her own coat over Gwen's shoulders. I danced from foot to foot and shouted impatiently, "Mother! We have to go," and then I yanked her out of the door.

The child started crying. "Sh, Rosa-May, it's all right. We'll be all right." My mother smoothed the little girl's hair from her forehead.

She named her baby after me. My heart swelled in my chest and I laughed, while Gwen and Mother gave me concerned sideways glances. That must have killed Paulo!

We took off for the gate to Ring Three, which was closest. Denis caught up with us, a group of about thirty people at his heels.

"We need to run faster," I wheezed. My mother struggled to keep up, her tiny legs tangling in her long skirt.

"Take Rosa-May, please. I can't keep up," she urged, handing the child to me. I grasped at the child with desperate fingers while running and secured her to my hip, her weight immediately slowing me down. Gwen grabbed my sleeve and towed me along. We were all attached, moving towards the gate like a blob of fear, knocking each other's shoulders and scooping each other up when we stumbled.

As we ran, I kept thinking of the things I wanted to tell my mother. But I'd have time. After this was over, I would sit down with her, and we'd have time.

Right now, the second hand was beating down on us.

49

Things We Do

JOSEPH

We ducked low and crept towards the dark machine. Our camouflage stood out against the shiny, reflective plastic of the chopper. My reflection looked enormous, and I tried to make myself smaller. An impossible task. Through the clear windows, I could see the pilot sitting with his legs up, staring blankly at the concrete wall in front of him. He seemed too relaxed for the current situation. Rash put his hands on the back of the craft, waiting for me to catch up.

I took a breath, ready to talk him out of it, but before I could say anything, he gave me a sideways grin and slammed his palms down on the lightweight panel, making a loud thwack and sending vibrations through the chopper.

The door rolled open. "What the hell was that?" a male voice asked.

"Could've been a bird, calm down," a low female voice replied dismissively.

Rash whispered to me, "You take those two. I'm going for the pilot."

I shook my head vehemently. "I can't *take* two armed soldiers," I said as I snatched a quick glance of them venturing away from the chopper and searching the tree line.

"Uh, yes you can," he stated, and left me standing there.

Gus was creeping silently towards us but I couldn't wait for him, Rash was already at the pilot door. He flicked his fingers behind him, one, two, three, and we moved together but in opposite directions.

I jumped out from behind the rear of the chopper and yelled, "Hey!" My gun out in front, raised and shaking like I had nerve damage. They spun around, and I shot the gun at their feet. The imprint of the trigger burned my finger.

"Drop your weapons!" I demanded, my voice booming, sounding strong like it didn't come out of my mouth.

The man dropped his gun on the ground as if it were too hot to hold. The woman was less eager, and she stepped towards me threateningly. Gus ran up behind me, his weapon ready. She raised her eyebrow. With two guns trained on her, she lost her bravado and crouched down carefully, placing her weapon neatly on the ground and standing back up with her hands in the air.

"Good decision," Gus said.

It was too easy.

The sound of Rash's scuffling shoes preceded him dragging a pilot by his twisted arm towards the other two soldiers.

Much too easy.

"I don't get it. That was too easy. And the soldiers from before…" I said.

The woman raised her head from where she was kneeling with her hands folded on the back of her head. "Our soldiers?"

Her dark blue eyes were wide with concern. "Your soldiers will live," Gus grunted. She hung her head and sighed with relief.

I ran my hands through my hair, confused by what was happening. This was not like any fight I'd been in before. Where men threw themselves at me, where they attacked first without thought for their own safety.

Gus's attention was on Pelo, who was stalking up to the wall when he said, "Find some rope and tie them up."

Rash jumped into the chopper, the whole thing jerking and tipping as he rummaged around in the cabin. A coil of rope sailed through the opening. His muffled voice flowed out of the door. "This is so cool, man. You have to come see."

I ignored him as I bound the soldiers' hands behind their backs with my eyes on Pelo. He hugged the shadows—almost as thin as one. He quickly dug at the dirt, his hands scurrying between his legs like a dog. Pulling out the bomb, he pushed the button and buried it, running like hell away from the wall. He must have pushed the minute button.

Bracing myself for the explosion, I squatted down with the bound soldiers.

I knocked into the female soldier, and she grunted but made room for me next to her.

I looked sideways at her curiously. "Why did you surrender so easily?"

She frowned, her face creased with confusion at what her mouth was about to say. "We were taught to use force when necessary, to be unforgiving in the face of defiance. But this... not one of us wanted to be a part of this." Her eyes were distant as she stared over the wall to some unknown point.

My heart picked up a new, frantic rhythm. "Part of what?"

The bomb detonated, making words impossible. I covered my ears as the wall split open and debris spewed across the ground.

But then the ground shook under our feet. It didn't just rumble. It quaked. Metal creaked in agony and screams. Screams came from everywhere, like the Rings were acting as a megaphone, amplifying peoples' pain for the whole forest to hear. This wasn't just our blast. Something had happened inside.

50

The Tip

ROSA

The ground hummed like the leftover sounds of a twanged rubber band, a sharp vibration that traveled up our legs and into our mouths. I swallowed. A puff of dust like two giant chalk dusters being smacked together appeared several hundred meters down the street. A rumble made us stop and attempt to brace ourselves against... nothing. The earth started to shift under out feet. I stopped breathing, willing myself to be weightless, to take my sister and the others and just float away.

The noise was alien, a loud pop! And then screams. Endless screams.

I turned to my mother as the ground tilted down. "We have to get to the gate," I yelled, though she couldn't hear me.

She was frozen, listening to the mouths screaming in wide-open horror, feeling the earth destabilize. I shook her shoulder violently. "Move. Now!" She nodded minutely and shuffled towards the gate.

A bin rolled past me on its side, tumbling and clanging down as we ran up a sudden incline. I couldn't look, but I could hear the sliding, the metal creaking and fighting against gravity, and thousands of people holding on and losing. Somehow, the world was crumbling, the roads were tipping, and everything and everyone was fighting against slipping into the ground.

We were so close now, the black gate shone like a dull beacon. *Freedom.* Locking us out of freedom. Hundreds of people were cramped around the locked gate. Ring Two was the Ring for young families. There were children and young people, clinging to each other in fear. So many tears and cries for help, even the sound of buildings being crushed and smashed against each other couldn't drown them out.

We thudded against the edge of the crowd. There was nowhere to go. People were wedged against the locked gate like scavengers, beggars. I looked through the bars and more people crowded on the other side, hands reaching through the gaps, fingers grazing against desperate fingers. I turned around and wished I hadn't. Two houses on opposite sides of the street had collided and had momentarily jammed the mechanism that was pulling the floor out from under us. Once they fell, we would fall.

My mother reached forward and tapped a large man on the shoulder, her voice loud and strong. "We need to get the children over the gate first."

The words spread like a secret and soon, everyone was saying the same thing. Parents locked their arms together as the ground crumbled not fifty meters away.

I looked to my mother as she stepped back. Grabbing at her, I missed her shirt by an inch.

"No. No. Don't give up. Mother, please!" I croaked.

She shouted out to those closest. "Please help my daughters."

Someone took my arm and pulled Gwen, Rosa-May, and me up over the heads of the people. They'd formed a human hill and children were being passed up to the gate and over it. Gwen grabbed the hand of a small boy and hoisted him over the gate in front of her. Denis had two children under each arm and he used his taller frame to hoist them higher. My eyes frantically searched for my mother as I reached the points of iron. On the other side, people had stacked tables, chairs, whatever they could find, to try and breach the gate. Now that most of the kids were over, adults were following. Mother's face was determined. She tracked me with her eyes, and I breathed a huge sigh of relief as I saw her working her way closer. She was going to make it.

The buildings streaked against each other, a shrieking, shredding sound as the walls tore open like a paper bag. The ground rattled, and the mound of people slipped. I slipped. My hands gripped tighter around my screaming sister. Someone above shouted, "Throw her over." A man, standing atop a pile of broken, teetering furniture, his hands just grazing the top of the gate. I put both hands under Rosa-May's butt and pushed with every ounce of strength I had. She tumbled through the air and landed on the man's chest.

She was safe. I got her out. My lips pressed together to suppress the panicked howl I wanted to loose. I spun around to tell mother, but she was lost in the sea of slipping, desperate people. People who were now truly panicking. People I was standing on top of.

The houses finally gave way and smashed against each other, a large section of wall shooting up like a buoy released from deep underwater. I clung to the gates as it sailed passed me and hit the wall to my right. Gwen and Denis stood on the other side, their hands wrapped around mine. My face creased with exertion, my breath stinging like pins in my throat.

"Just jump," Gwen screamed over the crashing. But I wasn't a grasshopper like her. I wasn't strong enough. I held fast, unwilling to let go as the world suddenly dropped beneath me. Someone grabbed my leg like it was a rope. My limb stretched and strained as I wound my arms around the gate bars and locked them together, my skin tearing as the weight dragged me down the rusted iron. The person slid down, pulling my sock and shoe with them. My leg felt like it would pop from my hip socket at any moment but then my shoe slipped off my foot, and the weight was gone. My floor of people was gone.

She was gone.

A tight sob caught and made a nest in my throat. One I would never dislodge.

I closed my eyes tight. If I looked? If I watched the source of what was ringing and slicing at my ears? I might as well let go.

The camera above me zipped and focused in on what was beneath me.

I clung ten feet up a gate with nothing but air below me. A neat circle of metal lined the crumbling dirt like a cookie cutter. Water rushed below, the screaming had stopped behind me, but was only just starting on the other side of the gate. On the safe side, where children had watched their parents disappear into the ground.

My arms pulsed. I couldn't hold on much longer.

I'd lost my mother.

Lost her.

Rosa-May's screaming pierced my ears and I opened my eyes, searching for her in the crowd. People were running scared. They didn't know it was just Ring Two; they could probably feel the earth about to dissolve under them. Gwen had been knocked back by the crowd, but she had Rosa-May safe in her arms. Safe.

I'll keep her safe for you, Mother. I promise.

My thin knees pressed between the gaps of the bars, the cold, and the pain of everything trying to engulf me like the yawn of a lion. Slowly, my body slackened. My arms couldn't hold on any longer. My fingers loosened. Gwen stood beneath me, screaming, with a small child clutching her who looked just like me but with warm brown eyes. I couldn't even see Denis.

"Here." A warm voice, so familiar it was like a blanket thrown over my shoulders. It was a ratty chair I sunk into, arms I sought forever. "Rest your knee on my shoulder."

I looked down, to see a round, muscled shoulder pushed against the bars. I let my knee fall to rest, my muscles screaming relief.

Old eyes blinked up at me, green eyes with flecks of gold in them. Rippled, golden hair with streaks of grey. A perfect, unbroken nose. The eyes crinkled into a smile and my heart opened, filleted and bared.

"My name is Jonathan," he said, deep and rumbling, and I almost slid off the bars because I was melting.

I summoned my strength, pulled my foot up to his shoulder, and stood. "You're Joseph's father," I whispered in wonderment. *Was I imagining him?*

He wobbled a little in shock, and I leaned away from the gate. Strong arms grabbed my ankles.

"You knew my son?" he asked as he helped me climb over the gate.

I love your son.

I reached the top and between bursts of shocked breaths and tears, I managed to say, "I know your son, Jonathan," as I flopped over the top of the gate and landed on him.

He laughed, and I found it hard not to hug him. To let the warmth of his laughter cover and protect me.

A small, gentle voice came from behind him. "Jonathan, we need to leave."

He pulled me up to standing, and I rushed to Rosa-May and Gwen. I tugged on her little arms, checked her legs, and squatted down to dust the tears from her face.

"I'm your big sister. My name's Rosa too." She nodded shyly, her plump stomach swinging back and forth under a tight grey jacket. "I'm going to take care of you now."

"Where Mama?" she asked, though I think she knew.

My heart sliced into a thousand pieces, and I handed one large part to her to keep. "It's just going to be you and me for a while, but I promise I'll look after you," I said, barely managing to speak. My eyes connected with Gwen's, who mirrored my sorrow. But the strength behind them was burning.

"Do you think they'll follow through with the plan?" I asked.

"They always do."

Jonathan stepped forward. "What plan?"

"Our friends and your son are going to free us from this place," Gwen announced.

My eyes followed the streams of fleeing people getting further and further away from us.

The woman tugged on Jonathan's large arm. "Jonathan, even if it is *our* Joseph she's speaking of, we still need to leave right now," she urged. Her eyes flicked to me briefly. "Please girls, come with us but come now. It's not safe here."

"Wait Steph," he said, putting his hand up. "What does she mean by free us?" he directed to me.

"There's a lot to explain, too much, but for now… just follow the people," I said, pointing towards the last stragglers running away from the shattered Ring.

I picked Rosa May up and swung her onto my back. Her wet face rested in my hair. I swore I would find a way to ease her tears but right now, she had every right to them. I dried my own and walked towards the outer Ring. My eyes to the sky.

51

Hush

ROSA

I'm too used to grief. I expect it. It's a sad friend that wraps itself
around my ankles and makes me drag it through the streets. These
empty, ghost-like streets.

Back in this grey world, I felt like a child.

"He's gone, Rosa," Gwen said lightly, like she knew it would happen.

"Huh?" I could barely concentrate on putting one foot in front of the
other.

"That Denis guy, your friend." She swept her head back and forth,
her plait snaking up and down her shoulder, an offered rope of safety
withdrawn, her eyes running over empty doorways and doors half-
cracked. She winced every time she saw a body in the street. Trampled. I
swung Rosa-May to my hip so I could shield her eyes.

"He wasn't my friend, not really." *He used me. I used him*. I wasn't
surprised that he took off.

Rosa-May kept saying Mama over and over again as we passed
through gate after gate. It was like a steady flow of small punches to the
stomach. I crumpled deeper at each repetition.

Joseph's parents were quiet in their horror. Several times, Jonathan
ran to a trampled body to check their pulse. Every time he returned,
shaking his head. Steph kept her hand over her mouth like that would
stop fear from winning, horror from slipping out. Pau Brazil was now a
hollow shell. Footsteps sounded like single stones falling from the sky.
Solitary, too loud.

Everyone was gone.

Everyone.

I checked every few paces, but the sky remained clear. The Survivor's video hadn't started, and I worried something had gone wrong. That he wasn't here. That they got to him first. My feet sped up, my leather shoes squeaking on the stones. Gwen and Joseph's parents kept pace with me and soon, we were running. We caught up with the noise, the panicked screaming, and were sucked into the thrashing fishtail end of thousands of people fleeing the compound. They had to be heading somewhere. I jumped up to try and see over the sea of heads, but I was too small. Jonathan stood behind me. He shielded his eyes with his hand, the sun casting a plane of light right into his face.

"There. Up ahead. I'll be damned. Someone's blown a hole through the wall."

I squeezed Jonathan's arm. "He's here." The words a balm, a medicine to keep me from liquefying into a pool of sadness.

I clutched Rosa-May tighter, grabbed Gwen's hand, and moved with the crowd, losing Joseph's parents in the throng.

52.

Broken

JOSEPH

After the blast, Pelo made it to us and we crouched down behind the chopper. Waiting. Watching for people to start coming over the rubble and into the open. A lid flipped open near the nose of the chopper, and the little guy with the case popped his head out of the ground like a mole. He took one look at the wall blown to pieces, swung his head to the chopper where he saw us crouching over the bound soldiers, and disappeared back into the ground before we could really register his presence.

In the other towns, people had warily picked their way over the broken wall and peeked their heads out like nervous mice. They tested the air. Sampled the freedom. Some had retreated. Some had stepped over carefully and wandered out. My eyes rested on the pile of rubble, anticipating the same kind of reaction.

A bald head poked its way up from behind the hill of twisted iron and concrete dust. Eyes squinted and blinked behind round glasses. The old man put his hand to his brow, searched the horizon, and was flattened. I surged forward but Gus grabbed the back of my shirt and yanked me back. Hundreds of people flurried over the debris, trampling the man. Desperate, dirty faces, women clutching children to their hips, others chained to each other by tight, clasped hands as they pulled loved ones through. They poured over the breach in the wall like an avalanche. People tripped, their legs getting stuck in the gaps between the rubble. They were run over before I could blink.

I tensed and clenched my teeth. *What the hell had happened in there?* These people weren't just escaping the compound; they were running away from something. Running for their lives.

A young woman with golden brown hair scrambled over the edge of the debris. People streamed passed her, yet she held still. Another girl came behind her and put her arm on the woman's shoulder, pulling herself up and passing her a small girl about Orry's age. I squinted. I knew that face.

"It's Gwen," I said to Gus, elbowing him.

Gus shook his head in disbelief and whispered, "It can't be…"

My excitement overcame any other panic. We'd found Gwen. I rose from my crouch.

"Joseph, look…" Gus said, pointing at the woman standing next to Gwen. She still wasn't moving, standing atop the pile of rubble, looking down at the small girl who clung to her leg. She leaned down, spoke to the girl, and then she flipped her hair, put her hands on her hips, and smiled wide.

The sun crossed her face and those eyes… those eyes I'd wanted for so long, flashed defiantly. A revolution standing in front of me. Rosa.

ROSA

This was what I had wanted. To stand atop the crumbling wall and watch the Woodlands disintegrate before me, turned to dust. But not like this. Terrified people clipped my shoulders, and I struggled to hold my ground. I clung to Rosa-May, keeping my body rigid, a barrier between her and the crush of the crowd. She wouldn't stop crying, that sticky, hick, hick, hick, hitching her breath. I had run out of tears. I was an empty drum with salt lines running around my walls.

Gwen spoke, though I could barely hear her through the screaming. "They have to be here. Let's go."

Rosa-May's perfect little jacket was smeared with dirt and blood. I leaned down and dusted it off, carefully checking her for injuries. My heart broke as I said, "It's okay, little sister. Hold tight to my hand. Don't let go." I was all she had left. I tried to smile for her sake.

Gwen tugged on my arm, but I wasn't ready to tumble into the crowd and lose my perspective. From here, I could see for miles. I put my hands on my hips and scanned the area, a smile still stuck to my face so Rosa-May wouldn't be scared. They had to be nearby.

My heartbeat grew steady as I took in sections of the forest. Like the pie of the Superiors' compound. I broke it up and searched each piece thoroughly. The black rocks were clear, the forest line seemed clear, although they could have been hiding behind the bushes. A soldier shoved past me, scrambling down the rubble and knocking others out of his way as he went, his uniform in tatters. Someone had pulled all the gold decoration from it, and now he looked like an urchin. He disappeared into the crowd. He was just the same as the rest of us in this situation, frightened, trying to survive.

My eyes landed on the chopper. I moved sideways, keeping my legs as sturdy as steel beams. The shadow of a person somehow shone behind the rear of the black angel.

The air around him was brighter, shining, pulsing like golden brushstrokes. Joseph.

JOSEPH

She looked thinner, her eyes ringed with dark, her clothes an odd combination of a delicate dress, torn to shreds as it reached her upper thighs, and a thick, grey wool jacket. I remembered that jacket. The way she had cursed the gate for giving her rust stains. I wondered for a second if she was an apparition, a memory, but then I would never imagine her with dyed hair. *What was she doing here?*

"It's her. Let's go," Pelo urged, pushing me forward.

But I froze, my feet stationed, burning a hole in the ground. Her eye's fell on me. They ripped me open and cut me a million times with every dusty-lashed blink.

What does she see?

I am broken.

ROSA

He looked the same. His beard scruffy, his hair knitted over his brow in that delicate balance. But when he looked up at me, his eyes were deep green, ringed with sadness.

What does he see when he looks at me?
I am broken.

JOSEPH

I forced my legs forward. Something stronger than any shame, stronger than any fear I had of what she might say or do when she met me, pulled me towards her and suddenly, I was running.

She was here. That was all that mattered.

ROSA

"There," I said as I pointed to the group of Survivors who were now approaching us carefully as the people of Pau Brazil spilled around them in scattered lines. Except for Joseph, who was flat out sprinting.

I handed Rosa-May to Gwen and helped them climb down. Slipping through the cracks, something snagged my leg, tearing my dress even further. I pulled my jammed leg out and scrambled down, holding Rosa-May's hand, keeping us connected. Her wide eyes were open to the chaos. She sniffed, but she didn't cry.

"You're so brave," I said, patting her head. Her gaze did something strange to me. Her eyelashes stuck together with salt water, her brown eyes, my *mother's* brown eyes, blinking up at me like I was *the* one. The *only* one she trusted. It filled me with hope.

I took a deep breath and crossed my arms over my chest. Something pulled at my body, elastic getting tighter and tighter. I found him. He was here. I was broken, but I could still run. My feet hit the frozen grass and my body surged towards him, my hand still wrapped around Rosa-May's as I dragged them with me. I wasn't in control anymore. He was here, here, right here in front of me. My heart. My hands ached for him; everything I wanted was wrapped in a green shirt and a dark jacket.

"Joseph," I whispered, as if it were my last breath. My first breath.

JOSEPH

If she knew of my crimes, she didn't seem to care. And I wasn't sure

I cared either. She was here. Impossibly. She ran towards me as fast as a heartbeat. As strong as warrior. My Rosa.

My brain couldn't take in anything other than her tiny form streaking across the muddy land with Gwen and the child behind her. Nothing could slow us. She was five feet away from me, her face dirty, her hair wrong, her mouth open and panting. "Jose..." she started, letting go of the child's hand for a moment.

I reached out and grabbed her, pinning her to me. Squashing our bodies together and hoping they would never part. I wanted to feel her heart against my own.

"I found you," I said.

She gasped as I squeezed her tighter, her face buried in my chest. Forcing her face upwards, she blinked up at me.

"I think I found you," she said stubbornly, her voice like ringing bells in my ears. I had wanted to hear her voice forever.

ROSA

Joseph's chest rattled with a chuckle. It felt old and new at the same time, like he hadn't used it in a while. I let the vibration fill me, let the cymbals crash against us both, the sparks fly. I felt his lips press down on the top of my head, felt him breathe me in. Every brush of his skin was killing me. We were ending and beginning. There was so much more to do but right then, the force of what we had wanted, the stretching sound and the feel of our hearts being sewn back together, was as painful and pleasurable as any emotion I'd ever felt, would probably ever feel. It was all I *could* feel.

"Say it," I said, my teeth glistening whiter than the ice, my smile too big for my face.

He grinned. "All right, all right, *you* found *me*." *Talk forever, never stop.*

I was done being apart from him.

JOSEPH

"Jooosssephh!" A woman's scream managed to fight its way through the crowd. I lifted my head from where I was staring at the part in Rosa's hair like it was the map to my heart. Rosa leaned back from my embrace and turned in the direction of the screams. She waved her hand, calling someone over to us.

"Oh yeah, and I found your parents too," she said, her eyes crinkling in the corners in the most perfect way.

"You're my hero," I said softly, my smile cracking me open.

You save me over and over again.

5·3

After

ROSA

I knew conversations had to happen. Big, serious conversations. But right then, all I wanted to do was make myself flat as a piece of paper, slide under his shirt, and live against his chest.

Joseph flapped a clean sheet in front of my face. It pushed scents of clean skin and smokiness that never washed out of your hair sailing towards me. I inhaled deeply.

A knock on the door disrupted my roaming thoughts. I moved through this stranger's house we'd commandeered, scared to touch possessions that didn't belong to me and had their own lost history.

A ratty hall runner rug gritted under my bare feet. I opened the door, and a gust of rust and smoke met my nose.

"Here." Gwen pushed an armful of children's clothes towards me gently. "A woman had these in her bag for her... but she doesn't need them anymore." She sniffed, and I knew the rest. "Anyway, you might as well take 'em for the kid."

"Thank you." I grasped the clothes from her cold hands. "How's it going out there? And how are you?" I asked, motioning to the gaping hole and the glow of hundreds of campfires outside the wall. Sad murmurs echoed into the blank sky.

I'd wanted to sleep under the trees too, but it was crowded out there. Most of the citizens were too afraid to step back inside, despite our assurances the rest of the town was not going to sink into the ground. Weirder still was the fact that they were looking to us for answers.

Gwen grimaced. "It's settling down, I guess..." She hesitated and then said, "I'm good. I'm back with my people. Best feeling ever!" She put her thumbs up, though her eyebrow arched sarcastically. We both knew it would take time for both of us to be 'good'. "The news of the Superiors' deaths has caused a lot of mixed emotions. Superiors…" she scoffed. "More like inferiors, idiots, imbeciles… uh… Matthew said I have to stop calling them names in front of the newbies," Gwen said, winking, her cheeks flushed and pinched with new freedom as she rolled her eyes at the word 'newbies'. She amazed me.

"You can call them anything you like in front of me," I said warmly.

"I know," she replied, gazing at her feet, still wearing my mother's shoes.

Whispers of Este and Grant's deaths had grown quickly to loud truths, rolling over the huddles of people like galloping clouds. It caused relief, fear, and displacement. I felt little relief. My own hand shivered from the cold of being dipped in Grant's blood. I stared down at it, and Gwen dipped her head lower to make eye contact.

"Anyway…the soldiers, Gus and the others disarmed have corroborated our story of the video the Superiors wanted to make and the purpose of it. Man. I think I kept hoping it wasn't going to happen, that they wouldn't go through with it, and then… *boom*." She made an exploding gesture with her hands, and I flinched. "There were other ways, you know?" she muttered, her voice cracking under the weight of it all.

"I know," was all I could say.

"Matthew says this kind of grief, this massive loss of life, will not be easy to overcome. It's going to take time and help. I'll help." Sadly, thousands of displaced, scared, and grieving citizens was a familiar situation for us.

"Do you want to come in and rest for a minute?" I asked as I yawned a hole in my body.

"Nah, I'm good. I have accommodation. You two deserve and *need* some time alone," she said, a slight edge of concern underlining the word 'need'.

"Oh okay," I replied doubtfully. "Thanks for the clothes."

"S'ok. Rosa. I'm sorry about your mother," she said as she walked backwards down the path.

A thread of ice worked its way through my heart, and I shuddered.

"It wasn't your fault."

She frowned, her cheeks dimpling, her eyebrows working. "It's just what you say, when there's nothing else you can say," she said, giving me a sad smile.

I choked on a weird laugh that wanted to escape. "Thanks."

I waved as she strolled quickly down the street like she owned it. My eyes tracked her down the road and up the path of another home, a few doors down. The world was inverted, Survivors on the inside and Woodlands' citizens on the outside.

"Grace!" she shouted.

"Huh?"

"It's a song. Look it up... but later." She shut the door. I pocketed the name, knowing it would tear me open—a song for another time when I had the chance and space to grieve.

Passing Rosa-May sleeping on the couch, I placed the clothes at her feet. I sucked in a sharp breath at the memory of my mother. There one second, her face determined, some fight still in her. Then gone. It hurt, but the weight of responsibility to my sister was a round, smooth thing, a warm reminder that kept me from sinking. I pictured her with Orry and it made me smile. It made me frown too. My mother should have been there to meet him. I hugged my body and returned to Joseph.

He glanced up from tucking the sheets in, lifting the mattress with one arm like it was made of cardboard. *I* was made of cardboard. A cut-out of myself. Everything overwhelming. Feelings clashing, crushing me flat. My body mushy with hugs, sharp with betrayal, on fire with desire, and shivering with worry.

"Who was at the door?" he asked, his beautiful eyes pulled back with distance. Too, too far away.

"Gwen."

"Oh."

After his parents, my parents, everything. He hadn't said much. But then, neither had I. I gulped down my pain in one lump as I recalled telling Pelo about Mother. Hurt and reassurance as I understood that he truly loved her, and now it was too late.

Joseph ran a calloused hand over the sheets and patted them once. He moved to where I stood frozen in the doorway, caught in a memory.

"You looked tired," he said, eyes glowing. He put his hands on my shoulders and assessed me, words trembling on the edge of his lips. "Are you all right?" His eyes darted away when his gaze reached my injured fingers. I shoved them behind my back. He wasn't ready for those answers. The ones that came with screams, ice, beggars, and fear.

I shook my head. "I'm fine." I wasn't sure I'd ever be fine.

His shoulders slumped. He knew I was lying. I knew *he* wasn't fine either.

"Do you still have it?" I asked, my eyes searing holes in his pockets.

A distant rumble of a laugh echoed in his chest because he knew exactly what I was asking for. He fished my handheld from his pants pocket, and I snatched it from him hungrily. My palms dipped with the weight of it, heavy with my promises. I turned so we could both see it, nestling the back of my head into his chest. He brought his hand under mine, holding the screen up closer to our faces, and when our fingers touched, my skin hummed golden songs.

The red light blinked an answer to my question. Joseph leaned down and whispered in my ear, his lips grazing my hairline.

"There he is." He pointed to the red dot resting in one place. Goosebumps rose on my skin.

I tried to nod but I was too torn, too eager to run out of the door and into the forest, climb a mountain, whatever I needed to do to get back to Orry.

"I know he's okay," Joseph said, putting both of his warm hands on my shoulders and spinning me slowly to face him. I put my fingers to his chin, running over the stubble. He leaned into my hand and closed his eyes. "Just like I knew you'd survive. I never doubted it," he whispered without looking at me. My finger ran over his lips. His posture was relaxed and guarded at the same time and I wished I could dive into his head to know what he was thinking.

JOSEPH

I couldn't look at her. The damage to her hands, the hollowness of her eyes. Torture ran all over her face in messy lines. I knew what she wanted. I wanted it too, but I was afraid of her lips. Or I was saving them. I wasn't sure. All I knew was those lips would undo me to the point where a confession was all I was, and I wasn't ready.

ROSA

I wrapped my arms around his waist and put my ear to his heart, the beat unsteady.

"You know me," I quipped. "Stubborn to the last."

He chuckled hollowly, and I felt it was the wrong thing to say.

"Always," he replied.

He turned off the handheld and put it away. We couldn't do anything tonight. We rocked back and forth, holding each other, the floorboards creaking rhythmically. On the wall, a cross-stitched picture of a house with the words *Home Sweet Home* sewn underneath it glared at me.

"I'm sorry," I said to his shirt.

"I'm sorry too."

The reasons behind the apologies were too long and too numbered.

He gathered me up, my bones sagging in my skin, my energy sapped. I ate for the first time in twenty-four hours just before, and it had stretched my shrunken stomach.

"Sleep," he ordered, laying me down on the bed and folding the sheets and blanket around me. He stroked my horrible hair from my face, his expression conflicted.

Kiss me.

My eyelids fluttered from pure exhaustion as I tracked him walking slowly around the bed. I felt a moment of peace that I held onto. He was here with me.

I was asleep before he had even crawled into the bed.

Just before dawn, I woke. My heart stuttering in my chest as the events of the last few weeks collided in my head. I closed my eyes, and my fingertips pulsed with twinges of pain. I curled them under into a light fist. The insides of my eyelids were a screen, projecting bursts of blood, instruments glinting on a tray, pins, and shiny black doors.

I drifted off to sleep after my momentary panic only to be woken minutes later. Joseph's hulking body seized next to me, flinging my hand from his sweat-soaked side. He screamed once, low and strangled, and then his body went slack.

It reminded me that we were not a magic cure for each other. There were things I needed to tell him and words he must have for me. I was scared of those words, but I wouldn't be able to avoid them.

54

Lift

ROSA

The world wants a piece of me, I know. But until I have my son in my arms, it's like tugging on a curl of steam.

I'm insubstantial.

Ineffectual.

Three pieces out of four.

The white rays of a cold dawn piercing the thin curtains of the bedroom shed unwelcome light on our situation.

So much confusion. So much to do.

I stretched out and the cold, empty place beside me sent a shot of fear through my body. My hand wavered over the cool sheets and for a second, I thought I was back in the Superiors' compound, but then I heard Joseph in the lounge, talking to Rosa-May. I padded out of the bedroom, but hung back, resting against the peeling hall, and listened to their conversation.

"So you don't like toast?" Joseph squatted down with his back to me, hanging his arms over couch. Rosa-May shook her head, gazing at the floor. "What about toast with…" He got up, moving out of my sight to the kitchen cupboards. Jars clunked against each other, boxes scuffed the shelves. "I know. Toast with detergent?"

Rosa-May perched on the back of the dusty pink couch like a monkey ready to jump, her watchful eyes twinkling but her lips set in distrust. She shook her head, her mouth tugging into a very brief smile.

"No. Okay, what about toast with…" He shook a box. "Dried pasta? With drawing pins? Ouch, that'd hurt. Um… sardines?" With each ridiculous suggestion, her face relaxed a little more, her smile growing as she watched him dance around the small kitchen.

She lifted her hand and pointed. "Jam."

"Jam. Really? Well, it seems a little unorthodox, but jam it is," Joseph said as I pulled around the corner and met his eyes. His gaze dropped to my bare feet, his fingers flexing at his sides, a jar of strawberry jam in one hand. He seemed to check himself, cracking his neck to one side, and then took a deep breath. Stepping towards me awkwardly, he swept me into his arms and held me close. He breathed in my hair as if he were memorizing me, saving me, like I would disappear. I felt bendy and squeezed of air in his arms, but happy.

The jam jar knocked the back of my skull with a light clunk. I felt Rosa-May's eyes on us. "Ouch!" I exclaimed, though it didn't really hurt, and he broke our embrace, leaving me wobbly and rubbery, liable to bend to the ground.

"Sorry if I woke you," he said, his eyes running over my body slowly. I couldn't quite work out what he was doing. Or thinking.

"You didn't," I replied politely. In agony. Rosa-May clambered over the back of the couch and ran to my side, wrapping her arms around my legs like a vice. I bent down and smoothed her hair, feeling a grief-coated lump rising in my throat.

Joseph's eyes were sadness rounded with distress when he caught my expression.

"What can I do? I don't know what to do," he said, expelling the thought desperately, without meaning to.

I wiped my eyes before my sister could see my tears and we both looked up at Joseph, our faces two halves pressed together, two parts of a whole.

His smile was a clash between guilt and love.

"God! She looks so much like you. She's beautiful." He kneeled down and tucked his large finger under her chin. "You're beautiful, Miss Rosa-May." The 'Miss' sent me tumbling towards a dark tunnel, but I braced myself against the sides.

She narrowed her eyes for a second, like she was sizing him up, and then she barked, "Toast." Like that, she pulled me back from the edge as we all laughed, truly laughed.

Joseph turned to make breakfast, and we discussed what we needed to do next.

We needed to find Gus and Matthew.

We needed to leave Pau and get Orry.

We stepped from the thin home and into a grey dawn. I tripped and stopped to roll up the long legs of the pants Joseph's friend Elise had lent me. The shirt she gave me hung over my hands and the boots were two sizes too big, but it was so much better than the torn dress I'd been wearing. Joseph waited, his eyes out over the fuzzy sky, his mouth pulled down.

I knocked his arm to startle him back to the present. "You still asleep or something?"

He dipped his chin to me and forced a smile. "Sorry."

"No need to be sorry." I smirked, and he sighed like he'd just expelled a large ghost from his chest. The sigh flapped around me and I pulled my grey jacket tighter around my middle, hoisting Rosa-May onto my hip.

Last night, we'd left everyone to sleep, to rest. This morning's light showed a world turned upside down. All the Survivors inside the walls, and most of Pau Brazil milling around outside, completely lost.

Matthew appeared from the mist, striding down the dreary street, his face etched in tired lines of worry and held up with purpose. I waved him over.

"Oh good, you're up. We're meeting outside to discuss our next move. Joseph, I believe your parents are waiting for you out there too." His smile was wary.

Joseph tensed at the mention of his parents. Their reunion last night had been joyful but brief with Joseph making excuses and whisking me away before much could be said. I think he was happy to see them, but I also understood his reluctance. We were not the same people who left here two and a half years ago.

Matthew turned, expecting us to follow.

"Where's Gus?" I asked, running to walk beside him.

"Hunting," he replied with a hint of amusement in his voice.

We parted the mist and climbed the crest of blown-apart concrete.

The view shocked us to a standstill. Thousands of people huddled in small groups, spread out below us like a herd that had lost its alpha.

I gasped.

Matthew heard me. "Yes. It's quite a sight."

We moved to the left, hitting the grass and walked towards the chopper. Matthew gestured to Gus, who was squatting by the wall, knife in one hand, the other pressed to the ground.

"What is he hunting exactly?" I asked both of them.

"That little man that went underground, I guess," Joseph answered.

Matthew nodded. "He has to surface eventually."

"Oh," was all I managed before I was swept into a tight embrace yet again.

I thought we'd done all this last night: The hugs, the kisses, and the happy reunions, which lacked happiness. But Rash had me off the ground, with Rosa-May still in my arms, before I could stop him.

We teetered together.

"In the cold light of morning, your hair really does look like shit," he joked as he planted me back in the grass. His eyes darted to Joseph, who shook his head.

"I know," I said, attempting to tuck it back and losing.

Joseph marked my side. "Considering everything she's been through, actually, despite any of that, I think she looks incredible."

Rash scowled. "Enough with the sappy romantic crap dude, I just ate," he said, holding his stomach and pretend-retching. Rosa-May giggled as I scowled at him.

Rash winked and pinched her cheek. She smacked at him with tiny fists.

"Whoa! Got your sister's temper I see, mini-Rosa."

Joseph loomed over Rash. "Don't call her that," he threatened.

I waved them both off. "Calm down you two." Their interaction was strange and left an icy, acid feeling in my stomach. I left them exchanging frigid stares and peered over Rash's shoulder to see Pelo and Joseph's parents talking seriously. I'd forgotten they knew each other. The image of a parent-teacher conference hovered like a bubble over their heads. When Pelo noticed me, he broke his conversation and strode over, the sun spilling through the frosted leaves and dancing off his dark hair.

"How are you, my girl?" he asked, bending down to peer into my eyes like they somehow held the answers more than my mouth could. Rosa-May pushed his face back from mine protectively with her chubby fingers. Pelo's eyes were strained, his mouth fighting to turn down, despite his best efforts.

"I'm fine. I'm good actually." Today, I was going to get my son and the dark blades of the chopper loomed with promise. "What about you?" I asked. Joseph's arm crept over my shoulder and grounded me.

"I have no right to be as sad as I am. You," he poked my chest and I stumbled back, "you have *all* the right, *all* the permission, to drown in your grief, yet here you are, stronger than ever." So many pages of lies piled on top of each other they were as thick as a textbook.

I ran my fingers along the side of the craft. "Do we have the pilot?" I asked, changing the subject.

Pelo nodded, for once understanding that now was not the time.

Deshi approached us exclaiming, "Remarkable. She looks just like you, Rosa." His expression was tired but cheerful. He held out his hand to Rosa-May, who inspected it and passed it back with a brief grin. She hadn't said anything except 'Toast,' and 'Jam,' since yesterday, and it worried me. I pressed my cheek to hers. It was very cold.

"So you're thinking what I was thinking, then?" Deshi continued. "This would be perfect." He slapped the black plastic and the whole craft wobbled, distorting the reflection of the forest that called to me.

Jonathan appeared, inserting himself easily into the conversation. "Is it safe?"

I almost laughed in his face. Nothing was safe. I didn't know what *safe* was.

Joseph spoke through tight lips, standing behind me like a solid wall. "I'm sure it's fine, Dad." Jonathan slapped a reassuring hand on Joseph's back and chuckled.

He was about to say something when Matthew cleared his throat and called us to him. The Survivors pressed their backs into the trees, like me. It was reassuring. A reminder of home.

"We need to make a plan going forward. We have thousands of people here looking for guidance, support. We also have an unknown number who have fled into the forest. I know the original plan was to move onto the next town, but that seems impossible now. After the information Rosa and Gwen have given us about the new Superior Grant and after…" he shook his head and ran a hand through his hair, grey strands belying unease, "after Olga, we have to assume that they will anticipate our planned moves and may retaliate against the people in the remaining four towns. I can't see any other option other than to abandon our plans for the other towns. We need to help *these* people *now*. We need a Woodlands' liaison and a spokesperson for the Survivors."

Scrabbling feet and muffled breathing.

Gus pulled the small man with the silver case by the collar, holding him off the ground like a kill to be skinned. The little man fought listlessly against Gus' firm grip for a moment, before his head sunk below his shoulders. Some people turned his way in disgust, but most ignored his presence.

"I move that we stay put. Organize ourselves. Recruit and assist the citizens of Pau Brazil. I truly feel we shouldn't risk anymore lives," Matthew finished.

"Rosa would rock it!" Gwen shouted enthusiastically. Alarmed, I found her face and shook my head at her hopeful, dimpled expression. "…or not…" she muttered. I rolled my eyes to the sky, wondering whether she had just said that to get out of it herself. The clouds were streaked, combed up like a wave threatening to crash down over us, and it seemed fitting to our enormous task.

There was little discussion. A few murmurs. But everyone seemed to agree that I was a good spokesperson. Matthew invited Joseph and me to the front. I placed Rosa-May gently on the grass, the wet blades darkening her tights with moisture. I opened my mouth to speak and Jonathan interrupted me, both he and Pelo pushing their way to the front.

"Don't you think these kids have been through enough?" Jonathan said, his voice secure. "It's too much. Too much responsibility to place on such young shoulders."

Stephanie "Mmhm-ed" in agreement, her body swaying as if she were a wispy, willow tree in the breeze, her branches clasped neatly in front of her.

"Wow," I said before I could stop myself. Jonathan was being the parent in this situation, and it didn't fit. It was too late for permission slips and groundings. I looked out on the concrete walls blown apart, the scattered souls unanchored, and considered it. *Wouldn't it be nice if we could hand over our troubles, our burdens to them? Could I just stop being the adult now?* The temptation was there, wafting thinly in front of my eyes, teasing me. I blew it from my vision. Our childhoods were over. And I was okay with pressing my lips to that shred of time and kissing it goodbye. The arms wrapped around my legs, and the arms reaching for me from the mountains, made the choice not a choice. My task was to give Orry and Rosa-May some of what I'd had, and most of what I'd never had—a good childhood.

I blinked a few times at the expectant eyes before me, wondering why they even listened to me, and said, "I can't agree with Jonathan. For better or worse, sadly, we're not kids anymore. But there *are* other reasons why I'm not the best person for the job. Though, that's not why I can't accept your nomination." In the crowd, a pair of green eyes framed with short, pale blond hair crinkled at my words. Elise smiled, and I smiled back warily.

"I can't *do* anything. I can't *be* anything useful until I have my son. If you don't need the chopper, I would like to request it and the pilot to retrieve Orry, Hessa, and the others. I promise, when I return, I'll help you as much as I can. In the meantime, I nominate Jonathan and Pelo." They would do a much better job than I would. I was not the one to put faith in. I was like two smashed plates. Broken and mixed together so much that I didn't know which piece went where or even where to start.

Joseph's hand wound around mine, and it lifted me a little. His hand shook in mine, my hand shook in his, our balance unsteady. But I gripped it tightly anyway.

Elise swept her delicate hand in the air and Joseph sucked in a breath before she said, "Aren't we forgetting what an asset this helicopter could be? We could fly over the Superiors' compound and blow them all to hell!" He exhaled, relieved.

Gus stomped his foot. It didn't make much noise in the damp ground, but his anger pulled everyone's focus to his words. "No more! No more death. If there is to be more fighting, it will not start with us. The only way forward is negotiation." The Survivors bowed their heads in agreement.

Elise shut her mouth with a snap, and I felt bad for her. She was new. I got that.

It was a simple decision, which I knew they would support. They were as anxious to see the boys as we were. If we could convince the pilot to fly us, we could go.

"Where's the pilot?" Joseph shouted. Someone pointed.

Deshi, Joseph, and I walked around the other side of the chopper where the soldiers and pilot sat, bound to trees.

Olga sat away from the others; her sorry head slumped between her shoulders as if it were hanging by a thread. I wanted to ask her—why? How could she do it? But I also didn't want to hear her excuses, her reasons for telling the Superiors where we were, for making it possible for them to murder thousands of their own citizens. That, and I was afraid of my own anger towards her. Because a large part of me wanted to stomp on her until she was parts, not a whole. Pieces lying cracked and open in the mud.

They had their video now. I shuddered at the thought of them showing it in the other towns. I saw my mother's face again and squeezed Rosa-May's hand. She put us first. She entrusted her little girl to me. My sister. It proved something I was never sure of until now.

"Do you want to talk to her?" Joseph's voice was edged sharply in anger.

I contemplated it and decided no. "There's nothing she can say."

Joseph moved his arm around my shoulders, a beat of hesitation there like there was a bubble of air between him and me he had to push through to touch me. I was trying to ignore it, hoping it was just concern.

"There he is." Joseph pointed to a man in his thirties, his head against a trunk, his eyes rolling with the swish of the frozen leaves above him as if mesmerized.

I squatted down in front of him and sat back on my knees.

His head snapped to me.

"I didn't know," he said quietly as his eyes lolled back to the leaves.

"They didn't tell me what they were planning. I just fly the choppers and follow orders. I swear. I didn't know they would do this." His head rocked back and forth in unison with the dancing branches. I shuddered as the wind picked up, hooking into my skin and reeling me into his swirling eyes.

I reached out my hand and touched his arm. "What's your name?"

"I didn't know. All those people. Did you hear the screaming? I didn't know," he muttered. Something in this guy's head had snapped. My hope slipped away with the threads of his sanity that someone had cut loose.

"Well, I really want this guy flying me hundreds of feet over pointy trees and jagged rocks," Deshi muttered sarcastically.

A rustle in the trees caught my attention, and I jerked to standing.

"What is it?" Joseph asked, his fingers digging into my arm.

"You're hurting me," I whispered, irritated.

"Damn it." Joseph let me go suddenly and walked away. He was acting so strange. He pulled his hands through his hair, turning his back to me. I placed a hand on his back, feeling it tense under my fingers.

"It's okay…It was an accident," I whispered.

"Denis?" Deshi's shocked voice carried suspicion and hope.

We swung around and watched as Denis carefully picked his way towards us from the bushes, his long legs slipping gracefully between the plants without touching them.

"I can fly it," he said, his bruise-shadowed face pulling between grave and nervous.

55

Lists

JOSEPH

I wish so many things. Mostly, I wish for time.
To go back. To savor. To fast forward. To control.
I want to tell them everything and nothing.

"Matt!" I jogged to catch up with him as he headed into the crowd to check more people for injuries. He paused. Soft gazes swung our way. The people of Pau Brazil were soaked in grief. But some were starting to move, to question and interact with the Survivors. There was no anger, only curiosity at the moment. I prayed it would stay that way.

"Joseph!" Matt's voice was welcoming. My words for him were lead-coated.

"I need to tell you something."

"Mhm..." Matt fumbled around in his pack for his stethoscope.

"It wasn't Rosa. It was me and Deshi." I breathed the words out slowly, watching them turn to steam.

Matt's gaze was kind. "I know. Deshi told me what happened. I know you can't see it yet, but you'll get through it." He placed a reassuring hand on my shoulder that may as well have been a sharp hook. "Have you spoken to your parents?"

"My parents are already upset with me. They feel like they only just got me back and now I'm leaving again. I don't think I can add any more stress to their lives right now," I blurted.

Matt nodded, doctoring me. I could almost see him taking notes on my PTSD in his head. "And Rosa?"

"I don't know how." *I don't know where to start.* Matt didn't even know about Elise. I'd made a mess so high and so deep I didn't know how to wade out of it or even if I deserved to.

"You'll figure it out," he said, unperturbed, like it was a given.

56

Leaving Pau

ROSA

I watched Denis and Deshi carefully as we prepared for our journey. They seemed friendly enough but there was no tearful reunion or any obvious evidence of a romantic relationship. Denis revolved around Deshi as if he were the sun, but he never touched him. When Denis climbed into the cockpit of the chopper, my eyes fell to Deshi as I tried to decipher something that was possibly never there.

"Rosa, I can feel you staring at me," Deshi growled while he was bent over his pack.

"You're just so stunning in those camo clothes!" I joked.

He stood up and grinned at me. "I missed you." He paused, his eyes softening.

I stepped closer to his side, our hips touching as I wrapped my arm around his narrow waist. Unlike Joseph, I could probably wrap my arms around Deshi twice.

"Did *he* miss me?" Our eyes rested on Joseph, who was talking to his father near the bombsite. Really, I knew he had. I don't why I needed the reassurance; things just seemed a little off with him.

Deshi wiggled out of my grip and faced me—in his expression lay all the truths and answers I wanted and didn't want. I looked away.

"I don't even know how to express to you how much he missed you, blamed himself, and almost died without you. Rosa, he's struggling. Even with you back, I'm worried about him."

I didn't need to hear that. "Is it because of what he did?" I asked, my heart pounding, shock waves running through me as the hours spent watching video after video of Joseph killing those soldiers rose like magic ink in my brain.

Deshi's eyes bugged out in a surprise and for a second, his mouth hung open. It was very unlike him and he quickly composed himself.

"You know what he did?" he asked, his voice high and cracked.

"Please, don't tell him," I pleaded. "Part of my tort... I mean, interrogations, was watching the surveillance from that night. I saw myself... dying." I kind of gulped dryly at the memory. It was physical, running through me like the knife that killed me. "And I saw what Joseph did after. They showed it to me... a lot."

Deshi sighed. "Oh..." There it was again. That beat of silence like there was a missing word lying flat on his tongue. "Jesus, Rosa, that's horrible."

I nodded, trying to slow my breath and stop the shaking. Joseph walked towards us, a determined look on his face. He stomped through the grass loudly, and I wondered what his father had said.

I whispered to Deshi as he gripped both my wrists reassuringly. "I know what he's like, I know he's probably been beating himself up about what he did, but he didn't have a choice. He would have died."

Deshi let me go as Joseph brushed through the spindly trees bordering the chopper. Ice crept up their trunks and froze their shoulders. I breathed in the smell of icy pine and smoldering fires as if it were a drug I couldn't get enough of.

"You're just going to have to talk to him," Deshi said with urgency winding round and round his voice.

I bowed my head. The words *how* and *when* pushed their way out of the dirt like spring flowers at my feet.

"What are you two talking about?" Joseph smiled, and the sun peeked out between his lips.

I tried it out; I let the golden rays hit my face and warm me.

"You," I teased. Something like panic and fear swept across his face like a breeze, and then it was gone. "It's okay. Nothing bad," I said, my hands up in defense.

"Nothing bad, man." Deshi backed me up.

Denis poked his head out of the cabin. "Are you ready to leave?"

I jumped, feeling on edge. "Is Rosa-May still with Pelo?" I asked Joseph.

"She is. Are you sure you want to bring her?" He brought a hand to my hair, and I felt like I might cry because there was air and awkwardness between us. His touch was comfort and heartbreak. It reminded me of things I'd lost, and it brought me back home.

"I'm not leaving her behind. I'm all she has." I set my mouth.

He grinned. "So I have a daughter now?"

I laughed at his acceptance, his readiness to let Rosa-May into our family.

"Well, technically, she's sort of like your sister-in-law. Is that right, Matthew?"

Matthew handed me a sack full of food and smirked. "I don't think there's a traditional word that fits your situation. All I know is, she's lucky to have you both."

The others gathered around to say goodbye. Gwen knocked my shoulder and whispered, "Good luck."

Everyone exchanged looks as the blades began to churn and distort the air and words became too difficult. Deshi slapped Elise on the back, rather hard, and she pursed her lips at him before breaking into a stunning smile directed at Joseph and me.

Pelo handed me Rosa-May and yelled to me, "I want to come with you."

I shook my head. He was needed here.

Jonathan and Steph held hands and waved to their son. When Steph's eyes caught mine, they narrowed suspiciously. I got the feeling I wasn't what she'd hoped for as a match for her son.

The air buzzed. Joseph grabbed my waist and hoisted me into the chopper, bending his head and following me inside. Deshi strode to the co-pilot chair and strapped himself in, busily connecting my handheld to the choppers' navigational system. I strapped Rosa-May in, her face flushed and confused. I wished there was more I could do for her, a way to explain. The craft rattled and did a one-legged dance as it jerkily lifted into the air.

Joseph closed the door and fell into the seat next to me, strapping himself in just as the craft became airborne. I wanted to say, *Remember the last time we were together in one of these?* But no words came. I was overwhelmed with the memories of our past. They hit me fast like rocks spitting up into a windshield. Fear of what was ahead, excitement at leaving home and Paulo behind, and an aching for my mother. But all of those memories paled to one—Joseph's hand over mine like a golden barrier, shutting out all my harried thoughts and warming me to my spindly core.

This was where we started. This was how we spread out over the wilderness, a thousand stretching strands. So many plotted points, missed and taken, that brought us right up to now.

His ribs nudged my side as his chest expanded with deep breaths next to me. I put my hand over his and curled my thin fingers over his tensed knuckles like a cage. We watched the people turn to ants and the forest swallow them whole.

Deshi pointed north and we swung around in an arc, the edge of Pau Brazil just visible. Concrete, I once thought impenetrable, was cracked and spilling into the grass.

57

A Kiss

ROSA

Denis and Deshi chatted happily in the cockpit because they had those headphone things on. It was as noisy as a windstorm in the back, the blades ricocheting off the low clouds like they were made of rubber. Silence suited us anyway. After we found Orry, we were going to have to find time to talk. Just not now.

Rosa-May's head lolled against my ribs. She'd slept for hours. I wished I could do the same. I sighed and looked down at our hands lying over each other's like soft blankets. Calming.

I turned to the window and felt Joseph staring at me. But I liked being under his gaze, so I didn't move my head for fear he'd look away.

Below, the wilderness stretched endlessly. Creeping up with fronded fingers as we ascended into the mountains. I chewed on my nails as I willed the chopper to move faster.

The chopper dipped suddenly, and we all gripped our harnesses as we flew out of our seats.

"We need to land!" Denis shouted over his shoulder.

It lurched and dove as if it were sitting in a sea storm. My stomach floated along with it. Finally, it touched down awkwardly in a tiny patch of wild grass surrounded by trees.

When it was quieter, Denis removed his headphones and explained. "The battery is flat. It needs to charge for the rest of the day. We'll have to... camp?" He said it like a question, like he'd never used the word before.

The blades slowed, and we unclipped our harnesses. Joseph stood and stretched his back, raising his arms up to the ceiling and pushing on it. I bit my lip while I watched his arms flex.

His eyes twinkled as they gazed at the sleeping child at my side. Gently, he unbuckled her harness and scooped her into his arms, her dark hair splaying out behind her head as it swayed from side to side with his movements.

We shuffled out of the chopper and as soon as my feet crunched the earth, I felt small. The forests around the settlements were lush, dominating, but new. This world was old. The trees were elders, their gnarled, enormous trunks scored with age and experience. The air had a cold quiet about it, like through the gaps in the trees, eyes were watching us. I jogged to one of the trunks, hopping over ferns and mossy plants. Joseph's chuckle pulsed through the air in fresh waves. My hand connected with the immense bark, deep cracks running through it like river canyons.

"Wow!" I said in awe as I craned my neck to stare up the branches spinning out and up, up, up.

Both Deshi and Joseph laughed.

Denis asked, confused, "What on earth is she doing?"

Joseph answered. "This is like Rosa's idea of heaven."

I wanted to press my whole existence to the trunk and hug it. It felt like it had been years since I was in the forest, even though it had only been about a month. One month of people trying to pull my spirit from my body. I rubbed my face on the mossy bark and breathed in the pungent smell of rotted wood.

Deshi coughed. "Ok, now you're just being weird. Did that tree give you consent?"

I blushed and stepped back. Under the cover of the immense canopy, the air was warmer. We were protected from the wind and the sprinklings of snow. I gazed up at the small patch of winter-white sky. Unfortunately, we were also hidden from the sun.

"How's it going to charge?" I asked, pointing at the leaves above. The whole clearing was in shadow.

Denis stared at the soggy ground, not quite sure which way to go. He decided to stand still. "Someone has to climb up there with the panels," he said, pointing to a tree behind us. The branches were slightly lower but still really high.

Joseph balanced carefully on a stone, with a sleeping Rosa-May still in his arms. "Of course," he grumbled. "Maybe we should make the Superior's son climb up there." His was voice terse with aggravation.

Denis' face registered alarm at the suggestion.

"I would," he mumbled, "but I'm injured. Besides, I think we all know who has to go." His eyes swung to me, my moss-stained hands clasped behind my back.

I would have volunteered anyway.

"Is there any point in saying no?" Joseph asked, his hair shielding me from his annoyed eyes.

I shook my head. "Nope. You ready to throw me?" I needed Joseph to hoist me into the branches. I was smallest and lightest. It made sense that it should be me. He groaned in response.

Denis backed into the chopper like the squidgy ground scared him and sat on the edge, unraveling the wire that connected the batteries in the chopper to the foldout solar panels beside him. Deshi held out his arms for Rosa-May. Her body was still slack with exhaustion, and I started to wonder if maybe she didn't want to wake up. When she opened her eyes, she would be met with more strange places and missing faces. I understood that feeling. Joseph handed her to Deshi.

Denis leaned over me, showing me how to unfold the panels and where to plug the wire in while Joseph hovered. Then, he rolled them up and put both in a backpack.

I took off my jacket, shoved my overlong sleeves to my elbows, and marched to the tree behind the chopper.

"You ready?" Joseph asked, his green eyes pulsing gold, his eyebrows drawn together in worry.

"It's fine. It should be easy," I replied, knowing nothing ever was.

He grabbed me under the arms and lifted me onto his shoulders.

I ran my fingers through his curls briefly before placing my hands on the trunk to balance and standing up on his shoulders.

"You're lighter," he remarked.

"She never ate much," Denis said, and Joseph turned suddenly.

My hands scraped down the bark, and I nearly fell backwards before he grabbed my legs. "Sorry."

The rich food they'd offered me had often made me sick. I ran a hand down my hip and noticed the sharpness of it, the way it almost pierced my skin. Was that why Joseph was being so careful with me? Did I look frail to him?

I glanced down at Joseph's head. His shirt flapped open and a series of scars running down his chest shocked me. *Another thing to ask about.*

"The food was fatty and gross," I snapped in Denis' direction. I reached out for the lower branch, but I couldn't quite reach it. "Throw me," I said to Joseph.

He put both hands under my butt, counted, "One, two, three," and hurled me at the branch. I got my arms around it and scrambled against the trunk with my legs until I was up.

"You okay?" Joseph shouted breathlessly, staring at me from below.

"All good!" I said.

I tucked my hair behind my ears, it swung back out, and I climbed.

Each brush of leaves raises my skin. Each crumble of bark beneath my fingertips brings me closer. I'm climbing to the sky, yet I feel closer to home than ever.

The air cooled as I ascended. The old tree's branches were so thick and sturdy it was an easy climb. Soon, I was in the canopy watching Joseph pace anxiously below.

Breathing in the frosted air, I let it woo me. I let it rescue me from the disasters, the wounding memories, and let my mind empty. The breeze crackled through my head and blew out the musty corners. They were huddled stubbornly and not easily moved.

Carefully, I unfolded the panels and nestled them in a branch that caught the sun, even in this late afternoon. I plugged the wire in and let it drop to the forest floor.

I straddled a branch and waited. Waited for the wind to pick me up and take me away, waited for the unease in me to blister and pop. I waited until someone yelled for me to get down.

Climbing down was harder. I was descending into a darker world and my eyes took time to adapt. That, and my feet were reaching out blindly, searching for branches, scraping the air sometimes and slipping.

Joseph swore as I reached the last few branches.

"You're nearly there," he said nervously, his hands out in front, ready to catch me. Taking the last branch slowly, my feet slipped on the slimy moss. I let go of the branch above to grab the next one when Rosa-May screamed. My limbs jerked in surprise, and I fell.

It was only a few meters but those seconds felt unending. My arms flailed up, still reaching for something to hold onto. My mouth clamped shut, my eyes scrunched tight, and I landed with a thump. Strong hands gripped my bare back.

I opened my eyes, my lips forming the words *thank you*, but rendered mute. Joseph's face was white, his freckles standing out strongly against his horrified expression. His thumb brushed the ropey scar across my stomach like a kiss. *A terrifying kiss.* And then he dropped me to my feet, my shirt falling back into place. I gripped the material in my fist, tears scraping at my eyes like thorns. I didn't understand his reaction.

He stared, his eyes wide but looking right through me. As he backed away, his head sweeping back and forth, he muttered, "I can't," before he turned and stormed into the forest.

Maybe I should have left him, but I couldn't stand the look on his face. I couldn't leave it like that and not try to change it. I chased after him, leaving Deshi attempting to calm Rosa-May and Denis standing still as a statue, so out of place in this world that he might have been one of Grant's garden sculptures.

58

Confession

ROSA

Deshi shouted at me as I reached the tree line. "Rosa, take this." He threw me a pack. When I shot him a confused look, he added, "Just in case." I didn't like the expression on his face. It was unfamiliar, frightening, because it was mix of disappointment and regret. It hit me like a plank peppered with nails because it wasn't directed at me. His disappointment was in Joseph.

Joseph's blond head bobbed through the trees, the distance between us stretching long as a highway. I called out to him, which spurred him on. *Was he running away from me?* It was a terrifying thought, which I shoved down as I picked my way over the dense vegetation. Shadows wrapped around every plant, trapping them in the dirt. The sun split its way between the trunks of the great trees as I used them to support me, warning me night was coming.

While I was staring at the sky, I lost him. Suddenly alone, with the dark, dank forest pressing around me, I shivered for fear of finding him. Because I felt there was a slimy, threatening truth waiting for me when I did.

My hands scraped along the slick trunks, the bark so large I could sink my whole hand between the gaps of the trees skin. Wrinkled like an old woman. Like Addy. God, I missed her advice. Her humor.

My breath formed mist that hung in the air too long. My sighs were heavy clouds floating to the sky. I paused at a tree, bracing my arm against it as my eyes ran in vast semicircles, sweeping the terrain in front.

Tree, tree, bush, tree split down the middle, Joseph, tree.

He sat restlessly, head down, leaning against the trunk of a stout tree plucked clean of leaves like a bird for the oven. It was dwarfed by the giants around us and by his own size. It reminded me of when I'd found him at the Classes, just before my assessment, talking to himself, huddled awkwardly under a Pau Brazil tree. It was a conversation he later explained as him choosing to tell me how he really felt.

It was too late then. It was not like that now.

He heard my foot suck out of the mud with a slurping sound. He looked up, and his face was a battering ram pushing me back. His eyes, the color of the bright green moss that crept up every trunk, were washed with a deep sadness. He was truly unhappy to see me. My heart tore like paper. Just a small edge at the bottom, which if he didn't explain himself, would rip all the way up.

His head dropped down again and I stopped, midstride, several meters from where he sat, afraid to approach and equally afraid to walk away.

I brought my legs together and took one more timid step towards him. My eyes never left his hidden face, hair curtaining his eyes as he hung his head between his knees like it was just too heavy to hold up. A strand of blackberry dragged across my face as I said, "Joseph, why are you running away from me? Ouch!" I lifted my hand to my cheek, a small stain of red coloring my fingers. The branch stuck in my hair. I tried to move forward and couldn't. Putting my hands up to my head, I attempted to pull it out, only to tangle it further.

Joseph stood up and sighed in exasperation. *Was he sick of me?*

"It doesn't matter what I do. I'm always hurting you." His voice plummeted like a stone dropped down an endless abyss. There was more regret than I could understand in there. He came closer and helped me pull the thorns from my hair.

As we stood chest to chest, I gazed up into his face. "That's not true." My own voice wavered like a feather tossed down the same abyss. Falling, but slower, hoping the wind might still pick me up and save me.

"Look," he said, running a finger under my eye and holding it in front of my face like proof. "You're bleeding."

"It's nothing," I whispered, knocking his hand away and forcing a smile.

He exhaled through his nose in frustration. "Yeah, it's nothing.

Nothing compared to what I have done, to what I'm going to do." His sarcasm was pointed and tipped in bitterness.

My ribs clamored and braced my heart, tightening a protective cage around me. He went to put his hands on my waist but stopped himself, his hands hovering there, hopelessly.

I don't want to ask. I have to ask.

"What are you talking about? If it's about what you did after... after I died, I know it's hard, especially for someone like you, but it wasn't your fault. You would have died if you hadn't defended yourself." I hated the sound of my voice because it was pitched with fear, uncertainty, and panic.

He glanced up from the ground, the cool dawn of realization rising on his face. Words had slipped out. It was too late to collect them. "Wait, how do you know what I did after? How could you? You were, were..." He stumbled over his words like boulders in the road.

I placed a hand on his chest and felt his heart galloping. "I was dead."

He shook once, all over, like the memory still shocked him. "So how?"

I swallowed, carefully picking out what I would tell him and what I would save for that nonexistent time—*later.*

"They made me watch the surveillance video." *Over and over, until it was scratched into my brain with their perfect, clean fingernails.* "I saw it all happen. They attacked you, and you fought back. You need to know, I don't blame you. I don't think anyone could blame you for what happened. It hasn't changed the way I feel about you."

My heartbeat stalled in my chest as those pictures flipped through the backs of my eyes. But as violent as they were, I knew he hadn't had a choice. Hesitantly, he placed his hand over mine. A gold flash slapped me across the face and he withdrew, stepping back and throwing his hands in the air. Whatever he'd been holding back was rumbling and growing now.

"Jesus, Rosa!" His voice angled towards the sky, and he clasped his hands behind his head. "I don't understand how you're okay."

I'm not... and you know I'm not.

He turned away from me, *stop turning away from me,* and I could see his ribs expanding, his back muscles tensed like they could barely hold him in any longer.

"Joseph, what's wrong? You can tell me," I pleaded, my hands limp at my sides, my body not daring to come closer. Electrified words piled up between us, jutting out of the mud like thrown-down axes.

He just shook his head over and over like the sad elephant at the zoo. *What did you do?*

He faced me, his eyes throwing warnings, and I felt the need to cover my ears, to run before his words caught me. "I wish it were just about that night. God, Rosa, if only it was just that. If only I had known before, maybe I wouldn't have... wouldn't have..."

The ground softened under my feet, turning to quicksand that tried to swallow me. *Don't ask him.* I picked my way over the obstacles between us. He stood like a statue, a Joseph statue carved from bleeding rock. I put my hand to his jaw, forcing him to look at me. "Wouldn't have what?"

His head fell. He didn't want me to ask either.

There were tears in his eyes, running hard like bullets, one, two, three down his cheeks. "Rosa, I was almost unfaithful to you," he whispered.

I laughed awkwardly, my lips curling and catching on my teeth. *This was a joke, right?* I swept my eyes around the forest like I was checking to see if anyone was listening. The trees seemed to lurch backwards, splaying like I was a bomb that had already gone off. But I didn't really understand him.

I attempted to calm myself, planting my feet firmly, and the ground steadied for a small second as I replayed the word *almost, almost, almost.* But it was such a brief reprieve. That second word swung around on chains strung from the clouds and blared in front of my eyes, bigger than the sky. I wished I could un-hear it, shove a cloth down its throat and throw it away, but it was too late. The bottom of the world slid away like a pullout tray, leaving me suspended in the air, my feet hanging limp below. My scrabbling fingers dug deep into the word *unfaithful.*

My hand dropped from his face. He was stone, the color and the feel. I shook my head from side to side, as if I could dislodge this thing rattling around in my head. It had sharp angles, and it was wedged into the soft corners that were once his. Now, they bled raw. *Almost unfaithful.* I didn't know what that meant. The sharp thing bashed at my thoughts. It was a box I didn't want to open, even as I pried at it with desperate, chipped fingers, because I didn't *want* to know what those words meant.

I stepped back and hit a tree with a thud. Little pieces of bark rained down my back and fell into my too-big shoes. My chest felt hollow; my heart and lungs had dissolved. I opened and shut my mouth, mechanically doing the things to keep me alive. *Breathe in, breathe out.* I didn't know how to react because I never expected him to say that. I cycled through every emotion and came back to nothing. I felt nothing. Bloodless, aimless.

He stood in front of me, bewildered and waiting. The words pinned to his shirt like a note for the teacher.

I thought nothing would come out of my mouth until everything poured from my lips like an avalanche. Suddenly, the questions were in my hands and I hurled them at him: *When? Why? Who? With who?*

He took each word like a spear to the chest, stumbling backwards until he was on the ground and I was standing over him, breathing hard. My legs trembled, and I swayed. I was going to be sick. Covering my stomach with my hand, I felt my insides twist like snake.

He knelt over, his hands pressed into the dirt, looking like he was going to be sick too.

He whispered her name into the tiny palm fronds that jabbed out of the mud, and when the name floated up to my ears, I couldn't stand it.

When he told me he kissed her, that he almost… I actually screamed. The details were a knife that kept on stabbing, through, through, through to the other side of me.

"Stop," I gasped, the bile burning a path up my throat. "Please. I can't hear anymore." His mouth clapped shut. His face was a broken bruise I shouldn't have to heal.

The smell of lemons, detergent, and chemicals brought me back. I was wearing her clothes. I shrugged off my own jacket, and my furious hands started unbuttoning her shirt because her clothes were burning my skin. It was a stupid thing to do. It was freezing and only getting colder, but I felt stupid wearing her too-long pants and her shirt that left so much air between where my chest ended and what it allowed for. I bit my lip and stared at the darkening sky. There should have been black, angry clouds pulsing with lightning, but it was clear. Empty.

My eyes snapped to Joseph as he rushed towards me.

"I'm so sorry, Rosa," he said, his beautiful, lying eyes tortured. He took both sides of her shirt and held them together, over my chest, in his fist. I tried to struggle out, but his grip was too strong. "You can't. You'll freeze to death," he whispered sadly.

I shoved him, screaming, "I can't wear her fucking clothes!" He staggered back in surprise. I'd never spoken to him, or to anyone, like that. I stood there, feral and angry, my shirt open, revealing my scars and frozen skin.

I started unbuckling my pants, but stopped. I didn't know what I was doing anymore.

He removed his jacket and started unbuttoning his shirt, calmer than he had a right to be. "Take mine," he offered.

Scowling, I snapped, "Then you'll freeze to death." My teeth were already chattering.

He smiled sadly at my obstinacy. I couldn't look at his mouth so I turned my eyes to his chest and the deep scars running down his skin.

"I guess we're at an impasse then," he said.

"What are those?" I asked, pointing at his scars. I needed to break the conversation in half, just for a moment.

"Polar bear attack," he said, gazing down at the dark purple parts of his skin. He carefully removed his shirt and handed it to me. Snatching it, I ripped her shirt from my body, the sleeve snagging at my wrist. I tugged at it until the cuff tore and released me, letting it fall to the dirt. Stepping on it, I screwed my foot into the ground, just to make sure it soaked up plenty of mud. I put his shirt on quickly, my movements jerky from the cold, and then put my own jacket over the top. His clothes enveloped me in the warmth and smells I'd craved and wanted. It reminded me that I loved him. *I love him.*

He pulled his jacket over his bare skin, his scars, and zipped it up. "What do we do now?" he said in a croak of sadness, reaching for my hand.

I withdrew. I was angry. Torture. That was all I could see in his eyes, across his mouth, in his tense jaw. He was torturing himself.

Good.

He walked away from me, pulling his hands through his hair. Sadness punctuated every movement. After everything we'd been through...

No. Not good.

I did the same as him, pulling my hands through my messy hair, trying to tease out my anger. Soon, night would pull down like a blind. The grey shadows were fast turning black.

"Please just give me a second. I don't know what to do." I put my finger up in the air. Exasperation tinged my voice because it seemed unfair that I should be the one to decide what we did next.

I stepped further away and watched him pace like a man possessed, in front of a backdrop of red-brown bark slathered with woolly, green moss. He became smaller and smaller in my vision as I disconnected. I walked backwards until my ankles hit a log, and I was forced to sit down. I was blank, my thoughts like startled birds, cruelly anchored to the ground, jerking up and scratching against each other. Feathers flying. Nowhere to go.

I stared at him for an hour or so, my eyes tired, round discs that begged for tears that wouldn't come. I stared at him until the sun disappeared and the coolness of the earth rose around us in sheets. Until one thought snapped its strings and whirled into the sky in broken-winged arcs—*you love him*.

He stopped pacing and sat opposite me. Only five meters away, but the distance between us seemed so far, perilous, flawed, and spiked.

I stood and his eyes followed me, the hope in them wounding me. "I'm going to light a fire," I announced, approaching the broken ground between us for the pack.

His eyes fell to his hands and I wondered—*did he see blood on them like I did on mine?*

I hurt for him, I hated him, and I loved him. I wanted him. Always.

Sighing, I began building the fire.

"Can I help?" His voice was meek, and I loathed the sound of it.

"Get some of the bigger wood, over there." I pointed to a fallen log. It was damp but hopefully, it would burn.

He stumbled off, always breaking branches and crushing plants in his wake.

I coaxed the flames; the wet, smoky smell filled my head with other nights, nights before he ruined things. My eyes watered as the breeze blew smoke in my face. I rubbed them with the back of my hand.

Returning, he placed the wood by my side. He sat closer, edging towards me like I might bite him. I did feel rabid. Angry and confused. I wanted to hate him, but I couldn't. I wanted to forgive him, but I couldn't.

"Rosa, say something," he begged.

"Like what?" I snarled into the fire that was more smoke than flames. Leaning down, I held my hair in one hand while I blew on it.

He didn't know what to do with his hands—in his lap, behind his back, in his hair. Every now and then, they reached for me, and I inched away.

"Do you hate me?" he asked

"No…"

"Do you still love me?" He was an idiot. The doubt in his voice almost broke my heart.

"Don't ask stupid questions," I snapped.

"Right, sorry."

I picked up a small branch. It crumbled in my hands, so I sprinkled it on the fire. Slowly, the flames were building. It was simple in there. I could have wished for my life to be simple, but it was like asking a meal to drop from the sky. It wasn't going to happen.

Joseph dragged the pack towards him, bumping it over my feet, and retrieved some food. "Are you hungry?"

"No."

"You can't even look at me, can you?" His voice was sliced-up pieces of what it used to be.

If I looked at him, my anger would melt away.

My eyes snatched a glimpse, a profile of his tormented face, and I was reminded just how much we'd both suffered, the things we'd had to do.

When I was in Grant's home, my only thoughts were getting back to him and to Orry. I just couldn't understand how he could do it. How, after only a month apart, could he have put his lips on some stranger's? But then I thought about how lost and alone I was and I wondered… *If someone had offered me comfort in my weakest moment, would I have taken it?* It had been so hard to hold out hope that I would see him again, when it seemed impossible. I tried to squeeze my feet into Joseph's worn-out shoes. I tried to understand why. I didn't want to understand, but I needed to.

"If I look at you, I'll forgive you. I don't want to do that yet," I said through a grimace.

"Oh, okay. What can I do?" His voice was a peak of emotions, each one tumbling down a cliff and landing in my lap to sort through.

I shrugged hard, my whole body feeling exhausted by all the words, all the apologies, and all the promises broken.

"Explain it to me."

The world slowed. The arms of the clock rewound as Joseph took me back to that first night when he'd left me because he had to. I listened to his anguish and I started to understand the pain, the hopelessness, he had felt. The burden of believing everything was his fault alone.

The shadows of the trees curled around us, protecting us, and gave us this time to absorb each other's lost days. It was so much more than I'd realized.

His face got sadder and longer with every day he went through.

After hours of listening, questioning, he reached the part of the story I had been dreading.

"She offered me a way to forget, and I took it. I was selfish, stupid, drunk. None of that is a good enough excuse, but that's the truth."

"And it was just a kiss?" I winced, anticipating the answer to a question I shouldn't have asked.

"Rosa, I'm so sorry. It was a kiss that would have led to more if Rash hadn't stopped us." He wrung his hands out, squeezing the last bit of blood and tears onto the soaked ground. "I'd like to think I would have stopped, it all felt so wrong, but if I'm honest, I just don't know."

I knew. "You would have stopped."

His laugh sounded like a sorrowful hiccup. "I can't believe you have faith in me after everything I've put you through." His lips were set hard with harsh memories of the past. "I killed people, men with families like me. And whether or not it was in self-defense, I'm not sure it matters. Every time I closed my eyes, I saw you dead in front of me, then I'd blink and they joined you, this pile of people I'd hurt, killed, left behind. When I did what I did, it was because I couldn't stand myself. I didn't want to see your face and their faces anymore. It was killing me. I needed you and you weren't there and it was my fault."

He poured his bad dreams out. They landed in the mud for me to inspect and maybe to bury. And because I still loved him, I felt awful that I hadn't been there to help him through it.

My head collapsed in my hands, and I stared into the fire. "Don't get me wrong, I'm really angry about what you did, but you're not a bad man, Joseph. You're messed up, not bad. You need to understand that not *everything* is your fault. Some things just happen."

I wished I had a higher horse to stand on, a step, anything. But after all the mistakes I'd made, the promise I'd broken, all I could do was look him in the eye and try to understand.

He put his hand over mine and although my instant reaction was to snatch it away, I let it stay. I let his warmth soak into me. It lifted me even as I fought against it.

I floated outside of my body, my mind begging for perspective because it seemed unreal. *My* Joseph couldn't have done this. But with every passing second, I understood, as I watched his grief-stricken body heave in breaths he didn't think he deserved, that *my* Joseph was broken and I couldn't walk away from him.

5:9

Move Through

JOSEPH

I'm trying to convince myself it's a dream. A fast, hollow dream. Because I hurt her. I hurt us. And I should have been better than this. She didn't cry much. She was holding herself together, holding herself away from me as if I were a fire and she needed to lean away from the heat.

She listened, nodded, and shifted.

My words felt like knives, cutting me first and then her.

The world slept and soon, we caught up with it. Slowly, she unraveled. Her body loosened from exhaustion, from everything I'd just put her through. She turned towards me, her face flushed from the fire, and put her hand on my leg. I stalled, scared I'd frighten her, when all I wanted was to press her to me and never, ever let go. Then all her angles and sharpness melted as she crawled into my lap, pulling my arm over her like a blanket and laying her head in arms. I felt her tiny weight, draped across my legs, her hair waving over my arm and tickling my skin, and absorbed every detail I could. She glanced at me briefly, a look of love behind confusion, and closed her eyes.

I flipped my head to the sky. I wouldn't sleep tonight. If this was all she was going to give me, I wasn't going to miss one second.

I stroked her dyed hair and wondered what they did to her. And stopped. One thing at a time. "You were in the sky. Now you're in my arms." I sighed like I might perish. *She was in my arms.*

Her lips fell open as she dozed off. My fingers burned to touch them, but I didn't.

I fed the fire.

I wasn't sure I even blinked for fear she'd disappear.

Her eyes opened slowly to the dawn. She coughed, and I tightened my grip on her. She moaned, snuggled closer, and my chest started to open. I smiled, my face feeling waxy and dry from the fire. She smiled back quickly, a flash across her face.

"Morning, sleeping beauty," I said, in agony from all the words I wanted to say, and all the parts of her I couldn't reach.

She stretched out her limbs, and I cracked my stiff neck. I'd hunched over her like a shelter all night, and my body felt like stone.

"Morning," she yawned. And then, as if she suddenly remembered, her face creased and she started to wiggle out of my arms.

"Rosa." She froze, scowled, and stayed half in my lap and half out.

She picked up the last of the wood and threw it on the fire. "Why did you tell me? You could have lied. Kept it to yourself," she asked, pinning me with her midnight blue and sunlit warm eyes.

I swallowed my dread and answered. "I don't know. It was selfish, I guess. Do you wish I hadn't?" I risked a hand to her hair and shuddered with relief when she didn't jerk away from me again.

She was quiet for a long minute. I listened to her breathing, heard her thinking in the silence that only Rosa could sustain.

"No and yes," she said, finitely, straightening her back. "It's a weird kind of feeling. I wish you hadn't, but I'm glad you did. It would have come out eventually. And lies grow like cancer, don't they?"

I nodded. "They do."

Her voice was low, sad, punctuated by my actions. "It would have poisoned us."

I leaned towards her desperately, forgetting myself. "Rosa, I promise it will never happen…"

She leaned back from my intensity and put her hand up to my face, her fingers grazing my open mouth. "Don't. I don't need you to. I know it won't."

I sat up straight and clasped my hands together, mostly because I didn't know what to do with them. I didn't deserve to touch her. I didn't deserve... her.

She narrowed her eyes, and I prepared for venom. "Joseph. Stop looking at me like that."

I raised my eyebrows in surprise. "Like what?"

"Like you think I will disappear. Like you think it's over."

My heart started beating so fast I must have been running towards that hope like it would save me. *It would save me.*

"It's never over." Slowly, she brought her hands to my face, wincing when she touched me. *How could a touch feel like guilt and redemption at the same time?* Her eyes fell to my lips, and I sensed the pain, the reluctance. "I still love you."

My stupid face, my stupid eyes, started crying. A tear ran down my cheek and over her finger. She stared at it curiously. I wanted to say, *I'm sorry, I'm sorry, I'm sorry* until the words had lost their meaning, but I knew she didn't want to hear it anymore.

My voice cracked all over the place as I said, "You're it for me. Don't doubt it. That never changed. The only thing that changed was how much I hated myself."

She dropped her hand and bowed her head, playing with the sleeves of my shirt, which hung so far over her little fingers. The milky light of the morning filtered through the trees and lit her face, shining over her eyelashes and making it hard for me to breathe normally.

"Okay," she mumbled, her toes touching, her knees pressed together. She was so small and so strong.

I want to kiss her. Though I know I have to wait until she comes to me. It has to be her decision. I pray it won't be long, but I'll wait a year if I have to.

I. Will. Do. Anything. She. Wants.

Funny thing was that I knew she wouldn't want much. She wasn't the kind of girl to make demands.

It was one of the many reasons I loved her so damn much.

ROSA

I needed time to let the images settle at the bottom of my brain. It was too fresh and it kept snapping at me, begging to be viewed. I needed her blonde, freckled face and light green eyes to become a transparent memory.

Joseph scooped me up and stood with me still cradled in his arms. Gently, reluctantly, he allowed me to fall to my feet. The ground felt firmer, still a little shaky, but not crumbling away.

I let him take my hand. It was a strange feeling, stinging for a second before it melted into what it was before. I hoped that would change.

We smothered the fire and walked back to the chopper.

60

Open

ROSA

We trudged through the clearing, and Deshi shot up from where he was squatting over a gas burner and saucepan. A plume of steam and the tinny smell of canned food heating welcomed me. He glanced from my face to Joseph's, down to our joined hands, and rushed us both, throwing his arms around our necks and knocking our heads together.

"Okay, okay..." He panted breathlessly. "Well, she didn't kill you. That's a start." Joseph managed a weak laugh in response.

I broke away from Joseph, his fingers gripping my hand until the last second, and let them talk. Everything was packed and ready to go. I wandered up to Denis, who was perched on the edge of the chopper cabin, poking food around his small, metal bowl. I threw the pack in the back of the craft.

"You'll get used to it," I said. Rosa-May's shadow stepped forward from within, the light hitting her frowning face. It was amazing how much she looked like me, especially when she was angry. Paulo was completely absent in her. A good thing. I bowed my head in thanks that she never knew him. She held out her hands for me. In only two days, she'd come to trust me.

"I doubt I'll ever get used to this," Denis replied smoothly, reaching for his headphones that were no longer there.

"We have music too. I'm sure Gwen could help you with that when we get back." My chipper voice was more like soggy bark chips, dull and unconvincing. Besides, I didn't really care whether he was comfortable or not. It was never a concern he had for me. I was about to add that maybe he shouldn't ask Gwen for anything, considering he'd abandoned her to die. But I left it, feeling a prickle of evil satisfaction at the fact that she'd probably tear him apart if he did ask her for something. My smile was dipped in acid sugar and he gave me a peculiar look, as if he knew there was a nasty thought lurking behind it. I shrugged, picked Rosa-May up, and squeezed her middle. "I'm sorry I was away for so long." She nodded, her roundish chin touching her chest. Still no words.

We waited the two hours needed for the batteries to charge before I retrieved the panels. During the wait, we ate our breakfast, plotted our course, and then, after they were reattached, we left. We rose up, wobbling between the trees like a puppet on strings.

Skimming through the air like a bug, I decided I liked this untouched-by-humans part of the forest. The hand of our inferior species hadn't razed this corner, stumped its growth. It meant the trees were full. The world was wild and how it should be.

I focused on my sister, purposefully seating her between Joseph and me. Unspoken, un-dealt-with things stacked between us. Just because I was willing to stay, to hold onto him, didn't mean I was fine. Every time I let my thoughts drift, they kept wandering back to the same place like a self-destructive homing pigeon. Him and *her.* It turned my stomach over once and then knotted it tightly.

I put my hand in Rosa-May's hair mindlessly stroked the top of her head as we whirred over the tops of the trees, the foliage of each touching the other like a dense, squidgy floral arrangement.

"Look down there," I said, pointing to a large gap in the trees. She glanced at it unenthusiastically and then went back to her fidgety fingers. She had half-moons in her fingernails, just like me. I thought of Mother, trimming her nails and mine. Chastising me when I had chewed them, sighing, always sighing at my defiance. Her memory coated this child like an extra layer of skin.

A smashed section of mirror lay on the land—a lake, reflective in the middle and frozen around the edges. The ice crept inwards like white ghosts racing to the center of the water. I craned my neck and could see the black underbelly of the chopper reflected in the water.

Joseph pinched Rosa-May's elbow and winked at her. "See over there?" He pointed to the middle. When he spoke to her, he forced air and light into his tone and it lifted her head. "They say there's a monster living in the bottom of the lake, and when children laugh, it jumps out of the water and does a flip."

I wanted to ask, *Who's they?* I wanted to play along, but I didn't.

I rolled my eyes, but Rosa-May looked up from her lap and pressed her face to the window behind us, twisting in her harness. While she peered out of the window, Joseph tickled her. Her laugh was husky, chords running side by the side. I laughed too and Joseph caught my eye, grinning. My stupid heart kicked into gear.

"I saw it! Did you see it?" he shouted. She shook her head, pouting. We passed over the lake and brushed the tips of the trees again. "Well, on our way home, you better look more closely." She nodded, very serious.

I covered my mouth but a small giggle slipped out.

The air cooled as the chopper climbed, the green forest gradually swallowed by white. I put my arm around Rosa-May's shoulders and rubbed her little arms. My hand brushed Joseph's elbow, and he sighed loudly when I withdrew sharply.

"Sorry," I shouted.

He shook his head. "Don't be," he said, reaching for my face.

I let him touch my cheek briefly before I twisted away. The feelings were the same with just this one obstacle: A paper-thin picture I couldn't get out of my head. This was difficult, wanting and not wanting out of principle at the same time.

The angle of the chopper changed abruptly, and we were scaling a mountain. I laughed and both Rosa-May and Joseph gave me a curious look. Pietre had certainly taken me literally when I'd said take Orry somewhere 'up'.

The higher we climbed, the thinner and shorter the forest became. Evidence of humans sprung out of the ground in black and rust. Seats hung from wire strung between long poles, moving independent of the wind like the spirits of the past were swinging their legs in them. I shuddered as we flew directly over the wire. These were the skeletons of a life and culture long gone.

Near the peak, the straight, flat lines of multi-story buildings peeked out from beneath lumps of snow. Deshi waved his slender arms about, pointing through the front window. Below, a building with a faded, red H painted on the roof rose out of the white like a dirty, grey building block no would want to play with. Denis nodded and swung over the top of it.

The chopper swayed and wavered in the wind, easing itself down clumsily until its legs hit the concrete roof with a plastic slap.

Deshi turned, his dark brows raised in excitement. "This is as close as I could get us safely. We'll have to walk from here," he said with an edge of a squeal lurking behind his expression.

"How far?" I asked, my legs burning to run.

Deshi beamed. He understood. Soon, he would see Hessa and I would see Orry.

"Not far at all."

61

The Best Of Me

ROSA

I stepped out of the chopper and slammed into a cold wall of air. The sun was deceivingly bright and glaring, bouncing off the white and stabbing my eyes. Denis quickly unfolded the solar panels and left the battery to charge. We piled on every item of clothing we had. With my overly padded arm, I snatched the handheld back from Deshi as soon as he pulled it from the chopper console, switching it on like a greedy child. I needed to see the red light. Search for it. Focus on it. The best of me was floating on a red light somewhere out there.

"Wait. Shouldn't we turn it off now that we're on the ground?" Joseph asked, placing his hand on the screen and resting it over my palm.

Denis gave a tight, condescending smile. "We are the Superiors last concern right now. I wouldn't worry."

I slapped Joseph's hand away. The light blinked, still in the same place as before.

We shuffled on the icy concrete towards an old, green door that seemed to stick up out of nowhere. Joseph kicked the rotten wood, his foot going straight through without any effort. Rosa-May dug her fingers into his neck. I pushed the rest through with my hands. It felt like an old sponge and smelt about as bad. Flicking a torch on, we walked down the slippery steps. The thin streams of light revealed nothing but dingy corners and prints of people flying through the air with long planks attached to their feet. Black mold framed the edges of the shots, spreading like a disease cloud.

"I'm guessing this used to be a ski lodge," Denis announced as he paused at one of the dimpled photos. When none of us responded, he said, "I'm also guessing none of you know what that is?"

"You guessed right," Deshi replied with a smile on his face.

Denis' face lit up at Deshi's smile.

I tuned them out as they politely conversed about a sport where people propelled themselves down a snow-covered hill on things called skis for fun. I was still trying to decide if Denis had made up for all the horrible things he'd done to me—let *them* do to me. Gripping the railing, I stilled as memories of every time he'd dropped me at that black door started assaulting my head. I swayed from side to side, trying to clear it. Like if I tapped hard enough, I could somehow evacuate the images from my head like sauce stuck in the bottom of a bottle. I lost my balance, and Joseph caught the back of my shirt before I fell down the stairs.

"Rosa, what's going on? Are you ok?" Joseph leaned over me from the step above as Rosa-May's small face peeked over his shoulder. She squinted under my torchlight.

Denis and Deshi froze a few steps above us, their eyes wandering as they tried to avoid intruding on our conversation.

"I'm fine," I replied, because I didn't know how to be honest with him. Even though he had hurt me, I had no desire to hurt him back with images he couldn't rid himself of. The torture and pain were a steady flow of horror I still wanted to protect him from.

"You're not," he said flatly, his eyes rolling to the crumpled roof that sagged over our heads. "I want you to tell me what happened to you." My face felt smooth like a rendered wall. I couldn't. He sensed it and added, "But I'll wait until you're ready."

I gripped his arm and gazed into his eyes, crisscrossed with torchlight, dark with shadows. "Thank you. I just want to get Orry back. After that..." I didn't want to say 'we'll have time' because I didn't know what the future held. Once we had Orry, who knew what we would be returning to. Hot tears welled like a candle fighting the breeze, but I snuffed them before they could fall.

He seemed to understand. His eyes darted to the men behind us briefly, but then they settled on me. *Drowning in gold would be a good way to go.*

"I love you, you know."

I didn't say it back, even though I wanted to. Stubbornly, I pursed my lips, nodded, and turned around. But I let him keep his hand on my back, to connect and stabilize me. I was a crooked, splitting trunk. I couldn't pull together by myself. Unfortunately, I needed help.

We followed the very convenient green exit signs, traipsing through several levels of soggy roofs and mold spreading over the wall like art.

The last door, painted with zebra stripes, celebrated the end of the stifling building. The light seemed brighter when I pushed down on the big, metal handle and shoved the door open. I felt closer. I pictured wrapping my arms around Orry and never letting go. Fear pricked the edges though. *What if something had happened to them?* I peeked at my handheld. The red dot hadn't moved at all. Shouldn't it have moved a little?

I traced the dot with my finger as if it were him, pausing in the snow. "What if he doesn't remember me?" I whispered.

Deshi uncharacteristically leaned his cheek to mine, his wiry hair brushing over my ear. "What if he doesn't remember *me*?"

Joseph hoisted Rosa-May higher up his back and flicked his hair from his eyes. "You two worry too much. Who could possibly forget either of you?" I liked the old grin back on his face. *Too much.*

I glanced up from the screen. The arrow pointed towards lumps of white between old streetlights. I walked up to one and kicked the snow away from the base. A road. The arrow told me to follow it. "This way," I directed with excitement and trepidation staining my voice.

As we left the ski village, as Denis called it, the road tipped off the edge of the world. Sheer cliff face above and below that the snow could barely hug. As I trudged upwards, my boots gaining layers of ice with every step, I wondered how they'd got up here with Pietre's leg. It may not have been as snow covered but still, with two children, it must have been rough.

I turned to Joseph, breath clouds misting his face at every step. "Are you scared?" I asked.

"Of you? Yes! Of finding them? Definitely not." He smirked and adjusted Rosa-May on his back. "You need to hold on tight, Posie." The nickname ran warming hands on either side of my heart.

I snorted, rubbed my hands together, and walked. Deshi strode next to me, as anxious as I was. Denis lagged behind, his head down, watching his feet make imprints in the snow like it was a first. Like he was the first man to ever walk up here. I rolled my eyes.

JOSEPH

I know what she's doing. Turning the idea over and over in her head. Trying to decide how she should act instead of doing what she feels. It's unlike her. I kind of wish she'd just punch me and get it over with.

She brushed past me and pinched Desh's elbow, whispering in his ear. It annoyed me, even though I had no right to be annoyed. I scooted closer so I could hear what she was saying.

"So, you and Denis," she started, awkwardly winding her fingers together, a blush appearing in her cheeks despite the cold. My fingers ached to touch those pink cheeks, but thankfully, they were holding on tightly to Rosa-May.

Desh's head jerked up in surprise. "Huh?"

She pursed her lips. I could tell she was thinking of a way to back away from whatever it was she was going to say, but then she blurted, "You know. You and him, uh, together..." She clapped her palms together. The sound echoed over the desolate-looking land.

The Superior's son was behind us, walking painfully slow. Desh jerked his head around to look at Denis and rolled his eyes. "Rosa, just because Denis and I have that *one* thing in common, it doesn't make us a good match. Besides, he's not really my type."

I suppressed a chuckle.

"Oh," she said, looking down at her feet as she shuffled through the snow that came up to her calves. "Sorry."

Desh slung his arm over her shoulder and laughed. "Don't be. You're being uncharacteristically sweet, and I don't mind it." Man, I wanted to be Desh right about then because she turned, poked her tongue out at him, and gave him a real, rare, Rosa-smile.

It killed me, because by the time her face had come back to me, the smile was gone.

ROSA

At midday, we stopped for food and drink. I scanned the thinning buildings. Only the occasional bump in the cold landscape showed any evidence that people once lived there. A broken roof, a car. The terrain flattened out, still a cliff face above, but below us, trees punctured the snow and a gentle slope drifted away from us. We sat on our packs, in the road, and ate quickly. Rosa-May refused food, but she drank a little. It worried me.

"She needs time," Joseph whispered as I tried holding the bread to her lips. She clamped them shut, shaking her head like I'd just waved a dead rat under her nose.

I put my hands on my hips and let my head fall in frustration. The air was clean, fresh, wet pine and snow creeping up my nose carried on a thin waft of wood smoke. "Smoke," I said, my voice shaky as a crackle in the fire. "I smell smoke!"

We all turned in circles, searching for the source. The smoke wafted under my feet, pushing me higher. It had to be them. My eyes skimmed the trees but I couldn't see anyone.

"There!" Joseph yelled, pointing down and northwest through a collection of leafless, blue-grey trees clothed in knitted, yellow moss. I didn't wait. I tumbled off the road and sunk knee-deep in the snow, following the imaginary line Joseph had pointed out. It ran like crimson ribbon in front of me, melting an imaginary path in the snow.

"Rosa, wait!" they shouted, but I couldn't stop. I ran, pushing my way through the snow like a plow, streams of sunlight piercing the gaps in the trees like the spokes of a wheel, strong and hopeful.

My legs were frozen, I think. I couldn't feel anything except the warmth of Orry's skin when I eventually held him. I couldn't hear anything other than the sound he would make as I squeezed him, and the tears I would try not to cry. My eyes lifted to the soft rise and fall of the land. He had to be just over there, just past that ridge of trees. The smoke smell strengthened. My heartbeat did too, pulling out of my chest and pulsing for home.

I pulled at the tree trunks like they were the rungs of a ladder. Bark scratched my hands, and birds startled away from me. My breath was hot, my vision sharp as icicles.

A flap of wings and children's laughter weaved its way through the trees. A sound I knew, like bells underwater. I halted. Snow seeped into my pants, my boots. I tucked my hair behind my ear and listened.

Two distinct laughs sailed up to the sky. Unfettered, unworried. Perfect.

I slowed, creeping towards the sound like a tiger stalking a deer. Afraid somehow that I would frighten them away.

My head poked past a frozen blackberry bush and I saw them, my heart breaking and melding back together. There they were, Hessa and Orry, playing together in the snow. It was an extraordinary, ordinary scene that slotted in my brain and took up permanent residence, knocking one old, bad memory out.

I crouched down behind the bush before they saw me. Scared of him. Scared to see if he was damaged. Orry grabbed Hessa around the neck, and they fell together in the snow. I carefully counted his fingers, checked his face for scratches, cuts, and bruises. His face had lost some roundness. But mostly, he was the same child. He was my baby, unaffected, like he'd been on a trip this whole time.

Alexei came striding through the trees, clucking his tongue. "You two are too rough with each other. And I've told you not to run off like that."

The boys ignored him.

I shifted on my haunches and knocked a branch. Snow fell from it and made a slight noise. Alexei's eyes snapped to the origin of the noise and found mine. I scrunched them tight and took a breath. It felt like a dream. *Don't be a dream.* I put my finger to my lips to stop him calling out and stood. I could hear the others tromping through my path behind me.

I strolled out, trying to look casual, and smiled down at the two boys. My voice shook like the branches around me. "You want to see a trick?" I asked, bending down to meet their eyes. I pressed my fingers to my side to stop myself from reaching out, grabbing them, and smashing them together in a crushing hug. They both nodded eagerly.

Long ago, my father had showed me how to do this in our front yard. I wasn't allowed to keep it. Mother had stood impatiently at the door, tapping her foot and waiting until we had kicked it in and smoothed the snow over, like it had never been there. But for that brief moment, where I was falling and laughing, free, I had pure joy and no fear. I was a normal child, doing normal things. The boys blinked up at me expectantly. I put my hands out at ninety degrees to my body and let myself fall back into the deep snow, swishing my arms up and down. The boys watched in fascination. While I was lying there, flapping like a wounded bird, Orry jumped on me, his tiny body making little impact.

"Mama," he whispered, grabbing my cheeks and squeezing them together. I was crushed leaves, bleeding sap into the snow.

I sat up and pulled us both out of the hole I'd made.

Alexei stumbled over to me, smothering me with a hug as I managed to splutter through my tears, "See the shape of the snow? It's called a snow angel, I think."

Orry scrambled out of my arms and dived face first into the snow to make his own, with Hessa following him.

"You're here," Alexei said into my hair, his stuttering voice as comforting as a warm drink.

"I'm here," I whispered, wiping my eyes with the sleeve of Joseph's shirt.

Joseph stomped through the snow. His worried face suddenly smoothed of concern as he eased Rosa-May from his back and lifted Orry up by his jacket, peering underneath to catch his son's eyes. "There you are."

Orry laughed again, and the feeling it created in me was huge. Bigger than the mountain, rumbling and shaking the snow from its back with laughter. Because Orry was *fine*. Our son was absolutely fine.

Joseph snagged my arm and pulled me close. I thudded against his chest and all four of us, me, Rosa-May, Joseph, and Orry squished together in a messy, perfect hug.

62.

The Bit After

ROSA

My heart split like a broken zipper every time Deshi approached Hessa. The boy didn't know him. It had been over six months since they'd seen each other, and Deshi was a stranger to him.

"You can hate me if you like," I whispered as I watched the painful exchange of Deshi holding out his hand to Hessa and Hessa hiding behind Alexei's leg.

"Don't be ridiculous, Rosa," he snapped. "I'm happy for you. God knows, you deserve some happiness."

"Yeah, but so do you." I thought about my month in the Superiors' compound, understanding more than most what Deshi had been through to get here. I repeated back what Joseph had told me about Rosa-May. "He just needs time."

Deshi waved me off, though I could tell his heart was punctured with a thousand holes. "I'll be whatever he needs. If that's no longer a father, I'll accept that. I just want to be a part of his life."

Joseph reentered the room, his face grave.

"How is he?" Alexei and I said at the same time.

Descending the stairs two at a time, he collapsed on the leather couch. He stared into the potbelly fireplace, which grinned ghoulishly back as he spoke. "Lucky we got here when we did. I've given him antibiotics. Now we just have to wait a few days to see how he responds."

Pietre had bacterial pneumonia. I wasn't sure what that was but from the coughing and swearing coming from the room, I assumed it was pretty bad.

Past the large, double-glazed door, piles of skins burdened the railing of the deck of the cabin.

"Where is she?" I asked Alexei about Careen.

He patted my arm. "She spends most of her day hunting. I don't think she could stand to be here and watch him... but now that you're here, things will be much better," he replied, as if he were trying to talk himself into it.

I leaned my head on his rounded shoulder. I couldn't believe I was here. It seemed unfair in a way that somehow I'd managed to get back to my family when so many had lost theirs. I had to be thankful that my suffering, my fight, had a good end. It brought me to the top of a mountain and to the boy sitting in my lap. Orry clambered off my leg and ran to Rosa-May, who was sitting on the edge of the rug, staring out of the window. He grabbed her arm and dragged her onto the deck. She went with him, still quiet but warming a little. I didn't explain to them who they were to each other. They wouldn't understand. All they needed to know was they were now family.

Denis hovered in the background, uncomfortable. We existed in a bubble he was unsure whether he should be in or outside of.

Alexei's eyes slipped to the window, where a shock of red hair stood out against the white snow.

"Here she is," he said happily, clapping his hands together and shaking them once.

I tripped over the solid wood coffee table and ran to the window, waving gawkily. Her eyes flickered up as I banged on the window. They widened with surprise, and I sprinted for the door. Joseph chuckled as my blunt footsteps made the glasses in the cabinet vibrate.

I sunk into the snow like a hot coal. She dropped her kill and glided gracefully towards me as if the ground were a meadow and she, a gazelle. We slammed into each other, and I felt the air leave her body. Dropping to her knees, she made an ugly gasping noise, tears pouring down her cheeks.

"You're here. You're alive," she cried as I knelt down beside her and hugged her close, her heaving sobs reminding me that while I was being tortured, so was she, thinking Pietre might die and that we would never come home.

"Thank you so much," I whispered, pulling her curves towards me.

"Thank you so much for taking care of my son." I owed her everything.

She pulled back, her big, blue eyes glistening with confusion.

"I said I would, didn't I?"

I collapsed over her, laughing, my arms wings ready to fold her into my heart. "Yes, you did."

Her voice was muffled by my shoulder, but I still heard her say, "Your hair looks very strange, Rosa." Our giggles rattled and shook the little hooks of pain that hung from my ribs, a few falling from my body and burying themselves in the snow.

It was strange and right, sitting around a chunky, wooden table, warm light bouncing off the timber that lined every part of what Alexei informed me was a ski chalet. It didn't sound like the name for a building; it sounded like one of the pretentious dishes Grant would have served. At the thought of him, chills crept up my spine, ruffling my skin and making me shudder.

The surviving members of our original group of escapees sat at the table. And despite their physical absence, the spirits of Apella and Clara were still there, in Hessa's eyes and Alexei's sad, wandering smile. Every time he shook his head slightly, or closed his eyes longer than normal, I felt he was having an invented conversation with her. It caused an aching and a comfort in me like a pillow stuffed with spiky grass.

Over cooked game and tinned vegetables, we talked about what had happened and what was yet to happen. We couldn't leave until Pietre was well enough, in a few days, which was fine by all of us. It gave us sorely needed time to prepare ourselves.

"I can't believe they went that far, to kill that many citizens in one dreadful act," Alexei muttered into his food. "I also can't believe two Superiors are dead."

Joseph and I exchanged a glance that spun and collided. Words traveled silently, bouncing off each other, in the space between our gaze.

"And four towns are free?" Careen asked Joseph, her elbows propped up on the table, leaning forward intently.

He shifted uncomfortably in his chair. "I think they are at least on their way to being free," he answered.

"I wish I'd seen it," I mumbled.

Joseph's gaze folded over me, a scorch, a cinder, an ember. "I wish that too."

"So much has changed in such a short period of time!" Alexei exclaimed. "It's unbelievable."

"It sure is," I said, my face pulling into a nasty frown that I directed towards Joseph. He leaned back, his face drowning in hurt and regret.

He stood up suddenly. "I'm going to check on the patient."

I stood too, glancing at the rabble of three children getting to know each other the way they knew best, tumbling in a ball and throwing things around the room. "I think I'll put the children to bed."

We left a cloud of concern hovering over the table.

I had more hands to hold than I could manage, and I beckoned Deshi to help me. We scooped the children up and climbed the short flight of stairs to the room that Hessa and Orry had been sharing.

Rosa-May undressed herself easily. The boys needed help, and I was glad to see Hessa allowing Deshi to help him pull on his pajama top. I felt sure they'd get there.

We tucked them in, their eyes already heavy as the light was turned down low. I kneeled down on the floor, my eyes finding each sleepy face. I kissed them. Deshi sat neatly beside me, his arm loosely on my shoulder.

I opened my mouth to say goodnight, but music flowed from my lips instead. "*Once there was a way to get back homeward.*

Once there was a way to get back home."

Orry's eyes were pools of innocence, cool blue and rich brown. Pure, muddy waters.

"*Sleep pretty darling, do not cry,*

And I will sing a lullaby."

Hessa's face was at peace. He smiled drowsily and dug his head deeper into his pillow. His mother's face rose from him.

"*Golden slumbers fill your eyes.*

Smiles await you when you rise.
Sleep pretty darling, do not cry,
And I will sing a lullaby."

Rosa-May's husky voice whispered through the dark, "Guhnight," and my smile glowed like a nightlight.

JOSEPH

I didn't know it could hurt this much, to hear her voice. Because I'm scared she won't ever look at me the same. I'm scared I'll only ever get to hear her from a distance now.

I was outside the door, shamelessly listening to Rosa sing, when they both backed out and smacked into me.

She turned suddenly and was pressed against my chest, her beautiful eyes fluttering up at me. I could feel that she loved me, wanted me. But she would always fight against it, and she had every right to be angry.

My eyes slipped to her lips, pursed in frustration, and I wanted to kiss her. Every minute of every day, I wanted to kiss her. I cursed myself for not doing it when I first held her, dirt-crusted and wearing that hideous dress. But that kiss would have been a lie. Until I'd told her the truth, everything would have been a lie.

"I'm going to bed, guys," Desh muttered, squeezing passed us.

"Night," I said without looking at him.

She brought her arms up to my chest. I breathed in, hoping she was going to lean towards me, but she pushed us apart.

Alexei clattered in the kitchen, wiped his hands on a tea towel, and looked at us both over his glasses.

She squirmed uncomfortably. "You look tired. You should go to bed too," she said, flustered. At least I think that was what she said. I was watching her lips move but not really listening to her words. I couldn't stand this barrier between us. I didn't want to be in the eye of her storm, where it was calm, still, infuriatingly quiet. If I couldn't be out there with the rain stinging my face, the wind sending a blur of leaves and debris dashing in front of my eyes, then I wasn't really *with* her.

"Joseph...?" My arms had wrapped around her waist of their own accord. She wiggled out of my grasp and walked down the stairs to the lounge area where Careen sat, sipping tea. I shrugged and went to the room we'd been given. I promised I would do what she wanted.

I flicked on the light by the bed and undressed. It was so warm in the chalet that I only needed the lightweight pajamas I found in a drawer. I slid under the warm quilt and praised the Survivors for their planning. This place was like their other hideaways, well stocked, comfortable, and like home.

I turned off the light and lay on my side of the bed, leaving wishful room for her. Staring out of the window at the moonlight reflecting off the snow, I hoped the door would creak open, that she'd crawl in beside me, wrap her arms around my shoulders, and the last month would just melt away.

ROSA

"I made you some tea," Careen said, blowing steam over the top of the mug cupped in both her hands and nodding towards another on the coffee table. Candles waved indecisively in the corners of the room.

"Thanks." I took the mug and let it heat my fingers.

"So what's going on with you two?" she blurted, pointing her finger between me and the closed bedroom door before I could even take a sip.

I gulped the scalding water and coughed. The sweetness fuzzed my teeth instantly.

"Seriously, Rosa. From what I can gather, you've been apart for only a month and now you're acting very strange with each other." *That's right; it was only a month.* "Shouldn't you be in there with him right now, you know..." She waggled her eyebrows, looking more confused than suggestive, though I knew she was going for suggestive.

I snorted. Careen was always very good at cutting right down to the bone truth of things. "A lot has happened in that month."

"All the more reason for you not to waste time," she said matter-of-factly. "Who knows what will happen next? You're here, together, now."

She was right.

The closed bedroom door seemed to pulse like a steady heartbeat. "He did something. I just don't know..."

She leaned forward, placed her mug on the table in front of us, and turned to me intensely. "What did he do?" Her voice was a stick of shock, stirring intrigue.

I dipped my head and spoke to my mug. "He was almost unfaithful to me."

Her laugh ripped through me, pulling my clothes and leaving me vulnerable.

"What the hell does that mean?" she managed through her giggling.

I laughed too, in a false kind of way, because even though it sounded stupid, it didn't feel stupid. It just hurt.

I sighed. "He kissed another girl."

She took a breath and calmed herself, tapping her chin. "And this was when you were captured, when he didn't know if you were dead or alive, when he was grieving you, apart from Orry too, just, well, completely lost and alone?"

I nodded.

She put her hands on my forearms and squeezed. "I could rip his lips off for you," she said, her eyes twinkling with mischief.

I grinned, covering my mouth, but it poked out both sides as if it were bigger than the room. "That won't be necessary but thanks." I loved his lips.

"Okay, then you need to decide right now if this is something you actually care about. After everything you two have been through, together and apart, you need to decide what you really want and what you're willing to lose."

Not him. Not over a kiss.

She just stared into my eyes as I thought about what she said. What did I really care about? It wasn't him kissing that girl.

And the truth was that I didn't need Joseph.

I *wanted* him.

It was a choice I had to make. I wanted love in my life, happiness, laughter, and warmth. Need could be a dirty, greedy little feeling. It was what drove Grant to do horrible things, and it may have been what drove Joseph to do what he did.

But I knew he wanted me and only me.

He was not *why* I lived. Without him, I would go on. It would be a sourer, hollower existence, but I could endure. Joseph was how I *wanted* to live.

She cocked her head to one side and smiled at me. "So...?"

"I don't care," I whispered.

6·3

The Ending

JOSEPH

Boards creaked as a slit in the door revealed a bar of golden light. She barely made any noise as she padded to the bed. She didn't get in on her normal side. Instead, she moved around to my side and crouched down. The moonlight streamed over her shoulder, her angles, so sharp and delicate at the same time.

She flicked on the bedside lamp. It lit up her face in golden hues. It took my breath. She stole it and wouldn't give it back. She could have it.

I wanted to, so badly, but I was scared to touch her, worried it was the last time. My hands stalled, pausing on the edge of the bed. Lying there, I felt bare. Without a word, she turned back the covers and tugged at the hem of my shirt, pulling it up to my neck. I followed her lead. I would do anything she wanted. I took the collar in one hand and pulled it over my head.

Her fingers danced along my scars as she whispered, "I don't care." Three words that could heal and harm me.

I was too scared to respond. Scared she could see how broken I was. How much I'd changed and that what was left of me was wanting.

She took my hand, guided it under her shirt, and pressed it to her warm stomach, forcing me to touch her scar. Her warm skin was strong, like everything I wanted. I closed my eyes as I let my fingers explore that new part of her. It was a rope, holding her together. It could bind us too. I fit my hands to either side of her waist and pulled her closer, my head, her head, hanging over each other's shoulders. She gasped at our closeness.

She murmured into my hair, "After everything we've been through, I just don't want to care about it, Joseph. I won't. It's not worth *us*. It's not worth losing us." There was a small pain in her voice. I vowed to scuff away that sound, live through it until it was just a memory.

But I'm lost.

She pulled back, searching my face with her amazing, piercing eyes, and said softly, "You know, you were always so perfect. Too good for me." I shook my head. If only she understood how wrong she was. "And I loved you for it." She tucked her unkempt hair behind her ear and the earnestness in her expression jumpstarted my heart. She could see me. All of me. "And now you're a bit broken, and I'll love you for that too. And maybe, now that we're both broken, we can kind of stick each other back together. You know, like glue." Her face twisted adorably, and I could see her internally kicking herself for saying it like that.

Something I thought was lost rumbled to the surface. "Glue?" I smiled. Then the rumble made its way to my mouth, and I laughed out loud.

That beautiful pinch between her eyebrows appeared, and she threw her hands in the air. "Oh crap, I don't know! I'm no good at metaphors. All I know is that I love you. I don't care if you're broken and stuck back together all misshaped with drips of glue showing through the cracks. Whatever happens, whatever it is, we'll work it out. We always do."

She loves me. Nothing I knew or would ever know compared to that realization.

My laugh grew. She had cracked me open, or glued me back together because I was hysterical, and I could feel myself letting a bit of all the bad things I'd been holding onto go. I stopped hesitating and reached for her scowling body, pulling her onto my chest. Her heart beat strong over mine.

I calmed myself enough to say, "No. Glue is good. It's perfect." *Perfect. We were broken and perfect.*

She smiled and thumped my chest lightly with her fist. Her hair fell on either side of me, blocking out the world. All I could see was her dark face, her pointed nose, and proud cheekbones that held up even prouder eyes. She dipped her mouth to mine and our lips touched. It was the beginning. It was a promise. I let the moment roll through me, existing only in this point in time. Not looking forward or backward.

She drew back and cocked her head, a delicious revelation of a smile dancing across her face. "You're an idiot," she whispered.

I nodded, trying really hard not to kiss her again, and gave up.

I knew she meant it, but I also knew she loved me for it.

ROSA

He is dented, golden light. I am light, redder than blood. Always, we will come together, strike orange flame, and sink below the clouds with the sun.

EPILOGUE

ROSA
SIX MONTHS LATER

The Woodlands was a beautiful idea, twisted into something gnarled and rotting. Because a settlement based on the rings of tree trunks should have grown. Each ring marking a passing year, new leaves and branches spreading past the trunk, touching other branches like resting arms.

What happens when you control a tree's growth? Its roots either become so netted, so wrapped around each other, that it dies... or one finds that tiny crack to push through and breaks free of its containment

The four of us looked up from our breakfast at the timid knock on the door. Rosa-May was the first one up, rushing to the door and swinging it open. Odval stood in the entrance, a shy smile on her face. Her baby was strapped to her chest in a complicated sling.

"Where are the others?" I asked.

"Pelo is watching the other two back at home," she answered. She had her hands full with the three lost children from the nursery she had adopted. Almost every Survivor had taken in a child. We had a few here until they were found permanent homes. Plenty of hands had gone up to take them.

This was the beautiful mess we lived in. Four free towns. Four under extremely shaky Superior rule. When they showed Grant's video, it had the opposite effect to what they had hoped. It had enraged the people. Superior Judith Grant was 'stood' down, and now only Poltinov and Sekimbo remained.

"Matthew has asked me to pass on a message to join him at the break this morning," Odval hummed.

"Now?" I asked with a mouth full of cereal.

"Yes, now." Odval nodded solemnly.

Joseph chuckled lightly, quickly clearing the dishes. "You heard the lady!"

Odval lingered in the doorway. "I love what you've done, Rosa…" I waited as she formed her request. She didn't need to be weird about it. "I don't suppose you could come help Pelo and me finish off our extra bedroom? Three children in one room… it's getting rather cramped," she asked quietly.

I laughed as Joseph's arm snaked around my waist. "Of course I can!"

We stepped out of our newly built cottage and I closed the heavy, wooden door behind us. Its solidity reassured me. I'd wanted to be near Pau but not inside the walls. I just couldn't go back in there after what happened to my mother. I couldn't make Rosa-May go back in there either. Cottages spotted the woods like they'd always been there. A lot of the citizens shared our feelings on living inside Pau Brazil after Ring Two was destroyed.

Joseph batted at Rosa-May's legs. "So Posie, you want a ride?" She grinned. She was still mostly silent, but a new word appeared every few days or so. I understood. She kept them treasured and secret. They were her one way of controlling things, and I wouldn't push. I wouldn't take that away from her.

He swept her up and hoisted her onto his shoulders.

Orry and I held hands and swung them high as we found the new road that led from Pau Brazil to Bagassa and walked towards the break in the wall.

We approached the gathering crowd and like a bright torch in a tunnel, my vision flicked to one glowing image, a personal, everyday moment that meant so much more: Their foreheads touching gently, brushing like bending bows. Deshi then lifted his face and kissed the top of his son's head. There was a small explosion in that kiss. Healing stars that spun out and spread. They told me that with time, with love, any relationship could be repaired. It was a hope I held for all of us.

Matthew stood in front of the break, scratching his leg nervously, the breeze causing the thousands of red death marker ribbons to wave and jump from the twisted concrete like they were alive. Survivors crowded around closest to him. The citizens of Pau formed an outer shell. Except for where Gwen stood, surrounded by kids from the Classes. They pierced the unspoken thin-film barrier that stood between Survivor and Woodlands Citizen. They padded after her and hung off her every word on music and culture, and she loved it. If they ever reopened the Classes as a university, whatever that meant, like Matthew wanted, she would make a great Guardian.

When Matthew saw me, he smiled and ran over, pushing his way through the crowd.

"Look at Gwen," I said. "Wouldn't she make a great Guardian?" She smirked at me and gestured to all the eager eyes on her.

"If we manage to re-open the Classes as a university, we'd call them counselors, Rosa," Matthew corrected. I rolled my eyes. I didn't care what word we used—I was counting on the meanings behind them changing.

Matthew took my arm, his eyes widening in nervous panic as he took in the large group of people whose faces had followed him to me. "I can't do this. I'm a doctor, not a politician."

"They chose you," I said, sweeping my arm in an arc over everyone who had voted for Matthew, almost unanimously, to be our representative in the negotiations for peace with the remaining four settlements that would take place in the now-empty Classes compound.

"I wish you were coming with me," he said, pumping his injured hand to steel himself.

I paused. He had asked. But I couldn't leave my family again. He understood. I was helping here, doing my small part and stepping into the background, into the shade of the others who would lead. They didn't need me. It was a wonderful, all-encompassing feeling of release.

"You don't need me," I said, smiling, real face-full-of-teeth kind of smiling.

Joseph leaned over my shoulder and whispered in my ear, sending that golden thrill through me that only he could, "I need you." But I knew what he really meant was he *wanted* me.

"You're doing fine without me," I managed, winding one hand through Joseph's and pushing Matthew forward with the other.

He nodded. "Okay. Thank you," he said, bundling his nerves together and placing them in his shirt pocket.

Matthew strode back through the crowd, climbed atop a broken slab concrete, and turned to address the watching eyes, the waiting hearts,

"Citizens of the Free Woodlands..."

Acknowledgments:

This story is for the readers who have stood by the series and by me over the last two years. Without your encouragement and support I never would have got this far. You've been an inspiration and a comfort on those doubtful days. And lifted me higher on the joyful ones. Thank you.

I'd like to thank my family, Michael, Lennox, Rosalie and Emaline for cheering me on, for being patient when I vagued out in the middle of conversations because I had disappeared into the world of the Woodlands. For understanding my need to finish, my compulsion to write and my crankiness at being interrupted. You've made it all worth it with your pride and belief in me.

Chloe, my critique partner and dear friend, has been a constant source of help. She has worked through this manuscript and picked up all those little annoying things like punctuation and spelling that I'm terrible at (though I'm trying to learn). But mostly, I appreciate her for understanding my crazy.

Finally, thank you Clean Teen Publishing. Courtney, Rebecca, Marya, and Dyan, you have been amazing to work with, you have assuaged all my fears about publishing, and made it an enjoyable experience from the first word to the last.

About the Author

Daughter of a physicist father and mother, Lauren Nicolle Taylor was expected to follow the science career path. And she did, for a while, completing a Health Science degree with Honors in obstetrics and gynecology. But there was always a niggling need to create which led to many artistic adventures.

When Lauren hit her thirties, she started throwing herself into artistic endeavors, but was not entirely satisfied. The solution: Complete a massive renovation and sell their house so they could buy their dream block of land and build. After selling the house, buying the block and getting the plans ready, the couple discovered they had been misled and the block was undevelopable. This left her family of five homeless.

Taken in by Lauren's parents, with no home to renovate and faced with a stressful problem with no solution, Lauren found herself drawn to the computer. She sat down and poured all of her emotions and pent up creative energy into writing The Woodlands.

Family, a multicultural background and a dab of medical intrigue are all strong themes in her writing. Lauren took the advice of 'write what you know' and twisted it into a romantic, dystopian adventure! Visit Lauren at her website: www.LaurenNicolleTaylor.com.